T

Darkest

Day

The Darkest Day

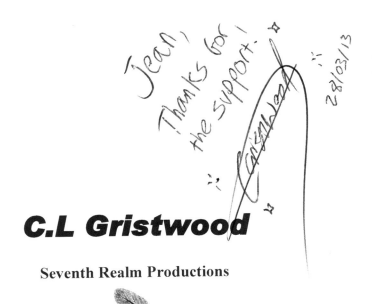

C.L Gristwood

Seventh Realm Productions

First published by C.L Gristwood 2012
This edition published by
Seventh Realm Productions 2013

Copyright © C.L Gristwood 2012
Cover Design Copyright © C.L Gristwood 2012

ISBN: 978-0-9559785-3-1

In loving memory of
Imogen Diana Gristwood
24th December 1931 – 16th February 2011

Kenan's first and biggest fan

Prologue
2300(ad)

"Faster, faster!" Liz had to scream for Kenan to hear her over the explosions. Kenan ran towards his wife carefully shielding the small bundle in his arms.

"How much further is it, Liz?" he shouted as he reached her side.

"It's just around the next block, we can make it if we run!"

"Okay, let's go!" The young couple began to run around a block of flats. As they rounded one side of it, the whole building was hit with another bomb and it exploded in a deadly shower of glass and debris. Liz shielded Kenan from the explosion whilst he held the small bundle even closer to him determined to protect it. When the smoke cleared, Kenan could see what Liz had been talking about. Before them, was what looked like a huge, half finished, multi-story, car park. It was raised several feet from the ground on huge concrete blocks and taking shelter in the space between the ground and first floor, was a group of about ten people. They were huddled round an old oil drum, in which was a fire. All of them were dressed in rather ragged clothes and none of them noticed the couple.

"Hey, Liz," came a harsh voice. Kenan saw a lean looking man walking towards them wearing an old torn, trench coat. He looked like he was in his mid thirties, his black hair untidy and thinning. "It's been a while," he muttered coldly, his brown eyes studying the two young people. Liz stepped forward.

"Damien," her voice had a slightly worried note to it. "Where are the others? I expected more people to come with-"

"Dead," replied Damien coldly. "They're dead. Bombed two days ago. It's just me."

"You can get him to the safe house on your own?" quizzed Kenan. Damien glared at him. "Your lack of trust in me is a little insulting, boy," he growled. He turned to Liz. "So where is he then?"

It was now that Kenan revealed what was in the small bundle he'd been holding so carefully... inside was a baby boy, just a year old, his blue eyes wide with fright and confusion. Damien wrinkled his nose before reluctantly taking the baby in his arms.

"Name?" He muttered.

"After his father," smiled Liz..."Kenan."

"We're counting on you," added Kenan, as Damien's face seemed to harden. "It's only until we get back from war remember, but if the authorities knew who we really, are, he could be kidnapped or worse." He handed Damien some papers and when he next spoke his voice had a strangled note to it. "You're his father now," he murmured. Damien smiled, a sickly smile.

"The kid can stay at the centre," he muttered. "I ain't responsible for what happens to him there." Liz and Kenan froze.

"What do you mean not responsible for him?" growled Kenan.

"Well, boy," snarled Damien, "as much as your papers here state that I am Kenan Wheeler, this kid isn't mine, therefore, he is not my responsibility. I said to get him to the safe house that's all." There was a stunned silence.

"You promised you'd pay us back!" Shouted Liz. "All that we did for you and you- you...!" Kenan looked first at Damien then at Liz, turning back to Damien.

"Give him back," he growled. A malicious smile grew into Damien's face.

"I will," he said. "For a small fee perhaps. Or maybe I'll just hang onto him here." That said he turned and ran! Kenan and Liz took off after him. Damien made for an open lift at one side of the building. He jumped over the rail and hit the button to reach the top floor. Kenan reached the lift, seconds too late. The lift began to ascend on its journey of over one hundred feet. Instinctively

Kenan grabbed onto the wire grating that was the floor of the elevator, and hung on, unnoticed by Damien. Slowly he began to work his way up over the side of the bars. Halfway up Kenan leapt over the side into the lift. Surprised, Damien hit a button and the lift jolted to a stop. He managed to escape into the car park with Kenan in hot pursuit. Damien ran to part of the building that had not been finished, and stood there...baby Kenan still in his arms! Kenan slowed his pace as he neared Damien, before stopping completely. Both stood frozen with tension. Damien knew that one false move would be taken as the wrong one and Kenan wouldn't think twice if he thought he was going to drop his child. Kenan didn't dare to break eye contact with Damien. He knew that the man holding his baby had the advantage, he had to be careful.

"Come on Damien," murmured Kenan. "Just come away from the edge, we can talk this over." Damien didn't move. Kenan's voice sharpened slightly. "Damien, come back or..."

"Or what!" snapped Damien. "You kill me, boy...you kill your kid as well!" (By this time Liz had caught up with them and stood shaking a few feet behind Kenan). For a minute or so, no one moved or made any sound at all...even the bombs had stopped. Suddenly Liz rushed forward, shouting;

"If you won't give him back, then I'll take him from you!" She ran towards Damien but he was ready for her and moved swiftly to one side as she went past him. She spun round but having already lost her footing she disappeared over the side of the building!

"LIZ!" screamed Kenan. Forgetting about Damien, he ran to see if she was okay...she was...but only just. She had managed to save herself by hanging onto the edge of the floor by the ends of her fingers. She looked up at Kenan. "Help me," she whispered. "Please don't let me fall Kenan!"

"I won't," said Kenan, just give me your hand." Liz

3

started to reach towards Kenan but neither of them noticed Damien creeping up behind Kenan. Just as Liz grabbed her husband's hand, Damien kicked Kenan over the edge! With one hand Kenan made a wild grab onto the side of the building, with his other hand he held onto Liz tightly. Damien sniggered as he lifted Kenan up by his wrist, held him at arms length and whispered;

"I assure you, your son will get the upbringing he so richly deserves"...then he let go.

Baby Kenan's screams were mixed with both of his parents as they fell from Damien's grip down to the bottom of the half finished multi-story!

2315 (ad)
Chapter One

"Kenan! Hey Kenan!" The shouts came from a dark haired scruffy boy as he ran towards a teenager with messy blonde hair that almost hid his brilliant blue eyes. He looked up as his friend approached.

"Hey, Matt," he called cheerfully. "Haven't seen you all day what's up?" Matt slowed down as he approached Kenan. Behind him were three other teenagers all about the same age; between sixteen and seventeen. Two girls and a boy.

"It's my air-surfer," groaned Matt as he sank to the floor. "It's not working very well." He handed Kenan a flat object, that looked a little like a skateboard with no wheels. Kenan took one look at it, turned it over in his hands and shook it. There came a faint rattle from inside. He handed it back to Matt.

"The brakes are busted," he said. Matt peered at the disc in his hands.

"You sure, man?"

"Positive," replied Kenan. Then he smiled. "Guess you won't want to give us a race this afternoon then? Matt snorted.

"'Course I will!" he exclaimed.

"Against us too?" came a voice from behind him. A girl with cropped blonde hair in baggy jeans and t-shirt was talking.

"You bet, Samantha!" grinned Matt. Samantha rolled her eyes.

"I have told you before Matt to call me Sam," she grumbled. "That other name makes me sound so pathetic!"

"You said it," teased Kenan. Sam went red but didn't answer back, she never did to Kenan. But she did to everyone else. She was tough. A tough fighter with a

5

boyish attitude to everything, seemingly almost uncaring, she wished more than ever she could somehow find it in her to tell her friends what they all meant to her, especially Kenan... but she never could, she was far too proud.

"Well, what are we waiting for?" exclaimed Kenan. "I'm bored of sitting here in this dump all day. Let's go."

The group of five friends each stood on their own air-surfer and zoomed out from the blackness of under the car park into the hot summer sun. When they were all properly air-borne, Kenan looked at Matt.

"Where to?" he asked. Matt looked thoughtful.

"How about to the outskirts of town?"

"You're on!" laughed Kenan. And they were off.

Kenan, Matt, Sam, Nick and Lia.

The group was most unusual, considering they were very close friends. Kenan was a natural born leader. He loved teasing the others and telling them what to do. As he zoomed ahead of the others, his hair blew out of his eyes as they shone with the feeling of freedom. Matt couldn't have been more different looking, with green eyes and brown hair. His parents were American and Matt had picked up a broad American accent from them, which the others relentlessly teased him about. Yet if he had looked a little more like Kenan, you would have thought they were twins! Both said the same kind of things, and were rarely seen apart. Both had the same type of attitude to certain situations and both were very competitive against each other...especially when it came to air-surfing. The only thing Kenan and the others found infuriating about Matt was the fact he was almost always moaning about something. Just behind Matt was Sam. Her blonde hair cut very short in a boyish style. Her green eyes were gleaming. She loved racing with her friends...in fact, anything with her friends was okay in her book as long as she didn't have to look smart or watch her manners! Behind her taking the race at a more steady speed were the twins Nick and Lia. Both had black hair and brown eyes. Both were as timid as mice and never argued if they thought they were going to be proven wrong. Kenan,

Matt and Sam used to make fun of them so much, but at the end of the day it was all in good spirits. Kenan and Matt were continuing to race, as the outskirts of town loomed closer. Kenan knew that if he wanted, to win he'd have to play with wit. He waited a few seconds then started to wobble about, pretending to fall off. Matt noticed first.

"Kenan's in trouble!" he shouted to the others. "C'mon! We've got to help!" Kenan smiled to himself.

They're falling for it! he thought. He carried on the act for a few more seconds heading straight towards a skyscraper, when at the last second he pulled up sharply, laughing happily at the others.

"He's faking!" cried Matt. "The son of a...whoa look out!" He and the others missed the skyscraper by inches! By the time they finally caught sight of Kenan, he was much too far ahead to catch up with.

*

"Man! I can't believe we fell for that one again!" Matt was speaking. He, and the others, had decided to land when they had finally caught up with Kenan. Kenan himself was sitting on the ground grinning from ear to ear at his victory.

"You are such a cheat!" Matt whined. "You never play fair."

"Okay, okay," said Kenan. "Just chill out for a second and listen. How about I give you another race, from here to..." (He looked around him) "Say from here to the big place on top of the hill?"

"You mean snobsville?" asked Sam. Matt looked in the direction Kenan was looking. In the distance was a large house on top of a hill. It had huge grounds all around it. Matt smiled.

"Okay! You bet!" he exclaimed. He leapt onto his air-surfer and ascended a few feet before stopping. "What's keeping you?" he shouted. "I'm not giving you any chances!"

"Even if you gave me a chance, I wouldn't take it," said Kenan picking up his air-surfer. "I don't need it!" Sam and

Lia looked at each other and rolled their eyes.

"Boys," muttered Lia. Nick looked at her.

"What?" he exclaimed.

Matt and Kenan were well away by the time Sam, Lia and Nick were air-borne. They knew they no chance of catching them...still-

"C'mon," cried Sam. "Let's try and see who wins!" Kenan and Matt were pushing their air-surfers to the limits, racing furiously; each determined to beat the other! The house ahead of them loomed closer. Matt suddenly seemed to pull himself together and shot ahead of Kenan with a cry of:

"You LOSER!" Kenan couldn't believe it. Matt had never raced this fast before, for the simple fact it was far too dangerous. It was hardly thirty seconds before they reached the grounds. Kenan saw the gates before Matt and landed in front of them. Matt however forgot about the busted brakes on his air-surfer, tried to stop, but instead, flew over the gates at great speed, crashed into a tree, fell through the branches and landed with a thud on the well-kept lawn.

"That wasn't so bad," he said painfully. A second later his air-surfer crashed down on his stomach. He pushed it off. "This is BAD!" he groaned. Kenan laughed at him through the gates almost in hysterics. As the others caught up, they too began laughing.

"You had no idea...how funny that looked...from where," we were laughed Sam, leaning against Kenan to stop herself collapsing.

"Ooh, very funny," growled Matt in a sour voice. "Bet you had no idea how painful that was either!" He picked up the mangled air-surfer, looked at it then threw it over the gates. It crashed to the ground with a splutter then died completely. "Guess I won't be needing this piece of crap anymore," he muttered.

"What do you think you're doing here?" a voice made them all look up sharply. A girl who looked about the same age as them was standing a few feet away. She had shoulder length tawny hair and was dressed in fashionable clothes. Her hands were on her hips, and her brown eyes flashed angrily at the company. Kenan stepped forwards.

"Err, sorry kid but we were having a race and our friend here lost control of his air-surfer...he crashed...-"

"I can see that! Snapped the girl. "I'm not stupid, just get out of my garden!"

"Say please," muttered Sam.

"I am not saying please to people like you!" exclaimed the girl. "I've seen you before. You live with those tramps under the multi-story don't you?"

"Tramps?" shouted Sam. "They're our friends and families, you stuck up little brat!" Matt who was still inside the garden looked nervously from the girl to Sam, he could see that if they didn't leave there was bound to be a cat - fight!

"Well, um, look um ma'am," he said trying to sound calm. "If you just open the gates we'll leave quietly and won't bother you again."

"I ought to give her a slap round the face before we leave," shouted Sam angrily. Kenan hastily jumped off his air-surfer and dragged Sam away from the gates.

"It's not worth it," he said quietly. "Just cool it." Sam sighed, she shot a filthy look at the girl but started to calm down. The girl nervously opened the gates and Matt ran out very relieved that a fight had been avoided.

"You'd better share my air-surfer," said Sam. "I think it's big enough for two." Matt accepted gratefully. He climbed on as Sam, Nick and Lia started to take off from the ground. The girl looked at them somewhat entranced.

"What are they?" she asked Kenan who had stopped to tie up a lace on his trainer.

"Air-surfers," muttered Kenan.

"Yo Kenan, c'mon man! Let's go!" called Matt.

"Wait a sec!" yelled back Kenan.

"I'd love one of those, for myself," mumbled the girl, still looking at the board.

"Well, it takes skill to ride one," said Kenan standing up. "Not that I'm saying you haven't got skill," he added hastily. "But they are pretty cool to ride." The girl managed a smile.

"I saw the race from my window," said the girl awkwardly.

"Those were some pretty impressive moves you pulled off there." Kenan only grinned.

"Nice to know someone appreciates talent," he laughed. The girl smiled back.

"Whoever taught you did a good job," she continued. "Did your parents teach you?" Kenan shook his head. "I taught myself...my parents died when I was little." The girl looked shocked.

"Oh. Oh I'm so sorry. I had no idea." Kenan laughed lightly.

"It's all right," he said, "I'm used to it." The girl still looked guilty.

"I'm sorry I insulted you guys..." she mumbled, "it's just that my grandmother is ill in hospital, very ill, and we don't know if she'll pull through. I'm just uptight please forgive me." The girl's eyes were wide with shame. Kenan looked at her then smiled.

"No problem," he said.

"I still feel awful," muttered the girl. "If there's anything I can do to help in return, then just call round and ask for Naomi."

"I will," replied Kenan as he took to the sky. He took off to catch up with his friends. Naomi watched him go holding the iron bars of the gates longingly looking out at the group of five teenagers get smaller in the distance.

"What a life," she whispered.

The evening was drawing in when Kenan and the others got back to the car park. Matt had been moaning about his busted air-surfer all the way home and was seriously getting on Kenan's nerves. When they landed, Nick and Lia went off on an errand of their own. Sam volunteered to help Matt try and fix his air-surfer. Kenan was happy to be by himself for a while. But before he even had a chance to think about relaxing, he heard a short, sharp barking noise. He sat up to see a big black and brown Alsatian thundering towards him.

"Oh No!" shouted Kenan, knowing exactly what was coming next. The next second he was pinned to the ground as the dog landed on his chest... and licked him happily. "Oh! Get off you great lug!" laughed Kenan. "I know, I know I'm back! Buster, get OFF!" Buster obediently jumped off and ran round in circles chasing his tail. He stopped and lay at Kenan's feet looking very humble, and jumped up again his tail wagging. Buster was truly Kenan's dog. He had been found by Kenan when he was a puppy. He'd been hit by a car and was seriously injured. However with some help from the others, they'd all managed to nurse him back to health but Kenan was the one Buster latched onto. He was always happy to see Kenan and now was no exception.

Kenan finally got Buster settled down and was lying down to have a doze himself, when he heard someone else.

"Kenan! Kenan you gotta look at this." It was Matt. He was running towards Kenan with a look of worry on his face.

"What is it now?" groaned Kenan.

"What is it?" shouted Matt. "Only the biggest piece of news everyone's talking about. Watch!" In his hands was a flat grey box, known as a holo-box. He lifted the lid of it displaying a kind of three dimensional picture of a news reporter who looked like she was in mid-sentence but frozen in time. Matt pushed a button underneath on the bottom of the box and the reporter started talking.

"In more local news, it looks like the end of the line for the multi-story car park in the centre of town. The one-hundred foot building is hardly ever used for its purpose as drivers are two afraid to park their vehicles because of the group of tramps living underneath it although there has never been a robbery of any car in the building, it has become noticeable that the younger generation may pose more of a threat. Because of its neglect, business plans are being drawn up by the council to destroy the car-park by blowing it up with nearly a quarter of a million pounds worth of dynamite. If all goes according to plan, the building will be destroyed within the next four weeks."

Matt stopped the recording and looked at Kenan, his eyes blazing.

"Can you believe that?" he exclaimed. "They're going to

blow up our home, and the cheek of calling us tramps, pieces of scum. What're we supposed to do now?"

"Well, a reality check," said Kenan. "We are tramps Matt, but I don't know, well really what can we do?"

"Oh come on Kenan you're smart!" exclaimed Matt. "Let's sort something out, let's take on these guys, dynamite and all…"

"Yeah I'd love to see that," muttered Kenan quietly. "Can see the headline now, tramps take on city council, who would honestly win that one Matt?" Matt paused in mid moan.

"Oh come on Kenan," he exclaimed, "this is our home!"

"It probably won't even come to-"

"Oh god you're such a quitter!" complained Matt.

"Listen!" Shouted Kenan, jumping up suddenly. "I've had it with your whining, just back off okay!"

"Pardon me for caring what happens to my folks!" glowered Matt. He shut off the box and stood up. Kenan glared at him.

"At least I'm lucky enough not to have that worry," he growled at last.

"Hey, just 'cos your parents got drunk and jumped off the top of this building...-" shouted back Matt. That was the flip switch. Kenan stood up so he was level with the dark haired boy.

"My mum and dad didn't get drunk!" He screamed. "Just leave it out!" Matt realised he had gone too far.

"I'm sorry man," he mumbled. "I just-"

"Oh sure!" shot back Kenan sarcastically. "Everybody's sorry for poor little Kenan. The youngest one here...who doesn't belong to anybody. The orphan! I don't need your pity on top of everyone else's! Get outta my face Matt! Leave NOW!"

Matt took a step back. He looked at Kenan and ran. His pounding footsteps faded. Kenan's eyes were wet with tears of rage. He stood still for a few minutes before turning in the opposite direction away from the building. He knew he had over-reacted and he knew that he shouldn't have been so hard on Matt but he'd had enough of his whining for one day and as for the comment about his parents… a fresh surge of anger ran through him… then he shook himself, he had to clear his head. He continued walking until he came across a stack of old crates and boxes. There he sat miserably and buried his head in his hands. He was sitting on exactly the same spot where his parents had died. Kenan couldn't remember what had happened. But someone else did. Damien, the self-appointed 'leader' of the group, had told him just exactly where and what had happened:

"You were just a kid," Damien had said. "Just old enough to walk when one night you wondered away from your parents and somehow found your way to the top floor of this car park. You were walking around up there with no safety around you as the barriers were not then set up and it was a very foggy unclear night. Your parents finally found you, and begged you to come back, away from the edge, but you didn't listen. They tried to come after you but the fog you see… and they couldn't see where they were going until it was too late…they fell Kenan. I heard your parent's screaming and rushed to help them, but I just wasn't quick enough. I managed to catch you Kenan, only just. But if I had been there sooner, I could have saved them… along with you…"

Kenan had never forgotten a word of this awful explanation. As he had grown older the words had slowly sunk in meaning more and more each time he thought of it. He was constantly haunted by the words; what if, and in his darkest moods, Kenan knew that if it hadn't been for him, his mum and dad would have still been alive. How he wished Damien had never saved him that night. Sometimes the guilt became unbearable. Everyone made up their own stories about what had happened that night to try and make it easier for Kenan, but sometimes the stories they came out with, only made him feel worse. Just like Matt telling him his parents got drunk. Although Kenan couldn't remember them, he just knew they wouldn't have been alcoholics; otherwise they wouldn't have bothered trying to save him…

And wouldn't have died! Thought Kenan miserably.

He didn't know how long he sat there. But by the time he

lifted his head, night had fallen over the city and it was beginning to get quiet. He stood up and wondered whether he should go and apologize to Matt. He checked his watch. It was late though, he'd been sitting there a lot longer than he had first thought; maybe he'd wait till morning. He slowly began to walk back to the car park; it stood out against the starry sky a black shape, somehow looking twice as big as normal in the dark. He was almost there when he heard something that made him stop. Buster! Buster was barking, but it wasn't his normal happy bark...he was angry. It took Kenan a minute to determine where the sound was coming from, it echoed so much. Then it hit him; Buster was actually in the car park! He ran to the nearest staircase and ran up it. He found the first floor and wondered round. A few cars were parked but not as many as Kenan thought there would be. There were even a few hover-cars, locked in place by metal clamps on the walls.

Hover-cars had been invented and marketed within the last century, and in that time they had become increasingly popular. The main reason for them being invented, was for people to avoid traffic jams by simply flying over them, but the sales had rocketed. New and faster models were being built and other floating vehicles appeared. Taxis, camper vans, buses and even lorries. This was why Kenan and the others only preferred to do their air- surfing at weekends when there wasn't too much traffic about. Otherwise it was just too dangerous.

He could still hear Buster barking.

"Where the hell are you?" murmured Kenan. He kept on looking. He didn't find Buster on the first or second floor. But when he reached the third floor the barking was louder than ever, he had to be around there somewhere. "Buster!" Kenan shouted. The barking stopped for a second then carried on. Kenan followed his ears until he could make a faint outline of the Alsatian standing next to a hover-car barking for all he was worth. "What is it?" asked Kenan as he approached. "Buster. What's wrong?" Something was beside the car. It was a small silver crystal. It was more like a sphere shape and wasn't very big...not much bigger than a tennis ball. He went to pick it up, but as he did Buster snapped at him. "You little sod!" shouted Kenan. He clipped the dog round the muzzle and picked the object up. As he stood up looking at it, something else in the car caught his eye. In the front seat sat a well-dressed gentleman, his eyes, were right on him. Kenan jumped then seeing no reaction took a closer look. The man's eyes continued to stare but they were glazed... and that was when Kenan saw the blood dripping from his neck...he was dead!

Chapter Two

It was getting late when Naomi's parents returned home. As usual, she was sitting at her computer when she heard the hover-car entering the garage. There was a pause then the sound of the front doors being opened, another pause before a long silence. Naomi was used to this sort of treatment when her parents returned home from any 'day out.' As far as she knew that day her mother had dragged Naomi's father, Lord Henderson out for a day of shopping in the big city of London. They lived on the outskirts of the city, but their hover - cars were so fast it didn't take them long to reach the fancy big shopping streets like; 'New Bond Street' and 'Second Oxford Street.' Naomi quite liked days like this. She was allowed to eat what she liked, get up at what time she liked, and watch any amount of television she liked. Normally in the evening she'd do her homework ready for the next morning, but that evening she hadn't been able to focus on anything...she didn't know why. All she could guess was that it was something to do with the five teenagers she had met earlier that afternoon. She leant back in her chair. They seemed so happy, so carefree, they didn't have boring lessons the next day, they weren't trapped in a house because their parents were over protective of them...well, apart from that boy who had stopped to talk to her. He had no parents. Naomi tried to imagine what that would feel like...even to lose one parent would be bad, but to lose them both and at such a young age...Naomi wished that she hadn't been so insulting to them, but what was passed was passed. Now she had to focus on her work, her parents would be up any minute to check that she had done her assignment. Naomi sighed. She pushed her notebook under her computer and made sure she logged off the Internet properly. The notebook which she had hidden was very important to her...she loved looking for Internet sites which seemed like they held any top secret information, about a government conspiracy or top secret terrorist plans...she never found anything, but she liked to be called a hacker by her friends, the few that she had. Naomi didn't go to school, she had private lessons in the mansion and the only friends she had were the children of her parent's friends...but they didn't seem to like Naomi very much. They always seemed to be talking about the tropical holidays they had been on and the cruise ships they had sailed on. Naomi had heard it all before...almost as if she had lived life to the full already...and she was only fifteen.

"Naomi," a voice called her from downstairs.

"Coming, mum," she called back. She walked out of the room down the stairs. Her mum was flouncing about holding a loud coloured dress against her, as their butler staggered through the hall with yet more bags all looking like they contained shoes or more clothes. Naomi caught sight of her Father's expression behind her mother...he was trying not to laugh.

"Well, what do you think?" said Lady Henderson. "Tell me honestly." Naomi bit her lip.

"It's erm, very colourful," she said truthfully, adding, perhaps, not quite so truthfully, "it suits you." Naomi's mum beamed.

"I'm glad you like it," she said, "because I got one exactly the same for you." She reached into a bag and pulled out the same dress, a few sizes smaller. Naomi blinked. Lord Henderson spoke up.

"Erm Audrey, I feeling quite hungry, do you think Pierre has dinner ready yet?"

"I'll go and check," said Audrey, hurriedly packing the dress back in the parcel, much to Naomi's relief. Lady Henderson swept out of the room, leaving Lord Henderson, Naomi and, the butler standing in the hallway.

"James," smiled Lord Henderson turning to the Butler, "could you pack those terrible clothes away, preferably in a dark part of the wardrobe where she won't see them and hopefully forget about them?"

"Certainly," replied James who had been trying not to laugh himself, through the ordeal. He picked up the packages and trekked up the stairs. Lord Henderson turned to Naomi.

"Are your assignments finished?" Naomi looked at the floor. There was no point in lying. She knew she was lucky her mother wasn't in the same room at that moment; otherwise she would be in really big trouble.

"No," she murmured. Lord Henderson's face fell.

"Why," he scolded. "You've had all day."

"I know," stuttered Naomi, "but something's playing on my mind...and I'm not sure what." She told her Father about her encounter with Kenan and the others as they walked upstairs to her room.

"And how does that stop you doing your work?" insisted Lord Henderson.

"It doesn't," said Naomi, "but...but...I don't know." She sat down at her computer and began to open up a program with her work on it. But before she got started, her father said something that startled her.

"I feel it too, Naomi." Naomi turned around.

"What do you mean, feel it?" Lord Henderson walked to the window overlooking the magnificent grounds. There was a far away look in his eyes.

"I can feel it...in the air and in the sun's rays. It's approaching us. But it's hard to say what it is exactly and when it will strike."

"Is it bad?" murmured Naomi. Her father nodded.

"Very. We're talking about a world - wide catastrophe here. But as I say it's hard to tell exactly." Naomi shuddered. Her father walked out of the room. "Get your work done quickly, I'll call you for dinner." He shut the door behind him. Naomi leant back in her chair. *Get work done? How could she?* Only she knew what her father had been talking about. It was something he had passed onto her...a sixth sense. Both she and her dad knew when things were wrong and when things were going to happen. Their life style had tried to crush this brilliant ability out of them, but it had failed, the sixth sense had never left her. Audrey Henderson, refused to believe that this ability was true, and told everyone who questioned it that it was just her husband's overactive imagination and Naomi was playing along with him. But truthfully, she was nervous, there was no knowing how far this ability could take her husband and daughter...they may even become obsessed by it, become reckless...Naomi knew, of course, that she'd never let this go to her head but she often wondered if she liked it; she didn't like the fact that things were happening in the world, and didn't know exactly what they were. Sighing, she began her assignment... it was going to be a long night.

*

It was midnight. Dressed in a warm dressing gown and slippers, George Henderson was sitting at the kitchen table a mug of hot chocolate in his hands. It was his third cup. He could not sleep. The kitchen door creaked and Audrey walked in. She looked sleepy and confused.

"What are you doing down here?" she mumbled.

"I can't sleep," replied George. "I thought a hot drink would help."

"Well, come to bed, when you've finished," grumbled Audrey. "I was worried waking up, and you weren't there." She shuffled off. George downed his drink and placed the cup in the sink...it could be washed tomorrow. It was too cold to sit here, but he was awake. Awake with worry. He wondered if Naomi was asleep. He was worried about her as well. She seemed very unsettled. Not just about something he too, could sense. She had seemed almost reluctant to do any work that evening. Every time he had checked to see how it was going she was either stretched out on her bed, or sitting back in her chair looking out of the window. She had never been like this before. He thought about this as he went into his darkened bedroom and tiptoed across to the bed. Audrey had fallen asleep already. George lay there for a very long time, his hands behind his head looking up at the ceiling...thinking...

Across the landing, Naomi turned over again. She had been doing so for two hours, and still hadn't been able to get to sleep. She cuddled up to her toy husky dog, trying to get warm. It was strange that it was summer yet it seemed so cold. What was wrong with the weather anyway? She was too cold and too tired to think about things she couldn't sort out. She snuggled down under the covers with an unhappy sigh as she tried to warm up.

"God I'm lonely," she whispered.

*

"And that's all you saw?" Kenan nodded quickly, he was still shaken up. The police officer looked suspiciously at the fifteen-year-old boy with his innocent blue eyes, stopped typing, and shut the small laptop with a click. "Well, thank you young man, we'll tell you if anything comes up." And with that the policeman whisked off leaving Kenan alone to go over things in his head. When he had seen the man in the car, all he could do was stand and stare, before running as fast as he could to the nearest pay phone. He dialled '999,' and waited. Within minutes the multi-story became a hive of activity. Police were everywhere and the press arrived taking pictures of everyone and everything. They had even interviewed Kenan. The police asked for a report. It was now two 'o' clock in the morning and things were finally quieting down. Kenan knew there was nothing he could now do except maybe sleep and try to get over the shock, but every time he closed his eyes he could see the body with the empty soulless eyes staring back at him. Did he have any family? How long had he been there alone in that dark, empty car park? Kenan didn't want to think about it.

As he lay there trying to get the image out of his head he suddenly remembered something. He dug his hand into the deep pockets of his sweater and pulled out the crystal sphere he had claimed from Buster. It had been the last thing on his mind when everybody had been questioning him and now as he sat there looking at it, he wondered if there was any connection to it and the body. He couldn't think straight. He needed a time out. Slowly he closed his eyes and fell into a troubled sleep.

Later that morning everybody was talking about the previous night. Matt completely forgot about being angry with Kenan, and he, Sam, and Nick tried waking him up at half past seven. Kenan sleepily pushed the moth eaten blanket from him and looked up at his friend's worried faces.

"Are you okay?" asked Sam worriedly. It took Kenan a moment to focus.

"I'd be fine if I had some more sleep," he groaned.

"We're waiting for the news," said Matt. "I reckon it'll be everywhere today."

"What're you talking about?" groaned Kenan.

"Last night, you fool!" exclaimed Nick. "You know the body and everything? Do you reckon they'll suspect it was any of us?" his tone of voice growing anxious at this.

"Probably," replied Matt. Kenan pulled the blankets back over his head with a sigh. He was too tired to face the world at that moment.

"Just make sure you let me know what happened," he said his voice muffled by the blanket. "I just need another five minutes."

"Too late!" exclaimed Matt. "The news is here already!" Kenan shoved the covers off him and looked up. Lia was running towards them with what looked like a small disk in her hand.

"I've got it!" she cried. "We had just enough, to get the local one." Matt quickly set up the holo-box as Lia approached her friends. "Okay," she said smiling. "Get ready for our five seconds of fame." She put the disc in and the holographic words flashed up...'London News.' A pause, then a news reporter flashed up.

"Good morning, this is 'The City of London,' morning news... What followed shocked everyone. There was no news of the body and nothing about any of the interviews or reports Kenan and the others had given.

"Maybe it'll be in the evening disc," said Lia. "I think we've got just enough money for that if we all contribute."

Kenan slept through most of the long day huddled into his blankets, for although it was summer, he felt strangely cold.

Finally, the waiting was rewarded. At seven 'o' clock, the group of friends once again gathered around the holo-box as Lia loaded another disc containing news into it.

"Good evening," blared the newsreader, "this is 'The City of London' evening news. The main story today is…:"

Nothing was mentioned. There was news of a huge drugs raid, some news about the economy and a piece about an elderly resident named Terry Orkas being attacked. "He was in a terrible state claiming that the world would be at stake if the police did not help him find the culprits," droned on the reporter. "Mr. Orkas was disturbed from his work at about ten 'o' clock this morning when he heard the sound of his front door being kicked down. He states: 'it was terrifying, I had no idea who or what it was. There was a crash as the door fell from its hinges into my hallway. I saw several people enter my flat then completely ransack it. I didn't have a chance to try and stop them -they knocked me to the ground and gave me a right bruising. When I came to, they hadn't taken anything, they just left, that was when I called the police.' Terry was taken to hospital and it was announced that his condition is stable.

In other news, a body has been found in the Queens Way multi-story, car park. The victim who cannot be named for legal reasons has been identified and the discovery is being treated as a suspicious…."

"W-wait!" exclaimed Kenan, "you're not saying that was it right?"

"All those interviews and questions?" exclaimed Sam.

"This has to be some kind of joke!" shouted Lia.

"Maybe there'll be some more details in the news tomorrow," reasoned Nick.

"Maybe," muttered Kenan.

"What do you mean maybe?" exclaimed Sam. "This stinks!"

"I'm going," grumbled Lia getting up.

"Me too," muttered Nick. The twins left, leaving Kenan, Matt and Sam alone.

"I think I'll go to," said Kenan after a few minutes, "I need to clear my head a bit." He kicked up one end of his air-surfer and it flipped over. The board didn't fall back to the ground, but instead hovered silently in mid air. Kenan mounted it and with a quick wave to his friends he flew out from under the car park towards the northern borders of the city.

Although times were bad, murders weren't an everyday occurrence, and Kenan couldn't see why a robbery on an elderly person - bad as it was - could take over the headlines of a murder. He racked his brains trying to think of how and why it could happen as he carried on gliding smoothly through the evening air, towards the borders of the city. He knew without doubt where he was headed, towards lookout point. Lookout point was commonly known as make-out point but it was normally quiet this time of day and Kenan loved to watch the sun set over the city and just sit and think about things, but when he reached the spot that evening he couldn't settle, something was pre-occupying his mind. It wasn't just the body; he didn't know what it was. He looked out at the city but it was just the same as always, the sun sank lower, an orange ball on the horizon, as the city lights became more visible, dots of light in a black concrete jungle. But even the beautiful sight didn't lift Kenan's spirits.

This is going to be my whole life, thought he to himself. *I'm going to grow up a nobody. I'll probably die in ten years time, or I'll be slung in jail. This is not where I belong...there has to be some way I can prove that I am a somebody, not just a homeless nobody.*

Wondering where he would be in ten years time and became lost in a sea of thoughts. When it became too cold to sit around any longer he headed back to the multi-story, hoping to get some sleep, but instead he found Buster asleep on his bed.

"Get off, you freeloader!" exclaimed Kenan. Buster obediently jumped up, it was then that Kenan noticed something was tied to the dogs' collar; it looked like a tiny CD, the same type they received the news on. He quickly took the disc and inspected it carefully. It wasn't labelled but Matt and Sam had left the holo-box lying around so Kenan quickly put the disc into it and after a few seconds, an image flashed up. It was blurred and Kenan couldn't very well see the speaker but he could hear him this is what was said:

"Kenan, I hope this message found its way to you safely. I need to talk to you. You don't know me but I know you and knew your parents very well. I cannot tell you too now much in case this disc falls into the wrong hands but if you can meet me and we can talk face to face. Time is off the essence, if you do not meet me soon, the fate of the world will be bleak. Kenan, I am counting on you. I know I can trust you. My address is one two eight, block 'Three A' The Square. I and the rest of the world need your help...NOW!" The image disappeared and a deafening silence followed. Kenan's mind buzzed. He felt worried, anxious puzzled and terrified all at the same time. Who was that? Was it safe? Was it some sort of trick or a prank? No, no that voice was far too genuine, pleading almost begging him to believe them. He had seen the time on the tower clock on his way home, and guessed that it was about nine thirty. He hesitated and paced up and down a few times before reaching a decision. Nine thirty or not, if it was that urgent they'd be grateful he'd got the message at least.

No time like the present, thought Kenan grimly. And with that he picked up his air-surfer and flew off towards the city.

Chapter Three

Damien and Vicky watched the news quietly. As the newsreader finished her sentence, Damien smiled.

"That's disgraceful," said Vicky, "A stupid robbery takes the headlines over a murder. People don't get killed every day."

"Yes, they do," said Damien, "but only one gets mentioned on the news." Vicky shook her head and pushed her long red hair off her face. Damien smiled at her.

"You just wait," he grinned, "not long now, then we won't have a care in the world about things like this... or anything at all." His dark eyes glinted in the light of the fire that crackled in the oil drum. "We can forget about them all and start a new life together...just you and me." Vicky grew uncomfortable, it was unlike Damien to be so happy, it normally meant trouble for someone else.

"I, uh, need to go for a walk," she said. Deep in thought, she walked away.

Damien and Vicky, had been together for nearly twenty years. The relationship had always been difficult for numerous reasons. She had met Damien when he had been sacked from his job in a factory. Vicky had been made homeless when the flats where she lived had been bombed in the war that had only ended fifteen years ago. The government was practically non-existent then and most of the borough councils were not open any more, after the workers fled the city. There was no help for the victims in these times, they stood alone. Only if they found someone they could trust, did they stand any chance of survival. Vicky and Damien with a few of their friends had decided to make a temporary home under the multi story car park that was being built, hardly a house but with a war raging, places to stay that were especially free, were hard to find. However, what should have been shelter for a few weeks had now turned into a home for all of them. Vicky had only been sleeping rough for a few weeks when she became ill. Damien had nursed her back to health and throughout this, a friendship had begun to grow between the two and soon they were a couple. It wasn't unexpected when Vicky announced that she was pregnant. They were given a flat, somewhere safe and warm but their time on the streets had led to petty crime and no-one wanted to employ ex crooks. Still Damien refused to take help from anyone convinced they would be able to look after themselves. Nine months later Vicky had a little boy. Both parents couldn't have been prouder and for about six months things seemed fine. Then the unthinkable happened. Damien and Vicky's child became very ill. They tried everything to make him better, but unable to afford proper medical treatment the situation only became worse until finally, one cold winter's morning the baby died. Vicky was heartbroken and Damien barely spoke or ate for a month. Then he became a very bitter person. He disappeared for nearly forty-eight hours and came back very drunk. He blamed Vicky for the baby's death and shouted abusively at her for hours. But the situation still hadn't hit rock bottom until finally, both evicted from their flat, they returned to their former shelter under the car park. Times had always been hard on the streets, but never this bad. One evening Damien came back to Vicky carrying a small bundle in his arms. It was a baby, blonde hair and blue eyes.

"I found him," he said. "He'd been abandoned. What about we take him in?" Vicky had stared at Damien. He just seemed a completely different person. "I thought," continued Damien sitting down next to her, "that by helping him, we could help ourselves a little bit...we could put the past behind us." Vicky had agreed and gone with Damien's suggestion of Kenan for a name. The years passed and Kenan, under the watchful eyes of Liz and Damien, had grown until as now, approaching his sixteenth birthday. Kenan didn't like Damien that much, sure he had taken him in, when he would have died, but still he just couldn't shake the feeling that Damien couldn't be trusted. Vicky, however, treated Kenan like he was her own. Kenan never forgot her...after all she was, to a certain, extent his mum, and Kenan guessed that she must've known his parents. One day when he was small, he had thought about asking

Vicky about them, but he only found Damien. Kenan had decided that Damien would know about his parents too, but he had been given the awful and graphic tale of how they had sacrificed themselves to save him. Kenan hadn't been able to take it in, he just sat there thinking. He had tried not to cry. "Now boy," Damien had hissed. "I suggest you tell no-one about what I have told you. NO ONE! Especially Vicky, she knew your parents well and if you bring them up in conversation, well, she may remember that it's your fault they're not here and that could well lead to her taking a dislike to you." Especially Vicky, she knew your parents well and if you bring them up in conversation, well, she may remember that it's your fault they're not here and that could well lead to her taking a dislike to you." So from then on, Kenan had not only had to live a life of terrible guilt, but he hadn't had anyone to confide in, except his four friends, Matt, Sam, Nick and Lia...but they sometimes made it worse than it was. All Kenan had told them, was that Damien had found him in the nick of time and his parents were already dead, but nothing else, so he had lived with his guilt in secrecy...and Vicky, like most of the others suspected nothing about what Damien had told Kenan.

Vicky decided to go a speak to Kenan as she hadn't seen him all day, but when she reached where Kenan and his friends usually were in the evenings she found everything quiet and deserted. This didn't surprise her much, after all they were probably out having a lot more fun than she was. Reluctantly she turned around and made her way back to where she had left Damien. To her surprise, when she got within a few feet of him she saw him walking around appearing to be talking to himself. She edged closer and noticed he was holding a tiny cell phone to his ear.

How on earth has he got hold of one of them? She thought to herself. She shrugged, thinking Damien had probably mugged someone for it. Keeping within the shadows she crept closer. Damien didn't notice her. He was talking into the phone rather worriedly. Vicky heard the following:

"The thing is Lance, if I do, and it's any time too soon it will just look suspicious." There was a pause. Then; "Oh no no no! I will do it, but I just think that well, the old geezers son..." Another pause. Vicky crept closer and strained her ears. She could just make out a faint voice on the other end of the phone it sounded angry.

"I don't care okay. I don't suppose you thought to take care of the kid to?"

"Well-l no," said Damien, "I didn't...it's been difficult Lance, they're always surrounded by people..."

"I'll call you back in twenty-four hours Damien."

"No!" exclaimed Damien. "Lance wai-" but Lance had hung up. Damien looked like he might throw the phone on the floor, but then he pocketed it looking extremely fed up. Vicky summoned her courage and came out of the shadows.
"Who was that then?" she asked coldly. Damien looked up sharply.

"How much did you hear?" he snarled. Vicky didn't flinch. She stood her ground.

"It has to stop, Damien, this little secret gang work you do. I know you're good at it Damien. I know you make it look like accidents and that you've been getting away with it for years...but at the same time it's getting too risky...if you get caught..."

"I won't get caught," spat Damien. "Not unless some little dog turns me in!" He glared at Vicky. She said nothing and instead walked off towards the town centre deciding she'd have to try and find something decent to eat...anything to get away from Damien. She hated him sometimes, she hated the work he did, the people he hurt, but if she left him, if someone did turn him in, she would be the first person he'd come after. It wasn't so much herself she was worried about... it was Kenan. If nothing else she had to keep him safe, or at least stay around to keep an eye on him and if you lived on the streets of London, Damien was a good person to know... as long as you didn't get on his wrong side. Leaving the darkness of the car park, she began to get worried. Killing adults was one thing but who was this 'Kid,' he and Lance had been going on about. Surely it was someone important, it had to be.

Apparently they were always with people (probably bodyguards) she thought. But who was that important in such a low-rent part of London?

She pulled her tatty coat tighter around her as the wind picked up.

Had Kenan not had the address of the flat from his mysterious caller, he was sure he would never been able to find it. The Square was filled to bursting with blocks of flats that looked one hundred stories high. Eventually, Kenan found block 'Three A,' and pressed button 128. After a pause, a voice came through on the intercom badly muffled because of the bad quality of the system.

"That you Kenan?"

"Yeah," replied Kenan. "How'd you know it was me?"

"A guess. Don't hang about come in...twelfth floor." There was a click and the speaker went dead. Kenan looked a little nervously up at the tower block then back in front of him as the metal doors shot back and a dark dingy hallway was revealed.

Life on the streets of London had taught Kenan a lot, and he was used seeing people and places that had seen better days. Even so, he cringed as he entered the block and a horrible smell wafted through the air. Sacks of rubbish littered the small hall leading to a lift, which, being 'out of order,' forced him to take the stairs. It took a while to reach the twelfth floor when he finally did reach it adrenaline fear, and anticipated pounded through every inch of his being. He quickly walked down another corridor lined with numbered doors on either side.

One two five, one two six one two seven...AHA One two eight, thought Kenan. He knocked on the door. A sound of shuffling footsteps was heard. They gradually grew louder. Kenan swallowed as the door opened. A figure stood silhouetted against the darkness of the corridor.

"Come in, Kenan." He obediently followed not really sure what to expect. The two walked in silence down a short hallway and turned right into an average living sized living room and ad-joining kitchen. The room itself was very interesting. It was lined with hangings. Some looked African, a couple of others looked South American there was even one that looked ancient Egyptian. There were shelves lined with strange looking stones and wooden figures. A strange but pleasant fragrance was coming from an oil burner. Kenan looked around him in wonder, but a voice suddenly snapped him out of his spell.

"You take coffee black?" Now Kenan saw him. He was an old man not much taller than himself and made Kenan's slim figure seem quite fat compared to his frail structure. His old, kind face was covered with tell tale lines, making one wonder just how old he was. He smiled as he looked towards Kenan. "Well," he said, "black or white?"

"Bl- black," stuttered Kenan, not really knowing why he said that, as he had never tried coffee in his life. The man spoke clearly into a small box mounted on the wall:

"Black coffee, no sugar." A whirring sound came from the box. A hot black coffee in a polystyrene cup dropped out of the bottom. He handed it to Kenan and gestured to him to sit down. "I hope you didn't want sugar," he said sitting down in an old armchair with a sigh. "I'm all out at the moment." Kenan sat nervously on the edge of an old couch and watched the old man light a cigarette, take a puff of it and smile. Kenan opened his mouth to ask what was going on but his host suddenly leaned forward in his chair and stared in him in such a way Kenan closed his mouth very quickly. The old man continued to squint at Kenan then smiled. "There's no doubt about it," he said. "You are the very image of your parents."

"What's this about?" asked Kenan, not really wanting to start a conversation on a subject he hated.

"It's about what I told you in the disc," came the reply.

"You told me sod all!" exclaimed Kenan. "Some crap about the future of the world, and how the hell were you connected to my parents?" The man's face didn't change, he sat calmly and took another puff of his cigarette.

"Kenan," he began, "I have a lot to tell you. My name is Terry Orkas and, as I understand it, you found a body in a car the yesterday, is that right?" Kenan nodded. In the excitement of that evening he had almost forgotten. "Well," continued Terry. "That young man who they refusing to name was my son." Kenan gulped.

"Sorry," he mumbled, but Terry continued talking.

"I take it you saw that I was robbed earlier today...it was spattered all over the news this evening?" Kenan nodded. "Well, the people who robbed me were the same ones who took my son from me. They ransacked my flat because they didn't get what they killed him for." He paused taking another long breath on his cigarette before continuing. "You see Kenan, I come from a long line of protectors, guardians if you will, dedicated to keeping safe a shrine...A shrine underneath this very city, but one that is not a place for gods or spirits. It was created by a few select people who worship the very earth itself and how each of the seasons guide and provide for us through our lives and ultimately with both the giving and taking life. The shrine is so secret not even the government knows about it and inside are five glass spheres." Terry took a piece of paper and pencil and began scribbling. "Each one of the spheres represents a season, spring, summer, autumn and winter. They are all placed in a circle, like so," he quickly paused so Kenan could see before carrying on. "The fifth one goes in the centre of this circle. That sphere represents the actual earth itself. As long as these spheres are kept safe and properly aligned with each other in the shrine, earth is safe..." Terry's voice echoed in Kenan's ears. He could hardly keep up, his own thoughts were full of so many questions, he could hardly hear the old man properly... yet somehow, for some insane reason, he found himself believing Terry, who was still talking quickly. "Now it so happens that a few nights ago, an organization of terrorists found the temple and took the treasures. My son was able to track them down and find the centre sphere, the one that represents the earth. However he only reached the car park... but he had the sphere with him, and that's what the gang who came here earlier were looking for. But they didn't find it. So if I don't have it and the gang didn't get it from my son, then who has it?" Kenan was already reaching into his pocket.

"You mean this thing?" he held out the sphere he had picked up the night before. Terry's face lit up.

"I knew you had it, Kenan and I knew you would keep it safe thank you. Hold onto it, I still need to tell you some more."

"You said that the world was in danger?" started Kenan.

"Yes," said Terry and here's why Kenan. As long as the spheres are aligned in the shrine, the seasons of earth will be in order and function properly but if the spheres are out of place then the seasons will be also. You could wake up one morning and it would be a hot summer's morning, but come the afternoon you could be sitting in three feet of snow! It depends on how long we leave this chaos for. But I'm warning you Kenan, the longer it's left, the worse it will get! A storm, one like nothing anyone has ever witnessed, will rip across the planet, bringing with it death and destruction. No-one will be spared. We need to act now, we need..."

"W-wait a second!" protested Kenan. "You said we...how am I involved in this?"

"I need your help Kenan," said Terry. "My son would be the one but I he's not here. I can think of no-one else..." The old man trailed off. He sighed unhappily. "There are rare occasions when I plead...and I will now. Please Kenan. Believe me! I need you on this." Kenan looked at Terry for one long minute.

"What do you want me to do?" he asked finally. Terry smiled.

"Go back home and get some sleep," he said. "I will be there tomorrow at nine 'o' clock. I want you up and ready."

"Ready for what?" asked Kenan.

"To help me find these terrorists and try and find out where the other spheres are," said Terry. Kenan nodded and looked out of the window of the apartment. Night had now truly fallen and it was very dark outside.

"I need to get going," he muttered

"You haven't touched your coffee," said Terry.

"I don't drink the stuff," said Kenan. Terry smiled.

"Neither did your parents," he said. Kenan didn't want to pursue the subject. He allowed Terry to show him out and ran down the flights of stairs and out of the front doors. Terry watched him go from his window. He sighed.

"It's him," he murmured to himself. "How I wish it wasn't..."

Chapter Four

When Kenan awoke the next morning, he was convinced that
the happenings of the previous night were just a dream. He
even told Matt when the friends made their way into the city
centre towards a luxury looking trailer with the words
'Breakfast Bar' emblazoned down the sides of it. The breakfast
bar sold everything that the word 'breakfast' meant. Fried
eggs, bacon, fried bread, toast, sausages, cereal, waffles,
pancakes and every drink from water and orange juice to hot
tea. Kenan and Matt loved going there, providing they had
enough money...and this was one of the rare occasions they
did. Getting money was mainly Kenan's responsibility. As
everybody knew, he was a natural acrobat, especially when it
came to air surfing. He'd pick the time of day and place where
he knew most people would be, and he (and sometimes the
others) would go into a show of daring stunts, tricks. Some
days were better than others. They did this Fridays and
Saturdays when they knew people would have money and
they usually had just enough by Saturday night to last them a
week. Today however, they got within a yard of the breakfast
bar and gasped. The man who usually ran it was being
completely ignored by his customers, who had assembled in a
crowd looking standing looking up, at one of the tower blocks.
What looked like hundreds of feet above him was a hover-
ambulance and police unit. As Kenan watched a horrible
feeling flooded through him. He knew that flat! He hardly
dared to read the name of the block...there it was on a board
high above them 'The Square'...' The tower block itself had,
over the main doors the number and letter 'Three A!' Terry's
block!

"Stay here," he told Matt. Without another word he ran
towards the doors of the block wishing more than ever that he
had his air-surfer with him. Almost falling over in his hurry,
he ran up the stairs to the twelfth floor. Sprinting out into the
cold dark corridor he made his way to Terry's apartment. The

door had been knocked off its hinges and lay in the hallway. Kenan ran towards the front room. A scene of utter chaos greeted him. How could so many people fit in here? Kenan didn't know. Nobody noticed him as he searched frantically for any sign of Terry. He saw the ambulance near the window...that had to be... He rushed towards it, the back doors were still open and sure enough Terry was in the back and he was in a bad way. Someone had clearly come back to finish what they had started the other night but had they succeeded? "Sickos," muttered Kenan. Terry was an old guy who was just trying to live out the rest of his life in peace. "Terry!" exclaimed Kenan. "What happened?" He immediately felt stupid asking this question. It was obvious what had happened. Terry could hardly speak, but he was clearly pleased to see Kenan. He smiled weakly and muttered;

"I was shot, I tell you Kenan, my life flashed before my eyes."

"Why'd they do it?" demanded Kenan. "Who are they? I'll get them for this."

"Kenan, you can't merely fight these people," gasped Terry, weakly "they're too many and too strong... you have to find their leader, and confront him..." Before Kenan could ask any more the paramedics arrived and tried to shoo Kenan away, but Terry grabbed his wrist as he reluctantly turned to leave. "Take this," he whispered pressing a small strip of paper into Kenan's hand. "Find the address, it'll tell you what you need to know, about everything." Kenan scanned the paper it stated simply:-

Orkas@tomicweb.co.uk
Password: Candyfloss

"Candy floss?" enquired Kenan. Terry shrugged managing a smile.

"My favourite," he said weakly, before the ambulance doors were shut and the unit pulled away disappearing northwards. Kenan stood looking at the vehicle unable to believe what he had just seen, when he felt a heavy hand on his shoulder.

"Now son," said a gruff voice, "what exactly are *you* still doing here?" Kenan turned to see a tall policeman towering above him his face partly obscured by a large moustache. He came back to his senses.

"I was uh- just leaving," he said trying to sound casual as he scrunched the piece of paper tighter in his fist. He made his way out of the apartment still packed with police officers, ran down the flights of stairs and out of the metal doors. He found Matt looking both disgruntled and confused.

"Fine," he said as Kenan drew nearer almost bubbling over with

excitement. "Why don't you just bugger off somewhere and not tell me what's going on." Kenan grabbed Matt's jacket sleeve and steered him through a mob of people until they were more or less away from the hustle and bustle of the crowd. "What's happening?" protested Matt.

"I've got a lot to tell you," said Kenan in a low voice "get your breakfast, I can't eat right now, and get back to the car park."

*

Kenan sat down, and got up again. He lay down on his blankets and he got up again. He couldn't settle. He had the piece of paper still clenched in his fist and he was facing a large dilemma. When Terry had given him the paper, Kenan thought that all he had to do was look up an internet site and get some information, but as Matt had pointed out a computer was very hard to get hold of when you lived on the streets and worse was Kenan didn't have the money to access an internet cafe and use a computer there. He really was at a dead end. He was also worried about Terry. Although he had seemed chatty and still alert, Kenan had seen how bad he really was. He remembered the bruises on his face and his chest covered on blood, he suspected that someone had shot him then beaten him just to make sure. He had to hand it to him; Terry must have been a real fighter to deal with those sorts of injuries at his age. But now it was three hours since he had seen him, he was getting worried.

Matt hadn't been exactly helpful in the matter either. Kenan had told him about everything Terry had said, but Matt although he had listened, hadn't really believed him. Kenan had seen him trying not to laugh in some parts of the story, finally making up a lame excuse to leave and left Kenan to worry about things on his own. He looked at the web address again. 'Orkas@tomicweb.co.uk' Surely Terry knew that Kenan wouldn't be able to get hold of a computer easily...after all he knew no-body who owned one...- The thought hit Kenan quicker than the speed of light. Why hadn't he thought of it before? It was the most obvious solution. But then, what if she didn't want to help...but she had said ...'just call round and ask for Naomi!' Surely she would have at least one computer he could use. Kenan decided it had to be worth a shot, it was his only option he could see that held a small chance of success. He looked at his watch; it was one 'o' clock. With any luck Naomi had stopped her lessons for lunch. He had to go now. He grabbed his air-surfer, pocketed the e-mail address and flew towards the outskirts of the city.

Kenan hadn't noticed the other day, just how big and fancy the Henderson estate really was. Beyond the ugly black iron gates was a gravel driveway flanked by beautiful willow trees. Numerous flowerbeds were dotted about on the lawns that looked like they had never seen a weed in their life. The driveway ended in a large circular area in front of the house. A white stone fountain, featuring mermaids and dolphins sat in the centre and a flight of steps led up to the large white colored house itself. With its large oak doors and two lion statues on either side of them, Kenan wondered just how immaculate the inside of the house itself was. He also wished more than anything that he wasn't wearing the same clothes that he had worn when he had met Naomi the other day. It had to be bad enough to come up here being from an average working class family... but from the streets...? Would Kenan ever persuade Naomi that he was here purely to help Terry and not to rob her? He honestly wasn't sure. As he landed in front of the gates, he wondered whether it was all just a bad idea and tried to decide if it wasn't too late to go back or not. He pulled himself together. He meant them no harm, he was innocent, and all he wanted to do was just ask them for some help in helping someone else...

There was a small intercom box mounted on the right hand pillar supporting the gates, taking a deep breath he pressed a button marked 'Talk,' and nearly got the fright of his life when a small television monitor slowly appeared with a mechanical whirring from inside the pillar. There was the longest five-second pause ever, and then the face of a forty something year old, balding man appeared on the screen.

"Can I help you sir?" he asked. He could clearly see Kenan through the monitor as his nose was wrinkled in obvious distaste. He obviously had a security camera with him in the mansion somewhere but he could probably have seen Kenan without it, as he was sure that someone had appeared in the main hall window dressed in the same dark suit as the butler's (he assumed he was a butler anyway... no one had ever called him sir before.)

"Err, I'm a friend of Naomi's, I need to speak to her very quickly concerning something important," he said, his voice far too nervous for the butler's liking.

"You know Miss Naomi?" he said looking shiftily at Kenan with his messy hair and scruffy clothes.

"You may not believe me," said Kenan, "but if you could just go and get her...she'll recognize me I promise." The balding man seemed to be looking past Kenan nervously. Kenan turned around. Had Matt and the others followed him? He really would have liked to keep this visit to himself.

"You're sure you're alone out there?" said the butler.

"Absolutely," said Kenan. The butler still didn't seem totally convinced but then he shrugged.

"I'll fetch the young miss, but if I find out your lying kid, there'll be hell to pay. Wait there." He walked away and the monitor now focused on a large marble staircase sweeping down into a large hall with two crystal chandeliers hanging from the ceiling. Kenan whistled under his breath.

That's just the hall, he thought to himself. He looked back up at the house. *No wonder the butler's nervous about letting me in, he probably thinks I'm here to pull off a raid or something, though I can't blame him for thinking that...I probably look like a piece of...*

"Hello?" Kenan's attention went back to the monitor. Naomi was standing there her face at first puzzled then brightened. "Kenan!" she exclaimed. She turned to the butler standing beside her. "Oh James, you should have let him in. Of course I remember him." Kenan tried to remember introducing himself to Naomi but couldn't...then he remembered...Matt had called him to hurry up, while he'd stopped to tie up a lace on his trainer.

This girl, he thought smiling at Naomi through the monitor, *must have a pretty good memory...maybe she's worth all of the private lessons here after all.* "Hold on," said Naomi. "I'll open the gates for you."

"No need," said Kenan hurriedly, "I brought my air-surfer along. I can fly over them."

"Oh wow!" exclaimed Naomi. She turned once again to James. "Have mummy and daddy seen these things?" she asked. "They are so cool- watch Kenan!" Red with embarrassment Kenan climbed onto his air-surfer, rose above the gates, dropped gracefully and skimmed steadily over the gravel driveway towards the house. As he approached the double doors, James slowly opened one of them and Kenan slowed his air-surfer to a halt and jumped off it, a foot or so from the ground. Naomi was waiting in the hall, but she seemed a little nervous now that Kenan was actually standing a few feet from her with no gates or T.V monitors between them. Indeed, Kenan felt the same...how on earth was he going to explain that he needed to visit an e-mail sight and if he didn't, the fate of the world was at stake? Even Matt didn't believe him. James stood aside to let Kenan in. Kenan stepped into the richly decorated hall and stared, it looked twice as big as it had done on the monitor outside. The crystal chandelier sparkled and the white marble floor and staircase glistened. He was snapped out of his daydream by Naomi's voice.

"Well, what can we do for you?" she was standing to his left her arms folded but a smile on her face. Kenan decided not to beat around the bush.

"I need to use a computer if you've got one," he said. "I need to find this e-mail address."

"Is that it?" asked Naomi, she sounded, strangely, a little disappointed. "You just need to surf the net?" Kenan nodded. "Well, there's a spare computer in the study," said Naomi, "but why don't you stop and have a bite to eat first. I was just about to go on my lunch break."

"Oh err sorry," said Kenan. "I thought you would have had lunch already."

"Well I normally do, at half past twelve," said Naomi, "but I've had to make up for time lost over the past few days...I haven't been feeling myself lately." Kenan nodded, but deep down he didn't know what he should be doing. Naomi had invited him in, said he could use her computer and asked him to stay for lunch, all in the space of two minutes, while he couldn't think of anything to say at all.

At that moment a tall smartly dressed lady swept into the room calling for James.

"Didn't I hear the intercom a few minutes ago?" she asked. Then her eyes fell on Kenan. Kenan grinned sheepishly and waved. "Who is this?" she asked not attempting to hide her disgust at all.

"Oh. Hi mum," said Naomi wearing the same expression as Kenan. "This is Kenan, you know the boy I told you about." Audrey managed a sickly smile.

"Oooh," she said a fake grin plastered on her face. "The tramp, yes. I remember you said that he and his friends were the ones who wrecked the flower beds the other day."

"That was an accident, err Ma'am," said Kenan. "My friend lost control of his air-surfer and he crashed...-"

"Never mind that!" snapped Audrey. She turned to Naomi. "May I have a word with you Naomi, just for a second? Excuse us young man." Turning to James, she hissed: "don't let him out of your sight!" With that she ushered Naomi into the study and closed the door behind them.

"What on earth do think you're doing?" she growled.

"Helping him out," answered Naomi.

"You've just invited him in," snapped Audrey. "I hardly call that helping him outside, where he should be."

"Mum, stop being so sarcastic and just listen to me, for a moment" said Naomi. "Kenan's not what you think, yes he lives rough but he seems nice enough..."

"How do you know?" whispered Audrey. "Have you actually spent any time with him?"

"No," said Naomi "just let me finish, please. I insulted Kenan and his friends the other day, and I felt horrible afterwards, so I just said to Kenan that if I could do anything to make up for it then all he had to do was to pop round and ask for me. All he wants to do is spend a few minutes on the computer. I swear he'll be no trouble m-"

"He *is* trouble!" shouted Audrey. "He's from the streets! He's a tramp, a reject a...a-"

"And you think that he's living like that by choice?" exclaimed Naomi, fighting to keep her temper under control.

"Nonetheless," snapped Audrey, "he's been brought up by thieves and beggars. I've seen them all, standing around, scrounging for money from decent people."

"But they-"

"Be QUIET! I'll let him use the computer on the condition...that he never sets foot in this house again, and if I find one thing gone or out of its place, I'll have the police onto him so fast, and he'll be in jail so quick, that his feet won't touch the floor!" She said this all in one breath her eyes blazing. Naomi couldn't be bothered to argue back so she nodded glumly and walked out of the study. Kenan was still standing in the hall nervously. Audrey walked off towards the kitchen and James, after a quick nod to Naomi followed her. Naomi blew out her cheeks with a long sigh and then turned to Kenan.

"All sorted," she grinned.

Chapter Five

Afterwards, Kenan wasn't sure that he should have let Naomi look at the website, but it seemed wrong *not* to let her look at it seeing as it was her computer. They had the study to themselves, which relieved Kenan as he suspected he would have had a hard time explaining to Lady Henderson what all this was about. He was connected to the page that displayed a bland grey page with a little boxed stating;

Enter Password for Approval

He typed in the word 'candyfloss' and waited. Five small file boxes appeared on the screen. Each one labelled 'blog,' with past dates and times underneath them. Instinctively Kenan clicked on one dated the day before he found the body.

"So what exactly are you looking for?" asked Naomi as a sign on screen displayed a 'loading' icon.

"I'm not sure exactly," said Kenan. "There's a lot of background information which you probably wouldn't believe."

"Is it something to do with the weather?" asked Naomi suddenly. Kenan looked at her sharply.

"How do yo-" his sentence was cut short by the computer interrupting him. Appearing on the screen, was Terry's face. In the background was his flat, obviously before it had been wrecked. Terry had a lit cigarette in his mouth and was speaking to the web cam.

"I've just had a phone call," he said. "Tony should be arriving in the city tonight with the centre sphere. I have been watching the news and checking on the internet for any sign of who could have robbed the shrine but so far have found nothing. Will add more data at twenty-one hundred hours." Kenan quickly clicked the next icon. This one was much more serious. Terry's face was drained of colour and he seemed very uptight. "I've tried to get hold of Tony, but he's not answering his phone or anything. It's twenty-three hundr- Oh to hell with it! It's eleven p.m and I daren't leave my flat in case he turns up." The screen went blank. The third video was disturbing. It was also the shortest. Terry had obviously hit the record button on the camera as a gang of five people crashed through into his front room. All had faces hidden behind Halloween masks. Two of them proceeded to beat Terry while the other three trashed his flat. Naomi was mortified. Even Kenan who was used to violence after a life on the streets was shocked. One of the men grabbed the computer and sent it to the floor. The picture and sound died. After a pause, Kenan clicked the fourth box. Terry was now covered in bruises; his eyes were red and swollen. He had another cigarette in his shaking hand, and just managed to stutter: "Tony's dead... killed by the gang. I am ninety-nine percent sure of who did this now." With shaking hands Kenan clicked the last box.

"I think I have found him. Spoke to him last night. His name is Kenan. He seems a nice enough lad, very well mannered, considering he's been bought up on the streets. The only trouble is, that if he is the one I am looking for, and the prophecy comes to pass, then...what the-" His sentence was cut short as someone stormed through the door aimed a gun at Terry and shot him! Terry gasped and fell to the floor! The person who had shot him was wearing a balaclava with just his eyes showing. Kenan caught a glimpse of them as the villain unwillingly looked for a split second at the web-cam, not realizing it was on. He turned to Terry and kicked him a few times. Kenan and Naomi couldn't see what was going on but Kenan knew what had been done to him...he had seen the injuries. Naomi covered her eyes with her hands. Finally the intruder stopped kicking Terry and left. The web cam was left running. Kenan and Naomi held their breath. Suddenly a bloody hand appeared reaching up to the desk. Terry's battered face came into view. Breathing badly he didn't speak a word but shut the web-cam off and the computer screen went blank Kenan and Naomi both stared in silence at the screen for one, long, minute. Finally without a word, Kenan logged off the site. His face was drained of colour and he was shaking slightly. He looked at Naomi, who looked twice as bad as he did.

"I'm sorry," he said finally. "You shouldn't have seen that, but I had no idea..."

"It's okay," whispered Naomi still staring at the computer. "It's just that...well, who could do that to an old guy like him?"

"I know," muttered Kenan. "They're obviously sick."

"But what do they want from him?" pressed Naomi and what's all this stuff about a temple or shrine or whatever it is, and what about YOU? How are you roped in with this?" Kenan hesitated. He didn't really want disclose everything to Naomi about Terry and the legendary shrine deep under the city. She'd never believe him. He smiled to himself. If she wouldn't believe him then what was the harm in telling her? So Kenan launched into the story trying to make it sound as casual as possible. Naomi listened, her brown eyes shining with excitement. When Kenan finished, he was surprised to find that Naomi had actually been hanging onto every word he'd been saying.

"Wow!" she exclaimed when he'd finished. "This is just so exciting!"

"Y- you mean you believe me?" asked Kenan, suddenly wishing he had something that could erase Naomi's memory.

"You bet!" she cried. "I mean it's just so uncanny that my father and I have been feeling, if you'll excuse the expression, under the weather..." Kenan half smiled..."and we both know it's something to do with the seasons, you see, we both posses a sixth sense. We know when something's wrong, or about to go wrong." Kenan raised his eyebrows. He didn't disbelieve Naomi; after all he was surprised that he believed everything he'd been going through in the past few days. As if to deliberately steer the conversation away from the subject, Naomi said;

"Do you want talk some more outside? It's getting too stuffy in here."

"Sure," replied Kenan, as the same thing was going through his head as well. They walked out of the study Kenan

44

still had his air-surfer under his arm. Naomi was eyeing it longingly. "I hope you don't mind me saying this," said Kenan suddenly, "but you're very gullible aren't you." Naomi looked at him sharply, but the faint trace of a smile was in her face.

"What do you mean?"

"Well it's just, you met me two days ago, you invite me into your house today, you ask me to stay for lunch, you've let me use your computer and you believe a story which I've told you while I'm not even sure that I believe it myself." Naomi continued to look at Kenan, started to giggle, then she laughed loudly.

"You really don't get it do you," she said finally. "I told you I know when things are wrong, but it also helps me judge character. You see as soon as I met you, I knew you were different, not just from your friends but there's something about you, and it's something only I can detect. You have potential, Kenan, a great gift, I don't know what it is yet but I have a very good feeling about you. And I'm pretty sure you wouldn't have told me what you did if you didn't think I'd believe you."

"Well actually I didn't think you would believe it," admitted Kenan sheepishly, as they walked down the stone steps, at the front of the mansion, "but," he continued, "you're the first person I've told who does." Naomi smiled.

"Well, at least you're honest," she said. At that moment a black hover-car appeared at the front gates. "Oh no," groaned Naomi. "Kenan quick! Hide somewhere!" But before he even had a chance to look around, Naomi was already dragging him to one of the nearby statues that had a place on the lawn. Both teenagers hid as the car glided gracefully up the main doors of the mansion.

"Who's that?" asked Kenan, as a rather fat boy, a little older than them, got out of the car. His brown hair was plastered down with gel and even though they were a fair distance away from him, Kenan could see he was quite spotty. He had a parcel and what seemed like a bunch of flowers in his arms. James was standing on the steps and as the conversation started the boy looked rather happy, but a few seconds later, his face fell. He handed the parcel and flowers to James and hopped back into the hovering car that glided back over the gravel drive and through the iron gates. The gates closed behind it with a clang and then silence. "Err, what just happened?" enquired Kenan, as they emerged from behind the statue.

"He's a friend," said Naomi casually, not making eye contact with Kenan.

"Oh yeah? A really good friend?" said Kenan grinning. Naomi raised her eyes to the sky.

"It's the third time he's been round this week," she groaned. "My mum introduced me to him at a dinner with some friends of hers a few months ago. After they'd gone, she just launched into how lonely he is as he's the only child in the family and how wealthy his family is. She said 'Oh you two look so lovely together, daaaarling!'" She mimicked her mum's voice perfectly. "Then a few days later she said, 'Oh I've booked for you and Cedric, at the theatre tonight, but don't tell him I arranged it." Kenan was desperately trying to keep a straight face. "So," she continued, "I was polite for just the one evening and now he won't go away. I mean, he's nice and all, but, well....not for me. I mean do you know what his idea of fun is Kenan?" Kenan shook his head. Naomi sighed again as she said blankly; "Going through his baby photos with me and telling me how cute he looked." Kenan stifled a case of the giggles. Naomi glared at him. "I need something to do," she said suddenly eyeing the air-surfer under Kenan's arm again. "Kenan, will you teach me to fly?"

Kenan looked startled.

"Well uh...you don't have an air-surfer or anything do you?"

"No," said Naomi "but could I use yours?"

"Well..." Kenan thought.

"Well what?" persisted Naomi. Kenan stared at her. He had never quite known anyone quite like her. She was so outgoing and up front. He liked her attitude. He smiled; after all he had nothing else to do.

"Okay," he said. "Do you want to start now?" Naomi nodded eagerly. "Well," said Kenan unsure of exactly *how* to start. "The first thing you need to bear in mind is that every air-surfer has, a device which can monitor your brainwaves. This enables it to multiply its gravity to suit your needs."

"Gravity?" questioned Naomi.

"Yep," said Kenan. "Each and every air-surfer built can manipulate the gravity holding you on, depending on how confident you are. For example, if you're terrified of falling off, the chip that monitors your brainwaves, can pick up on this and the gravity around your feet, is changed to be very high so you have less chance of falling off. But the more confident you become, and the more you trust yourself, the less chance you have of falling off anyway. I suppose it's a little like riding a horse, you following so far?" Naomi nodded slowly.

"Right," said Kenan. "Let's see you try then." He laid the air-surfer on the grass and gestured to Naomi to stand on it. Naomi did so and for a moment nothing happened. "Focus on hovering a few feet above the ground," said Kenan. "It'll pick up on your brainwaves, but it may take a minute or so." But to his and Naomi's surprise, the object floated smoothly off the grass nearly six feet from the ground without any trouble at all. Naomi squealed with laughter. "You're a natural," said Kenan. "Now focus on moving about. You should be able to do that well." But this was a lot harder for Naomi to get the hang of.

"How do you steer it?" she called.

"You just lean from side to side," instructed Kenan.

"But I'll fall," insisted Naomi.

"No you won't," remember the gravity around your feet. But Naomi wouldn't dare to try it and bought the air-surfer to the ground looking glum.

"I'm sorry," she said. "I guess I'm just too tense."

"I think you may be," said Kenan. He looked thoughtfully at the air-surfer. "I wonder," he murmured. Naomi looked at him. "Naomi, could you hop back on a sec but keep it on the ground?" asked Kenan. Naomi did. "I think," said Kenan, "it may be able to take two of us." He stepped up behind Naomi and focused on moving the board up. It lifted off the ground again. "Right," he said. "What's going through your head when you turn it?"

"I just...seize up..." began Naomi.

"Wrong!" exclaimed Kenan. "You've got to loosen up. Try and relax. Naomi concentrated on leaning and this time the board turned gracefully to the right.

"I did it!" shouted Naomi. "I actually did it!" she tried to turn around to face Kenan but began to lose her balance! Instinctively Kenan reached out and grabbed Naomi round her middle and pulled her back. Naomi caught him off guard and she fell back against him. Kenan looked at her anxiously but she was grinning broadly. As she looked back at him her wide grin subdued to a small smile. "Thanks Kenan," she murmured. Kenan felt himself blush.

"C- carry on," he said. Naomi focused on turning the air-surfer left and right while going forward. She really began to get the hang of it. After about fifteen minutes, she was flying at quite a speed, zigging and zagging, all over the place. Kenan still, ready to catch her if she lost control again, watched her face as they flew along. He could tell she was really enjoying herself, maybe for the first time in a very long while. The expression she was wearing said it all and, like him, she was a natural. Finally though, she a dip and spin in mid-air, making herself (and Kenan) too dizzy to control the disc! They both fell to the ground. Luckily only a few feet below they landed on the soft grass so they weren't hurt. Naomi was giggling non-stop, her breath knocked out of her. Kenan sat up watching her as she calmed down.

"I thought, you said the gravity..." she began. But Kenan stopped her.

"Losing control of it doesn't help," he smiled. "The only times you can come off it is if you are pushed off by a hard impact, or you lose your sense of direction," (Naomi smiled sheepishly) "which is what you just made both of us do," he finished.

"That was cool though," said Naomi happily. Kenan

shivered.

"Speaking of cool hasn't it gone cloudy all of a sudden." Naomi looked up at the sky. They hadn't noticed while they were flying but dark threatening clouds had quickly blotted out the sun. Before she could agree with Kenan, Naomi looked suddenly towards the house as though she could hear something.

"What?" said Kenan standing up. "Do you hear something?"

"Yeah," said Naomi. "I think I'd better go in, they'll be wondering why I'm not studying... " she made a face as she finished this sentence.

"I'd better get going then," said Kenan.

"Oh why don't you stay?" said Naomi. "I could still chat to you whilst I do my essay." But Kenan shook his head firmly. After all he didn't feel like he could stand Naomi's mum glaring at him like earlier. Naomi shrugged.

"Um Kenan," said Naomi looking a little awkward. "I was just wondering if possibly...you could come round tomorrow afternoon and we could practice flying again?" Kenan stared at her.

"Really?" he asked at last. "I mean if you want to... I've got nothing planned." Naomi nodded in response.

"If you don't mind," she added hastily. "I really enjoyed myself today." Kenan nodded.

"Okay. About four?" he suggested.

"Yeah sure," smiled Naomi, "thanks." Kenan gave her a wink.

"See you tomorrow," he grinned and with a deft movement of his feet, kicked the air-surfer up so it went back to hovering a few inches from the ground and mounted it before sailing gracefully over the gates. Naomi watched him go then walked back to the house deep in thought. She let herself in and made her way to the kitchen to get a drink. She had just finished a glass of water when she heard her dad's voice calling her, which struck her as odd that he would be home this early. She ran up the small flight of steps from the kitchen, checked in the study, and in the luxurious sitting room. Both her parents were sitting down both looking very grave. James was with them. Naomi looked at them all; suddenly she guessed what was wrong.

"Look," she began. "If you're worried about Kenan then let me put your minds at rest. He's a really decent guy. He's been teaching me how to air-surf but gone now, so you don't have to worry, and for your information he's coming back tomorrow. I happen to be in a very good mood at the moment so don't start – please." There was a silence.

"Sit down Naomi," said Lord Henderson softly. Then it hit Naomi...this was something serious, and she already had a horrible feeling she knew what it was. She sat down trembling suddenly. "I'm sorry, Naomi," said her father taking a deep breath, "but it's happened. She's gone. Grandma Henderson passed away at the hospital this afternoon."

*

Kenan reached the multi-story later that evening. He hadn't gone straight back to the car park but had instead been air-surfing around an old abandoned industrial estate. His lessons with Naomi had left him feeling elated for some reason and the old yard with its concrete pipes, pit falls and scaffolding, provided the perfect obstacle course allowing him to run off some energy. His mind was still buzzing as he alighted his air-surfer and he didn't realise he was smiling until Matt pointed it out to him when he saw him five minutes later.

"Hey!" he exclaimed. "You happy sod! Where you been? We've been looking everywhere for you!"

"We?" enquired Kenan. Matt pointed behind him. Vicky was there looking both worried and relieved at the sight of Kenan. Kenan smiled.

"Alright Vicky? I haven't seen you these last couple of days."

"I'm fine," said Vicky, "Damien's the one who's worrying me at the moment."

"Why?"

"He's on one of his missions, I think he's trying to pick

people off again." Kenan shook his head.

"Why did you pick the psycho Vic?" he muttered. "We really should turn him into the police."

"I'm too afraid," said Vicky. "If he ever got out and found out we tipped him off…" She didn't need to finish the sentence, Kenan knew all too well what would happen if that were to happen…. that was what made it difficult. "And also," continued Vicky lowering her voice, "I think he had something to do with the body you found in the car-park the other day."

"What do you mean?" asked Kenan. In as few words possible, Vicky told Kenan and Matt, about the conversation she had overheard the night before and asked them if they could think up and explanation for it. They couldn't.

"Well whoever this Lance is," said Vicky, "he's phoning Damien back tonight and I'm going to try and find out some more."

"But what if he spots you?" said Kenan. "It's too risky. Listen, let me keep an eye on him and I'll tell you anything I think is worth getting stressed out about."

"But how will you manage to get within earshot of him without him noticing?" asked Vicky.

"Same way you did," said Kenan. "Hide and hope for best." Vicky still looked uncomfortable. "Don't worry," said Kenan, winking at her. "What's the worst he can do?" Vicky smiled vaguely but still didn't answer. "When's this guy supposed to be phoning back?" he asked.

"It was about sevenish last night," Vicky replied "and he said he'd ring back in twenty four hours."

"Right," said Kenan standing up, "that gives me ten minutes to find Damien and a decent hiding place."

"Can I come?" asked Matt. Kenan looked doubtful. Matt was his best friend, but he did have a habit of messing things up.

"Well alright," he said finally, "but don't screw it up okay."

"As if I'd do something' like that," retorted Matt.

"You would," teased Kenan. Then in a more serious tone

he said; "Come on, let's find Damien."

"What'll I do?" said Vicky.

"Stay here," said Kenan, "just until we get back. We won't be long."

Chapter Six

Kenan and Matt were becoming stressed. They had searched everywhere under the multi-story and had seen no sign of Damien at all. They only had a few minutes left.

"This is pointless," moaned Matt. "We're not gonna find him in time."

"You may be willing to let him kill innocent people," muttered Kenan. "But I'm not! We have to keep looking!" Matt raised his eyes to the sky then looked twice as something grabbed his attention on top of the car park.

"Hey," he said. "Isn't that him up top there?" Kenan followed his friend's gaze. There was no mistaking the torn trench coat blowing in the night breeze. It was Damien!

"Quick!" exclaimed Matt "the lift!"

"No!" ordered Kenan. "He'll hear us if we take that. We'll take the stairs!"

"You're kiddin'!" whined Matt. "That's like ten flights we have to climb!"

"You don't have to if you don't want to," said Kenan, already running towards the stairwell. Matt considered for a second before running after him. Kenan flung open the door and raced up the stairs. Although both boys were good as far as running went, it was noticeable that even Kenan was getting slower as they neared the top. They slipped out of the door as quietly as possible and ducked behind the first car they saw. Nervously, they peered over the bonnet and scanned the rooftop for Damien. He was still there. Pacing around, he was obviously still awaiting his phone call. It wasn't more than ten seconds before there was a ringing noise. Damien fumbled in his pockets for the phone, found it, and shakily held it to his ear.

"H-hello?" he said, his voice seemed to have an odd tone to it, like there was a lump in it. Kenan and Matt couldn't hear what was being said behind the car so, on Kenan's signal Matt followed him and both began to crawl towards the car parked next to it. They ducked out of sight as soon as they reached it but still couldn't hear anything that was being said on the other end of the phone.

"Wait here," said Kenan quietly, "follow me when I reach the next car." But this wasn't as easy as Kenan had hoped. There was an empty space between the two cars, which meant that he'd be going into open space and Damien was only yards away. Pressing himself against the low concrete wall, he slipped past un-noticed and took cover behind the next car. Looking quickly back towards Matt, he gestured for him to come over...but his friend didn't move. He was far too afraid of being seen in the space between the two cars and shook his head stubbornly. Kenan, slightly relieved, looked around for Damien. He was much closer now and although Kenan had missed a few seconds of the conversation, he could now hear the speaker on the other end of the phone.

"Yes, yes," Damien was saying. "Well, I know it hasn't been reported but he wasn't the only person to have been killed this week was he...London's a big place."

"That's not the point Damien!" shouted the voice. "It should at least have been in the local news. Are you one hundred and one percent sure that he was dead?"

"Err," Damien faltered.

"You incompetent fool!" screamed the voice. "And I don't suppose your any nearer to getting the kid either?"

"No," mumbled Damien, looking weedier by the second and sounding much more like a five year old child than an adult.

"The kid is the main problem here Damien. It poses a threat to us. Think of the status the parents had and if any of this gets out..!"

"But it won't," persisted Damien. "I promise you Lance, I'll have the job done within the time span even if it's on the day itself..."

"You've got a week Damien," said the voice, and the phone went dead.

Damien let out a shaky sigh and turned his back to Kenan...before he seemed to go rigid as he started to look

54

around him sharply. Kenan hadn't realized how far he had
come from his cover to hear the conversation. His heart
skipped a beat. He looked round for Matt hoping that he had
gone away, but he was still there. Realising Kenan was
nervous, he began to crawl towards him.

"Don't," hissed Kenan. "Go away!"

"What?" said Matt forgetting to keep his voice down.
Damien whirled around; his eyes fell on the two boys!

"Well, well, well," he spat maliciously. "What have we
here?" Kenan and Matt were stunned still with terror. As
everybody knew, Damien was a murderer. Kenan glared at
Matt, stood up and faced Damien.

"It stops here, Damien," he said stubbornly. "We all know
you're up to something big. Just give it up and think of your
family first."

"I don't have a family!" growled Damien. "And anyway
that's rich talk coming from someone who killed their own
parents!" Kenan flinched.

"That was an accident," he said, his voice catching
slightly. By this time Matt had begun to slip back towards the
stairwell, not running away, but to get help. Damien, however,
spotted him.

"And just where do you think you're going?" he snarled.
Matt picked up his pace not daring to look around. In a
second, Damien had reached for a gun inside his coat.

"Matt! Down!" shouted Kenan. But Damien clapped a
hand over Kenan's mouth, took aim and fired! There was a
faint whistle but no bang of any kind. Matt fell! "No!" shouted
Kenan. Wrenching himself from Damien's grasp, he ran to his
friend's side. "Matt? Matt! Come on mate don't do this!"
Matt's eyes were closed. He seemed oblivious to Kenan's
words. Kenan tried to shake him awake, but still nothing.
Behind him, Kenan heard Damien's laughter. "You!" shouted
Kenan. "You killed him!"

"You idiot," laughed Damien. "He's not dead, he's
knocked out. This gun contains two darts full, of five
millilitres of the most powerful sleeping draught you can get."

"B- but why did you give him that?" said Kenan, starting

to get confused.

"Oh, don't worry Kenan," said Damien. "You'll find out soon enough." He turned the gun on Kenan and fired! Kenan's vision went foggy almost immediately. He tried to hold on as long as he could but the floor came up towards him and then, everything went black.

*

Before Kenan opened his eyes he knew that he was definitely *not* outside. He felt no breeze and heard no traffic; by the sounds of it, he was alone in a very small space. He opened his eyes...and immediately wished he had kept them closed again. He was in a prison cell! The room was dimly lit by one light on the ceiling and a steel door was the only way in or out, there were no windows. Kenan jumped up of the floor and began pounding on the door.

"Let me outta here!" he shouted. "I didn't do anything! Let me out!" A groan made him turn around. Matt was just waking up. "What is this?" shouted Kenan as Matt rubbed his eyes and looked around.

"I think we're in jail," he said slowly. Kenan rolled his eyes. Although he was relieved Matt was okay, he always stated the obvious.

"You don't say," he muttered.

"But in jail for what?" asked Matt.

"I don't know," snapped Kenan, "but you just wait until I see Damien. I'll bet anything he's got something to do with this!"

"Probably," muttered Matt, slumping down on a bed on one side of the room. "But what can we do? I'd like to know what time it is."

"I don't think it's morning yet," said Kenan, it was impossible to tell with no windows or clock.

"No wonder I'm still tired then," moaned Matt as he slumped back onto the bed.

"How can you still be tired?" exclaimed Kenan. "We've been slung in jail and we have no idea what it's all about!"

"I expect we'll find out soon enough," said Matt. "We can't do anything at the moment." They did find out. No more than ten minutes had passed when they both heard a security code being punched in behind the door. The steel door slid back and a police officer stood there. Now Kenan had been in trouble with the police before, but never in jail so as he ran up to the police officer, only meaning to ask him what was wrong, a shock ran through his body, throwing him to the ground. A force- field was there. Matt laughed as Kenan sat up, so did the police officer.

"Okay," he said. "My apologies boys but we were under the impression you were tampering with a crime scene, but we've checked out some CCTV footage and it looks like you're innocent,- and your alibi, of course." He lowered the force field and gestured a very puzzled but relieved Kenan and Matt out of the station.

"Wait! Our alibi?" asked Kenan before they left.

"Terry Orkas," said the officer, "claimed he knew you quite well."

"But isn't he still in hospital?"

"He was, but not anymore. He discharged himself earlier this afternoon."

"But he was in a real bad way!" insisted Kenan. The officer shrugged.

"Don't question me. Talk to him." He led both boys to the station entrance and showed them out.

It was dark already. Kenan could hear the chimes of the town clock. It was only nine. Kenan turned to Matt.

"I've gotta find out what's going on," he said. "Go back to Vicky and please don't let Damien see you. Tell her what happened. I've got to go and see Terry."

"No way," said Matt. "I want to see this Terry dude as well."

"Matt, please. Vicky will be worried sick." Matt frowned, but he turned quickly and ran off towards the car park as Kenan made his way into the city centre.

Chapter Seven

Kenan had always taken his air-surfer's speed for granted and he was beginning to wish that he'd thought about visiting Terry the next day rather than that night. It took him almost an hour to get to Terry's block, and it was getting cold. He pressed the buzzer. No reply. He pressed it again. Still no reply. Kenan began to get worried. *If he doesn't answer this time,* he thought *I'll break down the doors.* With determination, he pressed the buzzer and this time it clicked.

"Terry?" asked Kenan. There was no reply but the doors flew open. Kenan took it as an invitation. He ran up the flights of stairs, down the corridor and banged on Terry's door. It opened and Kenan immediately bolted in his urgency to see if he was okay. As before the hallway was dark, but once in the front room, he was able to see Terry's face properly...and was alarmed to see he looked angry. "Terry are you oka-?" Kenan didn't get time to finish his sentence. Terry took hold of his shoulders and spoke to him in such a furious voice, Kenan was almost afraid.

"What the hell do think you're playing at?" he hissed. Kenan's eyebrows rose.

"Did I miss something?" he answered.

"Are you taking me seriously?" demanded Terry. Kenan still didn't understand.

"I don't get what you're saying!" he exclaimed.

"What I'm saying," said Terry, "is what do you think you're doing messing around on air-surfers with that girl from the Henderson manor earlier?"

"What?" shouted Kenan. "give me a break! She let me use her computer to look up your website, like *you* told me to do! I had to thank her somehow!"

"You didn't need to do anything of the sort!" shouted back Terry. "What's more important? Saving the world or hanging out with your girlfriend?"

"Well, obviously saving the world!" replied Kenan, "and

she's *not* my girlfriend...anyway," he found himself changing the subject far too quickly, "how do you know about this? You were supposed to be in hospital with a bullet lodged on your chest!"

Terry glowered at him.

"I've got more important things to worry about," he growled, "especially if you're not taking this seriously. My granddaughter saw you at the mansion. She paid a visit there today. You didn't see her with your racing around the grounds but she saw you."

"Look," said Kenan, not really wanting to fall out with Terry, "I'm still going help you, but right now, I just need a lead."

"Funnily enough," snapped Terry, "while you were playing kiss chase earlier on, I heard on the news that the power plant has been broken into. Nothing's been taken but it seems like someone or a group of people have been tampering with the generator."

"And?" questioned Kenan. Terry's voice seemed to calm down as he continued:

"The generator for this part of London gives a whole lot of power right?"

"Err right."

"Therefore it must give off a whole lot of heat energy, right?"

"You're the boss."

"Don't you see Kenan?" exclaimed Terry. "The spheres will only function when aligned deep under the ground in the temple. When in an atmosphere of their opposite season, the season they represent will go haywire, this may be explaining why the weather we've had lately has been so cold."

"Let me get this straight," said Kenan. "You think that the sphere representing winter has been placed, within the area of the generator in the power station so it will get hot and not function properly..."

"Resulting in the first steps to the Earth's destruction," finished Terry triumphantly. "Kenan it matters not that we find who is responsible for this now, what matters is we find the spheres as quickly as possible." Kenan's mind was buzzing, things were finally beginning to look up.

"I'll organize stuff for tomorrow night," he said finally.

"What do you mean tomorrow night?"

"You want the sphere don't you?" grinned Kenan. "Matt Sam and whoever else is willing to help will come with me to the power station and retrieve the sphere."

"K-Kenan," said Terry looking very taken aback. "It's too dangerous. I was thinking about an undercover job or...

"We don't have the time for that," interrupted Kenan, "I know it's dangerous but what's more important? Saving the world, or worrying about what might not happen?" After looking amazed, Terry smiled.

"Thanks Kenan," he said.

*

"We're doing WHAT!"

"Breaking into the power station tomorrow night," repeated Kenan. Matt, Sam, Nick and Lia were sitting in front of him looking as if he'd gone mad.

"You honestly expect us to help you break into the city's main power station for the sake of one little ball?" spluttered Matt.

"Please guys," said Kenan. "I wouldn't ask normally, but you don't know Terry. He's not just some dotty old guy. He's serious."

"Kenan, this Terry guy isn't the one we're worried about," said Sam slowly. "If he is serious then why, has he chosen you, of all people, to help him out?" Kenan shrugged.

"It's a question I've been asking myself," he said truthfully, "but I just can't find an answer that I understand."

"Two thousand five hundred pounds!" groaned Kenan.

"But look at it," drooled Matt.

"No way!" said Kenan turning away from the window of the air-surfer shop. Matt who was pressed up against the window didn't move.

"Matt!" said Kenan in a dangerous voice, "we are not stealing a two 'n' half grand air-surfer that we don't need."

"But we might," insisted Matt finally tearing himself away from the window. "We could use it tonight...you know for a fast get away-"

"We don't need it!" shouted Kenan. He looked at the time on the shop's clock, why was it taking so long for four 'o' clock to arrive? He and Matt had spent that morning walking around the city centre looking for things that would help them that night. So far they had either found or stolen, a torch, gloves, some rope and two sets of walkie-talkies. Matt had been trying to get Kenan to help him come up with a plan to get the air-surfer but Kenan refused, as he knew it was just pointless. "Err look," said Kenan, "We've got pretty much all we need. Why don't we start heading back?"

"I suppose," muttered Matt, a large amount of bitterness in his voice. They made their way back towards the car park Kenan thinking of only one thing... the coming afternoon. He liked air-surfing and teaching Naomi was not only fun but also a way to get away from Matt and the others. Still there was something else that Kenan couldn't put his finger on. A weird feeling he'd never really had before. All he knew about it was Naomi had something to do with it.

"Kenan!" he could tell it wasn't the first time he'd been called. Sam and Lia were running towards him. Matt was talking to Nick who seemed to be trying to lead him away from the group. Sam gave a quick thumbs up sign to Nick and slowed to a walk as she approached Kenan.

"What's going on?" asked Kenan. Sam quickly pulled a skateboard shaped object out from under her baggy jumper...an air-surfer.

"It's Matt's," she said triumphantly. Kenan looked confused.

"No, it's not," he said. "That's brand new."

"Well yeah," said Lia. "It's our present to Matt for tomorrow..." Kenan still looked confused... "His birthday, remember?"

"Oh Jeez!" exclaimed Kenan. "I totally forgot!" By now Matt and Nick had vanished.

"Calm down," said Sam laughing. "We'll say it's from all of us."

"You guys sure?" asked Kenan. Sam and Lia nodded.

"Thanks," sighed Kenan with relief. He double took at the air-surfer. "If that's brand new," he said, "how did you get it?" Sam grinned.

"How else? Five fingered discount." She winked at Kenan. Kenan shook his head but smiled. In the distance, he heard the clock chime half past three with its distinctive two rings. An idea suddenly came into his head.

"Hey," he suggested to the two girls. "Can I test this thing out? You know how Matt is with new stuff. I'll give it a run in yeah?"

"Why?" asked Sam. "You've never checked out new air-surfers before."

Kenan faltered.

"Well, yeah," said Kenan. "But y'know…"

"Well no I don't," said Sam. "Come on what's up?"

"Oh, let Kenan test it," said Lia nervously not wanting an argument to happen.

"Alright," muttered Sam. "Just make sure you hide it until tomorrow." She and Lia walked away. Kenan looked at the board in his hands. It was nice. Much better than his...still he knew he wouldn't like a different one. His had a 'feel' that he was used to. Quickly jumping on his air-surfer while still holding Matt's, he flew off towards the Henderson's manor.

Chapter Eight

When Kenan landed before the gates that afternoon, he knew something was wrong. Several classy looking cars were occupying the driveway outside the house. One he recognized as Cedric's he'd seen the day before. Deciding it safer not to ring, he flew over the gates and around the grounds high above the manor. A part of the grounds he hadn't seen were the back gardens. As he got a bird's eye view of the place he saw them now, then something else caught his attention. He was sure he heard the sound of a door slamming and a girl rushed out of the back of the house and down the back garden. At the end of the garden was a stone bench hidden by rose bushes with a beautiful fountain before it. A fat figure followed her for a few yards followed by someone else. The two seemed to stand still before retreating back to the house leaving the girl alone. Checking the coast was totally clear. Kenan slowly sank downwards. He was only a few feet from the ground when he realized that the girl was Naomi…and she was crying.

"Naomi?" he exclaimed jumping to the ground and running up to her. Naomi lifted her head, her eyes bloodshot.

"She's dead," she sobbed as Kenan slowed to a stop.

"Who?" asked Kenan.

"My Gran," answered Naomi in a choked voice. "She died yesterday."

"Oh man!" groaned Kenan. "That- that oh I'm sorry…did you get to see her?"

"No," said Naomi, "I was air-surfing yesterday, wasn't I?"

"You mean she died when…" Kenan couldn't finish the sentence. A suffocating guilt swim over him… he felt responsible for keeping Naomi from seeing her Gran in her last hours. He bit his lip. As though reading his mind Naomi sniffed; "it's not your fault, I should've gone when I had the chance earlier on in the day." She buried her head in her hands as Kenan sat beside her.

"If you want," he suggested, "we can arrange air-surfing

for another day." Naomi looked at him.

"No," she said defiantly. "You took time out to come here. Anyway it may clear my head a bit."

"I still feel bad," muttered Kenan. He felt the air-surfer under his arm. *'No!'* screamed a voice inside his head. *'You can't!* Kenan looked at the board then at Naomi. *'I've got to!'* he thought furiously to himself.

"Err, Naomi," he said, "I brought you something." He handed her the board without looking at her. Naomi looked in disbelief at the air-surfer.

"Is this..." she whispered," an *air-surfer*?" Kenan nodded.

"You bought this for me?" Kenan couldn't lie.

"It's supposed to be for one of my friends," he said. "But they don't know about it yet." Naomi looked shocked.

"Kenan," she said. "It's brilliant but I can't accept it...my parents could buy me one this afternoon if they wanted to..."

"Take it," said Kenan still not looking at her.

"But your friend..."

"Take it!" exclaimed Kenan. Naomi knew to stop. For a moment she seemed happy beyond words and gave Kenan a hug, which made him go bright red.

"Thank you so much," she sniffed happily.

"No problem," said Kenan. Naomi pulled away. She also had blushed. There was a moments' embarrassing silence. Then; "Right let's see how much you remember, err where can we practise?"

"What do you mean?"

"Well, it looks like quite a lot of people are here and if they see me with you..." Naomi laughed.

"Don't worry," she said. "I told my parents yesterday that you'd be coming round...that was before they told me..." She hid her face as she looked at the floor. Kenan, awkwardly, put his arm around Naomi's shoulders.

"Cheer up Naz," he whispered. Naomi looked at him.

"Naz?" she enquired. Kenan shrugged as he tried to hide a smile.

"Your new nickname," he said innocently. "Like it?" Naomi pretended to be insulted.

"Well I never," she said putting on her haughtiest voice. "The cheek of it. Naz indeed." She grinned as Kenan laughed at her.

"Come on," he smiled "let's take this baby out for a run!"

"You know, it's odd but I think I've had one too many," said Cedric to a rather plump girl he was standing next to.

"Why do you say that?" asked the girl.

"I swore I saw Naomi fly past the window," said Cedric. The girl laughed.

"I think that's enough wine for you," she said lightly, "with you and your vivid imagination." She grinned. "Was she flying past on silver wings?"

"Oh ha-ha," muttered Cedric. "I don't know about my vivid imagination Delia, but if I don't leave this house soon I'll go mad...it's so morbid."

"What do you expect?" said Delia. "A member of the family has died and it was your idea to come and pay sympathy."

"I only did that to see Naomi," muttered Cedric bitterly "and she just ran out on me."

"Well, surely you can understand that," said Delia. "She's just lost her Gran." Cedric half nodded. Then he double took as he stared outside the window.

"Look at that!" he exclaimed "there's a boy chasing Naomi round the garden on some flying board!" Delia looked as well and gasped.

"We must tell George," she hissed. "But quietly don't make a fuss." She and Cedric sidled through flocks of people talking in sad hushed voices until they spotted Lord Henderson sitting alone. He was very quiet and solemn faced quite the opposite to his normal self.

"Errm, George sir," said Cedric. "We believe that, errm, an uninvited guest has turned up here."

"Wha' doya mean?" slurred Lord Henderson.

"Well, he's quite scruffy, and he's on a flying board kind of thing outside with Naomi." Lord Henderson looked bleary-eyed at Cedric. It was clear he had been drinking heavily...after all it was his mother who had died.

"Kenan," he muttered "donworry." Cedric decided not to pursue the subject.

"Well," he said turning to where he thought Delia was, "it seems we need not worry..." he stopped short. Delia was over by the window with a strange expression on her face. She had a very clear view of Kenan and Naomi now, but she was more focused on Kenan. "Delia," asked Cedric. "Are you okay?"

"I'm fine," said Delia her frosty glare never leaving Kenan.

Kenan and Naomi were sitting on the grass having just finished a furious race against each other. Kenan had won but Naomi was insisting he had taken a short cut somewhere along the line.

"How could I have?" laughed Kenan for the third time. "There was no way I could have unless I flew straight through the house."

"That's probably what you did," teased Naomi. "But I think we should have another race...somewhere different." Kenan hesitated. Although the grounds were large it didn't beat flying through the city. Personally it didn't worry him, but Naomi had only just managed to control her air-surfer. It was too risky and he said so. "I know of a different place," smiled Naomi mischievously. "My parents own it a few miles out of town. Acres of land, nothing but open fields." Kenan's eyes grew round. He had, of course, heard of fields but like trees, but as they were a sort of luxury, because there were so few of them left anywhere near London, he had never really seen one. He jumped up with excitement.

"Well then, let's go!" he exclaimed. "It sounds cool!" Naomi laughed at Kenan's enthusiasm.

"Okay, okay. Calm down!" she laughed as she stood up.
"It's only a field after all."

"But I've never seen one before," said Kenan, "only on the holo-box and even then so it's not very often." Naomi stared at him.

"You've never seen a field before?"

"Nope," said Kenan. Naomi shook her head.

They made the journey to the fields in silence. Inside, Kenan was bubbling over with excitement but he didn't really want to show it. He followed Naomi out of the city and slowly the apartment blocks and skyscrapers began to thin out. These eventually gave way to towns, growing more rural at each one they flew over.

"Nearly there!" she called to Kenan. They were approaching a blind summit of a hill, but as they reached the top Kenan's jaw fell open. Never before had he seen such an expanse of open land. Acres and acres of green fields spread out before him. Beyond them was woodland stretching away on the horizon. "My parents own that to," smiled Naomi looking at the amazed Kenan. It seemed as though an electric charge had gone through him he shot off with a burst of speed. He had only once felt like this, the first time he had ever ridden an air-surfer since then it had become like riding a pushbike and with buildings springing up and space becoming a rare thing in the city, he really did feel free. He did one circuit of the field then slowed to a stop as he reached Naomi. A huge smile was on his face and he was shaking... a new surge of adrenaline was in his veins.

"That was..." he didn't finish the sentence, his words were lost in laughter. Naomi was laughing at the state he was in.

"Come on," she said happily. "Let's have a proper race!" Kenan regained himself at the thought of a challenge.

"You're on!" he said. For the next hour and a half the two friends raced round the perimeters of the fields and beyond. They flew over the woods then actually through them, dodging trees and undergrowth as they went before going back round the fields. Slowly the sun began to be blotted out by giant rain clouds but they didn't notice until a drop fell onto Kenan's face.

"I think it's time to go," he said looking up at the black sky.

"I guess," said Naomi looking disappointed. But she could see it was pointless staying out if they were going to get wet. As it happened they both got caught in it anyway on the way back. Naomi had never flown in rain before and even Kenan knew to be careful. In fact neither of them saw the Henderson mansion through the thick sheets of rain until Kenan shouted:

"We're here already! Slow down!" He braked sharply but Naomi panicked, having seen how close she was to the house and lost control of her air-surfer. She dropped on it too fast and Kenan looked in horror. She fell to the ground and rolled over as the air-surfer clattered down beside her. Kenan descended and ran up to her. She was sitting on the wet grass clutching her ankle.

"Are you okay?" Kenan asked anxiously.

"No," whimpered Naomi. "It feels like it's broken."

"Try and stand up," said Kenan. Naomi wobbled to her feet but collapsed immediately. Kenan looked more closely. "I think it's sprained," he said, "maybe you've torn a ligament. Come on," he continued standing up. "I'll help you get inside." He picked up both air-surfers, supporting Naomi, who put her right arm over his shoulder, and with her other arm out for balance hopped over the grounds towards the entrance doors. Kenan was relieved to see all the cars had gone. He really didn't fancy the idea of a whole lot of people like Naomi's mum looking at him like she had done the first time he had met her. Naomi pressed the bell and a second later James opened it. At the sight of both teenagers soaking wet, he rushed them in quickly and into the empty sitting room, where a fire was burning. Kenan didn't feel right sitting down so he stood up as James rushed out to get a bandage and ice pack for Naomi. "I'd err better get going," said Kenan.

"In this weather?" exclaimed Naomi. "You'll freeze!" Kenan smiled.

"I've dealt with worse," he smiled. Deep inside though, he knew his real reason for going was he didn't want to feel anymore guilty than he did already, by intruding in a household that didn't really like him. Naomi could see that she wouldn't win this argument. She shrugged.

"If you're sure," she muttered.

"So I'll see you round sometime," said Kenan. "I mean you've mastered flying lessons easily enough." Naomi looked a little shocked.

"Kenan," she stuttered suddenly. "I err..." she trailed off.

Kenan stood suddenly very rigid and tense as he waited for

Naomi to continue... *what on earth is wrong with me?* He thought furiously. "I- I want to help you on this," said Naomi finally. "I honestly think I could be really useful, you know I could find out stuff on the net and help you out?" Kenan let out a discreet sigh then nodded smiling again.

"Well, what you need to do first," he said, "is rest that ankle. But if you're sure you want help us, well, you know where we are right?" Naomi nodded before defiantly attempting to stand up supporting herself on the arm of the chair...but she fell again. Kenan walked over to her.

"You don't listen do you?" he smiled. Naomi looked at him in a way that was supposed to look angry but she was smiling. She tried again and put her weight on her left leg so she was standing. Kenan looked impressed.

"Thanks for cheering me up anyway," said Naomi smiling.

"No problem," said Kenan, "you cheered me up." There was a moment of awkward silence. "I'd better go," said Kenan, looking at the floor.

"Yeah sure," said Naomi, who had also taken a sudden interest in the carpet beneath them. She hobbled over to the door and held it open.

"I think you've got that the wrong way round," said Kenan as he walked out. "A lady like you holding open a door for the likes of me?"

Naomi smiled, but said nothing. Kenan turned round to say a final goodbye to her but before he could, Naomi quickly gave him a hug. Kenan blushed redder than ever, and pulled away just as James came hurrying back.

"Miss Naomi!" he exclaimed. "What are you doing exercising? You should be taking it easy. I'll show Kenan out."

"No need," said Kenan. "I'll do that myself thanks." He waved at Naomi and made his exit. Outside the rain was pouring but he didn't care. A kind of energy was building up inside him. As he sailed over the gates he held his arms open wide and shouted the one word; "Yessss!"

Chapter Nine

It was still early in the evening when Kenan arrived at the car
park. He quickly packed his air-surfer away and hunted out a
ragged old towel, which he used to dry his hair. He was cold
and wet but, strangely, he didn't care. He lay back on the
blankets of his 'bed' and stared up at the ceiling above him.
The moment when Naomi had hugged him kept replaying in
his mind. *'Get over it,'* he thought. *'It's not like she's
interested. She's just glad of a friend to talk to...I mean look at
where she lives then look at me, hardly an ideal match...
besides it's not like we have anything in common, I hardly
know her, she's a good friend but that's it...'* Still it was a nice
feeling and he couldn't help smiling. He turned over on the
blankets and closed his eyes...

"Kenan, hey wake up already." Kenan slowly came to.
He'd been dreaming, about what, he couldn't remember but
he took quite a few minutes to wake up. Sam was gently
shaking his shoulder.

"Hey," she said in a low voice. "C'mon it's time."

"Time?" mumbled Kenan still in a daze.

"The power station," said Sam. "You know we've got to
go and get the sphere."

"You guys are going to help me?" said Kenan, pleasantly
surprised. He honestly didn't think they would have after the
reaction he had received when he told them. He hadn't had a
definite response from any of them after all, they had all just
made their excuses shortly afterwards and disappeared.

"Is there any reason why we shouldn't?" grinned Sam.
"It's just gone eleven thirty, we should be able to find it
within an hour."

"Half eleven already," murmured Kenan standing up and
stretching. "I must have needed that sleep."

"Mmm," replied Sam without much interest. "Let's get a
move on the others are all ready and waiting."

Matt had managed to fix up his air-surfer so it made
reasonable progress though it still was a little shaky. Seeing it

Kenan remembered (guiltily) about giving away his birthday present earlier that day but it was soon pushed to the back of his head as he remembered the dangerous situation they were about to venture into...

Kenan and the others had hardly ever seen the power station. It stood on the outskirts of city. As they approached it on their air-surfers, the building loomed up seemingly twice as big as it actually was. Everyone had been unusually quiet on the journey there. Even Matt, who always found reason to complain about something hadn't uttered a word and Kenan couldn't help feeling he was trying to avoid him. There was also someone else accompanying them on their journey...Buster. He had been on an air-surfer before, and was possibly the only dog that Kenan knew who was a perfect passenger. He lay between Kenan's feet very still and silent. Kenan had decided to bring him along just in case they ran into trouble. What with Buster's huge teeth, claws and strength, no one was going to pose a threat. Finally they soared over the gates of the building and circled it trying to find a spot where there was no security. It was surprisingly easier than anyone had thought. The south side of the building had no cameras or guards about and the five teenagers and dog quickly landed.

"Okay," said Kenan, when they had sorted themselves out. "I vote we split into one group of three and one of two, how about Matt with Buster and me. Sam, you with Nick and Lia?" Everyone agreed. "Right, we'll check the south and west side," said Kenan. "You guys check the north and east side." He handed Nick a set of walkie-talkies and a flashlight before him Matt and Buster set off trying to find an entrance.

"How do you think those guys got in the other night?" asked Matt after a minute.

"It may have been an inside job," said Kenan. "We've just got to find the generator. We get to that and we'll have already found the sphere."

"And what if it's not there?" asked Matt. Kenan didn't reply. He had been worrying the same thing but just didn't want to admit it. He, Matt and Buster wondered around the building looking for any sign of how they could get in…a window left open of a door ajar but the power station was locked up. Just as Matt was about to start moaning about what a waste of time it was, Buster put his ears up and growled softly.

"What's up, Buzz?" whispered Kenan. Buster stood absolutely still. The dog took a small step forward and another before breaking into a flat out run.

"Buster!" shouted Kenan and Matt. But Buster had disappeared into the night. With Matt holding the flashlight, the two boys began to try and follow, but there was no sign of the alsatian anywhere. Kenan and Matt stopped running and looked around desperately. "That stupid mutt!" groaned Kenan. "He might be seen."

"We didn't see any security guards though did we?" said Matt. Kenan didn't answer. Just then he heard a voice on his radio. It was Sam.

"Kenan, Kenan are you there?" Kenan grabbed the radio.

"We're here," he said. "What is it? Have you seen Buster?"

"No-o," replied Sam slowly. "You've lost him?"

"Never mind," said Kenan his hopes quickly vanishing. "What did you want?"

"We can't find a way in," said Sam, "it's hopeless."

"Right," said Kenan. "Go back to the car park, we'll find Buster and follow you. This wasn't a good idea at all."

"Okay." The radio clicked out and Kenan sighed. Then he turned to Matt.

"Come on, we're not leaving without my dog," he muttered. Before either of them could say anything else, they heard it, cutting through the night air, loud and clear. Buster was barking. Kenan's face lit up. "Let's go!" he shouted to Matt, "he's this way!" Again the two friends set off, in the direction of Buster's barks. It soon became very apparent why there were no security guards and only minimum amount of cameras, the power stations security was locked down and Kenan couldn't for the life of him think how the gang had

managed to get in or out at all. It didn't take them long to find
Buster. He was standing outside a separate building smaller
than the main plant. Upon seeing Kenan he stopped barking
and wagged his tail. "There you are," grinned Kenan, petting
him. Matt pointed the torch to a sign on the door it read:
Warning High Voltage Generator
Kenan turned to Matt grinning.

"That's it!" he exclaimed. "The generator isn't in the main
building... we've been looking in the wrong place."

Matt inspected the door, it had a card reader next to it and
not much else in the way of security.

"No wonder they managed to get in," he said aloud, "this
thing's practically prehistoric."

"Reckon you can get in?" asked Kenan.

"Only one way to find out replied Matt. He took a plastic
card out of his pocket and swiped it through the reader beside
the door. Nothing happened. "It's not working," he muttered.
"Guess we'll do this the old fashioned way. He slipped it in
between the door and door frame and slid it about for a
minute. The card in question was one Matt had found in
Damien's coat pocket some years before. It turned out it was
very handy and opened most doors in town. They didn't ask
how Damien had ever gotten it in the first place, but he had
never seemed to notice its absence so they had used it on most
excursions into 'missions.' Matt, however, seemed to have
'the knack' for using it on doors that didn't open. Suddenly
there was a click and the door swung open. A blast of hot air
hit them. Buster ventured in first as Matt swung the flashlight
onto a huge metal generator. It was whirring noisily and the
heat it gave off was like stepping into an oven. Buster sniffed
around busily while Kenan and Matt, with the aid of their
torch searched the surrounding area. Kenan saw Buster
barking again. Although they couldn't hear him above the
noise of the generator Kenan could see where he was and
quickly tapped Matt on the arm to follow him. They quickly
ran over to the dog and finally saw what all the fuss was
about. Glowing with a blue light just under the generator, a
sphere about the same size as the crystal one Kenan had first

found was lying there. Kenan grabbed it and looked with a feeling of utter victory inside him. Matt was awestruck at the sight, looking at Kenan with renewed respect. The two friends and dog quickly and silently made their way out of the building and Matt closed the door behind him.

"This is it," whispered Kenan hardly able to take his eyes off the glowing ball. "This is the winter sphere. Oh, wait until I show Terry tomorrow this is SO COOL!"

"Yeah great," said Matt but shouldn't we be making a hasty exit. "I don't think we ought to be hanging around too long."

"Oh right," said Kenan, "but where did we leave our air-surfers?"

"God damn it!" shouted Matt as a realization hit him, "back at where we ran after Buster!" Without another word, they set off again at a run back to where they had left the boards. Relief flooded through them as they saw them lying on the ground, indeed, where they had left them. Matt climbed onto his and Buster quickly lay down on the other as Kenan climbed on. With the sphere in his jacket pocket they took off.

That was easy, thought Kenan. *Way too easy it's almost like something else is going to happen tonight that'll make this situation a whole lot more difficult...*

"W-what did you say? Sorry I was miles away there," said Kenan trying not to let his voice go shaky.

"Matt's birthday present," repeated Sam. Kenan gulped. It felt like a ton of lead had been dropped over him, as he remembered Matt's birthday and more importantly the air-surfer, which he'd given Naomi.

Fake it,' he thought to himself. *You'll just have to fake it. It could've been stolen while we've been gone.* It was just gone half past midnight and Sam was insisting they give Matt his present now.

"Come on," persisted Sam. "Let's get it ready! Nick and Lia are bringing him down here in a few minutes. I managed to lure him away when you got back, y'know you were packing your air-surfer away."

"Oh right," said Kenan, getting up and walking over to the same box where he had put his own board, only minutes before. After a few minutes of pretending to look for it he turned back to Sam trying to look alarmed. "It's not here!" he exclaimed. Sam's face fell.

"W-what do you mean it's not there?" she hissed.

"It was here when I went to sleep, before we left," lied Kenan.

"Someone must've stolen it."

"Wait!" exclaimed Sam, her face clearing "I know where it's gone!"

"W-where?" asked Kenan, confused. Sam looked hard at Kenan for a minute before walking up to him until she was inches from his face.

"You know where you lying, selfish git!" she spat. Kenan gulped. "I thought it was a little weird," continued Sam. "You never thought to test out air-surfers before so I followed you...never suspecting you would just give it away to that little snob!" Kenan was speechless. What was worse was as he looked at Sam he saw three people show up behind her. Each of them shared the expression on her face. Sam had obviously told them too. No wonder they'd hardly spoken to him all night. Matt looked as though he wanted to hit Kenan. "So," pushed on Sam, "how long have you known her?"

"What?" shouted Kenan in disbelief. "You think I'm seeing her or something?"

"Duh," muttered Sam. Kenan couldn't bear to face them. He turned around with his back to the group. "So?" persisted Sam. "Don't keep us in suspense any longer, how long have you known her? Is this why you wanted to race to the mansion the other day?"

"She's only a friend," said Kenan quietly his eyes closing, hoping that this was all just an awful dream.

"A week, two weeks?" pressed on Sam, taking a step nearer to Kenan.

"She's only a friend." repeated Kenan, he tried not to keep clenching and unclenching his fist.

"Maybe you've fooled us all!" exclaimed Sam taking

another step towards Kenan. "C'mon Kenan, you've known her a month haven't you? A year?" Kenan opened his eyes and spun round. His arms were raised in exasperation and he didn't expect Sam to be so close to him. He knew what was going to happen a split second before it did…and there was no time to lower his hands. Sam shrieked as Kenan's hand came into contact with the side of her face. She fell to the ground and the others gasped. Kenan immediately knelt by her side. He had never meant to hit Sam but she had been standing so near to him. He knew that, but he also knew how it looked to Matt Nick and Lia.

"Sam!" he cried, "I'm so sorry! Are you okay?"

"Get away from me you freak!" she shouted leaping to her feet.

Buster, who had fallen asleep on Kenan's blankets, awoke with a start and quickly hid underneath them.

"Come on Sam!" Kenan exclaimed, "You know I would never hit you intentionally!" He stood up and went to move towards her but Sam only backed away from him.

"Stay away!" she shouted clutching the side of her face. "If you can't even admit that you're in the wrong without taking it out on somebody else…"

"Sam please…"

"Get away from her Kenan." Everybody stared as Matt stepped in between them. He glared at Kenan and when he spoke his voice was so quiet and his face so deadpan everyone felt uneasy. "I can take it that you've given my air-surfer to that kid, and I take it that you lied to us to try and cover your own back, but what I can't and never will take is you hitting a girl."

"For the last time I didn't hit her on purpose!" shouted Kenan. He picked up his air-surfer and flew out from under the car park. The wind screamed in his ears as he picked up speed and he didn't even realize where he was headed until he reached lookout point. He landed quickly and sat looking out at the city for a long time. *She was too close.* He kept repeating to himself. *But how am I going to convince the others it was an accident?* Would they ever speak to him again? The feeling he was torn in three different directions was growing inside of him. He wanted to help Terry, but his friends didn't. Nor did his friends have any time for Naomi, even though Kenan had learned she was a genuinely nice person. *How am I going to get through this without falling out with one of them... maybe all of them?* It was a horrible feeling.

He finally decided he'd have to return to the car park, he was too tired...it was definitely the early hours of the morning now. He rubbed his eyes as he reached for his air-surfer and then looked at his hand. It was wet...he hadn't even realized he'd been crying.

Chapter Ten

Not surprisingly Kenan slept through till very late the next morning. He awoke at near enough eleven and as the previous night came flooding back to him he groaned quietly to himself. With a jolt he remembered- it hadn't been all bad...he had still gotten the sphere. Immediately he leapt out of bed and reached for his jacket, as he had slept fully clothed. After a quick check to see if the sphere was still in his pocket, he quickly reached for his air-surfer and made for Terry's flat.

It seemed that Kenan wasn't the only one who had overslept that morning. When he finally got inside the flat, Terry was still wondering around in his dressing gown. He sleepily asked Kenan if he wanted any breakfast, Kenan accepted gratefully and showed Terry the sphere. The old man's face lit up and it almost seemed as though he had had an instant injection of caffeine. He told Kenan to help himself to breakfast while he got washed and dressed. He was so fast Kenan hardly had time to finish his plateful before Terry was back asking Kenan how he had got hold of the sphere. In as few words as possible, Kenan told him the previous nights events even about the Sam and Matt business. Terry didn't interrupt once but his eyes were shining and he was on the edge of his seat. Finally when Kenan had finished Terry shook his head, smiling, but in part disbelief.

"You really have to overdo it don't you?" he smiled.

"But I didn't mean to hit her," said Kenan, "she was standing so close behind me and I didn't expect her to be there."

"Oh I believe you," said Terry hurriedly, "it's just that only you could do something like that...I've never known anyone to have such bad luck." At that moment the intercom buzzed, and Terry quickly scurried out to the hall to answer it. "Yes," he said, "yes come on up, but I'm going out soon." He re-entered the front room. "My granddaughter's coming up," he said. "You won't have met her but her name's Delia...she's the one who saw you at the mansion the other day." Kenan nodded.

"Is she okay?" he asked tentatively. Terry looked at him questioningly.

"As far as I know," he replied. "Why do you ask?" Now it was Kenan's turn to look confused.

"Well I just, thought," he said quietly, "was Tony her dad?"

"No," replied Terry shortly. "I have a daughter as well, we don't speak that much. She said she didn't want to know anything about the shrine when I told her... she didn't even give me a chance. Told me I was just a crazy old fool. Like I say, we hardly talk any more but Delia did give me the chance and she comes in to see me frequently." Kenan nodded again.

"So why was she at the Henderson estate?" asked Kenan. "Is she a friend of Naomi's or something?"

"No no," smiled Terry. "As far as I know they met at a mutual friends birthday party a few months ago... some boy named Cedric, Naomi may have told you..."

"Oh yes," smiled Kenan, "I know about Cedric."

"Ah," exclaimed Terry, "so you must also know that he's, shall we say, pretty keen on Naomi. Now Delia knows this, she's been friends with Cedric for years and she feels the same way about him, so she's recently found every excuse to follow him and make sure that he doesn't get too near Naomi."

"A good thing too," muttered Kenan. Terry smiled again.

"Why do you say that?" he asked casually. Kenan suddenly realized what he had said. He checked himself.

"Well err, you see Naomi's not really keen on Cedric, so she's told me and err well maybe Delia will distract him from her or something..."

"Are you hot or something?" interrupted Terry.

"No. Why?"

"You've gone really red," laughed Terry.

"Oh give it a rest," moaned Kenan. Fortunately he was spared any more questions by a knock at the door.

"It's open," shouted Terry. A rather plump figure swept into the flat. She had short brown hair, and hazel eyes.

"Hi Grandpa," she started to say, then her eyes fell on Kenan. "That's him!" she exclaimed. "Grandpa, I'm telling you I saw him…"

"Calm down Delia," said Terry. "I've sorted out all the stuff with Kenan and there's no reason to worry. It seems he was only at the mansion to use a computer to access my website."

"But I saw him," insisted Delia. "He was there yesterday as well, racing around the grounds on some kind of board!"

"An air-surfer actually," said Kenan quietly. He had already decided to take an instant dislike to Delia…he didn't approve of people who never gave others a chance to explain their side of a story.

"Grandpa you said you were going out soon," said Delia. "Where?"

"You should know Delia," said Terry smiling again. He nodded in Kenan's direction.

"You mean he's got it?" exclaimed Delia, "oh wow! Was it in the power plant?"

"Yeah," said Kenan, "right next to the generator." He looked at Terry. "So where are you going Terry?"

"I think you'd know the answer to that as well Kenan." Kenan looked blankly first at Terry then at Delia.

"No," he said finally. "Don't know."

"Well, where else can the sphere go," said Delia. Kenan suddenly realized what they were saying.

"We're going to the shrine?"

"Yes," said Terry. "Deep under the earth's surface. Miles under the London underground system…only we know of its location…"

"Us and the guys who robbed it," Delia reminded him. Terry faltered.

"Hey Terry," said Kenan. "If we're going to leave this ball underground in the shrine, won't the guys come back for it?"

"I shouldn't think so," said Terry. "They're very well organised, I don't think they'll be stupid enough to try a prank like that in a hurry. Anyway I have my own method of guarding it but I never thought to set it up before."

"What are y-?" Kenan started to ask, but Terry was already putting on a coat. He also grabbed an old cloth bag.

"What's that for?" asked Kenan. But Terry only smiled.

"If you come with us Kenan I can show what's going to happen…it's kind of hard to explain if you don't see it for yourself. We've got to take the tube to the Old Piccadilly Circus, then…well you'll see soon enough."

Kenan was shaking with excitement about an hour later as they stepped off the tube onto the platform of the Old Piccadilly Circus. As the train pulled away, people began thinning away until soon there was no one left except for someone asleep in a sleeping bag at the other end of the platform, obviously a tramp. Kenan looked at him knowing how it felt, wondering if he'd turn out just like him…lonely…probably a drunk…

"Kenan!" Terry had obviously called him a second or third time. Kenan looked around and in surprise saw Terry and Delia stepping onto the tracks of the line.

"What are you doing?" he exclaimed.

"Shh!" hissed Terry. "This is the way to the shrine so hurry up."

"But what about trains?" insisted Kenan.

"That's why the phrase hurry up was invented," snapped Terry. "Trust me and follow." Kenan quickly hopped down on the tracks and followed Delia and Terry into the darkness.

Once they were away from the station pitch black surrounded them only occasionally broken by halogen lights on the wall. *This is crazy*, thought Kenan. *This is as crazy as you can get, following an old guy and his pudding of a granddaughter onto the tracks of the London underground!* He noticed Terry and Delia finally stopped and Terry began looking around at the walls.

"Now where is it?" he muttered. "I know it's around here somewhere."

"What are we looking for?" asked Kenan.

"A light that doesn't work," said Terry. "The only problem being that you can't see it very well because it's broken." Kenan nodded slowly.

"Uh-huh."

"Ah!" exclaimed Terry in a tone that made Kenan and Delia jump. "Here it is." He was looking at a light with no bulb in it. He took hold of it and turned it forty-five degrees clockwise. There was a faint rumble.

"Come on Terry," said Kenan, nervously. "There's a train coming."

"I don't think so," said Terry "you'd feel the breeze first. You might have a chance to get away. They move fast but obviously they slow down for the stations. As he spoke, the rumbling grew in volume and Kenan jumped back a foot as a panel of wall that held the dead light, began to slide upwards vanishing from sight. A gaping hole lay before them. Terry entered first followed by Delia who had obviously seen all this before then Kenan. Inside was no light at all and Kenan walked quickly to avoid getting separated from the other two. "Okay Kenan slow your pace," said Terry from in front, "just listen to what I say and you'll be fine. We're standing just outside a lift, just here," Kenan heard two metal clangs from Terry's direction. "It descends very quickly but I assure you it's perfectly safe okay? The only thing is, it can only take up to two people at a time. I'll go first and then you can follow with Delia." Kenan heard the sound of trainers on a metal grid then the sound the lift (which didn't sound that fast at all) descending downwards into the darkness. After a minute or two it came back empty. Delia walked in and Kenan followed. He waited as he heard Delia push several buttons on some sort of control panel. Then he heard her voice;

"You should hold onto something," and they were off on a roller-coaster ride downwards. He didn't think it could get any darker but it did. The wind blew his hair back and stung his eyes. It whistled past his ears as it had done the previous night when he had been air-surfing. Travelling down the metal shaft further into the darkness, he seemed to go faster and faster with every passing second. Just as he was sure he was about to throw up they came to a surprisingly smooth stop at the bottom. Kenan staggered out of the lift, collapsed onto his back and lay there, trying to gain his breath. A laugh made him look up. To his surprise and embarrassment, Terry and Delia were both standing as though they did something like that every single day.

"What the hell was that?" demanded Kenan shakily getting to his feet.

"A very practical way of reaching out destination I think," said Terry grinning from ear to ear, "but Kenan we must hurry, follow me. Delia stay put for a second." Kenan studied his surroundings with interest. They were in a huge circular cavern lit by flaming torches around the room. In the middle was a huge chunk of rock connected to the main floor by only a small stone ledge. On top of this huge rock was the shrine! Kenan had never seen anything so magnificent in his life. It was so old yet the decorations that had been carved into it thousands, maybe tens of thousands of years ago were in perfect condition. The rock where the shrine stood was surrounded by a drop so deep that when Kenan looked down, while crossing the ledge, he couldn't see the bottom. He followed Terry into the shrine and saw before him a small stone, circular table. He gasped as he saw five familiar symbols etched into the stone, the same symbols that Terry had sketched for him only days ago. A snowflake, a budding flower, a fully-grown type of tree and an oak leaf were marked out surrounding another symbol right in the centre that looked like the Earth.

"Take the two crystals, and put them on the symbols," demanded Terry. Kenan obediently took the two spheres from his pockets and placed the silver one in the centre and the blue winter one on the snowflake. They seemed to glow with an eerie light before returning to their normal colors.

"That's it," said Terry looking happier with every passing minute.

"Right now to set up a protection system. You go and stand with Delia while I get it ready and whatever happens don't act alarmed or all hell will break lose!" Wondering what on earth could alarm him more than he was already, Kenan walked across the ledge to join Delia. Terry was looking in the cloth bag for something. To Kenan's surprise, he pulled out a large red book and placed it on the floor in front of him. He opened it and knelt before it. All was quiet then Terry's voice rang out loud and clear around the cavern in a language Kenan couldn't make out. It sounded like: "Tambingo sa nelcho kepa chule a sint ta knewle. Femba newall kerrupta."

"What's he saying?" he asked Delia.

"Summoning spirits," she replied, "in the ancient language."

"Spirits?" exclaimed Kenan.

"They used to guard the shrine thousands of years ago," said Delia, "then they were given rest when the shrine sank below the ground. It wasn't always here you know."

"Well as it happens I didn't," muttered Kenan. He didn't exactly disbelieve Terry was summoning spirits, after all he had seen so far he was ready to believe anything. There seemed to be a faint rumbling growing in volume as Terry continued talking.

"But why were they sent to rest in the first place?" asked Kenan his curiosity getting the better of him.

"A great priest was born," explained Delia. "He was greater and older than granddad. He was born nearly three hundred and sixteen years ago at the turn of the new millennium. He lived for decades and before he died he said that he had had a vision of something happening in the future that a great plight would befall the shrine. He said that the spirits guarding it would need to have rest so they could return to protect it with full strength when the incident arose." Kenan stared as the words slowly made sense.

"You mean he was talking about what's happening now?" he asked.

"Yes," said Delia, "a person of great importance would also rise up and help to save the earth from destruction. But in doing so they w-" She stopped talking.

"Well?" Kenan prompted, "What does this person do?" Delia didn't reply. She had gone very pale and her mouth was clamped tight. "What?" shouted Kenan. He could hardly hear himself think. The cavern walls were beginning to shake as Terry's speech became louder and faster. Suddenly a sound like thunder rang in his ears and a brilliant white light blinded him. He squeezed his eyes tight shut as the walls stopped shaking and the rumbling subdued. When he dared to open his eyes, Terry had made his way back from the shrine and was standing beside them looking very pleased at something. Kenan followed his gaze and almost jumped out of his skin. Two slightly transparent shapeless forms were silently gliding around the cavern. They weren't as Kenan had ever thought spirits would look like. They seemed to have no shape or sense of direction, they seemed more like cigarette smoke, just gliding around occasionally passing through each other. There was no sign of where they begun or ended, no human features at all. Just a mass of white, smoky, shapeless, beings.

"Well," said Terry. "That about wraps that up. Let's get out of here."

"Um Terry," began Kenan as they were walking up a concrete staircase that led up to the subway, "two questions."

"Fire away," said Terry.

"You know you said that those spirits are guarding the shrine."

"Yes."

"Well won't they attack us if they're protecting it?"

"They won't attack us, they recognize us."

"How can they?" persisted Kenan. "They don't have eyes."

Terry shook his head and muttered something about the youth of today and thinking outside the box. Kenan decided to let the matter rest and ask his next question.

"Terry?"

"Kenan."

"Next time we come back here, can we take the stairs down? That lift really messed up my stomach."

Chapter Eleven

"Nothing?" exclaimed Kenan.

"Not a thing," muttered Terry sitting back in his chair and looking blankly at the computer screen.

"Maybe another website," said Delia helpfully.

"I've checked all of them," snapped Terry. "Let's face it, the only information we'll get on these spheres is the stuff I already have. I don't know where the other ones are or how to locate them."

"Well, we know that they'll be in an opposite environment of what they represent..." started Kenan.

"Oh and that's going to help us!" exclaimed Terry jumping up from his chair. He storming out into the kitchen, he lit a cigarette. He leaned over a tiny table covered with maps and scrolls and studied them closely for a few minutes before shaking his head and turning back towards the living room. "They could be anywhere." He said finally. "I'm just fooling myself, I'm fooling you two. You can't tell me that we'll be able to find them in the next few days. Accept the fact the world's doomed. Mankind's doomed and that's final!" Terry wasn't the only one whose temper had worn thin. Kenan jumped up and faced him.

"We can't quit now!" he exclaimed. "After all we've seen and done we can't just give up halfway. We can do this we're going to save the world...I don't care what it takes." Terry was a little taken aback.

"B- But Kenan..."

"No 'buts' about it!" shouted Kenan. "You chose me to help you out for a reason, you told me yourself that you knew I could help you, and although I didn't believe it at first I now know you were right. If we work as a team we can pull this off." Delia, who had been sitting on the sofa watching the scene with an open mouth, suddenly said, possibly the first nice thing to Kenan:

"You tell him," she exclaimed. "You've got the right spirit

and I like it. It's just what we need to help each other keep together." Kenan turned round and smiled at her. Delia wasn't really that bad now that he'd gotten to know her.

"Now think about it logically," she continued, "we all need some more information but we don't have the time or resources available to us," she winked. "But we know someone who does." Kenan looked at her.

"Naomi?" he asked. Delia nodded.

"I'm sure she'd be willing to help out, wouldn't she?"

"She said she wanted to," said Kenan, remembering Naomi's words.

"Well what are you doing telling *us?*" said Delia. "Go and ask her for help."

"W- what sort of help?" asked Kenan.

"Well according to Cedric she likes to spend her free time on the net...hacking."

"Isn't that illegal?" asked Kenan.

"Yes but that's not the point," said Delia, "not when the future of the world is at stake." Kenan slowly nodded. "If you're nervous about asking her, then I'll ask her myself," grinned Delia.

"No, no, no," said Kenan hurriedly. "I'll ask her. I might as well go now, if that's all I have to do." Terry nodded.

"That's all. You don't have to come back at the moment. I'll contact you somehow if we need any more help. Thanks Kenan."

Flying towards the Henderson mansion Kenan couldn't help feeling a little uncomfortable. He felt he had visited Naomi way too many times in the last few days. He reached the estate and stopped at the gates, as he went to press the buzzer, something made him stop. It looked like Cedric's black car, that was parked outside the doors again. *Man this guy's persistent,* thought Kenan. *No wonder Naomi's getting tired of him...I wonder what Delia sees in him?* He decided it was safer to search for Naomi himself rather than ringing and have both Cedric and Lady Henderson glare down their noses at him. Kenan silently flew over the gates and scanned the floors, peering in at each window to see if Naomi was about.

It was when he was on the second floor that he thought he saw someone. He stopped and went back past the window and sure enough, sitting at a computer looking bored out of her brain, was Naomi.

Kenan waved to get her attention. She looked up and nearly screamed. Quickly she opened the window to let Kenan in. She was grinning but also looked a little cross.

"Jeez!" she hissed. "Couldn't you at least knock at the door like normal people? You scared me to death floating outside the window like that... I thought you were some kind of ghost!"

"Being normal is over rated," grinned Kenan deftly jumping into the room grabbing his surfer in mid air so as to bring it with him. "Where's Cedric? I saw the limo outside."

"Oh that's not him, thank goodness," said Naomi quietly. A few people downstairs that's all. They're arranging my Grandmothers funeral and stuff. They'll be quite a while yet."

"Okay," said Kenan, "'cos I've got a special assignment for you."

"Yeah?"

"I understand from a reliable source that you like computer and internet hacking," he continued. Naomi looked surprised.

"Yeah, but how did you know about that?" she asked.

"You know Delia?" asked Kenan. Naomi thought for a second, and then answered slowly;

"I've met her once..."

"Well she just happens to be Terry's granddaughter and long time friend of Cedric," explained Kenan "and she's heard through him, that you spend your free time doing that." "She's Terry's grand-daughter?" exclaimed Naomi. "Why didn't you tell me?"

"I didn't know until today," said Kenan. "I went round to Terry's and she turned up. Oh, I almost forgot to tell you what happened last night..."

He told Naomi all about the power plant and the sphere and what had happened with Sam. In fact he didn't stop once, he went right on about the shrine and what Terry had asked

Naomi to do. But although Naomi accepted to help on the net, he didn't notice she was also very angry about the whole Sam business.

"How dare she!" She exclaimed. "Well, if you ask me I think she got what she deserves. What on earth has it got to do if we're friends anyway? She sounds like an insecure, immature kid more along the lines of five years old rather than eighteen! Was she the one who had a go at me the other day?" "Yep," replied Kenan. "She has an attitude problem," muttered Naomi sitting down on the bed. "I think I should go and have a chat with her."

Kenan tried to interrupt but Naomi was still fuming. "And asking if we're going out! Even if we were, and, you know, obviously we wouldn't, what's it got to do with her? Kenan shrugged. Naomi sighed.

"If people like her are going to keep on interfering we're not going to get anywhere with this thing."

"I know," said Kenan "but it's just very difficult to keep stuff from her…she's very over- protective of her friends."

"From a girl's point of view," remarked Naomi, "I'd say she's jealous…" she trailed off into muttering." Kenan decided to change the subject.

"How's your ankle?" he asked.

"It still hurts," said Naomi. "But I'm so bored of being stuck in doors."

"Well get used to it," teased Kenan, "'cos you're going spend a lot of time helping us out from now via that computer…that is," he went on hastily, "if you don't mind."

"Hey," grinned Naomi, "I said I'd help yesterday didn't I?" She rose and hobbled over to the computer and sat down again.

"Right," she said, "let's see what we can find." She logged on to a search engine and typed in the words 'Orkan Shrine.' A second later, a message flashed up on screen. 'Nothing found for your request.' "Damn," muttered Naomi as Kenan pulled up a chair beside her.

"You didn't think that was actually going to work did you?" he asked. "They're much more than just watches," smiled Naomi, "they're phones as well. Look." She tapped a button on the one she was holding and a second later Kenan's beeped. "Press the green button," instructed Naomi. Kenan did, and to his surprise, a miniature three dimensional image appeared out of the screen, it was Naomi. "See the camera?" She laughed as the image did the same. "Hold yours up." Kenan lifted the watch and held it so the tiny camera focused on him. A second later, his own hologram appeared on the screen of the watch Naomi held. He laughed in amazement. "Oh and you see this flashing book symbol?" continued his friend. "That's your phone book, you can call not only other types of these things but also original mobile phones and landlines, and you can text other people to − or e-mail... I think you'll find it's quite up to date. Your number will already be in mine and vice versa." Kenan gaped.

"You mean you want me to have one?" "Well, what did you think I was just showing them off?" grinned Naomi. Kenan looked in disbelief then smiled.

"If you're serious I'll take whichever one, seeing as they're both the same." "Might as well keep the one you've got," she shrugged.

"How do you set the time and that?" he asked as he put it on his right wrist. Naomi, who had just done the same with her watch, picked out a manual from the cabinet drawer and sat down next to him. After about five minutes of reading, they had both managed to learn the basics of their new gadgets. "But I don't get it," said Kenan as Naomi replaced the manual. "If these were given to you last month, how come you never used them?" Naomi turned away to hide her red face as she said;

"I never really had a friend who I liked enough to give one to." Kenan smiled.

"And you picked me of all people," he said lightly trying to make a joke out of it out of the whole thing, more because he was a little embarrassed than anything else. Naomi only smiled. "I'd better get going," muttered Kenan at last. "I'll call tomorrow, yeah?"

"If you want," replied Naomi with a nod.

"I'll leave the way I came in then," said Kenan as he grabbed his air-surfer. "See ya." Naomi waved as Kenan slipped through the window and out of the grounds of the Henderson estate. He didn't notice it while he was air-surfing, but as soon as he reached the car park, he saw he had a message. He opened it and this is what it said;

'Hi Kenan, I think it may be better if I call you if something comes up. It's just if I don't' find anything you'll waste power on your phone. Probably speak to you 2morrow. Luv Naomi'

Kenan thought for a minute before replying;

'You got it Naz. Thanks 4 letting me know. I'll c ya 2morrow!

Kenan!'

A few seconds later another message bleeped up on the phone. Smiling Kenan opened it: 'Don't call me Naz! Luv NAOMI!'

Kenan laughed, then sent;

'Oh dreadfully sorry me-lady...I forgot you're not used to communicating riff-raff style.'

The next message he got back was the last one, which read;

'Hey I was just kidding. I luv that name, it's pretty cool. And any way you're a pretty decent person, not just any old 'Riff-Raff. Don't put yourself down, a lot of people like you because of who you are, that includes me. C ya 2morrow. Luv Naomi x'

Kenan read the message three times. He actually felt quite moved. Matt or Sam would never have thought of saying something like that. After a minutes thought, he sent back; 'Thanx Naz. K. x' After that no more messages came. He lay back on the blankets and stared at the ceiling. Evening was beginning to draw in but the last few days were beginning to catch up with him, he felt very tired indeed...still smiling - he fell asleep.

Naomi sighed and logged off the website. This was proving to be much more difficult than she had first thought. Getting any data on the Five spheres or the Orkan Shrine, was near enough impossible. Whether it would come up with useful information, was another matter completely. She thought for a minute then her. She logged onto the BBC website and looked up the latest news. Among the other headlines was the information about the other night when the power - station had been broken into, but there was now more information about it. Several clues had been found including a few shreds of clothing, an imprint of a trainer in the mud near the buildings, and the most significant was a Halloween mask. As Naomi read the last two words again she had a startling flashback…the people who had beaten up Terry…they were all wearing Halloween masks. She tapped the screen where it said 'View Pictures.' Three came up: the trainer print, a shred of a black sweatshirt and the mask! It looked like it was supposed to resemble a 'Punch and Judy' doll, with its huge hooked nose and eerie smile. It gave Naomi the creeps. She quickly opened another tab and went onto Terry's site. Her excellent memory remembered the password. She typed it in and the file came up with the little boxes in it. She clicked box number three and watched again the horrifying scene as five people stormed into the flat and trashed it. But she now took more notice of what the five people had over their faces…then she spotted it, exactly the same mask as what she had seen on the BBC's website. These were the same people who had attacked Terry! They had to be, she was certain. For a minute, she didn't know what to do first. Should she text Kenan? Or alert the police? Or neither? Maybe she should try and track down Terry or just carry on trying to look stuff up… no. There was no way she was going to sit there and pretend that a dangerous gang of people, (who wore freaky masks), weren't, in fact, dangerous. Should she tell Cedric? After all he knew Delia, and she was Terry's grand - daughter. Maybe that would help somehow. Did Terry know that the same gang who had attacked him were the same one's involved with the power – plant incident. *He probably does,* thought Naomi, *but this is the only information I've got so far. What else can I do to help?* She sat staring at the screen for a few more minutes. She was bought back to earth with a jolt as someone entered the room. She quickly minimized the window on her screen, so that it went into desktop mode. It was her mum. She looked suspiciously at Naomi who looked back wearing her best 'innocent' expression.

"What are you doing?" she asked looking at the computer screen.

"Nothing," said Naomi.

"I can see that!" snapped Audrey. "You've got three essays to do for your homework you know... are they done yet?" Naomi shook her head.

"I- was- just about to do them," she lied.

"Mm – Hmm," said her mum not looking very convinced. "Really Naomi," she lectured, "This attitude you've adopted lately has got to stop. If you don't do well in your studies you won't be fit to take on your Father's business. You'll have to get some low paid, mindless job, or worse still, no job, like those tramps in town... now how bad would that look on the family name...?" Naomi hated it when her mum gave her talks like this... as if they were above the rest of the world, but she kept quiet and bore it. "Maybe," continued her mum, "a talk from your Father wouldn't do you any harm..." the rest of her words fell on empty ears as Naomi suddenly thought. Of course that was who she could tell: her dad was more likely to understand (and believe her) more than anyone else. She smiled to herself as her Mother, still scowling, swept out of the room slamming the door behind her. Naomi sat in front of the computer patiently waiting, until sure enough, she heard footsteps coming down the hall. There was a knock at the door.

"Come in," called Naomi. Her dad came into the room. He was smiling despite the rough evening he had had before and numerous annoying relatives calls. This didn't surprise Naomi. She knew he wasn't in the mood to get all worked up and angry. He rarely did anyway. Of Naomi's parents, Lord Henderson was the more understanding one and he always listened to everyone's views before voicing his own. That was why he was such a successful businessman.

"So this is homework?" he said looking at the blank screen.

"Dad, I can't concentrate on it at the moment," explained Naomi. "I've got more important things to find...look." She opened the window of the news report and the one with Terry's website on it whilst explaining in as few words as possible all that had happened over the past few days and who was involved; Kenan, Terry, Delia everyone. "It's not as if I went out looking for it to happen," she ended. "It seemed to find me. I can't let them down now. Please dad. You know that there's something wrong in the air, so do I. That's the reason I believe all this stuff. There must be something we can do to help." George Henderson sat at the end of Naomi's bed looking straight ahead. Naomi was right. The feeling that he could detect was getting worse by the day. They didn't have much time as it was. What could he do? Then an idea struck him. Naomi looked hopeful as a smile began to appear on her father's face.

"I think," he said, "I may just have had a thought. I can't tell you what it is yet but if it works we'll have this sorted out in a very short space of time."

"Really?" exclaimed Naomi. She jumped off her chair and hugged him. "Do you think it'll really work?"

"I'm almost certain," he replied standing up. "But you have to do one thing for me on that machine of yours," he said gesturing to the computer.

"Anything," said Naomi sitting down in the chair a huge look of enthusiasm on her face. Her dad smiled as he went out of the door and said:

"Keep your mother off my back. Get your homework done for God's sake."

Chapter Twelve

Lord Henderson put the graceful white Lamborghini in reverse gear and backed it out of the garage. As soon as he was outside, the garage door closed automatically. Turning in mid-air, he skimmed over the gravel drive and through the open gates towards the city. On normal occasions he would have had the chauffer to drive him around, but he had decided it safer to go out alone that evening...he didn't really want anyone to know where he was going. He drove over huge blocks of skyscrapers and flats. Gradually these gave way to larger shops as he approached the center of London. More big department stores came and went. Big parks, and homes not unlike his own, soon replaced these. He now slowed the car's speed and descended a few feet. He knew what he was looking for, it wasn't exactly easy to spot, but then he saw it. Tucked away behind trees and rolling lawns, a mansion that was at least twice the size of his. Lord Henderson drove the car downwards till he reached the gates. He pressed the buzzer and waited patiently. A butler answered him with obvious recognition.

"Lord Henderson! Long time no see sir. It's been years! You've hardly changed a bit." George smiled.

"So you're still working here Stan. It must have been about fifteen years huh? I was just wondering, I need to speak to our old friend; Mr. D. Tainard?"

"Oh, you've missed him," said Stan. "You know how he is. He goes away for days at a time. It's a busy life being adviser to the King. Was it anything important?"

"I thought he might know something about the break in at the power plant the other night."

"Well of course he knew...it was in the news."

"Right... do you know if he knows anything about the Shrine of Orkan?" Stan's face seemed to freeze.

"How should I know George?" said Stan. His friendly nature had quickly disappeared.

"Do you?" Lord Henderson's eyes were fixed on Stan's.

The butler turned pale.

"I don't know what you're talking about George", he snapped. "Now if you'll excuse me, I can't hang about here all night, people to see to." The monitor went blank. George looked past the gates up to the big house.

"Yes," he said to himself, "I'm sure you have."

*

Kenan awoke with a start the next morning. Buster was sniffing his face and whining.

"Gerroff," he mumbled sleepily. He heard a voice.

"It's about time! We weren't sure whether you were alive or not." Kenan sat up quickly. Nick and Lia were sitting there with the holo-box and a disc with the morning news logo on it.

"Y- you guys aren't mad at me?" asked Kenan.

"We saw what happened," said Nick. "We tried explaining it to Matt and Sam but they weren't taking a bar of it. I think they know the truth but just feel pretty stupid about how she acted." Kenan smiled with relief. At least not everyone had deserted him.

"Check this out," said Lia waving the disc at Kenan. "Do you know Naomi's dad? Lord Henderson?"

"Never met him," said Kenan, "but from what I've heard, he seems like a decent guy…Why?"

"Look," explained Lia as she pressed play on the holo-box. "He's made headlines this morning." Throwing the covers off, Kenan looked at the 3-D image of the news reporter who was saying the following:

"Good Morning, London. The main news this morning: Questioning is underway, regarding Lord George Henderson and his whereabouts last night, which had the whole of the London police force up in arms when he sent them e-mail with 'news' about a place called The Orkan shrine. Lord Henderson, President of Henderson Enterprises, stated that the information from Terry Orkas, regarding the Shrine, was not to be taken lightly and that all help was needed to find the people responsible for ransacking it.

Although it is not yet certain how much of this information is true, an investigation may well be carried out into what officials believe to be a group with some kind of conspiracy about the shrine and Terry Orkas will be questioned when Lord Henderson is released." The holo-box shut off. All Kenan could do was stare.

"How does he know?" he said finally.

"Well, there's a pretty obvious answer to that isn't there?" exclaimed Lia. "Naomi's probably told him."

"She wouldn't," said Kenan. "She knows how important this is."

"Did she ever say she wouldn't tell anybody?" asked Nick. Kenan didn't answer. The more he thought about it, the more he had the horrible feeling that Naomi had let it slip. Finally he stood up.

"I'm going to talk to her," he said.

"Can we come?" asked Nick. Kenan hesitated. It wasn't so much that he wanted to be alone, it was just he didn't feel it would be in his best interest if Nick and Lia saw the mansion first hand as he did. If the truth were known he was proud, that he of all people was allowed to go in there, but he also wanted some straight answers from Naomi with no interfering.

"Maybe another time," he said, reaching for his air-surfer. To his surprise, Lia stepped in his way.

"We want to help you," she said. "I don't care if Naomi lives in a mansion and we don't. At the end of the day she's just a person. If she doesn't like us that's down to her! The more people you have helping you on this Kenan, the more chance you have of succeeding." Kenan stared at Lia. She had never sounded so positive before. She always agreed with everyone and hardly ever spoke her mind, only if she knew she wouldn't upset or challenge anyone. And yet here she was talking back to Kenan and giving him advice which he really couldn't argue with. Finally he smiled.

"Alright," he said. "Go get your air-surfers and you can come with me...if you can keep up."

*

"So tell me again just why did you find it necessary to alert the whole of London's police force about this shrine?" asked the officer. George groaned. He hadn't bargained on all of this happening at all.

"I told you," he said "I thought you'd take me seriously. Haven't you noticed the weather's been a little out of season lately?"

"I didn't ask you for a weather report Mr. Henderson," snapped the officer. "I am trying to find out about this so called shrine, you and that old man keep raving about."

"I can't tell you anything more about that," said George.

"So you don't even know where this shrine is?" smirked another officer. "You couldn't possibly show me and officer Barker here, where it is."

"NO!" exclaimed George. He was extremely tired and irritable. He glared at the identity badge on the officer who was questioning him. It stated 'Detective First Class Williams.' He had read it a hundred times already, he had been in here so long and he was bored. The other officer, Alan Barker sat next to him across the table from George. "Look," he said at last, "you'll have to ask Terry Orkas about that. I don't know any more." There was a long silence.

"Okay," said Barker. "We'll bring Terry in, but you'll have to stay at the station in the mean time." George shrugged.

"Works for me," he muttered. A female officer escorted him out of the room. Outside Terry was waiting. The female officer said nothing, but gave him a nod. Glaring at George, Terry stepped inside the room. The door slid shut behind him.

"Okay," he said slumping down on a chair. "Let's get this over with." Barker smiled.

"Fame getting a bit too much Terry? Are the paparazzi on your back twenty-four seven? Must be hard trying to guard a shrine with all that happening." Terry bit his lip.

"You must believe me," he said. "There is no need for the

whole world to get involved with this. If more people know about this... all hell will break loose!"

"Why did Lord Henderson provoke an alarm last night for all station's within a twenty mile radius to be alert?" shouted officer Williams.

"I have no idea..." began Terry, but Williams pressed on.

"Do you know how many people we had on a wild goose chase last night Terry? Twenty men and women were trying to find George, scouring the streets, tracing phone calls and internet sites. Ten of our police cars were also on the lookout. That's thirty police units, that didn't need to be out. They could have been saving lives or solving drug dealings, but instead we're investigating a stone shrine that doesn't exist!"

"It does exist!" shouted Terry. "The only reason I can't tell you where it is because if the media get wind of this, the people who raided it the other day will do it again! We'll be back to square one with less time to set this right... and then it will be too late."

"Too late for what?" asked Barker.

"To save the world from unspeakable terror," whispered Terry. "Havoc will wreck across the earth. Seasons will be thrown to opposite ends of the globe. A storm, unlike anything mankind has seen before will rip the world apart. There will be no stopping it. Legend says that it resembles a dark and evil creature that turns the sky as black as night and can cause earthquakes as it approaches. It would be then end of all life on earth. Armageddon. The Four Horsemen Of The Apocalypse." Barker looked at Terry then at Williams. Both looked as if they were beginning to believe the old man. Barker sighed.

"That will be all, thank you Terry." Terry stared at him.

"Y-you're releasing me? Just like that?"

"Would you like to be locked up?" smiled Williams. "We'll try and get a discreet operation underway to sort this out." Terry smiled.

"Thank you," he said as he made to leave, "this means a lot to me." The female officer escorted him outside closing the door behind her. Williams called out as they left:

"George Henderson. He can go as well." Barker looked at Williams.

"Do you believe him?" he asked. Williams shook his head.

"I think they both needed a bit of a shock, I can't see the point in warning either of them. Lord Henderson's obviously been taken in by the old crackpot. Hopefully they'll think twice before winding us all up again. Barker smiled.

"Let's hope," he muttered.

*

"Wow!" exclaimed Lia.

"It's even bigger than I remember," exclaimed Nick.

"We're not here to admire the scenery," muttered Kenan. "We need to talk to Naomi." Turning to the twins he said; "I've go find out if she's here. If she is I'll come back for you." Nick and Lia nodded. Kenan soared over the gates and into the grounds of the mansion, leaving Nick and Lia out of sight by the white, stone wall. He wasn't feeling that comfortable at all now that Nick and Lia were there with him, but he couldn't think of a feasible excuse to get rid of them. The only thing he could think of was to say that Naomi was out, but he needed to know for certain if she had told her dad about the shrine. He tried to remember where Naomi's room was. Second floor? Third Floor? He, honestly, couldn't remember. He decided his best bet would be to fly around the house and take a quick look through the windows, but before he could do this, he heard a short, sharp whistle. He looked up quickly - Naomi was leaning from a window grinning broadly and waving at him. Kenan didn't return the smile. He quickly ascended to the window and jumped into the room.

"What the hell have you been saying?" he whispered fiercely. Naomi looked confused.

"W-what do you mean?" she asked.

"Your dad is all over the morning news!" scowled Kenan.

"He alerted half of London police last night telling them about a certain *Shrine!*" Naomi looked guilty.

"I thought he'd be able to help us," she said sadly, "you

know with all the friends he has who are high in social status…"

"You've completely ruined this whole thing!" hissed Kenan through clenched teeth. "It was supposed to be a discreet operation with as little fuss as possible. Terry didn't want the public to be alarmed and now this has been broadcast all over London…tell me what's going to happen Naomi!" Naomi had never seen Kenan so angry before. His, once blue eyes, seemed to have turned black and he was shaking.

"I- I'm sorry," she whispered. "I just thought…"

"You thought wrong!" exclaimed Kenan. "I trusted you to keep this secret but I guess I was misled."

"Kenan please listen to me!" cried Naomi close to tears. "I didn't mean for you to find out like this- "

"Evidently not," snapped Kenan.

"But I couldn't think of any other way to help," said Naomi. "I'm trying my best and I really didn't expect dad to go off and do what he did." Kenan could see Naomi was genuinely upset and he began to feel a little bad but a he wasn't quite ready to forgive Naomi yet.

"You should have tried to contact me before you told him," he said.

"I know," said Naomi, "I was just thoughtless, I guess I'm just an idiot!"

"No! No you're not," said Kenan feeling more awful by the minute. He took a deep breath. "Please don't put this on my shoulders Naomi, I don't need it."

"You shouldn't make such a fuss out of it," said Naomi. "If you let me finish, I got some more information last night." Kenan couldn't stay angry for long. He knew Naomi was trying her best and, true she had slipped up but she knew not to do it again. The public hadn't believed Terry's rant about the shrine before; maybe it would be the same again. He sighed.

"I'm sorry," he muttered. "It's just my temper's worn thin over the past few days."

"Apology accepted," smiled Naomi. "We're still friends right?" Kenan couldn't say no.

"Yeah," he muttered, "I can't exactly tell you to stop helping at this stage now can I?"

"Oh you can," said Naomi, "It's just I wouldn't listen to you." Kenan looked at her. Naomi laughed. "I'm only joking," she giggled playfully punching him on the arm.

"Assault!" shouted Kenan. "I could get you arrested for that!"

"They'd have to catch me first," said Naomi. Kenan grabbed Naomi's wrist.

"Caught you," he grinned. Naomi twisted out of Kenan's grip but stumbled a bit a look of grimace on her face.

"You okay?" he asked.

"Yeah," said Naomi. "I forgot my ankle's still bad."

"You'd better sit down then," said Kenan. Naomi nodded glumly.

"That's all I seem to be doing today," she muttered. "It's so boring!" A cough sounded from outside.

"Nick! Lia! Sorry guys I forgot you were there." Naomi let go of Kenan and steadied herself.

"Hey I recognize you two," she smiled. "Weren't you with Kenan the other day?"

"Erm yeah," replied Nick, "when, err, Matt ruined the flowers."

"Come in," said Naomi, "make yourself at home." Nick and Lia both came in still on their air-surfers looking a little taken aback at Naomi's hospitality. Sensing their uneasiness, she laughed and said:

"Hey! You can breathe in here you know!"

"Well you guys didn't exactly hit it off very well did you," remarked Kenan.

"Yeah," said Naomi looking guilty, "sorry about that the other day you two. I was just a little bit uptight." Nick and Lia nodded.

"That's okay," smiled Lia. Naomi grinned and turning to Kenan said:

"So you want to look at what I found last night?"

Chapter Thirteen

"So far we're the only ones who know that the mask is our only connection to Terry's attackers and what happened at the power station the other night," finished Naomi, "but that's all at the moment."

"But Terry knows it was the same people who attacked him," pointed out Kenan. "He's said that already…"

"But the police don't know," said Lia suddenly. Kenan looked at her.

"And…"

"We can make the connection," said Lia, "and start making enquiries."

"I don't follow."

"I do!" exclaimed Nick. "Think about it. These people must live locally or they would have hidden that sphere much further away than at the power station. They can't have that much money. I reckon that they get by from stealing like we do right?" Kenan nodded slowly. "So," continued Nick, "they must have stolen that mask…things don't come cheap in London right?" Kenan nodded again, a smile appearing on his face as the words slowly made sense. "All we have to do is find out what shop they stole that and the other freaky masks from, and we may have an idea of what area we can find them living in." Naomi and Lia were also smiling along with Kenan now as Nick sat there grinning at himself. Kenan slapped Nick on the back.

"You two should become detectives!" he laughed. "You know, that could get us somewhere!" Lia was beaming at her brother.

"This is so cool!" she squealed.

"Absolutely!" said Kenan, "but do you know what makes it even better?" His three friends shook their heads. "You two," said Kenan, pointing at the twins, "are going have the important task of making these enquiries." Nick and Lia's faces fell.

"B-but we've never done that sort of thing without you

around," stuttered Lia.

"Well, there's a first time for everything," said Kenan. Lia looked at Nick who looked just as unsure. "Look," said Kenan. "You can't spend your lives living in the shadow of somebody else. You've got to go out and do your own thing sometimes. Just because I'm not with you doesn't mean I won't be there when things get real tough. I'm your friend and I'm not about to leave any of you. All you've got to do is just go into a shop and ask if there are any Halloween masks in stock like the ones on Terry's video. If they say yes just say you'll be back for them later on and walk out. If they say no just say…oh I don't know, something like 'well we saw them in here last week,' and ask what happened to them. Chances are that'll be the store they were stolen from." Nick and Lia still looked a bit unsure but nodded at Kenan with smiles on their faces. "So?" said Kenan, after a minute. "What are you waiting for? The sooner you get started the sooner we may be able to find something out."

"Oh right," said Nick, "c'mon Lia, let's go." The brother and sister both picked up their air-surfers, waved goodbye to Naomi and Kenan, then quickly vanished through the open window.

"You wouldn't believe they are actually both two years older than me," he smiled as he turned back towards Naomi.

"They seem pretty nice," said Naomi as she watched them get smaller in the distance.

"Well, apart from you, they're the only friends I've got right now," said Kenan. "Matt and Sam still aren't talking to me." Naomi shook her head.

"It's pathetic," she muttered. "Don't talk about them anymore." Kenan shrugged.

"Okay," he said. "What would you prefer to talk about?" Naomi smiled and turned her attention back to the computer.

"How about this?" she grinned. She tapped the screen a few times and bought up a new tab that she hadn't shown Kenan or the others. "I found this last night while looking for more stuff about Terry's attackers," she said "but I think you'll agree it's just as useful." Kenan looked at the page. It was another news website, that stated two words: 'Graveyard Robbers.' There followed a page of writing:

'Concerns are rising in London for not only the citizens being in danger by eccentric terrorists but also for those at rest! The famous cemetery 'High Gate,' has been vandalised by a group of individuals who have been digging up the grounds...but what is baffling detectives that the ground that's been disturbed, is the new ground, where the cemetery's been extended in recent years. Further more, it's unused. Several holes and a small trench have been found in ground yet to be used, but for no apparent reason. Police are still looking for clues.'

Kenan read the passage through twice, then looked at Naomi with a confused expression on his face.

"Well," he said, "it's interesting enough, but how does that help us out at all?"

"Think about it logically," said Naomi. Kenan's face still didn't clear, so Naomi continued. "Okay what spheres have we got so far?"

"The one that represents earth," replied Kenan "and the one for winter."

"Right," said Naomi. "So we still need the one for spring, summer and autumn. I thought about trying to track down the one for spring and had an idea. What happens to everything in spring? You know with nature stuff?"

"Everything wakes up," said Kenan slowly. "A new start, new life."

"Right again," said Naomi. "Think about it Kenan, where would the sphere have to be to be out of this environment? Somewhere where there is no life...only death."

"A...graveyard." Kenan grinned and clapped a hand on her shoulder. "You're getting good at this, Naz. I would never have thought of that." Naomi smiled.

"So what do we do now?" she asked.

"Well isn't it obvious?" replied Kenan. "We go to High Gate where these guys have obviously hidden the sphere." Naomi clearly hadn't bargained on this, her face fell.

"B- but we wouldn't know how to get there."

"Ever heard of a train and a wonderful thing they invented called a map?"

"Yes yes! But I mean High Gate a huge place. We'd need a day and a night to look for something the size of a tennis ball in there."

"Not with four of us looking," said Kenan. "You me Nick and Lia, we'd only need a night." Naomi's expression froze. "NO!" she said. "We are NOT going to High Gate in the MIDDLE OF THE NIGHT!"

"Okay," said Kenan. "You stay. Just the three of us can go, if you're scared."

"I'm not scared!" exclaimed Naomi hotly. "I just don't like the idea of walking around a graveyard in the middle of the night."

"Why not?" insisted Kenan, "there aren't any loud noises or anything to scare you. A graveyard like that would be *dead quiet*!" He nudged Naomi at the joke. Naomi rolled her eyes.

"Okay," she said finally. "I'll come with you but I don't like the idea at all." Kenan laughed.

"I knew you'd come round to my way of thinking," he grinned. Naomi half smiled and rubbed her eyes with a groan.

"I'm so tired," she muttered. "Do you mind if I take five?"

"Nah, of course not." Naomi eased herself off her chair holding onto the desk for support. She went and sat over on the bed and took a look at her left ankle.

"I think the swelling's gone down," she said as she took off the ankle support she was wearing.

"It has definitely," said Kenan. "It'll probably be a bit better by tomorrow." Naomi nodded. She closed her eyes and slumped back on the pillows.

"We've got my grandma's funeral in about a week she said. "I am really hoping it'll have cleared up by then. I'd feel bad if I wasn't the only family member not going."

"I suppose I'm lucky in that sense," said Kenan. "I've never actually been to a funeral before."

"They're not nice things," sighed Naomi. She looked at Kenan. "Never been to one…? But I thought that you said your parents…"

106

"Died before I knew them," said Kenan. "I don't even know what they looked like." Naomi bit her lip.

"Sorry," she mumbled. Kenan stood up and went to sit on the side of the bed.

"It might have been worse if I had known them," he said thoughtfully.

"Maybe," said Naomi. "At least it feels like that at the moment with my gran. At least she's not in any pain now, but...well you know." Both friends went very quiet for a moment then Kenan said:

"If it helps, I believe that when you die you see what you've desired all your life, if you deserve it."

"Huh? Oh like a heaven and hell thing?"

"Something like that," said Kenan. "Let's put it this way. Take a guy who's never seen his parents..." he smiled at Naomi.

"You," she said.

"Right," he replied, "now if I do what I can to help others out in life I'm hoping that at the end of it all, I'll get to see my mum and dad for as long as I want, whenever I want. But if I do something to hurt someone or some people I won't. I'll never see them ever...that's my idea of hell anyway... I just want to know if they're proud of me," he said quietly.

Naomi looked idly at her fingernails. She was considering asking Kenan a question, which he may not like to answer. In the end, her curiosity got the better of her.

"If you don't mind me asking," she started "what happened to...? Well I mean how did they...? Um hold on..."

"How did they die? That's what you're trying to ask?"

"Yeah," said Naomi looking phenomenally guilty. "Don't answer I shouldn't have..."

"It's okay," said Kenan not looking at her. "Matt, Sam, Nick and Lia asked. I suppose it's only fair you get the story to. I was too small to remember but a guy called Damien took me in...he told me. When I was just old enough to walk, I wandered away from my mum and dad. It was a really foggy night and I suppose a bit of a miracle I made it to the multi-story. I made my way up top not really knowing the danger…as I say I was only small. My parents came looking for me and saw me near the edge of the building. Th- they went to pick me up but misjudged the distance I guess. Like I say, it was foggy and they more focused on me than the edge… and they fell. I was a bit luckier. Damien was seconds too late to save them but not too late to save me." Kenan closed his eyes. "But at the end of the day," he said in a strange voice, "it's my fault they're not here." He turned his head away so Naomi couldn't see his face, but she read it anyway. She sat up so she was right next to him.

"It's not your fault," she whispered putting her arm around his shoulders. "That's what you were told. It may have been a little different. Maybe a lot different."

"I've only got Damien's version to go by," said Kenan, still not looking at her.

"His version maybe wrong," said Naomi, getting Kenan to face her. "He wasn't up on that top floor. He doesn't know everything that happened. What happened to your parents was an accident, not *your fault!*" She smiled. "And you're wrong to live in guilt of it anyway. Even if that *is* how it happened, like you said, you didn't know what you were doing right?" A strange feeling came over Kenan. Whereas before, everyone had made him feel bad about what had happened that night, Naomi had completely the opposite effect. He couldn't help smiling. A second later, Naomi gave him a cuddle, which he instinctively returned. For a couple of minutes neither of them said a word. Finally Naomi pulled away and opened her eyes. "You okay now?" she asked. Kenan nodded, for some reason he found it difficult to make eye contact with her.

"I'm very hot," he said after a minute. "Why did you close the window?"

"It's open," said Naomi. She looked at him. "You do look pretty red though." Kenan stood up quickly.

"It's the weather," she said. "The sooner we get those spheres sorted out we might be able to get some proper summer weather."

"Yeah," laughed Kenan. "Rain." Naomi giggled.

"Okay," she smiled, "when are we going to High Gate?"

108

"Tonight," said Kenan. "If you can get a map we'll bunk the train...you can get out tonight right?" Naomi nodded. "Great," said Kenan. "We would, air-surf but I don't know the way there. Take your surfer anyway," he added. "I've got and tell Nick and Lia what the plan of action is." He picked up his air-surfer.

"Can you text me later for times and stuff?" asked Naomi.

"Yeah sure," said Kenan, as he placed the air-surfer in mid air so it just hovered.

"Great," said Naomi. "I've got to do some homework or I'll be grounded for life," she said looking vengefully back at her computer. Kenan laughed.

"Good luck," he said as he made to go out.

"Same to you," smiled Naomi. She reached out and tapped him on the shoulder. "And thanks for taking my mind off next week," she whispered, and before Kenan could wave her thanks aside, Naomi had given him a kiss on the cheek.

*

Never in his life had Kenan felt so happy. He found himself smiling all the way back to the car-park and upon landing he found Matt and Sam, both with very sombre expressions on their faces waiting for him.

"Hey guys!" said Kenan. "What's up?" Sam ran forward and hugged him.

"I'm really sorry," she exclaimed. "I acted like a kid...I knew you didn't mean to hit me on purpose!" Kenan smiled.

"You could have just listened to me in the first place you know."

"I know I know!" groaned Sam, "but...well... oh Kenan I'm so sorry!"

"It's okay," smiled Kenan. "I shouldn't have lied." Matt stepped forward.

"Alright mate?" he said looking very guilty.

"Yeah," said Kenan. He gave his friend a playful punch on the arm. Matt retaliated with one. Within seconds, the two boys were having some sort of play fight as Sam rolled her eyes, though she was still smiling.

"So," grinned Matt when everything had calmed down a bit, "What's going on with this Terry guy?"

"Oh you don't need to talk about that right now," said Kenan.

"Yes we do," said Sam. "After all you do have to save the world pretty soon don't you?" Kenan didn't think he had heard aright.

"But you guys didn't believe me… did you?"

"Well we said the other night we were going help you." said Matt. "We haven't changed our minds just because of a row. After all that's what friends do right. They stick together, even if they think the other one is a bit mad." Kenan felt the happiness inside him swelling. Finally, things were starting to look a bit better.

"By the way," said Sam, "do you know where Nick and Lia are? We've been looking for them all day." Kenan nodded.

"They're in town somewhere," he said. "But I'd better tell you what's been going on first. We've got a busy night coming up…"

*

Nick and Lia made their way out of the fourth costume hire shop feeling sick and tired of asking the same questions over and over again and getting the same answers.

"I never knew," said Nick "that there were so many shops that sold masks in London."

"London's a big place," Lia reminded him, "and it's nearly twice as big as it was about three hundred odd years ago." Nick nodded, looked across the busy street then did a double-take. A very small and dingy looking shop was opposite them. A faded sign above it simply stated.

'Dave's Costumes'
For Sale and Hire
A Family Business Since The 21st Century

"Do you think..?" Nick looked at Lia who was obviously thinking the same because she was nodding slowly.

"Let's make it the last one," she said as they hurried across the road. "We may strike it lucky." The twins made it to the other side of the street and pushed open the door. The inside of the shop was most unlike the others. The other stores had been brightly lit and had big coloured posters advertising their best costumes for hire. This one was dark and quite small in comparison. No one was in it.

"Do you think it's even worth having a look?" muttered Nick looking at the dusty shelves. "It doesn't look like anything's been moved off these shelves for weeks!"

"You're right young man," said someone from behind a till who they hadn't seen when they'd walked in. "Nothing's much has been sold for at least a week now."

As the twins looked, a man who only looked a little younger than Terry came round from behind the counter. "All these big fancy shops like the one across the road spring up and people find they sell much cheaper stuff than me... none of it any good quality," he added bitterly. "My great-great- grandfather founded this business at the turn of the millennium and it's been handed down through our family since. But my two daughters don't want to take it on. They're still in university and want to become doctors. Fair enough I suppose. After all, the world needs them more than silly costumes."

"It must have been successful in its day," said Lia politely.

"It was!" exclaimed the old man. "But now I can't afford half decent stock. I have to literally give stuff away. It's the masks that are the hardest to sell. So many people prefer the face paints. Mind you," the old man paused with a smile; "I did manage to sell quite a few masks the other week." Nick and Lia exchanged glances.

"Like what?" asked Nick.

"Oh let's see," said the man thinking hard. "A man came in and said they were for some private function. There was about five in all. A witch, a monster and a Punch and Judy type one...I can't remember the other two." Nick and Lia looked at each other trying not to smile too much.

"What did the man look like?" said Lia trying to sound casual, then noticing the manager give her an odd look she blurted out "well we know our uncle uses this shop quite a bit... it might have been him you met." The old man's face cleared.

"Oh, he was about forties I'd say, but I couldn't really see him that well, the lighting's not that great in here as you can see."

"Did you manage to catch his name?" asked Nick trying not to sound desperate.

"I did," said the man. "He signed a cheque and I remember how unusual the surname was. Oh Tai- Tain-Tainard! That was it."

"Oh that wasn't him," said Lia quickly. "Thanks anyway." Nick nudged his sister and said with a wink: "Don't you think we should be getting back home? We'll be late."

"Oh yeah," said Lia quickly catching on. "We'd better get going."

"Okay," said the man going back behind the counter. "Good bye." The twins said their goodbyes and walked a few yards down the street both nearly bubbling over with excitement. When they reached a quiet part of the street, they both grinned at each other.

"Alright," laughed Nick. "This is getting better and better!" Lia couldn't stop smiling.

"Last one to tell Kenan is a rotten egg," she exclaimed sprinting off towards the car park.

"Yeah?" yelled Nick as he ran after her. "And the first one there has to eat it!"

Chapter Fourteen

"So it's agreed? You're all coming then?" Matt, Sam, Nick and Lia all nodded their heads. Kenan was beaming like a child with a new toy. News about the masks from 'Dave's Halloween Costumes,' had gone down very well indeed and the fact that the twins had returned with a name was even better. "We can work on that tomorrow," said Kenan, "depending on what we find at High Gate tonight." He saw Lia and Nick go pale. "Come on guys," he said. "The dead can't hurt you."

"It's just the thought of it," shivered Lia. Kenan shrugged.

"People live, people die, there's not a lot you can do about it," he said.

"This may be what you two need to toughen up a bit," pointed out Sam. "You've got to have some teen adventure in your life. It's not as if we're about to go grave robbing or anything..." She turned to Kenan..."right?"

"Course not," he replied stubbornly. "We'll just have a hunt around like we did at the power station, you know, behind headstones buried under old leaves, hidden in shadows..." he cast a look at the twins who were looking paler by the second. "Don't worry!" he laughed when he saw them. "We'll put you two near the gates so you can run out when you get scared!"

It was late when the group of friends left for the Henderson mansion. Kenan had decided it was safer for Naomi to meet them outside the grounds for two main reasons: There was too bigger risk of them being seen if all five of them went to meet up inside the grounds, and Kenan, as before, had decided to take Buster along with them, except Buster was on Matt's air- surfer. The Alsatian could become edgy if he didn't know where he was going, unlike at the power plant where he had been passed and seen it before. Kenan had already text Naomi and told her this and she had agreed it was probably for the best. Kenan kept checking his watch as they neared the mansion. They had agreed to meet at the bottom of the hill at eleven 'o' clock, and the journey seemed to be taking much longer than usual. He called over his shoulder to Matt.

"I'm going speed up a bit," he said, "just to see if she's there. You guys catch up okay?" Matt nodded and Kenan accelerated ahead of them. Instead of his usual route of high flying until he got near the mansion, he descended at the bottom of the hill and looked around for Naomi. A torch flashed from somewhere in front of him. A second later, his watch beeped. Kenan quickly tapped it and bought up a message which simply said:
'Down here...the torch. Where's everyone else?'

Kenan dropped down towards the torch's light and landed smoothly. He could just make out Naomi standing there smiling nervously with a small rucksack on her back.

"We're not going to the North Pole," he laughed. Naomi only smiled more.

"I've got some stuff I thought would help us," she said as she took some things out and showed them to her friend. "A map, a few more flash lights, train tickets..."

"I thought I said we'd bunk the train," said Kenan. Naomi shrugged. "Not too good if we all get caught though ," she said "so I ordered them on the net about an hour ago."

"That must have cost a fortune for all of us!" exclaimed Kenan.

"Not that much," said Naomi casually, waving this comment aside. She packed the things away but as she did, another piece of paper fell out. She made a grab for it far too quickly for Kenan's liking.

"What's that?" he asked suspiciously. Naomi looked around checking that the others weren't about. She held it out in her hand and shone the torch on it as Kenan took it.

"I was going give you this when we got back," said Naomi. "But you may as well have it now."

"Whose it meant to be?" asked Kenan as he looked at the small picture. It had been drawn very recently there was no

114

mistaking that, the pencil smudged slightly on his fingers. It was a portrait of a man and woman both quite young smiling back up at him.

"Well you know I said that I had a sixth sense?" Kenan nodded.

"Well in the past I've drawn these pictures of some of my friends relatives who I hadn't even seen before…it started out just as a joke but I used friend's faces and made them older or gave it slightly different eyes you know, and it turned out that they were quite accurate, in fact exactly the same as say an uncle or a cousin…even though I'd never seen them before. I suppose it's all part of this, gift if that's what you want to call it. I hoped you wouldn't mind…this is… at least I hope it is…I've only done a few drawings…it's your parents." Kenan stared at the two people in the picture. Something in his memory stirred. Had he seen them before? Was Naomi's gift and talent really this accurate? She was extremely good at drawing anyway. He tried desperately to remember any memory of his mum or dad from those fifteen long years ago, but to no avail. Naomi was talking again. "I know it's only shaded with pencil," she said not making eye contact with him, "but I think both of them had blonde hair like you but I reckon you've got more of your mum's personality, she's got the same smile as you, and your dad's eyes, they're like yours, I hope, I tried to do them the same shape but I couldn't quite remember." She looked at Kenan quickly to double check but her attention didn't go back to the drawing.

"What?" said Kenan after a long minute.

"I err, thought you… had something in your eye," lied Naomi. She quickly looked back at the picture. She seemed very embarrassed. "Anyway," she said quickly "you can keep that." Kenan looked at it for a few more minutes then put it in his back pocket.

"Thanks," he said quietly. "That, that's real nice Naz… I don't know what to say."

"It's okay," she smiled. "I wasn't sure whether you'd like it or not."

"Like it?" said Kenan. "It's excellent. I only wish I could

do something in return."

"You taught me how to air-surf," said Naomi, "that's enough." Kenan shook his head.

"This means a lot more to me than that," he said trying to keep his voice steady. Before he knew it he'd thrown his arms around Naomi tightly. "A lot, *lot* more," he mumbled. As he lifted his head and looked Naomi right in the eyes and said, his voice barley above a whisper. "Because it's the nicest thing anyone, and I mean ANYONE has ever done for me." Naomi seemed a little taken aback. There was a long silence - Naomi took a small step forward as he did the same...

"KENAN! You could give us a signal as to where you are, dude!" Matt was yelling along with Buster's barks, making a phenomenal noise. Naomi quickly took up the torch and flicked it on and off several times then switched it on so it was continuous. By that light she could see Kenan's face. He looked a little embarrassed but for once hadn't gone red. Matt landed on the ground and Buster jumped off at once. He made straight for Kenan, sniffed around his ankles and turned his attention to Naomi.

"Buster come here," muttered Kenan. But Buster sat himself next to Naomi and wouldn't budge. "Buster! Come here!" repeated Kenan. Everyone exchanged looks.

"Looks like you've made a friend," smiled Matt to Naomi. "Mind you," he said, "he doesn't normally warm up to strangers so fast." Naomi beamed down at the Alsatian and started scratching behind his ears. Buster's eyes half closed in bliss.

They hardly noticed the others land behind them until Sam's voice said:

"This isn't High Gate. Why are we just standing here?" Matt turned around.

"We're going sir," he teased, leaping onto his air-surfer. "AttennnTION!" he yelled. "Calling 'Buster unit' to accompany 'Best Looking Guy unit' to train station. That's the 'Buster unit' to accompany the 'Best Looking Guy unit' to station over." Sam rolled her eyes.

"Shouldn't that be the best jerk unit," she muttered.

"Well he can go with you if you want," he grinned. In a second Sam had gotten hold of Matt in a playful head-lock.

"What was that?" she demanded as Matt squirmed.

"Okay," he gasped finally. "Okay sorry!" Everyone laughed as Sam let go of Matt. He stood rubbing his neck muttering something under his breath, but the others could see he was trying not to laugh.

"Hey guys!" Naomi had spotted Nick and Lia standing quietly in the background. Nick gave her a nod, Lia just waved.

"Okay," said Matt after everyone had calmed down. Let's go...High Gate here we come!"

*

"Tickets please," the computerised voice came from the machines that blocked off the entrance to the underground station.

They had all had managed to find their way to the station they needed that would take them to High Gate with relative ease. Although Matt had wanted to lead the way, he had eventually admitted that they probably wouldn't get anywhere, because he didn't have an ounce of co-ordination in him. Kenan however, did. So he took the map and torch and by its light, led the others to the station within half an hour. Naomi had given them each a ticket and they were now standing at the gate into the station eagerly waiting to get through. Naomi, who had used the tube system before showed the others how to use the tickets which were scanned, confirmed that they were genuine, then returned. There was a bit of a delay when it came to Matt's turn and in his hurry put the ticket in the wrong way round, but eventually they all got into the main part of the station without too much trouble.

"We catch the 'eleven forty-six'," said Naomi looking at her ticket "and we should be at High Gate by around twelve."

"Oh great," muttered Lia. "Midnight...the witching hour." Nick shuddered as Matt rolled his eyes.

"You guys really believe in all that crap? The day I see a ghost or witch is the day either one of you two stand up to

Damien."

They had reached their platform which was empty apart from a middle-aged couple sitting at the other end. They lowered their voices as they talked over plans for the night ahead.

"When we get there," said Kenan, "we'd better split up. Nick and Lia you two can have Buster. Matt and Sam can go and check, say the west side, Naz and I can check the east. We'll meet up after an hour and..." Sam laughed loudly.

"Kenan!" she exclaimed. "Did you think this through before we left? High Gate is huge! We'll need hours to search it properly even with six of us looking." Buster whined from Kenan's side. "Oh all right even with *seven* of us looking," she sighed. Before anyone else could say anything else there was faint rumble, then a breeze followed by the sound of a powerful engine of the tube train. It slowed to a stop and the doors shot open. As hardly any of the carriages had people in them, they quickly boarded the nearest to them. Making a final check to make sure absolutely no-one was with them, they continued talking about the plans for the evening. In the end everyone agreed that they would each search different areas of the graveyard and meet back at the main gates after two hours. It seemed only a matter of minutes before the train pulled into their destination. The six friends, (and dog) tumbled off the train and made their way out of the station, secretly all feeling a lot more nervous than they thought they would have been. Naomi had printed out a map of the surrounding area of the station that included where they needed to go. There was a slight setback when Nick, who insisted he was best at reading maps, led them the opposite direction because he was holding it upside down... but eventually they found themselves before the tall gates to the cemetery. Using their air-surfers they quickly made it over and now it had to be said that no-one looked at all ready for what they were about to do. Buster seemed the most uncomfortable of all. He kept whining continuously and leaned against Kenan's legs trembling a little.

"Right," said Kenan. "You know what we're looking for. If you find it come back to the gates and DO NOT move until we come back at the agreed time."

"But what if we find it in the next ten minutes?" asked Lia. Kenan looked out over the headstones and monuments.

"Trust me," he said distantly, "you won't." After a minute of uneasy silence, the group of friends spilt up into pairs (Nick and Lia had Buster) and started walking around in between headstones and looking around trees, under leaves, anything that might look as if it could hold something the size of a tennis ball. Everyone knew it was going to be a long evening, but no-one knew, least of all Kenan, what else they would find.

"Matt, this is pointless," moaned Sam. "What the hell are we doing any way?" Matt looked at her. Sam continued. "It's dark, it's cold, and it's the middle of the night, why are we doing this?"

"I think Kenan's telling the truth," said Matt bluntly. "He's been my best friend all my life...I don't think he'd do something like this just for the hell of it."

"What about Naomi though?" persisted Sam. "Do you think she could be leading us all on...think about it. Our lives were normal before we met her and now..."Nah," said Matt. "She doesn't come across as being like that, she's pretty cool I think."

"You like her or something?"

"No...and even if I did..."

"What?" Sam had fixed Matt with a look that was neither jealousy or anger.

"Well Sam I don't like to say it, but I think she's got a thing for Kenan." To his surprise Sam laughed.

"Well that wasn't obvious," she said sarcastically. "The pair of them are so much in denial it makes me ill!"

"But I thought you liked him," said Matt.

"Yeah, 'liked' being the word," said Sam. "Once upon a time when we were kids, now he's more like a brother to me and I'm happy with that."

"So you're not interested in him?"

"What the heck has it got to do with you? No." Matt

grinned. He seemed to have gone back to his old self.

"Well I can't blame you," he said. "I am the better looking one wouldn't you say?" Sam looked at him as if to say 'You are joking?' At length she sighed and walked away.

"That wasn't a no," laughed Matt as he ran after her.

"It wasn't a flipping yes either," muttered Sam. Meanwhile, Lia, Nick and Buster were realizing that they seriously didn't like walking around large cemeteries in the middle of the night. Every small noise made them jump, and Buster kept getting under their feet making them more edgy and nervous. Nick eventually broke the silence by finally voicing not only his thoughts but those of his sister as well.

"This totally stinks! Why did we have to come along anyway?"

"Because we're friends," said Lia. "Remember...friends stick together, no matter what the circumstances."

"But normal people don't face these circumstances!" wailed Nick.

"We've got caught up with Kenan in some crazy wild goose chase," he continued, "and I'm getting sick and tired of it!"

"Oh for goodness sake" muttered Lia. "If you worked as hard with looking as you do whining we could have found it already! Let's just get this searching over with so we can get back to the gates and wait for the others." Nick nodded his agreement. At least they knew what was back at the gates; a street...lit by street lamps...a welcome thought for two teenagers (plus a dog) who were all scared of the dark.

*

"Do you think one of the others have found it yet?" Kenan turned around and shrugged. "What if they don't find it tonight at all?" continued Naomi. "What will we do then?"

"I don't know," sighed Kenan, "but it was you who pointed out that it might be here."

"*Might*, being the word," said Naomi. "And it wasn't my idea to come here at this time of night looking for it." Kenan turned around smiling.

"I've told you, if you're scared…"

"I'm not scared!" snapped Naomi "I just think that our chances of finding anything in this cover of darkness are…whoa! Look at that!" She pointed straight ahead of them. Kenan looked and saw a huge stone angel straight ahead of them standing atop a plinth. Its hands were cupped together and in the blackness of the night, they saw a pink glow coming from *inside* the figure's hands. Instinctively, Kenan ran towards it. Of course! A place no one would think to look…the headstone's themselves! But before he reached it, he found himself falling as he tripped over something in the ground.

"Are you okay?" asked Naomi.

"Yeah fine," muttered Kenan as he pulled himself to his feet. It appeared he had tripped over some kind of small hole. At the same time he and Naomi exchanged glances as they remembered reading: -several holes and a small 'trench' have been found-

"What do you think they dug them for?" asked Naomi.

"Probably thinking of the best place to hide the sphere," said Kenan thoughtfully. "My guess is that the police showed up, they panicked, and decided to hide it somewhere no one would guess, like…" he turned to the angel a few feet away… "That memorial."

Carefully checking for any more holes in the ground, he and Naomi made their way to the angel. There was no denying it was a fantastic piece of work, made in white marble and mounted on stone.

"How are you going to get it?" asked Naomi.

"Well that's obvious isn't it?" replied Kenan. He clambered up onto the plinth standing on tiptoe to reach the angel's cupped hands. Naomi stared.

"What are you doing?" she exclaimed.

"Isn't it obvious," grunted Kenan as he stretched himself even further in an effort to get to his goal.

"But you know what they say about if you step on a headstone - it's bad luck!" Ignoring her Kenan finally found what he was looking for. His hand clasped round something smooth and cold. It certainly felt like a glass sphere. He pulled it out and held it up triumphantly. It was the Sphere of Spring! It glowed with a slightly pink light as Kenan slipped it into his pocket. He jumped down and landed lightly on the ground. He faced Naomi.

"Okay," he said smiling, "if it's bad luck how come I didn't just break my leg then?" Naomi only scowled.

"I don't know," she muttered. "It's only what I've heard." Kenan took the sphere out of his jumper pocket again and looked at it intently. Naomi who hadn't, of course, seen the spheres at all took it for a closer look.

"Well, that's that then," sighed Kenan in satisfaction. He turned to the statue. "Thank you, Mr... whoever your name is," he swung the light from the torch onto the stone that bared quite a long inscription. As Naomi looked at Kenan she felt herself grow colder than she already was at the look on her friends face. The blood seemed to have completely drained from his face and the torchlight quivered as he shook slightly. "Kenan?" He didn't reply. Instead he took the drawing she had given him earlier and looked at it and at something right above the inscription. Although Naomi couldn't see properly she gathered it was some kind of picture, of the person buried there. Kenan looked at her

"Have you seen this picture anywhere before?" he whispered showing her the sketch. Naomi shook her head.

"Why?" Kenan shoved the torchlight in her hands with the picture.

"Look," he said quietly. Naomi shone the torch on a small photo of two people. She stared. She looked at the picture she had drawn and then the one on the headstone…it was IDENTICAL. Slowly she moved the torchlight over the inscription below:

In memory of
Kenan Wheeler -1st March 2270 to June30th 2300-
And His Wife:
Elizabeth Wheeler, -3rd May 2270 to June 30th 2300.

A Sad Loss To All Who Knew Them.
Stewards and Royal Councillors to H.R.H Lance I.
'Exceptionally Skilled' Pilots In The R.A.F.
Now Re-united With Lost Son And At Peace.

As she finished reading the inscription, Naomi was now the one who was shaking. She looked at Kenan whose face was deadpan. His mind was moving faster than it had ever done. Was this really his parent's grave? Were they only thirty years old on that night they had tried to save him? His second name? He had often wondered what it was. Wheeler? And his father, he had the same first name.

"I swear," whispered Naomi. "I have never seen this picture before." Without a word, Kenan took the flashlight from her and shone it back at the picture.

"This is my mum and dad," he whispered. "I know it. You've got a sixth sense Naomi you said it yourself...how can it not be them?" Naomi didn't know what to say, as Kenan continued talking. "I often wondered where they were buried. Who was at their funeral?" He read over the inscription again, and his eyes widened. "Stewards and Royal Councillors to H.R.H and pilots in the R.A.F? They were so cool!" he sank to the ground and buried his head in his knees, however he didn't make a sound or movement for a long time. Naomi decided to leave him alone. It had been a shock to her as well. After what seemed like hours, Kenan lifted his head but kept his eyes hidden in shadow. Naomi guessed why.

"We can't stay here," he muttered. "We'll have to meet the others soon." Naomi followed him back to the gates neither of them saying a word to each other. When they finally reached their destination they still said nothing. Kenan slumped down on the ground again and rested his head against the gates staring up at the starry sky. Naomi finally broke the silence.

"We found the sphere anyway," she whispered. "At least something good came out of it." Kenan looked at her...smiling half heartedly.

"And we found you've got a gift," he said looking at the

sketch he was still holding. Naomi didn't know whether she should try and steer the conversation away from the current subject. She closed her eyes as the evening breeze picked up. Kenan looked out at the cemetery and still not looking at her whispered, "Thanks."

Chapter Fifteen

Naomi had fallen asleep long before the others came back. She had started off with her head still against the railings then, moved her head onto Kenan's shoulder. Kenan was still lost in thoughts. He sat there his head whirling faster and faster. New questions were arising all the time. Apparently Terry had known his parents…why hadn't he told Kenan that they were advisers to the King…the Royal Family? Or that they had been in the R.A.F… - But the thing that bothered Kenan the most was another part of the inscription…. 'Re-united with lost son.' Did that mean him? Lost son? No one knew he was alive?

Next to him Naomi shivered. It was getting colder by the minute.

"Hey," Kenan whispered. Naomi's eyes flickered open.

"I wasn't asleep," she murmured lifting her head from Kenan's shoulder. "I was just resting my eyes."

"Sure you were," smiled Kenan. "Just like you weren't scared earlier on." Naomi scowled.

"W- well I wasn't," she muttered. "Don't believe me then."

"Fine, I won't."

"Kenan? Naomi? Are you guys there?" Lia's voice cut through the night air.

"Hurry up guys," yelled Kenan. "We're cold!" Through the darkness, Buster came bombing towards them. He had his ears and tail down and seemed to have come to the conclusion that he didn't like cemeteries. The light of a torch moved on the ground towards them. Seconds later Nick and Lia followed.

"Did you get it?" asked Nick as Buster landed on Kenan whining hysterically.

"We did actually," said Kenan. He took the orb from his pocket and showed it to them.

"Did you get it?" asked Nick as Buster landed on Kenan whining hysterically.

"We did actually," said Kenan. He took the orb from his pocket and showed it to them.

"Wow," breathed the twins.

"It- it's beautiful," whispered Lia. "Pink... my favourite colour." Kenan put the sphere back in his pocket.

"Where are Matt and Sam?" he muttered.

"They'll be here soon," said Nick looking around.

"They'd better be," grumbled Kenan. "I just want to get out of here."

"Are you okay?"

"I'm fine!" snapped Kenan. Nick actually took a step back.

"I just asked," he mumbled.

"Guys!" Matt and Sam appeared through the darkened mist.

"Did you get it?" asked Sam anxiously.

"Indeed we did," sighed Kenan, once again showing the pink sphere to his two friends.

"Hard to believe something that small can determine the fate of the earth," murmured Matt thoughtfully.

"Yeah sure," said Kenan hurriedly putting it back in his pocket. "Come on then we'd better be getting back."

"Are you okay man?" asked Matt. "You don't seem yourself."

"I'm tired," lied Kenan, picking up his air-surfer. Naomi wisely decided not to say anything. She knew that if Kenan wanted the truth told, he'd have told them himself. Buster leapt between Kenan's feet and in a few minutes they were all ready and flew over the gates of the cemetery (Nick and Lia looking more relieved than anyone else). As they lost view of High Gate, a blue light shone from behind them. Sam was the first to see what it was and swore.

"It's the police!" she yelled.

"What the hell are they chasing us for?" exclaimed Matt.

"Maybe they thought we were the ones snooping around the cemetery last time," suggested Nick. The hover – police car gave the sirens a short bleep.

"What do we do?" panicked Lia. "We've got no proof that

126

we're innocent, especially now that Kenan has the sphere.

"Split up!" shouted Kenan. "Me, Naz and Buster this way, you four the other. They were approaching a crossroads. Kenan leaned his air-surfer left and climbed higher. Naomi followed suit. Below they saw Matt, Sam, Nick and Lia veer right. The police car seemed to stop as if to try and decide where to go, then chased after Kenan and Naomi.

"Uh Kenan," urged Naomi. Kenan looked back past her.

"Oh crap!" he yelled. "Okay... top gear!" With a burst of speed, he took off Naomi just behind him. They took back alleys and side streets. But the car kept pace, suddenly with a horrible lurch Naomi felt her air-surfer begin to shudder violently.

"What's going on?" she yelled to Kenan. Her friend guessed in a second.

"You're losing power. It needs more time in the sun to collect excess solar energy. Hold on!" he slowed his air-surfer a little. "Jump!" he cried.

"Are you crazy?" shrieked Naomi. "That thing can't hold three!"

"I bet it can," shouted back Kenan. "Come on Naomi or you'll be going home in that thing!" He looked at the police car that was gaining on them. Naomi looked nervously at the distance between them and then jumped. Holding the air-surfer as steady as possible, Kenan watched. Naomi made a lucky landing on the board as Kenan held on to her. She laughed.

"We made it!" she shrieked hugging Kenan. But the blue lights still shone on them. Kenan dropped the board sharply.

"We're not out of the woods yet," he said. "Heads up." He caught something in his hand as it fell from the sky. Naomi's air surfer had fallen a few seconds after she had jumped and had only missed the police car be inches. He handed it to her. "Okay," he said. "Hold on." They dived down more as the police car spun round above them trying to trace their movements. "We've got them on the ropes," said Kenan. "Here we go." He dropped further vertically and with a burst of speed zoomed off. He didn't care in what direction he went, just anywhere apart from the same place as the police hover-car. Unfortunately, he was so busy checking behind him making sure they had lost the car he didn't pay too much notice to what was going on ahead.

"Kenan?" urged Naomi. "What's that?" Kenan turned around. Ahead of them coming out of the pitch-blackness, were more flashing lights, but these weren't police lights. They were orange and red…and not moving. It took a few minutes for the friends to realize what exactly was ahead of them. At the same time they both yelled;

"Level crossing! Straight ahead!" Kenan tried to stop the air-surfer quickly but this time he wasn't so lucky. His foot caught the top of the barrier and the next second, he Naomi and Buster were catapulted onto the tracks! Kenan picked himself up and looked up and down the line for the lights of a train. He saw them, in the distance but they seemed to be disappearing…a noise to the right of him made him look as the barriers lifted and the lights stopped flashing.

"Guess we just missed the train," smiled Naomi as dusted herself down. Kenan picked up his air-surfer and shook it slightly. His worst fears were confirmed as a rattle came from inside.

"We can't use this," he muttered. "Not in the dark any way, the brakes are broken… and I don't know where the hell we are! We're lost!"

"On the plus side," said Naomi looking around, "I think we also lost the police." Kenan looked now, they did appear to be completely alone – then they both looked down the line.

"I know where we are!" exclaimed Naomi. "Don't you remember we went over this level crossing on our way here?" Kenan now looked around with more interest. Now that Naomi mentioned it the crossing did seem familiar. Then he remembered. Although they had started and ended the journey in underground stations, there had been a period of a few minutes where the train had surfaced, before going back underground. Naomi who had the backpack with her torch and train timetable inside quickly dug both of them out and scanned a certain page before turning to Kenan and saying, do you want the good news or the bad news.

"Go on," sighed Kenan. "Make my evening complete...what's the bad news?"

"Well, the train that we've just missed is the last one tonight. But the good news is that if we start now we should be back at the station we started off at in about an hour. We'll just follow the track."

"Are you sure that was the last train?" said Kenan. "because if we're following the track and another one comes along behind us or in front of us..."

"No more trains on this line for at least four hours Kenan," said Naomi reading the page again. "The next one along here is the five fifty five from Kings Cross."

"Well if you're sure," said Kenan slowly.

"Of course I'm sure," smiled Naomi. "Not only that, but I'm right."

"Of course you are," said Kenan rolling his eyes. "You're female." Naomi ignored this last remark and by the light of her torch they both set off down the railway line.

*

"No, he's not here. Maybe he got on the earlier train," Matt slumped down in the comfort of the chair and groaned. "You had to have me search the entire length of this thing didn't you."

"You agreed you'd do it if you lost 'paper, rock scissors,'" giggled Sam. "So stop moaning already."

"You don't think they got arrested do you?" asked Nick.

"Nah," replied Matt confidently. "Kenan can evade a police car any day...the amount of close calls he's had, he should have either been jailed or killed himself trying to escape them."

"But he did have Naomi with him," said Lia, "and Buster." Matt bit his lower lip then shook his head vigorously.

"He'll be fine," he muttered. "There's not too much he *can't* do...except I can pick up more girls than he could handle." Lia snorted.

"You attract girls? Pull the other one!" Nick joined in the laughing but Sam sighed impatiently.

"Can't you guys go one minute without insulting each other?" she scowled.

"Ah leave it out, Sam," laughed Nick. "After all you're the first one to start throwing the insults round here."

"I just don't know how you can all be so happy when who knows what's happened to Kenan and Naomi, that's all," muttered Sam. After this remark however, she kept quiet and looked the other way down the carriage.

*

"Buster! BUSTER! Where are you?"

"Kenan, he's right beside you."

"Huh? Oh yeah so he is." Naomi laughed.

"You're so edgy tonight," she smiled.

"I'm still thinking," muttered Kenan. Naomi's face fell.

"Well, at least you know where they're buried," she remarked quietly. "And there's nothing to stop you going back there whenever you want."

"Yes there is," muttered Kenan miserably. "The police know I've been there."

"Well you don't have to go back there right now," said Naomi hurriedly, but Kenan interrupted her.

"Yes I do!" he exclaimed. "You don't get it Naomi! Nearly fifteen years I've been waiting to find them, hoping that I'd discover something about them. Now I know what they look like, how old they were when they died, what their names were and what they did for a living, I need to go back there before I find a reason not to and with the police skulking round there as they no doubt will be tomorrow I won't get a chance to visit them for who knows how long." Naomi sighed.

"But your not vi-si-ting them," she said slowly. "They don't know you're there."

"You don't believe in spirits?" shot back Kenan, but his voice was quiet. "Life after death? Even though you can tell if they're about with this sixth sense you posses?" Naomi didn't reply. Kenan nodded. "I thought so," he muttered. They walked on without a word. Finally Naomi broke the silence.

"Sorry," she mumbled.

"No problem," muttered Kenan. Naomi looked up at him surprised. Kenan looked back and gave her a wink. "Really don't worry," he said. "I'm just a bit…uptight right now…hey look!" Ahead of them was a tunnel sloping down, they guessed into the underground system.

"Okay not long now," smiled Naomi. "Only a few stops. We'll be back home before half past two. Good thing it's Saturday, my parents are out at a friends place till tomorrow lunchtime.

"What about James?" asked Kenan. "He's there somewhere," said Naomi "but he sleeps like a log. I know you may find it hard to believe but he's a pretty decent guy once you get to know him he's so funny. But the thing is he's been employed with us since before I was born so I'm kind of like a niece to him… he just doesn't like the idea of me mixing with 'lower class.' That's the only thing that annoys me about him and my mum for that matter. Dad's okay about it but mum and James are like two peas in a pod…obsessed with the whole social status thing."

They were now in the tunnel and although it had been dark outside it was nothing compared to the blackness that greeted them now. It wasn't far off (Kenan thought) from the lift leading down to the shrine. Naomi switched on the flashlight and with Buster now literally bolted to Kenan's side, they set off further into the darkness.

They had been walking about ten minutes when Naomi stopped for a second or two. She looked back at Kenan.

"Do you hear that?" she whispered.

"What?" said Kenan. "Come on, Naz don't do this."

Naomi looked past them, back the way they had come.

"It must have been my imagination," she muttered.

"It better have been!" exclaimed Kenan. They walked on a bit further. Naomi stopped again. This time there was no mistaking she had heard something… and whatever it was, it wasn't good. The colour simply disappeared from her face.

Apparently Buster had also heard it, because his ears were up and he looked as nervous as Naomi.

"Will you please tell me what this is about?" said Kenan, feeling more than uneasy. Naomi said nothing but looked at the ground. So did Kenan, the next moment he felt his blood run cold. The tracks were vibrating ever so slightly but getting a little louder each second.

"I don't know how to tell you this Kenan," said Naomi looking at him as he looked up but there's a train on our track, coming this way."

"From where?" said Kenan, trying not to panic. "I think from behind us," said Naomi.

"It's okay," said Kenan "I've got an idea that might just work."

"What is it?" asked Naomi.

"RUN!!!" yelled Kenan. Buster tore off ahead of them as the two friends followed. There was no mistaking it now. The tracks below their feet were well and truly shaking. Kenan could now feel a faint breeze on the back of his neck. If they could just reach the next station before it caught up with them. A horn blared through the tunnel seemingly magnified to be ten times louder than normal. They weren't going to make it. Kenan's lungs were already bursting; he was running as fast as he could. They were giving it all they could but no matter what the train was faster. Suddenly the light cast by the torch Naomi was holding seemed to go all over the place…it had gone from her grasp along with her air-surfer as she had fallen over: her weak ankle had given in at last. Without thinking what he was doing, Kenan doubled back and quickly helped her up, whilst also grabbing her torch and air-surfer. At that moment, he was thinking almost as fast as he was moving and as he saw Naomi limp and struggle to stand he only had one crazy idea left. He threw the air surfer a few feet ahead of them and saw it land with a shower of sparks right on target- on the electrically charged rails. To Naomi's amazement, it surged back to life. The light from the train was now approaching, Kenan knew they only had seconds. He half carried, half dragged Naomi towards the now recharged board and jumped on.

"Hang onto me and don't let go!" he hollered above the rumble just feet behind them. Gathering every ounce of mental energy he had left, he concentrated on moving, moving faster then he had ever gone before, maybe faster than sound itself, the air-surfer lunged forwards, Kenan couldn't believe it! He concentrated harder than ever whilst balancing to keep the board on the rail so they were now practically grinding along it. Less than a few feet behind them, the train horn screamed in their ears, but Kenan never lost his focus. All Naomi could do was hang onto him as tightly as possible, knowing that were she to fall, it was the last thing she would ever do. Kenan leaned to the right as the track curved round and up ahead he saw a glimmer of hope. A circle of light was shining up ahead of them…the next station! Just a little more. The board lurched as adrenaline pounded through his body. *Come on!* He screamed to himself, *lift up NOW!* With the last word the board did indeed lift a clear six feet up as Kenan threw his whole body weight left and they skidded sideways in mid air as the train thundered past just clipping the board, not enough to damage it but enough so it spun violently out of control and crashed onto the platform sending its two passengers tumbling to the ground. Buster, it seemed, had beaten them there with time to spare; he bounded over as Kenan lay there trying to get his breath back. Sweat cascaded down his face. Had they really made it? Were they really still alive? It appeared so. As he lay there he heard an odd noise from next to him that made him sit up.

"Naomi?" Kenan's eyes widened in worry. She was positively sobbing!

Chapter Sixteen

"For the last time Naz stop saying sorry," laughed Kenan.

"But we were nearly killed..." sniffed Naomi.

"But we weren't," interrupted Kenan, "and that's what counts."

"Look at my air-surfer!" exclaimed Naomi. Kenan stopped walking and looked. Where the train had caught it, there was a small scuff to the side. "If I had noticed that thing coming a second later we wouldn't be here," continued Naomi, "all because I read a time table wrong."

"You couldn't have," said Kenan, "I asked you to double check remember? Maybe it was a freight train...or ghost train." He raised his arms and moaned trying to make Naomi smile but to no avail.

"It was no ghost train," said Naomi as the Henderson Mansion rose up before them, "and freight trains don't move that fast..." Kenan stopped her:

"Naomi, it's three in the morning, you're tired I'm tired, can we continue this debate tomorrow or something?" Naomi looked at the ground.

"Okay," she muttered. "See you tomorrow huh?" then she stopped in mid-sentence. "Oh wait! I can't tomorrow evening."

"Why not?" asked Kenan, his curiosity getting the better of him. Naomi looked as un-enthusiastic as possible as she muttered;

"I'm going to the theatre with mum, dad... and Cedric." Kenan sniggered.

"Have a nice time," he grinned.

"Ha ha ha," grumbled Naomi. "Look, I'll text or ring you if anything comes up okay?" Kenan nodded. Naomi quietly tapped in the security code of the gates and they swung silently open.

"See you tomorrow...possibly," she said in a low voice, "and thanks."

"For what?" asked Kenan. Nomi smiled.

"Saving my life," she replied giving him a hug and she walked through the gates as they shut behind her.

"Naz?" said Kenan. Naomi turned round.

"Yeah?" she asked eagerly. Kenan gave her the thumbs up sign.

"No problem," he said.

It was half past three when Kenan and Buster finally made it back to the car park. Kenan couldn't be bothered too much else except throw the air-surfer on the floor and collapse on to his bed. What a night...why hadn't he tried to get some sleep during the day? However, they had one more sphere. Now only two left: the sphere of Autumn and Summer. He had barely closed his eyes before a shout made him open them.

"Kenan you're back!" Kenan sleepily raised his head. Matt, Sam and the twins were running towards him.

"Guys I'm not being rude," he groaned "but I'm so tired."

"So are we," exclaimed Matt. "We've been up waiting for you... what's wrong?"

"I'll tell you the whole story tomorrow," muttered Kenan, "but the long and short of it is, we nearly got arrested by the police, almost killed by a train and the brakes on my air-surfer are gone." His four friends looked at each other, then back at him.

"Guess you want get some sleep then," said Lia at last. Kenan smiled weakly and nodded.

"See you in the morning," murmured Kenan. No sooner had his friends left than something else got his attention. The watch/phone on his wrist bleeped...a message. Kenan hurriedly bought it up. It read:

'Hey, Kenan, just to say thanks again. I still can't believe I read that timetable wrong...it nearly cost the both of us. I'm off to the theatre at six tomorrow so you can come round just before if you need me to help on something else. Gotta go... need sleep luv Naz! x x'

Kenan finished reading the message, saved it and went back to the main menu. He smiled and closed his eyes. "Yeah, good night Naz," he whispered. He didn't wake until around lunch -

time that day, and when he finally did come round there was a nasty shock in store...his air-surfer was missing!

"No," he mumbled as he threw his blankets to one side and stumbled to his feet. He knew it had definitely been there when he had fallen asleep, and he felt sure Buster would have alerted him if someone had stolen it. "So where's it gone?" he groaned as he searched hopelessly around for it.

"Kenan," that was Sam's voice. He turned around. She was standing there with Matt next to her... and in their hands, each of them holding a side, was Kenan's air-surfer. The twins were behind them.

"What are y-?" Kenan rubbed his eyes. He really didn't have any mental energy only two seconds after waking up.

"We fixed it," announced Matt.

"Huh?"

"The brakes... I- we fixed them." Matt was beaming. Kenan was confused.

"No offence Matt," he mumbled, "but you don't know the first thing about how to fix these things."

"It's not really that hard," said Matt, as Sam handed the disc to Kenan. "See you just unscrew the bottom," said Matt pointing to the small control panel underneath, "and tighten up a part of the reactor that monitors your brainwaves, that's all that I had to do to mine."

"Well thanks guys," smiled Kenan. "But how did you know what you were doing?"

"I'm not as stupid as I look Kenan," said Matt sounding a bit hurt. Everyone laughed except Sam.

"You're very sweet when you get all defensive you know," she smiled nodding at him."

"Really?" said Matt. "You really mean that?" Sam looked at him sweetly for a few seconds before laughing out loud.

"Nope!" she grinned.

*

"Well, not bad for an evenings work wouldn't you say Kenan?" Terry was studying the pink sphere carefully. He set

136

it down next to him looking pleased. Kenan didn't answer at first. He was staring out of Terry's window that overlooked the city. Although he was happy that Matt and Sam had fixed his air-surfer he couldn't completely shake out of his head what he had seen only in the early hours of that morning.

"Kenan?"

"Wh- what? Oh yeah sorry I'm err…" and he was lost again.

"Okay. What's wrong?" asked Terry. Kenan sighed. It wasn't that he didn't want to tell Terry but he didn't think he could. He hadn't even told his oldest most trusted friends for goodness sake! He decided he had to, Terry had started all this anyway.

"Why didn't you tell me they were connected with the royal family?" he shot at Terry. Colour drained from the old man's face.

"Wh- who?" he stammered.

"Don't give me that bull!" shouted Kenan. "My mum and dad! Councillors to the late King!" Terry lowered his gaze. He looked ashamed. "You said you knew them!" Carried on Kenan, "and you never said a word to me!"

"You never asked," said Terry. "Would you have been so upset if they had been, forgive the phrase, normal people." Kenan stopped. He wasn't sure, how to feel at that moment as it was. He sat back in the chair with a groan and closed his eyes. He was still very tired and irritable but he knew it wasn't Terry's fault.

"Sorry," he muttered.

"That's okay," said Terry. "You've been under an awful lot of stress lately. But remember Kenan, two more spheres…then it's over."

"It's not that that bothers me," said Kenan. "It's how much time we have left."

"I don't know," sighed Terry. "I've been checking various weather- web- sites and they really can't give accurate forecasts because it's changing by the hour but look at this site," he opened a new window on the screen and Kenan stared as the old man pointed to an image over the atlantic ocean. "Here, he said, and here, and there's one here as well..."

"What are they?" asked Kenan looking at the complex diagrams.

"Storm systems," replied Terry. "If those two collide here and are joined up with this one -" he was moving his hand around the screen. "This could well be the start of the 'legendary storm' Kenan, and guess where it's going to hit first?" Kenan didn't reply, he didn't need to. It was out at sea, just off the east coast of America, maybe a few days away, no more. If Terry's calculations were correct, every second counted. "The MET office have mentioned severe weather already," he continued, "I think they know more than they're letting on. Probably don't want to cause a fuss, the media would have a field day... which reminds me, I haven't seen the news this morning, you never know, you and your friends maybe mentioned." Pointing a remote control at a holo-box that was a fair size bigger than the one Kenan and the others had, Terry bought up the lunch - time news. To Kenan's surprise and relief, nothing was said about any one hanging around High Gate in the early hours of the morning. Trains were on strike again, a celebrity had been found shoplifting, there had been some sort of charity event. He was just about to breathe a sigh of relief, when something else made Kenan's heart plunge as he stared at the screen.

"Now to our more local news," blared the newsreader. "Wealthy Lord Henderson of the company Henderson enterprises has been accused of breaking and entering when he was found trying to force his way into David Tainard's offices last night. George Henderson has refused to comment on his actions but has already been bailed out by his wife, Audrey Henderson. Here Lewis Richards reports." Kenan's eyes widened as a rather plump middle- aged man appeared. He was standing so that the Henderson mansion could be seen behind him but no - one was in the grounds. Lewis Richards had the sort of face Kenan could never get tired of hitting. He seemed to be looking down his pig like nose at everything and had a posh accent that sounded too over the top to be genuine. But it was the actual words that he said were the thing that made Kenan angry:

"Well yes, as you can imagine the Henderson family are now inside the estate behind me wanting to keep a low profile I should think. The recent behaviour of George Henderson has been questionable for some days now, though some people have pointed out that his mother died earlier this week..."

"But is that any excuse for breaking into the King's advisers offices?" interrupted the reporter in the studio, "bearing in mind the kind of information that must be kept there? Could this be maybe a gross neglect of security at the offices that should be restructured?"

"Well of course it's not a feasible excuse," replied Lewis smugly, "but no-one really has any valid explanation, the police say nothing was taken and George Henderson gave himself up without a fight when the police arrived, and I have been assured that he did *not* actually gain access to inside the building."

"Now there's talk that George is supposed to be accompanying his wife, daughter and a family friend, to a West End show tonight," droned on the studio reporter, "do you think this will still go ahead or will they be trying to stay out of the limelight for a bit?"

"There's no talk of plans being cancelled," replied Lewis. "But my guess is they will be going out tonight, regardless. Let us not forget what has made George Henderson such a successful business man and that is his attitude to any matter concerning him, he deals with in a calm and laid back manner."

"Lewis Richards, thank you," nodded the studio reporter. "We'll have more on this story and others in our evening news at six. Until then goodbye."

Terry turned off the holo-box and looked at Kenan, who was positively seething.

"This is a joke," he growled. Terry looked uneasily at Kenan and just managed to say (very timidly):

"I don't think it's a joke Kenan. The Henderson family is very much respected... this can't be some cheap story to be on the news."

"I'm going over there," said Kenan, standing up. Terry stopped him.

"And get spotted by the press? I don't think so!" Kenan turned to Terry.

"Well you think wrong!" he exclaimed. "I'm not having Naomi's family put down over something that isn't even true!"

"Didn't you hear me?" shouted Terry. "It's on the news Kenan... as much as you don't like it, it IS true I'm a lot older and more experienced in this world than you are...I know how it works! You're just a kid!"

"That's what you all think!" Kenan shouted back. "You think I'm just some punk kid who knows nothing! Well let me tell you something Terry. I think this whole thing is crazy! Let the world end! What have I got to lose..? Exactly... NOTHING! I've had it with you! You, Delia, Cedric even Naomi...yes Naomi! She's got so much to live for and I'm not cramping her style anymore!" The sooner she forgets about me the sooner she can move on... and make the most out of what time we've all got left. Kenan's eyes had gone jet black and tears of rage were streaming down his face. There was a long silence then Terry finally spoke.

"You really think that Kenan?" he muttered. "You really want to give up now, when we're halfway there. Naomi's helped you more than anyone... even myself, and this is how you thank her... by giving up. You were the one that talked me round the other day Kenan. I had to take a step back, regain some faith in myself and in you... now I'm asking you to do the same." Kenan sank down on the sofa, his head in his hands. "Get your head down," said Terry finally. Kenan looked up his eyes already bloodshot.

"What d'you..?"

"You're tired," said Terry giving Kenan a glass of water and tablet. "Take this and just kip on the sofa...I guarantee you'll wake up in a couple of hours feeling much better." Kenan took the tablet really too tired and confused to think about what he was doing. He barely put the tumbler down on the cabinet next to him when his eyelids began to feel heavy.

140

He lay his head down on one of the cushions and fell asleep. Terry looked at him. "I'm so sorry Kenan," he whispered.

When Kenan opened his eyes later on he couldn't for the life of him remember where he was. It was only as the foreign tapestries hanging upon the walls and ornaments on crammed shelves came into view that he remembered – of course, Terry's flat. He also remembered what Terry had told him before he had fallen asleep and he was right, maybe it was the tablet, the sleep, or both but Kenan felt a lot happier. He lifted his head and looked around. Terry was still there working silently on the computer. He turned as Kenan woke up.

"So you can move after all," he smiled. Kenan nodded and rubbed his eyes. "By the way," said Terry turning away to hide a smile, "your hair's a right state."

"What's new?" groaned Kenan as he sat up on the side of the sofa and stretched. A thought hit him. "Terry what's the time?"

"Half past four," said Terry. Kenan relaxed. "Why?"

"I've got to meet Naomi," explained Kenan, "find out if she's got anything else to help us out. She's leaving at six isn't she?"

"Okay," the old man turned back to the computer looking mystified.

"What's wrong?"

"My computer, I think it's just because it's an old model but it seems to be running very slow." Kenan stood up and walked over to the desk Terry was sat at.

"What's that?" he said pointing to a small envelope symbol in the bottom right hand corner of the screen.

"I - don't know. I hadn't noticed it until you pointed it out. It looks like an e-mail." Terry pressed once on the small envelope symbol and waited. At that moment and just for a split second, the monitor seemed to flicker on and off. "Oh no," groaned Terry. "Please don't let it be what I think it is."

"What would that happen to be?" asked Kenan. A small box appeared in the middle of the screen. For a moment there was nothing but a flat gray colour, before an image filled it.

Kenan and Terry could just make out the outline of a human figure but their face was hidden in shadow. Then it spoke: "Terry Orkas. I trust that is your name... unless I have sent this thing to the wrong person. Well hopefully I haven't, I mean a few of my boys have visited you recently haven't they? Yes Terry, I am who you think I am, and I am quite capable of carrying out what you don't think I could. You know what I want. The spheres. At the time I sent this, only two were in my possession, but they are now being hidden carefully, so your little 'helper' can't find them. Consider this a warning Terry. I want all five spheres in my possession very, VERY soon. If you fail to comply I will have to send some more people round...and you wouldn't like that would you? You know who I am. You know where I live and I just thought you'd like to know, that this message also contains a virus. Right now it is raging through your hard drive making it impossible for you to use the internet or access any of your pathetic research files any more. Well at least until you get the money to fix it, and I don't think that's going to be any time soon. Oh tell Kenan to watch himself... you know what could happen 'old friend,' because if I so much as get a smell of something wrong happening, it won't just be you paying. It'll be him, and his friends...including the ones at the Henderson mansion. I'll be waiting." The monitor flickered and the computer shut down. The screen, the sound the whole thing, just went out. Terry and Kenan stared at it then Terry put his elbows on the desk and put his hands on the top of his head groaning.

"This can't be happening," he muttered over and over again. "It just can't."

"Who was that?" asked Kenan. It took a long while for Terry to answer finally he said:

"You recognize his voice?"

"Well yeah...I think so... but I just can't think where I know it from or... who..."

"I wouldn't expect you to," said Terry, hardly able to speak now. "Kenan, he's the son of the King your parents served, he was prince at the time..."

"Wait," said Kenan, "but... that means..."

"Yes," whispered Terry, "Lance the second, our monarch, the King of England."

Chapter Seventeen

"You're kidding."

"No, Kenan, I'm not. I know him very well through your parents as it happens."

"But how did you know them?" Kenan couldn't resist asking now. The more he got involved with different people, the more tangled and secretive his and his family's history became.

"Because I taught them, and Mr. David Tainard and George Henderson at a university. You look surprised, Kenan. You can't just expect to leave school and walk straight into Buckingham Palace now can you? Yes. Your parents and Mr. Tainard were my top three students among a few hundred others. However, when George Henderson's father died he was given the business and everything. So because his future was well secured he left, though still stayed in contact with David."

"Did Lord Henderson know my mum and dad?" asked Kenan eagerly. Terry looked thoughtful.

"Yes he did but not that well. David was supposedly his best friend. Anyway your parents…they studied the hardest out of my whole class and ended up being just that bit better than David. There was a space of a few years where I heard nothing from them. One night I had a call from your father. All three of them had jobs at the palace. He and Liz, sorry, your mum, had made it to being actual stewards to our late King. You know what that means Kenan. If the situation had called for it, your own parents could have ended up running the country." Kenan raised his eyebrows, it seemed too insane to be real and for a second he felt very proud to have been the son of two such wonderful people. "Anyway," continued Terry. "They were not only stewards but royal councillors as well and David was their kind of second in command. But when they died David took over their job and has been doing it ever since."

"And that's the guy George Henderson has been trying to

144

dish the dirt on?" asked Kenan.

"Not necessarily him," said Terry mysteriously. "I think Lord Henderson knows the game Lance is playing. He's caught onto it and wants to talk to David...you know, see if he's in on it to." Kenan slowly nodded his head.

"I've got to talk to George," he said finally. "Tonight before they leave. Why doesn't he just speak to David face to face?" Terry shrugged.

"You've got a lot of investigating to do Kenan," he said. "And now that my computer's down Naomi's work will be doubled." Kenan nodded again.

"I'm going over there now then," he muttered, before a thought struck him. "Terry, do you have a phone?" Terry pointed to a small phone mounted on the wall that Kenan hadn't noticed before. "So have I," said Kenan pointing to the watch on his wrist. "Shall I call you with any information I can get tonight?" A smile crossed Terry's face.

"Sure," he said. "But Kenan, be careful. Tensions are a bit high all over the city tonight. Just watch out okay."

"Don't worry," said Kenan standing up to go. "If anything happens I can just sweet talk my way out of it." But Terry only half smiled.

"I'm serious Kenan," he said quietly. "Be careful."

All the way to the Henderson mansion Kenan had been checking his watch and as he flew over the gates he checked it again... five thirty. They shouldn't have left yet. He saw a white limo standing outside glinting in the golden rays of the sun. To his surprise, Lord Henderson was out and walking around the vehicle while James was polishing the chrome parts of bodywork. They looked up as Kenan slowed his air-surfer down. George greeted him with a smile.

"Hello. You must be Kenan, I'm sorry but we're going out tonight..."

"I know," said Kenan. "But I need to speak to Naomi for just a second, unless Cedric's here."

"Oh he's not due here for another ten or fifteen minutes," said James. Lord Henderson checked his watch.

"I could go and see if she's ready, come in." He ushered

Kenan indoors and made his way up the marble staircase. Kenan waited patiently in the hall. He knew one thing…he could never get tired of looking at this place. The crystal chandelier was now lit and looked twice as pretty as before, reflecting off of the sparkling marble floor. What he wouldn't give to live just for one day in a place like this. He heard footsteps on the stairs George was trotting down them.

"She'll be down in a second, she's just finished freshening up. Is there anything I can help you with?"

"Well no, I just wanted to tell her some news."

"Oh don't mention that word," groaned George. "I take it you've seen my antics last night made headlines?" Kenan nodded.

"Sorry sir," he mumbled.

"Oh please Kenan, don't bother with all that sir and madam talk. Just call me George." Kenan nodded again. He could now see why Naomi had been so laid back when he had first visited. But he was also desperate for more answers and he couldn't bear holding back any longer.

"You went to university with my parents?" he blurted. George Henderson looked at him confused… then his expression changed. He looked shocked.

"Kenan and Liz? Y-you can't be their son." Kenan smiled.

"Believe me I am."

"But how… they died, you were orphaned. Everyone assumed you were lost as well…. Where have you been all these years and how on earth did you find out your identity?" Kenan felt in his pocket for the picture Naomi had drawn for him and showed it to George.

"Naomi drew this for me. Apparently she's done similar stuff for other people as well." Kenan wondered whether Naomi had told her dad about High Gate. He decided to not mention her and just stick to himself.

"When we - I mean I went to High Gate, I found a picture like this on their headstone. There was no way on this earth that she could have copied it. She told me she knew nothing about it and I believe her." George simply stared.

"I can't believe it," he whispered. "You are aware that not

146

a single person is aware you're still alive? Kenan looked at the ground and couldn't answer. There was something about the way Lord Henderson asked him that which made him shiver. He simply said:

"Yeah. I've seen the headstone, I know everything about them." George just looked at the picture and back at Kenan. Finally he said:

"Visit tomorrow. I need to tell you something that I think you'll find interesting... now is not the right time." As he turned to leave, he stopped and with his back to Kenan, said something, which made Kenan, not only honoured but also uneasy.

"You're a good kid Kenan. I don't care what society or even my wife thinks of you... I know different. You helped Naomi through a tough few days when her grandmother died, they were very close. I have no purpose left really except to do the best I can for her and Audrey and no matter what she says... Cedric's not right for Naomi." He turned and faced Kenan. "If the media and law decide I need to be locked up," he said his voice hardly more than a whisper, "look after her... she needs a friend like you." With that, he handed the picture back to him and walked out. Kenan looked after him. If his head was a whirl at that moment, it was nothing to what happened next.

"Kenan?" he turned around looking towards the staircase... and his jaw dropped. It was Naomi only she looked so different. Her hair, which was usually lose, was now styled in a kind of French plait. She had a beautiful heart shaped silver locket on, but what was the most eye catching of all was the long red dress she was wearing which trailed along the floor after her, dotted all over it were delicate silver sequins reflecting the light from the chandelier. She had red suede sandals to match the dress. Kenan's eyes grew wide. Naomi smiled. "Well?" she said as she reached the bottom of the staircase, "what do you want?" Kenan pulled himself together and gulped hard.

"It's err Terry," he stuttered. "Well not really him it's more his computer's beutif- I mean buggered and you're going to have to do a lot more research than we first thought."

"What's wrong with it?" asked Naomi not noticing Kenan was still staring at her in disbelief.

"A virus," he said. "Some one sent him a virus through the internet and wait until you find out who it is Naz."

"Well who?" said Naomi. "Do you need a drink or something? You're really flushed."

"Yes thank you," said Kenan, following her out of the hall. "It's only the King... King Lance." Naomi stopped in her tracks as they entered the empty kitchen.

"You're kidding!"

"That's exactly what I said," said Kenan leaning against a work surface.

"B- but the royal family, they wouldn't...the King wouldn't..."

"I heard his voice Naz, it's him. He wants all five spheres in his possession very soon, and he said that if he doesn't get them, everyone will pay." Naomi put the empty glass tumbler on the side so it wouldn't tremble in her hands.

"I can't believe it," she murmured. "I mean I expected it to be some kind of big syndicate but not stretching as far as the royals. Now I know why my father went out..." she couldn't finish the sentence. Kenan hadn't thought to ask but it was clear she was more ashamed than upset. He put a hand on her shoulder.

"Don't worry about it," he said quietly. "Your family's got a very good reputation Naz. The press will forget about it next week, I bet you." Naomi nodded slowly, filled the glass with water and passed it to Kenan. "It's weird you know," laughed Kenan. "I'm not really thirsty." But he proceeded to drain the whole thing. There was a distant ring of the doorbell.

"I'd better go," said Kenan. Naomi nodded.

"You can leave through the back door if you don't want Cedric sneering at you," smiled Naomi as she pointed at a door at the other end of the kitchen.

"Okay," said Kenan. "Shall I text you later or something?"

"I'll text you," said Naomi, "oh Kenan, one more quick question."

"Go on."

"Give me an honest opinion, how do I look?" Kenan had hoped she wouldn't ask. Finally he said;

"Don't worry. You look stunning, and if you don't turn heads tonight then they must be blind."

"Creep," giggled Naomi.

"I'm serious."

"I know that's what I'm worried about," and she whisked off. Kenan sighed.

"You have no idea," he muttered.

That evening, however, Kenan couldn't settle. He was extremely restless and couldn't stop thinking about all he'd seen and heard. The King of England. Lance. He was in on this whole thing. How on earth could Kenan and the others overpower him? Well they couldn't...that would be treason. Then there was George Henderson. He had known his parents... an awful lot more than Terry had let on. What did he want to speak to him about? Kenan was certain his family history couldn't be much more tangled than it already was. As for David Tainard, that was another name that Kenan wanted more information on. Then he had an idea. He could ring Terry of course! He remembered how to work the phone but just as he was punching in the number a cold voice made him stop.

"Wotcha got there kid?" Damien. Kenan hurriedly covered his wrist with his jumper sleeve.

"Nothing," he said turning round to face him. "But I want to ask you some questions Damien. Why did you try and get me and Matt thrown in jail the other night?" As ever Damien merely sneered. In a blink, he grabbed Kenan's wrist and ripped the watch off. Holding Kenan back with one hand he studied it in the other.

"This isn't a bad bit of kit," he said. He turned to Kenan. "How much do you think I could sell it for?"

"Don't," exclaimed Kenan. "That thing means a lot to me, it was given to me... by a very good friend." Damien's sneer only grew wider.

"You'd be breaking my heart if you weren't so pathetic," he growled.

"Damien it's mine!" shouted Kenan, and with a sudden burst of strength he snatched back the watch and shoved it in his pocket. Damien reached for something inside his coat, but was stopped only by another voice.

"Where have you been?" it was Sam.

"Hey Sam," smiled Kenan very grateful she had turned up.

"What's up?" Damien looked disgusted and without another word he skulked away, his hands buried deep in his pockets.

"What was all that about?" asked Sam looking after him.

"I don't know," replied Kenan. "I think he's drunk." Sam nodded the smile returning to her face.

"We've been looking for you for ages," she said. "Where have you been?"

"Sorry," sighed Kenan, sitting down. "I was at Terry's this afternoon then went straight to Naomi's." Sam sat next to him.

"And?" pressed on Sam. "You've clearly found something else out, I can see it." After a deep breath Kenan told her everything: his parents, Terry, Lance, the virus, the conspiracy, George Henderson, everything. Relaying all this, he found was far more exciting than just hearing it. Sam hung onto his every word, right up until;

"So I came back here, but I can't relax Sam. Not while the fate of the earth's in my hands." Sam looked at him.

"There's something else," she said quietly.

"What?"

"Something else is bugging you," she said. Kenan went to interrupt but Sam smiled in such a way that he thought better of it. "Kenan, I've known you nearly fifteen years. What is it?"

"Well," said Kenan. "There is one thing. I'm really, well, confused…about Naomi." Sam's smile widened.

"Why?"

"Well it's just, I'm worried. All this pressure, she doesn't need it. I think she needs someone to talk to, you know just to offload a little bit."

"Why don't *you* go and talk to her?"

"I can't," said Kenan bitterly. They've gone out tonight haven't they?"

"Who's they?"

"Naomi, her mum, dad and Cedric to the theatre in the West End somewhere."

"Ooh," said Sam cunningly, "so they were all dressed up I bet."

"Hell yeah," said Kenan letting the sentence slip out of his mouth without thinking. "She had this long red dress on. Sandals to match, she looked stunning Sam..." he suddenly realized what he had said and hid behind his hands with an embarrassed moan.

"Well, I think I know the problem," said Sam after a long silence. "You're jealous."

"No I'm not!"

"Okay, let's put it this way. You don't think Cedric should be with them do you?"

"No."

"You think you should be there instead right?"

"Uh- huh, but Sam wait..."

"Don't interrupt, Kenan. You're feeling put out because Cedric's out with her looking like a model and you're not. Is that or is that not jealousy?" Kenan looked thoughtful. He lay back on the blankets and stared up at the roof.

"I can't believe it," he whispered at last. "I am jealous...and if I'm jealous...that means I'm in love." He covered his face with his hands again. "Oh Christ," he groaned.

Chapter Eighteen

It was getting on for midnight but Kenan was wide-awake. He was stretched out on his bed, hands behind his head…thinking…about what had been said not just that evening but that day. But for some reason all this seemed obsolete now, all he could think about was Naomi. His mind was running like a crazy blur he couldn't clear however much he tried.

"This is crazy," he said to himself quietly. "I'm supposed to be saving the world not hanging out with…" a sudden realization hit him. Even Terry had picked up on it before Kenan. He remembered the words: *What's more important? Saving the world or hanging out with your girlfriend?* With another groan, Kenan pressed his face into his moth eaten pillow. Two spheres short, Damien was acting oddly, The King of England was in with probably the biggest conspiracy of all time and on top of saving the world he had just admitted that he had made the fatal mistake of not only admitting to Sam, but also to himself, what he really thought of Naomi. A familiar bleeping sound bought him back to his senses…his watch. He sat up in a hurry and opened a new message:

'Kenan. It's me. The show was really good, but other than that the evening was lousy. Just about to look on my computer for some more info that could help us.'

Kenan immediately texted back.

'Don't worry about it. You've done way too much over the past few days and you can't tell me that you're not tired after last night. Leave research and stuff until 2morrow.'

A reply:

'Maybe you're right. O.K I'll leave it for tonight. I've had an idea though… I think I know where the sphere of autumn is. Come round at about one 2morrow and I'll probably have some info for you. C u then. Luv Naomi x'

Kenan simply replied:

'Ok - You're a diamond. C ya at one. K x'

But as soon as he had sent the message he felt butterflies in his stomach again. "What the hell am I gonna say to her?" he wondered. It was the first decent night's sleep Kenan had had for what seemed an age. When he awoke the next morning however he didn't know how tired he would feel only too soon after. He had barely gotten up and sorted himself out before he heard Matt calling him…he sounded as though he was in a right panic.

"Kenan! Kenan! Have you seen what happened in the night?"

"What?" Kenan knew it was more bad news and frankly he didn't know how much more he could take. Had Lord Henderson been out on a 'mission' again? Matt slowed his run to a jog as he approached his friend.

"You have to see this! C'mon!" Kenan followed Matt out into the bright but somehow cold sunshine and stopped short. There were thousands of them. Tens of thousands! Blowing along the floor almost looking like torrents of water:

"Leaves?" exclaimed Kenan. "But it's summer. The trees can't lose these for at least another three months!" Matt was staring as wave after wave of brown and gold blew past them.

"It's on the national news and worldwide," he said. "Every single tree in the U.K at least has just shed all their leaves."

"But they'll die," said Kenan. "They need leaves to photosynthesis especially in this weather! Come winter they'll have nothing left to live on!"

"Kenan," said Matt looking at him. "Since when did you become a scientist? Besides, that's the least of our worries…"

"No it's not!" exclaimed Kenan. "Did you forget? Trees produce oxygen! You know the stuff that keeps us alive! If there are no trees then there's no oxygen! No oxygen means no people Matt!"

"Oh yeah," said Matt quietly, "I forgot about that." Kenan shook his head.

"I'm meeting Naz at about one," he said. "Hopefully she'll have some more info for us. She said she had an idea about the sphere of autumn or something."

"I hope so," said Matt. "Because if we don't start to sort this stuff soon, we won't be around for winter."

"Delia? It's me Cedric."

"Oh hi, how'd it go last night? You have fun?" Delia held the phone to her ear speaking with hardly any enthusiasm at all. Cedric however didn't pick up on this.

"It was cool, I don't think Naomi liked it much, still she's been a bit off altogether lately."

"Don't you think you're making it a bit obvious?" said Delia unable to keep the anger out of her voice.

"W- what do y-?"

"You know what I mean! You hang around that mansion twenty-four –seven hoping to develop your little 'friendship' which she's putting the blocks on because you're in her face all the time!" There was a silence on the other end of the phone. Then:

"Delia. No offence, but you're the granddaughter of a priest, your mother hasn't worked in years. You have no idea about the minds of business families. We work in very different ways."

"But you don't even like her that much," exclaimed Delia. "You said yourself if anything was going to happen between you two, she'd have to calm down as she's much too fiery for you to handle!"

"Yes I admit to saying that!" shot back Cedric, "but I can calm her down a bit you'll see…now I did call up for a friendly chat but it seems you just want to lecture me on how I should swoon the ladies in my life and I have a lot to do."

"Cedric w- wait…" stuttered Delia but she was only left with the dialling tone. She slowly replaced the receiver and for the first time in that conversation looked across the room at her Grandfather. Terry looked expectantly at her.

"No luck?" he guessed. Delia shook her head.

"He needs to let go," she muttered. "If he gets any more involved he's going to try and tag along with her on these, these excursions to get these spheres he'll only end up getting in trouble to." Terry looked at his broken computer then back out of his apartment window.

"A lot more than just trouble," he mumbled. "A lot more."

*

"Well, I was sitting there, at the theatre last night, and it just came to me like that. It's so obvious Kenan."

"So tell us already, where do you think the stupid thing is?" exclaimed Kenan.

"Water," replied Naomi.

"Huh?" Kenan looked at Matt for some kind of clue but for once Matt was speechless. "Say that again," Kenan stuttered. Naomi sighed. "Water. Large amounts of water." Think about it like we did about the sphere of spring. What happens in the autumn?" "Trees lose their leaves? Birds migrate? Come on Naz put us out of our misery here." "I know," said Matt quietly. "Everything dies." Naomi snapped her fingers.

"Bingo!" she grinned. "Everything dies or hibernates... what ever way you want to put it, life slows down for a little bit."

"Well we know that," said Kenan. "What's water got to do with it?"

Naomi sighed again.

"Water is where all life came from. Where it starts. It's just a hunch but I reasoned if life slows up or stops in autumn then surely the sphere will be somewhere where it starts...like some form of water." Kenan smiled but shook his head.

"Yeah, good theory," he said. "But the only water around is in ponds in parks and stuff. Now they are way to public to go hiding something that important in and I doubt these clowns would try to hide the sphere in the sea...they'd never find it again."

"I never said anything about ponds or the sea," said Naomi her eyes gleaming in that mischievous way that Kenan didn't see very often. "I was thinking about the Thames," she said triumphantly. Kenan stared at her then very slowly a huge smile appeared on his face. He looked at Matt, who wasn't looking far off from ecstatic himself. "It'd be very easy for these goons to just drop something the size of a tennis ball in a there," continued Naomi. Think about it they weigh it down so it doesn't get carried away, and it's so easy to get to, a place everyone knows of should they have to return to get it. All we have to do is find a way of locating it and retrieving it..."

"Which could be a bit of a problem," said Kenan sheepishly. "I – err can't swim very well."

"I can," said Matt, "and the twins can to." But Kenan clearly didn't want the limelight hogged by the others.

"Well, I didn't say I couldn't swim!" he exclaimed. "I'm just a bit naff when it comes to swimming *under*water, anyway do any of you have any idea of just how big the Thames actually is?"

"I can hold my breath for just under a minute," said Matt, choosing to ignore this last question. "I'm sure we could find it..."

"Whoa, whoa! Time out!" interrupted Naomi. "Listen to what you guys are saying! I was thinking if we got some machinery stuff to pinpoint the sphere for you then you could go and get it... like a radar or something."

"But we don't have the money or time to get something like that," sighed Kenan. "Besides we've got the best radars money *can't* buy... our eyes and Buster! He's helped us find two out of three so far and the only reason he didn't find the last one is because he was over the side of the cemetery with Nick and Lia." Naomi still didn't look convinced but in the end she shrugged.

"Well if you guys are sure you could find it..."

"Of course I can," exclaimed Matt. Naomi looked at him.

"I wasn't just talking to you," she grinned. Matt turned red. Suddenly a thought hit Kenan... he needed to speak to Lord Henderson, with out Matt eavesdropping.

"Hey Naz," he started, trying to sound casual. "Is your dad in today?" Naomi smiled.

"No, he had to go to work, with such a hangover, he had best part of a bottle of wine before we went out last night and more when we got back."

"He was drunk?" Kenan felt as though the heaviest weight had been dropped on his shoulders. Did this mean that Lord Henderson had been talking rubbish? Naomi didn't pick up on his down tone and nodded.

"He was plastered." He acted really sober while we were out. Then when we got back and said goodbye to Cedric he came in and just slated the show... he was so funny! But why do you ask?"

"Oh nothing," muttered Kenan. "I just wondered." He pulled himself together. "Okay, Matt let's go and tell the guys the plan of action... I trust Naz can supply us with a map?" Naomi looked a little uneasy.

"I can," she said "but I don't think I'll be able to come with you guys tonight. My mum's beginning to get a bit suspicious as to why I'm so tired all the time." Kenan nodded. He felt a little relieved. The more spheres they got, the more dangerous it became. It was probably safer for Naomi to stay at home even if it was just for one night. "If you hang about for a second," continued Naomi, "I can print a map off for you now."

"I'll get going Kenan," said Matt picking up his air-surfer and headed for the open window. Kenan nodded.

"I'll catch up," he said, "see you soon," Matt gave a quick wave to Naomi and jumped lightly out of the window on his air-surfer and took off. Naomi watched him go then shook her head.

"What?" asked Kenan.

"You guys," smiled Naomi sitting down at her computer. "You really do have a thing against using doors don't you?" Kenan raised an eyebrow.

"Well not so much against doors," he said pretending to look thoughtful, "it's just I don't want your mum thinking I'm some kind of stalker." Naomi nodded slowly.

"Give me a second while I get a site with some maps and I'll print the best one." Kenan sat down beside her.

"Why are you doing this Naz?" he asked quietly. Naomi fixed a stare on him.

"What do you mean? I'm helping you aren't I?"

"But why?"

"I don't get you," said Naomi. "What is it, you don't want my assistance anymore?" Kenan sighed.

"I don't want you or your family in any more trouble," he corrected.

"I'm not in any trouble," said Naomi turning back to her computer.

"But your dad…"

"Isn't in the news today," finished Naomi. Kenan took a deep breath.

"Naomi. My parents were councillors to the last King. I don't know whether it's destiny or what but I feel like I'm responsible for keeping England at least, as safe as I can, and that includes you." There was a long pause. Naomi who had been working at her computer without so much as looking at Kenan turned to him and lent across so that her face was inches from his and asked:

"Do you believe in destiny?" Kenan nodded. Naomi continued. "You believe it was your destiny to grow up an orphan?" Kenan slowly nodded again. Naomi moved even closer. "So why are you worried about what you know is going to happen anyway no matter what you do to try and prevent it?"

"Because I don't want you or any of my other friends to suffer, if something bad happens," replied Kenan. "I'm not a person to abandon people. Yes I believe in destiny, but it's not fate, it can be changed." Naomi looked at him for one long minute. Kenan didn't break eye contact. He didn't feel anything at that minute and it showed in his face. All he wanted was for Naomi to stay out of the way for a little while at least until the press stopped following her and her family. A whirring from the printer made Naomi sit up and turn her attention back to the computer. A sheet of paper came through with a section of London on it. Naomi pointed to a little grey rectangle shape on it.

"That's the car park," she said. She moved her finger over to the other side of the map. "And that's the Thames," she finished. Kenan took it and stood up.

"I'll text you okay?" Naomi nodded.

"I'm sorry if I seem a bit off," she said. "But I've got a really bad feeling about something… something bad is going to happen, but I don't know what."

"Something bad is happening," said Kenan picking up his air-surfer. Naomi shook her head. "This is worse," she said looking at him. "Much worse. We're all in danger now...people want to stop us that much I do know."

"What are you talking about?" asked Kenan stopping short. Naomi looked at the floor.

"Among certain other headlines yesterday, one caught my attention, but I forgot to tell you last night. When we were on the tube track I was right. There were no trains scheduled for the next few hours. But yet one nearly killed us... that's because the person behind the wheel was trying to do just that. That was no near miss Kenan. It was in the news as a train had been stolen, yet found at the other end of the line the next morning. No clues have been found as to who stole it and tried to get us but I know we're being closely watched."

Kenan gulped. He felt dizzy. It hadn't been a misreading on the timetable. That train wasn't meant to have been on the tracks. It's sole purpose for being out was trying to kill them...or one of them. He nodded. "Thanks for letting me know Naz," he said finally. Take care," he put a hand on her shoulder. "Stay in the house with someone, anyone. Promise me." Naomi nodded.

"I promise," she whispered.

Chapter Nineteen

Desperately trying to think of what to say, Kenan waited as
Matt went to fetch Sam, Nick and Lia. His mind was so full of
what Naomi had said that he really didn't feel like talking ever
again, but he knew that he had to get the others to help him
and as soon as possible. He took the map out of his pocket and
looked at it again. The Thames was right out of their way and
he knew if anything bad happened, they would be quite a
distance from being close to people who could help them. He
shook his head, they would be fine. So far they had so far
been to a power station undiscovered, High Gate and escaped
police and even a tube train for goodness sake.

"Okay Kenan! We're here, what's up?" Kenan sat up.

"Sit down guys," he said smiling as best he could. "This is
going to be a bit of a tough one but I think we can pull it off!"

"Damien, what are you doing?" Vicky opened her eyes.
She had lost so much sleep the past few nights she couldn't
help but fall asleep during the day.

"Nothing," snapped Damien. "Do me a favour keep your
nose out alright?" Vicky raised her eyebrows but knew better
to keep quiet. Damien had a large haversack on his back and
was checking his coat pockets for something. Finally he
straightened up and looked at Vicky.

"I'll be back late," he said shortly.

"Where are you going?" asked Vicky without thinking. "Is
there anything I can do to help?" Damien turned and glared at
her.

"For God's sake!" he shouted. "Just leave me alone, you
stupid cow!" Vicky jumped to her feet. It was very rarely she
got angry but now she was...she hated being insulted when
she'd done nothing wrong.

"I just asked!" she yelled. Damien took a step towards her,
his fist clenched menacingly.

"And I'm just telling you," he spat. "Keep out!" Vicky

stood her ground. Damien looked at her for a minute then lowered his fist. His eyes opened a little wider and his sneer disappeared. "I'm trying to get some things sorted out," he growled. "Leave me alone, and I'll give you an easy life." He turned and walked away. Vicky watched him and sighed quietly.

"What are you doing?" she whispered. "Who are you going to kill now?"

"Well personally I think it's a bit risky Kenan but if you have confidence in us let's go for it." Lia nodded in agreement with her brother.

"I'm not that greater swimmer myself," she said "but I'll help…"

"No you won't," said Kenan. "You can't swim, you don't swim. Matt and I will look first, give us ten, fifteen minutes?" He looked at his friend who nodded as he said this. Kenan continued. "Sam and Nick then can go while we catch our breath, before me and Matt go back. If none of us find it in an hour we'll come back and think up another strategy." Everyone nodded. Then Sam spoke up.

"Is Naomi coming?" Kenan shook his head. Sam looked at him as if to say: 'What? You've had a row?' To Kenan's relief she kept quiet.

"We will be taking Buster though," said Kenan, as if deliberately changing the subject. "How much help he'll be in the water I don't know, but we'll try and see how things work out." None of them were really sure how 'things would work out' but as they set off that evening towards the river none of them suspected the evening would be far more surprising and dangerous than the previous two.

*

"That's it up ahead," shouted Kenan, as the others followed behind him.

"Wow!" yelled Matt, "It's huge, far bigger than it looks on the map." Sam laughed loudly.

"Of course it will be you idiot," she yelled. Buster was the first on the ground and ran about sniffing busily. Though the last adventures had been a little scary for the dog, he couldn't help but like them. That was the main thing that he and Kenan shared... their sense of adventure. The five friends walked quietly along the banks of the river all eyes on the unsuspecting alsatian. Quite suddenly he stopped and looked towards a certain point in the river, ears up and very softly growled. This was the sign Kenan had been watching for. He nudged Matt and pointed at the dog. Matt's face lit up.

"He knows," he exclaimed to Kenan. "He knows it's in there... guess this is the place."

"Yeah," agreed Kenan. "Alright, you ready for a swim? Ten to fifteen minutes?" Matt grinned.

"I can swim for much longer than that Kenan," he said, "but as you're a novice I'll let you off." Kenan bristled. "Hey," exclaimed Matt holding up his hands, "just kidding. Just do your best mate okay." Kenan sighed and nodded. With Sam, Nick, Lia and Buster (by now whining hysterically) sitting at the edge of the river, Matt took a deep breath, took one of the water proof torches and jumped in followed by Kenan who preferred to ease himself in using the large rings mounted in the stone walls. Gingerly he made his way in as Matt surfaced. "Man it's cold!" yelled Matt. "And it STINKS!" After this however, he disappeared back under, coming up a few seconds later. Kenan watched him in disbelief. Not only was the water a lot colder than he had predicted but none of them had any idea what else resided in there.

"Matt," he warned. "Be careful. We don't know what's at the bottom of this thing." Matt laughed, the torch still in his hands.

"It is deep," he admitted then laughed. "Ahhh," he teased. "Is Kenan scared of the widdle fishies swimming about? Kenan glared at him. He tried to look down to check for life in there, but it was impossible to see through the murky water with no light as Matt had the only one. He pushed off from the stone wall taking small strokes, not much more than doggy-paddle and almost immediately felt uncomfortable. But he was determined to try his best. Taking a deep breath, he went to go under faltered at the last minute and came up spitting water out of his mouth, clamouring back to where he could touch the wall. His pride was hurt more than anything and Matt laughing and still swimming as well as a fish made it worse.

"I thought I saw something," he lied. "Give me a minute."

"Yeah right," smirked Matt. "You went under like a brick!"

"Oh shut up," muttered Kenan, shaking his hair out of his eyes. Matt's laughing subdued.

"Alright," he said. "I've got a better idea. You search there where you're near the wall and I'll take a look around here." Reluctantly, Kenan agreed, but he could see the sense of the idea. He enviously watched Matt as he went under the water, but after such long periods, he began to get worried. He turned his attention to going under the water. It was humiliating because he could only stay under for a few seconds, and though every time he surfaced his lungs were bursting, it looked very poor next to Matt's controlled breathing. After about ten minutes of searching as much of the area as he could he felt exhausted.

"Matt," he yelled as his friend surfaced. "I'll give it one more try in a minute and I'll take five." Matt nodded and went under the water. As Kenan prepared to do the same, something made him stop. A sound he had never heard before. It was getting louder; a breeze was beginning to build up to. He looked towards the opposite waterfront and against the dots of bright lights of the city. Something brighter than those was slowly appearing like a sunrise over the skyline.

"What the-?" his sentence was cut short as a huge flying machine, not dissimilar to a helicopter appeared. Two gigantic and blinding lights were mounted either side of the craft and accompanying these were two barrel like objects. He watched each barrel crackle with an electric blue light as it approached the middle of the river… above Matt and himself.

"KENAN! Get out of the water!" screamed Sam. "That

thing's going to release an electric current down there!" Kenan turned and swum as well as he could back towards the wall. Sam and the twins helped him up. The machine did, indeed, seem to be positioning itself for an attack as the two barrels rotated towards the surface. Once he felt dry land beneath his feet, Kenan collapsed puffing and panting, but stopped. Something had just occurred to him.

"MATT!" he yelled. Matt had been underwater since the arrival of the craft and had no idea of the danger he was in. The others joined in with shouting for their friend. The craft was now hovering right over the middle of the Thames, the electric blue light growing denser and brighter every second.

"Look!" yelled Sam. "There he is!" Matt had just surfaced shaking water off his face.

"Matt, get out now!" shouted Kenan. Matt turned to their direction. He could barely hear them and hadn't noticed the craft over his head.

"Huh?" he yelled back. "Guys I can't hear you there's something making too much..." he slowly looked up as he realised what was going on. He caught sight of two blinding blue lights before a sound like a hundred fireworks went up as the electric current shot down towards the water.

"Matt! No!" they yelled. But it was too late! Matt cried out as the electricity swarmed over the surface of the lake... and straight through him! Kenan didn't think twice.

"NO!" he screamed. "MATT! HOLD ON!" He took off towards the edge but to his surprise and anger he found himself being held back by Sam and the others. "What are you guys doing!" he shouted. "Get off of me! We gotta help him!"

"Kenan No!" shouted Sam. "You'll only be hurt too!"

"Matt's gonna be DEAD if we don't do something!" shot back Kenan. "Get OFF!" But they didn't. All Kenan could think of was getting Matt out of the river. He forgot he couldn't swim that well. He forgot that electricity in water would paralyse and most probably kill him. All he wanted to do was help his best friend. But the twins had him by each arm and Sam had grabbed him around his middle, all of them and using their full strength to pull him back. Exhausted from the swimming anyway, Kenan couldn't protest any longer. He collapsed to his hands and knees (pulling his friends back with him) and stared at the horrific sight, helpless. Matt was still screaming as the electricity relentlessly coursed through him. He couldn't ever remember having felt pain like this. Despite he was in water it felt like he was on fire! But he knew his friends couldn't help so all he could do was yell as the pain grew worse and worse. Back on the shore, Kenan, Sam Nick and Lia couldn't do anything but watch as the craft relentlessly shot wave after wave of electric energy downward...but then something happened. The lightning changed direction. Someone was obviously trying to pull the current back to the water for the light shuddered but was pulled towards the shore. It went past Kenan and the others it made for a long metal pole in the ground that had definitely not been there on their arrival... a lightning rod! Standing next to it were two hooded figures, arms folded and motionless. The craft and light were held in place for a few more minutes, and then the lights died and went out. As suddenly as it had arrived, the craft left in a hurry, disappearing over the London skyline. Kenan pulled himself up and without waiting to see whom the hooded people were, jumped back into the water. Immediately Sam followed suit. Matt was motionless in the water. With Sam's help, Kenan managed to get him back the wall and Nick and Lia helped to heave him out.

"Matt," Kenan hardly dared to raise his voice above a whisper. "Matt. Come on Matt open your eyes." Nothing.

"Matt," Sam tried close to tears. "Don't... don't leave. Oh God! Please be alive." She checked for a pulse and held her hand over his mouth then looked up at Kenan. "I think he's stopped breathing!" she whispered.

"Hey, hey are you guys okay?" one of the hooded figures was speaking.

"Get an ambulance!" exclaimed Kenan. "My mate's in a real bad way."

"Already done," said the second figure holding a phone in his hand. Sam looked up at them.

"Please help us," she whispered. The first person knelt

down and felt around for a pulse, stopped and looked back up at Sam.

"Don't worry," they said. "There's a weak but definite heartbeat, and the ambulance will be here soon." Kenan stood up.

"Thanks guys," he said. "But we don't even know who you are." Slowly the first figure stood up and pulled the hood down. Kenan couldn't believe it.

"Delia?" he exclaimed. He looked towards the other person…it took him a minute to recognize who it was, "and, Cedric?" Kenan wasn't the only one who felt confused.

"Err Kenan?" said Nick timidly. "You know these guys?" Kenan nodded.

"This is Delia, Terry's grand-daughter, and Cedric a family friend of Naomi, I think."

"Well, actually a *very* good friend of Naomi's," sniffed Cedric. Delia nudged him in the ribs. But if anything had been going through Kenan's head that he wanted to say back to Cedric, he kept it to himself, after all there were more important things to worry about. An ambulance siren cut through the air in the distance, and in less than a minute it had arrived. For the next few minutes there was bedlam as paramedics rushed about for stretchers and other things.

"But I don't get it," said Kenan quietly to Delia. "Why did you two help?" Delia sighed.

"Grandpa told me I should keep an eye on you," she said.

"We're doing fine," said Kenan. But Delia shook her head. It was then Kenan knew that something wasn't right.

"Don't you think it's strange about what happened with that train?" she insisted. "And what's happened to your best friend?" Kenan stared at her.

"What do you mean?" he asked finally.

"These people are out to stop you Kenan, and they don't make mistakes. This is only the beginning, consider these things warnings."

"But-," Kenan couldn't think what to say.

"Excuse me?" a paramedic was walking over to Kenan. Kenan felt his heartbeat quicken.

"Is he gonna be okay?" he said. The paramedic looked at him gravely.

"It's hard to say… I think you'd better come with us."

"But he's still breathing? Right? He- he still had a heartbeat and that." The paramedic looked at Kenan. He then heard two words (but didn't dare to look at where they came from) that made him feel like he wanted to pass out:

"Okay. CLEAR!" His knees gave out beneath him and he sunk to the ground.

"Oh no," he murmured.

Chapter Twenty

Much, later, Kenan, Sam, Nick and Lia sat underneath the multi-story each lost in their own thoughts. Every so often, the twins looked at each other then at Kenan and Sam... it was hard to decide who was taking it the hardest. Both were unnaturally pale and their eyes reflected how they felt, cold and empty. Finally Lia spoke up.

"Sam? Samantha? Can you hear me? Are you okay?" Sam slowly looked up and nodded. Lia looked at Kenan.

"How 'bout you Kenan?" Kenan didn't answer. "Kenan?" Lia tried again, but Kenan was too far away.

His mind seemed to have travelled back to the hospital. Hours ago, when he had seen Matt rushed into accident and emergency. Kenan hadn't been allowed in. He found it completely wrong that he should go with them as far as the hospital then not follow his best friend in. But the staff were firm in saying that family only should be there. Kenan finally gave way and trudged back with the other three to the multi-story to tell Matt's parents as much as they could without giving the whole game away. They told them Matt had been swimming and that he had been attacked- unprovoked but nothing about the spheres. Matt's parents hadn't really taken the news well. They headed off to the hospital as fast as they could on foot... the same one Terry had been taken to. Now the waiting began.

The group of friends sat quietly in a circle not knowing what they could do to make the time pass any quicker. Even Buster was quiet, lying, just behind Kenan, evidently awaiting Matt's return. After what seemed like an eternity, Sam gently nudged Kenan and pointed in the twins direction... they had fallen asleep. Kenan half smiled but suddenly he felt a little angry with them... how could they fall asleep when Matt's life was hanging in the balance. Sam seemed to read his mind.

"Come on," she said, trying to cheer Kenan up. "It's been a long night for everyone. They're not used to staying up past their bedtime." This time Kenan didn't smile. Sam sighed. "Kenan, please you're not making this any easier." Kenan stared at the ground, Sam felt as if she was talking to a brick wall but she was determined to get him to acknowledge her. She put a hand on his shoulder but couldn't find the right words to say anything she thought would help. Kenan looked up at her.

"'S my fault," he choked. Sam immediately gave him a hug... more relieved that Kenan could speak again, than anything else.

"It's not," she whispered unable to stop herself crying. "It's those sickos who want the world destroyed."

"No," said Kenan. Sam looked at him. "They don't want to destroy the world Sam," he continued. "This goes much deeper than that, I mean the King is in on this one. His royal highness," he muttered bitterly, "Lance the second..." He was about to say something else when a horrible thought went through his head. A flashback had entered his head so crystal clear it was almost as if he had gone back in time and was re-living the whole thing again. Damien and what he had said that night at the top of the car park:

"I promise you Lance, I'll have the job done within the time span even if it's on the day itself..."

"No way," whispered Kenan to himself. "It can't be the same one."

"What are you muttering about?" asked Sam. Kenan didn't answer something else had come into his head. He looked like he was thinking hard.

"Sam," he started. "Do you have any idea what Damien's second name is?"

"Oh Jeez," groaned Sam. "I'm... not sure. Isn't it T- Tai Tainard isn't it?" She realised what Kenan was saying. She remembered the twins coming back from Dave's Halloween costume shop with the name... D. Tainard. It all fell into place. The masks! They were trying to kill Terry, to stop him trying to find the spheres and save the planet. Damien had obviously bought the masks, and if the King of England was in on it as well that meant that he was in league with Damien!

David Tainard was the name of the King's advisor. Was that
Damien's real name? Did that mean he was a fraud and didn't
really have to live on the streets? There had been times he had
disappeared sometimes for weeks and he had shown up
looking none the worse. Of course he didn't, not if he had a
luxurious big house somewhere. Sam's face was white. Kenan
couldn't take it in. It was bad enough he had to save the
world, but from Damien and the King? It seemed impossible!
Leaning against the concrete pillar, he stared at the ceiling.
    "We are now officially in trouble," he muttered bitterly as
he closed his eyes. I'll tell you something now," he continued,
"I don't think I can do this." Sam shook her head. For once
she was stuck for something to say. They sat in silence for a
long time. Finally Sam stood up. "I'm going for a walk," she
muttered. "I don't suppose you want to come to do you...?
Kenan?" She looked at him and smiled to herself. He had
fallen asleep. "Night Kenan," she whispered.

    "Hello? Kenan?" The voice was very faint like it was a
dream, but Kenan awoke with a start.
    "Wha-? Naomi?"
    "Were you asleep?" Kenan rubbed his eyes and looked
around sleepily. The twins and Sam had obviously gone
because apart from Buster, who was asleep, on his back, he
was alone... but where was that voice coming from? Had he
dreamt it?"
    "Kenan, your phone, look at your phone." Kenan glanced
down at his wrist and saw the tiny image of Naomi had
appeared out of the screen on his phone.' He realized that
Naomi must have called him and he'd hit the reply button by
accident. He lifted his hand so Naomi would be able to see
him and spoke to the holographic image of his friend.
    "Naz. Can you see me? Sorry I was asleep."
    "What?" exclaimed Naomi looking a little annoyed. "I've
been up waiting for you to text me. "You've had me worried
sick."
    "Sorry," mumbled Kenan running one hand through his
hair that had somehow found it's way all over the place while

he had been sleeping. Everything was slowly coming back to him. Suddenly he felt wide-awake again. "Naz! Jeez I didn't tell you what happened did I?"

"Huh? What?" Kenan took a deep breath; he sometimes wished that he couldn't work out things that took so long to explain.

Naomi patiently waited for the website to load, it was unusually slow. Or was just her nerves making her think that her computer was next to be taken out? After speaking to Kenan who was obviously in a bit of a state, she was now more determined than ever to try and find some thing that could help them. The news that Damien was also probably in with the conspiracy had been worrying and Naomi had repeatedly told Kenan to stay away from him as much as possible, but what had really caught her attention was Cedric and Delia turning up at the lake. How? How had they known they were there? Terry wanted an eye kept on him fair enough, but why would he send him out on this crazy thing if he knew Kenan was going to be in danger anyway? Naomi didn't like it. She didn't like it at all and she was determined to find out what was going on. She needed as much information as possible on the shrine, the spheres, anything that could help them some more. She logged onto @tomicweb then hesitated. She knew what she was about to do, and knew that if she was found out there would be big trouble but as she reminded herself what would happen of they were to fail, she pulled herself together. She went to the 'login' option and typed in Terry's username she'd copied from the piece of paper Kenan had when he had first asked to use the computer. She faltered again at the password before typing in 'candyfloss'.

It didn't work. According to a message on screen she only had two more attempts. "Typical," groaned Naomi. Clearly for whatever reason, Terry had changed it. She pondered this for a minute before typing in 'Tony Orkas.' Again the same message came up. Naomi swallowed hard, if this last one was wrong... The very slowly she typed in D-E-L-I-A and pressed enter with baited breath. The login screen disappeared to be replaced a second later with a page for Terry, that displayed a picture of him from, Naomi would have guessed, a few years ago now. 'The sub-site of Terry Orkas.' Naomi clapped her hands together She was in!

There were a lot of tabs on the site, a biography, blogs, pictures but it was all pretty boring and deceivingly normal. To an outsider, Terry Orkas just looked like the friendly old man living out his twilight years in peace, but Naomi knew differently. She scrolled through some more pages before leaning back in her chair with a sigh... it was then that her eyes fell on the settings option almost completely hidden away at the bottom of the page. Clicking on it, she was greeted with privacy settings, hoping that it wasn't password protected she clicked it... and was greeted with the following message; 'update, manage and view your personal files here,' she was in luck. Hands shaking, Naomi scoured the folders. Sure enough it was all here. The shrine, it's history, past guardians, the prophecy... she double took. Prophecy? She didn't know of any prophecy. Was it to do with what was happening now, or something that already passed? Did Kenan know about it? She doubted it, surely if he did he would have told her. Deciding to just double check she clicked on the file and a few seconds later, lines and lines of writing were displayed before her, written in an ancient kind of style but still understandable. She scrolled down browsing through at first then a word caught her eye and she hurriedly went back to take a second look at it. She read the context that the word was in and felt the colour drain from her face.

"No," she whispered as she read the line over and over again. "Please no."

*

"Kenan! Kenan! Kenan wake up! Quickly." Kenan jerked awake. How could he have fallen asleep again? The first thing that came into his head was Matt. He then realized that Sam had been calling him. She was beaming all over her face.

"Guess what?" she panted as she approached her friend.

"What? He's better? He's awake?"

"Even better than that!" exclaimed Sam. She stood to one side and Kenan could hardly believe his eyes. Matt was standing there as real as he could ever be looking, a little tired yes, but still he was there and looking none the worse from his experience.

"M- Matt?" Kenan couldn't believe it. He really hadn't thought he would have seen him alive again. Matt gave him a nod and simply said:

"Yo." He was a lot quieter than usual, true, but Kenan didn't care. He ran to his friend and embraced him quickly before resting his hands on Matt's shoulders grinning at him.

"But last night you were... but... I can't believe it's you... You're- you're really real."

"Of course I'm real," laughed Matt. "It's known as the National Health Service. Two hours in intensive care and I was stabilized. Soon I as I was able to walk, I went straight down to the main desk and discharged myself." Kenan couldn't stop smiling. He gave Matt another extremely brief hug as Sam pretended to look away. She smiled to herself. For all their toughness and arguments they were best mates after all and she knew that they were closer than brothers.

"What did your mum and dad say?" asked Kenan. "They didn't ask too many questions did they?"

"Nah," replied Matt. "They were just relieved that I'd come round. I think they believed your explanation that we'd been attacked for no reason... luckily." Kenan nodded slowly, before Matt reached into his jacket pocket.

"So, you want this sphere thing now?" he grinned.

"W-what?"

"This," said Matt. He held up a sphere an orange gold colour, the only difference that this one had to the others was that it had a long length of string attached it with a small thin metal emblem tied to the other end, a symbol Kenan recognized from somewhere. "They fixed this to it," explained Matt pointing to the emblem, "so they would know where to return to. We were right, it was held in place, they fixed it on

the hull of an old sub that must have gone down in the war. You should have seen it... it was massive, the perfect hiding place. It nearly defeated me though got to be honest, that's why I was so long, I had to detach it..."
He handed the sphere to Kenan, who took it unable to believe his eyes. "Don't ask me how," he carried on, "but they missed it when I was taken in, I got it just before that attack…it's been safely zipped up in my pocket since." Kenan smiled. He laughed he was so happy. The sphere had been the last thing on his mind for the past few hours and now here was Matt handing it to him.

"You… got it?" he stuttered, still unable to believe it. Matt was back safe and well and with the sphere as well? Kenan was still asleep and still dreaming, he was sure of it.

"Dude, what did I just explain to you?" laughed Matt.

"Well yeah but…" Kenan knew he wasn't showing it that well but he was thrilled beyond words. Finally he found his tongue. "Thanks," he smiled. "This is SO COOL!" He turned around and picked up his air-surfer. "I'm dropping this off at Terry's," he announced. "I'll be back soon guys." Sam nodded.

"We've got to go and find Nick and Lia anyway," she said. "They don't know Matt's out of hospital yet, we thought we'd come to you first." Kenan nodded. He grabbed his air-surfer and took off. Matt and Sam watched him go, Matt looking a little dejected.

"I come out of hospital, having nearly been killed and he takes off when I give him one glass ball."

"Matt, you may find this hard to believe," said Sam, as they turned and walked towards the other end of the car park, "but we were up all night worrying about you. He does care, he's like me… he just doesn't show it as well as he should."

"Well, I suppose you've got a point there," said Matt. "You never show your feelings to anyone. Sam stopped in her tracks.

"That's not completely true," she said indignantly.

"Well I've never known you say anything nice to me... ever."

Sam giggled.

"You're such an old woman," she laughed. "Always moaning..."

"And you don't?" shot back Matt, but he was laughing to. Sam shrugged.

"I suppose you could call us one of those old married couples," she giggled. Matt didn't get the joke.

"What you on about?" he exclaimed, turning red. Sam laughed as she strutted ahead.

"Nothing," she laughed. "It's just an expression!" But Matt didn't appear to hear her and ran after her.

"Come on Sam," he said overtaking her and walking backwards so he was facing her. "What are you on about?"

"Nothing," repeated Sam still laughing at the look on Matt's face.

"If you're saying what I think you're saying..." began Matt but Sam stopped him.

"Watch where you're going you..." There was a thud as Matt collided with something behind him.

"Ow! Ah jeez that hurts!" he exclaimed. He turned to look, and rolled his eyes, he had walked into one of the concrete pillars holding up the car – park and hit his head.

"Are you okay?" asked Sam urgently.

"Yeah," muttered Matt clutching the back of his head. "I don't think there's any more damage in there than there was originally!" But Sam wasn't convinced.

"Let's have a look," she persisted.

"I'm fine really."

"Let me have a look NOW!"

"Well alright...but I don't see what..."

"MATT!"

"Okay." Sam looked closely at the back of Matt's head, but there was, indeed, no sign of damage.

"See," said Matt turning round and smiling at her. "I'm right and you're wrong." Sam tried not to smile through a scowl. Matt winked at her. "Thanks for the concern though," he continued. "Anyway let's find the twins." And he walked off in front of her. Sam looked after him.

175

"You're welcome," she murmured.

*

Kenan arrived at Terry's block that lunchtime. He jumped off his air -surfer and immediately hit the intercom button...but there was no reply. As Kenan had had this experience before he patiently waited and tried it again. There was a click but no voice. Kenan began to feel a little uneasy. However, the doors shot back and he walked in. The lift was still out of order and it was one of the many times Kenan was glad he had his air-surfer with him. He made his way up to Terry's floor and walked down the landing. As he neared flat number one hundred and twenty eight, he slowed his pace. He could hear voices... angry voices, both sounded familiar. With a start he realized one was Terry's. The other was a female voice but he couldn't place it. He ran to the door, which he could see was already on the latch and pushed it open. He ran up the dark hallway and turned right, into the front room.

"Naomi?" he exclaimed. Naomi whirled around she didn't look that pleased at the sight of him in fact she looked more upset. Her face was the same as Terry's... Pale. Far too pale for Kenan's liking. "W- what are you doi...?" His sentence was cut short as Terry spoke up.

"Naomi please! Forget it! It's not worth..." But Naomi answered back. Kenan had never seen her so angry. She was positively on the brink of hysteria and shouting so loudly that his ears rang.

"Of course it's not worth it!" She screamed. "It's only a stupid legend... THAT YOU KNEW WOULD COME TRUE!"

"Naz, calm down," said Kenan.

"NO!" shouted Naomi. "Listen. You don't know what this son of a..."

"Naz! Calm down!"

"NO! LISTEN TO ME!"

"I FORBID you to tell him!" shouted Terry suddenly sounding panicky. Naomi looked around for something then

176

saw a sheet of paper on the coffee table.

"Fine! Then I'll SHOW him!" she yelled. She made a grab at the paper at the same time Terry did. Both tugged at the sheet but by now Kenan's curiosity had got the better of him. He too, grabbed the paper and with Naomi's help finally got it. Terry went to stop him again then sighed. He knew it was useless. He looked at the floor as Naomi glared at him. She turned to Kenan and nodded to him to read. Kenan did. It was obviously some kind of extract that Naomi had printed off of the internet. He read the following aloud:

'Since the dawn of time the seasons have been in a delicate balance with the earth, controlling life with spring and summer and death in autumn and winter.

The Orkan Shrine and its spheres were once worshipped by the ancients of the land for generations, but the more man began to overcome nature with harvesting and hunting, they began to mock the earth and her seasons and tried to take the spheres so they would have full overall control.

Angered by such ignorance and greed the Gods sent upon the Earth, a terrible storm that churned the land and seas causing death and destruction. The shrine was sunk below the Earths surface to be kept safe.

Only the oldest and most trusted family who still respected earth and nature knew of its location and passed the information down the generations. For they knew the time would come when they would need to fulfill the ancient prophecy of the
'Chosen One.'

For he will appear at the same time as a great evil, and when he does he, and he alone will be have to carry out the tasks ahead and make the most difficult of decisions to ensure our survival.

His journey must be one that is made alone, so closely is his fate tied to that of the Earth some say his life will be controlled by the effect of the spheres themselves for it has been written that just as the cruelest winter snatches life from the generous summer, a great evil will set out to snatch the life from the purest heart.

Chosen One, we pray to the spirits around that you find courage and strength to fulfill your destiny and stop the legendary storm that will surely be unleashed, and that evil will be vanquished from this land at whatever the costs. Search within your soul, for the answers and you will not fail, for they will be the right ones, and the only way to protect us from...
The Darkest Day'

Kenan slowly lowered the sheet of paper.

"Terry?" he asked finally, "what is this?" Terry shook his head.

"I'm sorry Kenan," he muttered finally. "There is a part of this prophecy that is 'Unheard.'"

Chapter Twenty-One

"What do you mean? Unheard?"

Terry sighed.

"I haven't been entirely honest with you…"

"Oh that wasn't obvious," cut in Naomi sarcastically. She faced Terry. "You knew he was out on this… this suicide mission from the start didn't you!"

"Naomi," Kenan got his friend to face him. "Please," he said. "This is just between me and Terry."

"But Kenan, you don't understand…" persisted Naomi. Kenan just looked back at her. He was one of these people who could say more with his eyes than he ever could with his voice. Naomi looked right back, and without a word sank down on the sofa between them. Kenan faced Terry. Terry took a deep breath.

"I knew you would be in danger," he said. "But the only reason I didn't tell you was because I wanted to try and find a way to stop anything… well before it happened without you knowing." Kenan didn't want to believe what he was hearing.

"Wait, wait, wait," he said. "Back up a sec. You think that I'm this… Chosen One?"

"Who else could it be," exclaimed Terry. "You've successfully retrieved three spheres…"

"Four," corrected Kenan, taking the sphere of autumn out of his jacket pocket. Terry stared at him.

"Good Lord," he whispered. "It is."

"And," said Kenan smiling at Naomi, "Matt's fine. He was released from the hospital this morning." Naomi managed a smile back. Terry looked from one to the other.

"Matt?" he asked at last. "What happened?" Kenan told him in as few words as possible about the performance and worry they'd gone through to get the sphere. At the end of the explanation, Terry collapsed into an armchair with a moan. "This is all my fault," he whimpered. "I shouldn't have contacted you at all…I should have done all this on my own."

"But Matt's okay," said Kenan. "We all are."

"That's not the point!" exclaimed Terry. "Didn't you see what was written on the paper? If you save the world, you could be in terrible danger, your very life..." the old man couldn't finish the sentence. He buried his head in his hands and Kenan sat down in the one remaining chair at Terry's computer and looked at him. For a few minutes or more, no one said a word. Naomi looked very pale. But to Kenan, Terry looked worse... so guilty, so frail and scared now. Kenan didn't like it at all... who would? Everything, right from the word go, had proved Terry right. Now here he was telling Kenan that if he saved the world he would pay the ultimate price... one way or another. Yet that seemed impossible. It was hard to see past that moment in time let alone a week. Finally Kenan stood up.

"I'm going," he muttered. "See you round." Terry looked up sharply.

"Where are you going?" he asked. Kenan shrugged.

"I'm going to see if I can find out where the sphere of summer is."

"You can't!" exclaimed Naomi. "Didn't you take in anything you just read?

"I read it alright," said Kenan. "But I'm not going to stop saving the world just because of that." He placed the sphere of autumn on the coffee table and showed himself out. Naomi and Terry heard the front door being opened and closed. Naomi rose. She cast one resentful look at Terry and followed Kenan.

"Kenan! Kenan wait up!" Kenan, who was halfway down the hall, walking towards the stairwell, stopped and turned around. To Naomi's surprise he was smiling.

"You coming back with me Naz?"

"How can you be so happy?" insisted Naomi. Kenan shrugged. In truth he didn't know. Finally he replied;

"Well, there's no good sitting and worrying about it is there? If it happens it happens. If it doesn't ...hey all the better." He pushed open the door to the stairwell and began to walk down them, with Naomi in hot pursuit. She had so many more questions to ask.

"So you're really going to finish this thing?"

"Hell yeah," said Kenan. "I promised."

"And you don't care about the consequences?"

"Nope."

Naomi shook her head. She thought Kenan just didn't believe
Terry. She thought he'd come round and refuse to complete
the task when he realised the risks... or at least, she hoped so...

*

"So, it's got to be somewhere cold, dark, and not very
lively, well that's anywhere in this city isn't it." Naomi looked
at the six faces looking back at her, nodding. Upon returning
to the car - park she and Kenan had called a hurried meeting
to discuss the next move they should try in an effort to get the
last sphere before it was too late.

"Well, we can't try every back alley and dark nook and
cranny in the city," grumbled Nick. "We don't know where to
begin looking for a start."

"But what if it's not in any old dark nook or cranny,"
remarked Sam. "It could be in someone's refrigerator for all
we know."

"That's stupid," exclaimed Lia. "Who'd do that?"

"I don't know, Lia," snapped Sam beginning to lose her
temper, "but don't call me stupid."

"She didn't!" shouted Nick.

"Hey," growled Matt, "don't you shout at her."

"She started it," shot back Nick.

"You're a fool," scowled Matt. "King of fools!"

"Say that again," interrupted Lia. "But how about you say
it with my fist in your mouth...?" A furious argument broke
out at this remark, resulting in a scuffle. Kenan and Naomi sat
there too stunned to move. It was more because the twins were
winning apart from anything else, then Kenan's eyes suddenly
widened.

"Hey," he said. No one heard him. "Hey!" he said a little
louder. The fighting continued.

181

"SHUT UP!" Yelled Naomi. Everyone stopped. The scene was quite funny. Lia had Sam in a painful looking headlock and Nick had Matt's arm-twisted behind his back. Matt's mouth was opening and closing but no sound was coming out.

"I know where it is," said Kenan. Lia dropped Sam to the ground and Nick twisted Matt's arm further in surprise.

"OuCH," whimpered Matt. Nick quickly let go.

"What do you mean?" asked Lia.

"I know where the sphere is," repeated Kenan. "Matt's provided the answer."

"I have?" stuttered Matt. "I mean of course I have… How?" He hissed.

"You called Nick a King of fools," said Kenan. "And that's given me the idea. King. King Lance has the last sphere."

"You're not serious!" exclaimed Sam, picking herself up. "What makes you think that?"

"I don't know," said Kenan. "But something tells me it's in his possession. He's had people watching us the whole time. Following us, toying with us…he wants a showdown… and he'll get one when I find him."

"Whoa, whoa hold on a second," exclaimed Matt. "Surely you don't mean face to face?"

"I'll do it alone," nodded Kenan. "If that's what it takes."

"No way," said Naomi standing up and facing him. They hadn't told the others about the prophecy but everyone could tell even without a warning that this was dangerous. Naomi's face told them more so than ever. "I'm coming too," she continued. Kenan went to shake his head but Matt was looking at him.

"Me too," he said. Kenan looked at him anxiously.

"And me," said Sam. "You can't play the hero on your own you know."

"We're all for it," said Lia with Nick nodding beside her. Kenan had never felt so supported. It had been a gruelling few days for them all and yet they were prepared to go on a mission with him one last time. Finally he had to give in.

"Thanks guys," he smiled. "Really…thanks."

*

"So what is it exactly you're hoping to find out again?" asked Kenan.

"Where he is," replied Naomi. He's not at the palace, that much I do know, but he has tons of places scattered throughout the city. We just need to find out where he is, and what it's like in terms of security. Not just in terms of guards, I'm talking cameras, infrared beams, any security codes."

"And you reckon you could get that?" Naomi nodded. The group, were on air-surfers heading back to the mansion. She had agreed that the others could come along as her mother was out for the day and even though Lord Henderson was going to be working from home that day as long as they were quiet, he probably wouldn't even know they were there.

"It'll be difficult," said Naomi, "very difficult, but give me half an hour to an hour, I'll do it."

"Naz the computer nerd," teased Kenan. "I like it." Naomi gave him a look but was once again trying not to laugh." They flew over the gates of the mansion and skidded to a halt outside the doors. Naomi glanced at her watch.

"I think James is out," she muttered. "Let's go round the back." They walked round the side of the mansion, all of them, except Matt, trying to get a look through the windows at the rooms inside.

"Don't," Kenan hissed at him. "It's impolite."

"Oh so sorry," sniffed Matt putting on an over the top, posh voice. Naomi looked round at him, expecting this was a dig at her. Matt grinned sheepishly but Naomi only laughed.

"Don't worry," she giggled. "I'm okay about it seriously." She took a key from her pocket and opened the door… at least she started to but it was already ajar. "Huh?" she muttered as she opened it fully. "They're out and they've left the door open? That's not like James at all."

"I don't think it was James Naz," murmured Kenan. "Look." Naomi did… and gasped. They were in the huge and normally immaculate kitchen, but now it looked like a scrap yard. Pots and pans littered the floor. Cutlery draws had been pulled out, tipped and emptied. Knifes, forks, spoons and various other cooking accessories were peppered throughout the room and the door leading out had been nearly knocked off its hinges! With Naomi in front looking deathly pale they slowly walked through. No one said a word but the worst was still to come. As they came into the hall, Naomi stopped short. She was looking at something on the other side of the room. Without a word she ran forward. Kenan saw what it was and felt as though a block of lead had been dropped over him.

"Oh no," he muttered. "It can't be." But it was. Lord Henderson was lying motionless on the marble floor badly hurt by a vicious attack from something...or someone! Naomi slowed her pace.

"Dad?" she whispered. No reply. His eyes were closed. Naomi knelt beside him and tried again. "Dad? Please. Open your eyes." Her heart felt as though it had jumped into her throat as George slowly moved his head.

"Naomi," he could hardly speak. Behind them Kenan and the others stood motionless not knowing what to do.

"He's alive!" she exclaimed. "Someone ring for an ambulance hurry!"

"No," gasped George. "No Naomi, it's no use. Look at me... I'm not going to make it."

"Who's done this to you?" stuttered Naomi holding back tears.

"The people you've been trying to track down," murmured her dad, "yes Naomi, they told me everything. But you must listen, these people... you need to be careful of...I can't protect you anymore."

"Yes you can," said Naomi. "You're going to make it dad...you've got to." But in her heart Naomi knew he wouldn't. His eyes kept rolling back and he couldn't focus on her for more than a few seconds. She took his hand and held onto it. "Why were they here?" she whispered. "Why did they do this to you?"

"They were trying to get you," mumbled George. "They thought you'd be here not me. I caught them ransacking the kitchen and one of them came at me with a knife. I told them

I'd rung the police, even though I hadn't and they ran. They want the sphere Naomi. They kept going on about the sphere of autumn…"

"But that's at…"

"It doesn't matter," whispered back her dad. "Don't say anything aloud in here… they may have bugged the place." His voice was getting quieter and his breathing more laboured. Naomi knew he was using up his last breath to help them as much as possible but she wouldn't show she was upset.

"Where's mum?" she whispered finally.

"Still out," mumbled George. "Tell her I love her Naomi…nearly as much as I love you…I'm so proud that you're my daughter…" Naomi closed her eyes tightly.

"I love you too dad," she whispered. George closed his eyes. Naomi kept hers closed, and the next minute she felt his hand slip out of her grip… he was gone. Naomi simply couldn't speak. Neither did anyone else. Very slowly, Kenan walked up beside her.

"Naz?" he whispered. Naomi didn't answer. "Naomi?" She looked up. Tears were streaming down her face.

"It's not fair," she whispered shakily getting to her feet. But she could barely stand. Kenan supported her. It was a major shock to him as well; he couldn't even try to imagine what was going through Naomi's mind. He looked at the others who were as white as each other.

"I'm sorry," he whispered. Naomi couldn't reply. The shock of it all was too much. She could hardly cry come to that, but when Kenan did the only thing he could think to do and put his arms around her, she broke down completely. She was shaking and hanging onto him tightly as her voice chocked with sobs.

"It's not right," she kept saying. "It's not fair." It was five minutes before anyone said anything else.

"We can't stay here," said Matt finally. Kenan looked up and nodded.

"I agree. Naz? We've got to go. We'll phone the police okay." Naomi nodded.

"Let's get out of here," she whispered.

*

"Well everyone, who needs to know knows. Everything's been done right. When will your mum be back?"

"Soon," mumbled Naomi. "But I don't want to go back in there Kenan." They were sitting a little way beyond the main gates to the estate. Police and forensics were everywhere, the scene was taped off. Matt, Sam, Nick and Lia had gone but Kenan had stayed with Naomi... the thought of leaving her alone here, was just something that he wouldn't even consider.

"I know what you mean," he admitted finally. "But this is being treated as murder Naz, you're gonna have twenty four seven protection for a while. They're examining the video surveillance that was running... I know it's easy for me to say but don't worry... you'll be safe."

"I won't feel safe though," argued back Naomi.

"Look," said Kenan. "I'll be here for you, no matter how far apart we are. If you want to go out anywhere tell me and I'll be here straight away."

Secretly if Kenan had had his own way, he would never have left Naomi's side again, as long as he could keep an eye on her he wasn't bothered. He didn't know why- because he knew that he stood no chance against an attack like that that had been carried out on George - but he just wanted to stay there, to check she was okay, to comfort her, just to be there. Naomi looked at him she knew he was trying to help her but her independence was higher than ever and she wanted to prove it.

"I appreciate it Kenan," she whispered. "But I don't need help right now from you or any of the others great as you guys are. I need to find out who did this so I can kill them with my own bare hands..." Kenan looked at her sharply.

"You can't," he said, firmly. "You know you can't that's grief talking..."

"I can," began Naomi, but Kenan cut across her.

"Naomi! Listen to me." He took a deep breath. "The other evening when I came round I spoke with your dad. He said to me that if he wasn't around to care for you in the near future, he wanted me to look out for you... I don't wanna let him down Naz." Naomi was staring at him.

"My dad said that to you?" she said finally. Kenan nodded. Naomi glanced at the floor. There was a long silence. "It's going to come true isn't it?" she mumbled with a lump in her throat. "This is how it starts, no-one's safe now." Kenan shook his head.

"No, it's not," he said defiantly, "and I'll tell you one thing Naomi, they may have started this sick little game, but they won't finish it... not while I'm here." There was another long silence in which Naomi moved her head onto Kenan's shoulder.

"Please Kenan," she whispered at last... "don't put yourself in danger. Not for me or anyone else. Promise me?" He could feel her trembling, he could almost smell her fear, he couldn't put her through any more worry and grief, no matter what that meant in the long term, he would not do that to her.

"Yeah okay," he muttered reluctantly as he put his arm around her and pulled her closer to him. "I promise."

Chapter Twenty-Two

Needless to say that Kenan was in no mood to be out for another night of danger after that. When he had left Naomi, he had headed straight for lookout point. He had sat there watching the sunset behind the city, and tonight it was more beautiful than ever. It was hard to imagine that five little spheres would eliminate something like this. Sixteen years before, people had been fighting a war for a right to live... now Kenan felt he was doing the same but completely on his own. Also Terry's warning was now beginning to shake him up a bit. It was strange, he didn't care less about what happened to him, it was his friends he was worried about, most of all Naomi. He headed back to the car park after a good two hours and was surprised upon his arrival. Matt, Sam, Nick and Lia were sitting there all looking extremely serious.

"What?" muttered Kenan making a smooth landing, "more bad news?"

"No," replied Sam. "Actually, we all need to suggest something to you?" Kenan gestured for her to continue.

"You don't want any more people hurt do you," begun Nick.

"No."

"But it's going to keep going on isn't it?" continued Lia.

"Until we stop them yes," said Kenan. "Believe me I'd do it tonight if..."

"Well why don't we?" interrupted Matt. "What happened to Naomi's dad was only the beginning. What happened to me was just a warning... if we don't stop them soon it's going to get worse... a lot worse." Kenan didn't respond. There was no doubt he wanted to stop Lance but he didn't want any more of his friends hurt.

"You can't do this alone Kenan," said Sam as if reading his mind. "We said we're going to help you and now we're going to stick to it- weather you like it or not." Kenan sat down heavily, looked at the five determined faces, (one belonging to a large, black and brown, Alsatian) but he still shook his head.

"We don't even know where Lance is right now," he pointed out quietly.

"No," said Sam, "but we watched the news from a couple of nights back when," she paused before saying quietly; "Naomi's dad tried to break in to David Tainard's offices. We did a little digging ourselves and, we know where the place is!"

"Are you insane?" exclaimed Kenan. "Are you forgetting who that guy actually is? If we're caught, I'd rather stay in prison than come back here to face him!"

"All we're after is information," said Sam. "It's not a house Kenan, it's an office block, people will have gone home for the night..."

"And the security guards?" snapped Kenan.

"Oh, Kenan come on," exclaimed Matt. "You've done your share of break ins, in the past – don't deny it!" Kenan grimaced at this. He remembered all too well only a few years before, when he had gone through a rebellious stage in his life... a time when he had actually followed Damien and his gang of street thugs out on various, drug dealings, and burglaries. He had seen first hand the real scourge of London. At first he had loved it. He loved the adrenaline, with Damien he felt safe, no-one would dare argue with him or threaten him. It seemed that Damien had rather taken to the idea of having Kenan be his second in command and would stand beside him as they watched baseball bats being swung and money exchange hands. It had only stopped when an operation into a deal went horribly wrong and two of Damien's followers had been killed in the conflict. Kenan saw it happen. He had seen the flash of a pistol, heard the sound of thuds as the bodies hit the floor. He had seen the blood mix with the rain on the sodden streets and the life drain out of their eyes. It freaked him out. It was only after that, that he deliberately started avoiding Damien as much as he could, that was when Damien's whole attitude towards him seemed to change, but Kenan was prepared to put up with any grief he

189

got than get involved with the gang again, sometimes the things he had witnessed still made him shudder...

"Okay," he said finally. "We'll leave tonight. We don't need a map . If you guys know where it is, we'll find a way in... I'm pretty sure it isn't protected from aerial trespassers."

*

Naomi lay silently in her room. Downstairs, she could hear the distant sound of various people milling around. The news that George Henderson had been murdered had spread fast and numerous relatives, friends and work colleagues had arrived to pay respects. Some had arrived with bags and had announced that they'd stay for as long as they were needed. James was in shock. He'd known and worked for Lord Henderson half his life and had taken the news very badly. Naomi just wished everybody would leave. Judging by the look on her mother's face, she felt the same. It seemed to be some sort of social event more than anything else. Naomi felt sick when she had seen people greet each other then lower their voices and whisper 'Isn't it terrible...' 'I heard young Naomi found him...' 'Didn't she have some friends with her?' When it had become totally unbearable, she had run upstairs and shut herself in her room she lay quietly on her bed looking blankly at the ceiling. She didn't feel like crying, or speaking to anyone, or in fact anything but to sit and think. There was a quiet knock on the door. Naomi didn't answer. The door opened a crack and Lady Henderson's face peered in.

"Naomi? Why aren't you downstairs?" her voice was unusually soft and calm.

"Why should I be?" answered Naomi bitterly. "You didn't hear what they were saying mum."

"Oh I can," said Lady Henderson coming into the room.

"But sometimes you have to understand that people are only trying to help."

"Well, they can just un-help," said Naomi. "I don't want to speak to anyone and I know for a fact Cedric's down there some where."

"Darling he just wants to make sure you're okay-"

"Well I'm not!" Naomi's voice was trembling. "Nor are you mum and no-one down there is helping that's for certain!" Audrey was silent for a minute then said:

"Why don't you go and speak to your friend, Kenan- that is his name isn't it?" Naomi didn't think she had heard aright. "What did you-?" she began. Lady Henderson looked at her kindly. "I know he's been round here, quite a few times as it happens. I only kept quiet because your father kept telling me not to worry. You're a good judge of character Naomi, and if you trust him, I guess I do as well. You certainly appear to have been happier since he's been around." Naomi half smiled at this but still wasn't convinced.

"I can't leave you here mum," she whispered. "Not alone." Audrey smiled again. "I won't be here," she said softly. "It was your father's wishes to be laid to rest in the town he was born in, you know the one my darling."

"But that, that's up north," stuttered Naomi. "Near my cousins..." Her mum nodded. "That's right. I'll be staying at my sisters overnight. I have to go up there and make arrangements over the next few days." Naomi was shocked. "But what bout me?" she exclaimed. What if I want to stay? What I *need* to stay?" Audrey sighed, then after another short silence, said;

"You can stay if you want. I'll go alone. James will still be here, he'll look after you... I'm setting off on the drive this evening," she finished, once the current party have gone. The police I spoke to earlier even recommended it, I really do need to see my family now Naomi." Naomi nodded hugged her mum affectionately. Audrey returned it and for two minutes, neither of them said a word. Finally they let go and Lady Henderson smiled at her daughter one last time before heading for the door. "Take care," she whispered and left. Naomi looked outside. Her head was teeming with different thoughts and emotions. Her first thought was to run and catch up with her mum, to go with her up north. Kenan would understand, they could do without her for a few days. Yet something was holding her back. Her father had given his life to help them, to give them a chance… she couldn't waste it, not now they were so close. She glanced out of the window towards the city in the distance. Should she call Kenan? No, no it would waste time, she could get to the car park easily and quickly anyway. Her air-surfer was in the corner of her room still fully charged. She made up her mind. She quickly pulled on a warm jumper and opened her window. Then making a final check to make sure all was clear, she took off into the gathering darkness.

*

Kenan scanned the area far below looking for any sign of an unguarded entrance or indeed open window into the office block. The trouble was he couldn't see much as it was. He and the others had arrived at their location under the cover of darkness. That was their only real defence. Kenan had made them all promise to follow him only if he was one hundred percent sure it was safe, but now he really had no idea and also had no choice but to descend slightly to try and get a clearer view of things. The others who were higher above him followed suit silently. They all knew the importance of this mission and were determined not to let Kenan down, even Buster, who was balanced on his master's air-surfer, was behaving. The building grew larger as they neared it. Kenan's eyes began to move over the area slowly looking for any sign of movement for that was what they wanted to stay away from. They were now directly over the roof. Surely they wouldn't have guards up there. Kenan made a decision. Signalling to the others to follow at a distance, he made his way to the top of the building and landed as softly as a cat and waited, hardly daring to breathe. One by one his friends landed beside him. Lia was the one who dared to break the silence.

"Well?" she whispered. "What now?" Everyone suddenly realized what she meant. It was easy enough to land on the roof without being seen, but how would that help them in getting into the building? Matt looked around then he double-took at something.

"Look," he hissed to Kenan. Kenan followed the direction Matt was pointing in and his eyes lit up. Two giant vents were sticking up out of the roof, they were the kind that stood up and curved round slightly so they looked a bit like upside down 'J's. But more importantly, they were big enough for every one to access.

"They must be ventilation systems," said Nick. "I'll bet we could get in through those."

"Err yeah, Nick we've figured that out already," muttered Sam.

"We'll have to be quiet though," said Lia. "With six of us going through the vents not knowing where we're going, we could get into enough trouble as it is." There was a short silence after this. Then Kenan shook his head.

"It's the only way I can see how we can get in," he muttered. "You don't have to come with me if you don't want to."

"Of course we're coming!" said Matt, "We're going to do this thing together!" The others nodded in agreement. Kenan nodded back at them.

"Okay," he said. "You guys wait here for me and I'll give you some kind of signal if I get anywhere." With that, he mounted his air-surfer, with Buster and ascended till he got level with the opening of the air-vent, then took out a flashlight and ventured into the darkness. He had to move very slowly, for although he had the light of the torch he really had no idea what lay in store for him or, how many shafts he had to explore... but he was betting it was going to be a difficult task.

Right at that moment, in a separate building not far from them, someone was watching Kenan and his friends on a small computer monitor in a darkened room.

"Look at him. He seriously thinks he's going to find me by snooping around in that office."

"But he has friends with him sir, there's five of them that includes him."

"Exactly... five of them and one dog. Don't you think

they're slightly out numbered Charles?" Charles glanced at the floor, a frown of embarrassment and anger on his thin face. "However," his master continued talking, "I think that he'll need all the help he can get until he reaches me, maybe we should turn the air conditioning onto cool for a little while…"

"Buster will you shut up or you're going back with the others!" exclaimed Kenan. Buster looked at him, obviously hurt. It was one thing for Kenan to get through the vents but a fully-grown Alsatian? The dog's claws kept clicking and clanging on the metal of the ducts and the echoes seemed ten times louder than they should be. Kenan wondered if he should call for the others yet. It wasn't that he didn't want their help, he just felt they would find it too difficult… it was hard enough for him, for although he was very slightly smaller than the others, it was tough making any progress in the cramped space. He decided to press on as far as he could. It was a good five minutes of crawling along on his front before he came to where the vent branched off into two different directions. He lay there looking down each one but even with the flashlight it was impossible to tell where each one led. He decided that he'd have to call the others then they'd have to split up and take the two different directions. His heart was pounding with excitement as he turned to make his way back, for although he was though wary of the grave situation ahead of them, he was aware of more adrenaline in his blood than ever before.

*

"Kenan? Matt? Is anyone here?" Naomi looked around surprised. She would have expected at least one of them to be there… even Buster would have been a welcome sight but where Kenan and the others normally were was deserted. She thought she saw someone move behind some boxes hardly yards from where she was standing. "Hey!" she exclaimed. "Is that one of you guys?" The figure began to retreat. Naomi

jumped over the boxes - and came face to face with Damien!
"Are you…" she began but in an instant Damien, who had
seen the phone on her wrist, had snatched her by the arm and
was staring at her in a very menacing way.

"Naomi Henderson," he spat. "I assume that's your
name?"

"I- it is," stuttered Naomi, "but what do you want… let go
of me!"

"Tell me where he is," growled Damien.

"I don't know what you mean!" exclaimed Naomi trying
to wriggle out of Damien's vice like grip.

"Kenan!" shouted Damien. "The guy you seem to like so
much… and his annoying friends! Where are they?"

"I don't know!" whimpered Naomi as the grip tightened.
Damien glared at her before pushing her away.

"Pathetic," he muttered. "I'll find him myself." Before
Naomi could see where he had gone he had disappeared. She
stood there holding her arm trying to take in what had
happened. Her eyes widened as two horrible thoughts hit her
at the same time.

"No," she whispered. Then shouted as she picked up her
air-surfer. "No! Kenan!"

"Ow! Matt that's my foot!"

"Sorry Sam, move faster!"

"Shut UP!" hissed Kenan. "Jeez I wish I'd never come
back for you guys."

"Well, if Samantha here moved faster," grumbled Matt.
Kenan shook his head in the darkness.

"I knew I should've gone with Nick, Lia and Buster," he
muttered.

"What? And leave me to look after our big baby here,"
grinned Sam. Matt went to hit her foot with his elbow but
missed and banged it onto the iron floor of the vent. It made
the most horrible noise and Kenan and Sam both glared at him
but hardly dared to say a word. Matt clutched his elbow
hissing through clenched teeth:

"Ah! Ow! Ooh! That was my funny bone!" Kenan was
just about to tell Matt exactly what to do with his funny bone

when they heard another noise... a different sound this time...
like someone, or something running around the other air-ducts
that branched off every now and then.

"Kenan," Matt hissed. "Do you hear that?"

"Yeah," muttered Kenan nodding.

"Do you think they're onto us?" asked Matt.

"I don't know, let's just slow it down a bit okay." They
slowed their pace right down as the banging grew louder. The
vent was now beginning to curve round and the noise was
getting nearer, then round a corner...

"Aaah!"

"Whoa!"

"Oh crap!"

"Nick?"

"Hi Kenan!"

If it hadn't been for the cramped space they were in, Kenan
would have probably hit Nick. They now knew that the
banging noise was Buster running around. It only sounded
louder because of the echoes.

"I guess these two vents are just one big circle," said Lia
from behind Nick.

"Did you find any way in?" asked Kenan. The twins shook
their heads. Kenan studied their surroundings. There was
another slightly bigger pipe, leading away from the system
they had just explored and it was the only way left to go. The
group began to move again. It was extremely tough on their
elbows and knees as they were crawling 'army-style' all the
time. Still they carried on in silence, even Buster seemed to be
making an effort, before a loud bang sounded from just ahead
of them. They stopped dead in their tracks.

"What was THAT?" exclaimed Sam voicing all their
thoughts. A low humming sounded.

"It... sounds like a fan," said Lia slowly.

"Whatever it is we can't stop now," said Kenan. "Come
on." They rounded another sharp corner and immediately the
vent branched out and became bigger. It was now a circle
shape as opposed to the horrible rectangle they had been
clambering in. But also, a very unwelcome sight met their

eyes. Lia had been right about a fan. It was there blocking their whole path positively huge! It was only moving slowly… slow enough for them to get past the blades one at a time but still very nerve racking. Kenan stood up.

"I'll bet we can clear that thing if we're fast okay," but even he looked nervous. "I'll err go first," he muttered. "You guys stay here until I'm through- whoa!" The next second his feet gave beneath him and he was laying on his front again facing the group.

"Look!" shrieked Lia pointing behind him as she too struggled to stand upright. As Kenan stared, Matt, Sam and Nick seemed to be having the same problem.

"No!" exclaimed Matt as he followed Lia's gaze. "Kenan get up quick!" Kenan tried but he couldn't even though he was moving slowly it was still difficult to regain…. MOVING?" he looked behind him and for the first time realised what the others had been trying to say to him. The blades of the fan were speeding up, moving faster and faster… they were pulling him towards it!

Chapter Twenty-Three

That was when Kenan panicked. He tried scrabbling to his feet again but the curved floor of the vent made it difficult. The fan was pulling him ever closer as the whirling blades moved faster and faster. Matt and the others stood there numbed with horror at the sight but one member of the party wasn't. With one agile leap, Buster ran towards Kenan and grabbed hold of his jumper between his sharp teeth and started to pull him back. But it only worked for a few seconds. As much as the Alsatian pulled, he too was dragged, inch-by-inch, towards the fan. Matt ran forward and grabbed Kenan's wrist. The other three quickly followed suit: Sam held onto Matt, Nick held onto Sam and Lia held onto her brother. That was how strong the fan's pull was…it was taking all of them linked together to stop it pulling them in. Very slowly they began to edge backwards… but it didn't last long! Matt tripped over Sam's feet and the whole party went down with him. With horrible speed, they found themselves being drawn in towards the blades, now rotating too fast for anything or anyone to survive. Kenan squeezed his eyes shut and waited for the worst to happen. The most horrible clanging noise then shattered their ears... at first Kenan thought that was it. They had failed, they'd died all of them and it was all his fault, but he began to realize they had stopped moving before he heard Matt's voice;

"What the…?" Kenan opened his eyes and gasped. An unmistakable board object was wedged in between the fan's blades at such an angle they couldn't spin round any more but shuddered violently. It was then, Kenan realized they had stopped inches away from a certain death. He looked closer… it was an air-surfer, but they had left their ones on the roof. He looked up the air-duct and there, running towards them, with a face white with fright but determination and relief was Naomi. Kenan jumped up and ran towards her as the others picked themselves up.

"Naz? What are doing-? Hey what's all this about?" he exclaimed as Naomi gave him a suffocating hug.

"You have no idea how relieved I am to see you," she exclaimed on the verge of tears. She was clearly happy to see Kenan and the others safe and sound but she couldn't believe that had she been a second later, she would have lost them all.

"Naomi?" exclaimed Matt. "Is that your air-surfer?"

"Uh-huh," sniffed Naomi as she let go of Kenan.

"It'll be mangled if the fan starts moving again!" said Sam looking at the blades that were still shaking.

"Come on then!" exclaimed Naomi. "Get moving through it." They wasted no time and barely seconds after Kenan got through; there was a cracking sound and the fan spun back to life. The force of the breeze now pushing against them instead of pulling them in caught them all off guard and they once again fell to the floor. Kenan saw a flash of white and blue go whizzing past him, grabbed it before it had time to hit the wall and held up a very sorry looking air-surfer. The others gaped. It was completely bent almost at a ninety-degree angle...beyond repair that was for sure. Kenan looked at Naomi who looked at the air-surfer then at him and shrugged.

"I can get another one," she said.

"You threw it in the blades... to safe our lives?" breathed Nick.

"Looks like it did the job huh?" she smiled. Kenan just stared at her.

"You didn't have to," he said. "You shouldn't even be here."

"I think he means thank you," said Sam glaring at Kenan.

"Oh yeah, yeah! I do mean thanks and everything," said Kenan looking guilty, "but... I just can't believe...hey, what's happened there?" He had caught sight of a mark on Naomi's wrist.

"It's nothing," she replied hurriedly pulling her right sleeve down over it. Kenan looked at her.

"Show me," he said quietly. Naomi looked back at him, sighed then lifted up her sleeve to reveal a red hand mark around her wrist. The others stared as Kenan's eyes narrowed.

"Who did this to you?" he growled.

"I don't even know," said Naomi shakily. "I went looking for you, only because I was worried, and he just appeared. He asked me where you were, I said I didn't know, but he seemed angry... I mean really angry. I don't think he meant to hurt me..."

"Not hurt you?" snapped Kenan. "Naomi that's going to bruise, he must have grabbed you pretty damn tight there!"

"I couldn't feel my fingers," whispered Naomi tearfully, "but I was so worried about you all, I just wanted to -" She stopped talking while she composed herself.

"What did this guy look like?" asked Matt suddenly. "Was he wearing a seriously outdated trench coat thing?" Naomi nodded. Matt looked at Kenan, who looked back an ominous look on his face.

"Damien," he muttered. "What the hell is he playing at?"

"Forget it," said Naomi. "We can figure all this out when we get out of here, but don't you think we should be moving on... Aah!"

"Naz!"

Naomi's eyes widened as something ripped through the duct and into her arm, it looked like some kind of dart.
Immediately she stumbled to stand upright. Kenan and the others tried to support her but it was no use. A second later another dart zoomed past nearly hitting Nick.

"I... think... we've been... discovered," whispered Naomi. Kenan shakily took the dart out of her arm. Sam took it from him and studied it closely.

"It's poison," she whispered in alarm. Kenan looked at her and shook his head.

"Please," he muttered. "Sam, it can't be!" Another two darts shot through the metal but missed them again. They hadn't realized how much noise they had been making since the fan incident and Naomi was right, they had been discovered.

"What are we gonna do?" whispered Sam.

"I'm not leaving Naomi," said Kenan. "You guys run, take Buster... ow!" Another three darts had got through. One had caught him and the other had got Sam. She immediately fell to her hands and knees. Kenan looked at her as his vision became foggy.

"This… can't be…happening," he whispered, as the metal flooring of the air vent came up towards him!

"Huh? We're still alive?"

"Kenan?"

"Hold on a sec Sam." Kenan's vision was still taking awhile to clear. As he regained his sight he realised that they were in a small dingy room with hardly any light and solid stone walls. Whilst this didn't really surprise him, he was a little taken aback that their lives had been spared. He looked around at the others. They were all looking a little dazed but at least they were all there: Matt, Sam, Nick, Lia, even Buster but…Naomi? Kenan shot up from his slumped position against the wall.

"Naomi!" he exclaimed. "Where is she?" Everyone looked awkwardly at Lia. Kenan looked at her to. "What's going on?" he demanded. Lia looked at Kenan trembling slightly.

"When you, Sam and Naomi got shot," she began, "It wasn't long before Matt, Nick and even Buster were. I wasn't but I stayed put and just lay there. About ten minutes later some security guys came up into the vents and carried us all off, but one of them took Naomi somewhere else, but I don't know where or why... I'm so sorry Kenan." Kenan, who by this time was on his feet was just staring at Lia. He shook his head and dropped to his knees.

"No," he murmured. "She can't be..."

"What do you think he's going to do?" asked Matt. Kenan looked up at him.

"Isn't it obvious," he whispered. "She poses a threat to him just like her father. George even said they were looking for her before they attacked him." Kenan swallowed hard before saying with a slight choke in his voice:

"He's going to kill her…if he hasn't already."

*

201

No one knew what the time was in that terrible stone room. Kenan's watch had been taken, which made it impossible to know what time it was. But what was bugging him more was he couldn't phone or even text Naomi to make sure she was okay, though as much as he hated to be pessimistic he seriously doubted it. The only way they knew it was still night, was through a small grate set in a wall, near the top of the room and through here they could see the night sky. There were wooden benches around a few walls of the cell and Kenan spent most of his time lying on one of these, his hands behind his head thinking: Thinking 'what ifs' and 'if we had done this.' But whatever way he looked at it, they could not get out of this mess. The poison hadn't fully worn off and all of them, with the exception of Lia were still very sleepy and kept dozing off. Sometimes for a few minutes, sometimes for an hour or so... However they soon lost track of time and hardly anyone spoke.

"You never know Kenan," said Matt as he sat down on the bench with him. "I reckon she's still alive you know... just got a feeling." He smiled as he looked at his friend but his face fell when he saw Kenan's expression. "Well, I'm just trying to stay positive," he murmured as he got back up and walked away. Kenan didn't respond, he just turned away miserably and closed his eyes tight.

It was well into the night when he opened them again. The others were asleep on the far side of the cell. Kenan couldn't be angry with them for finally giving in, he was still so tired but didn't want to sleep but at the same time he didn't want to lay there awake, worrying.

After a while, he got up off the bench and walked around the room quietly so he didn't wake the others. He stopped near the wall that held the grate in it, and there he stood looking miserably up at the stars through the iron bars. As breeze blew through, he closed his eyes trying to imagine he was air-surfing…it worked… but only for a second.

How are we going to get out of here? He thought desperately, *all of us. They put their trust in me and this is where I got them. It may be too late for Naz but I can at least help them even if I don't get out myself. I will get them out but... HOW?* That last word echoed in his mind for a long time. He lowered his head and stood there with his hands in his pockets...- then he felt something, it was a piece of paper. Quickly he pulled it out unfolded it and felt the muscles in his whole body tense. It was the drawing Naomi had done for him. It wasn't so much what was on the paper that made him feel an odd feeling building up inside him, it was the thought that Naomi had had far too much going for her, just for her life to be cut far too short. He looked up through the grate again and back at the drawing. A thousand thoughts and memories went through his mind in seconds. But one that stood out more vividly than the rest was at High Gate. The picture on the headstone... and the engraving:

Stewards and Royal Councillors to H.R.H Lance I, and 'exceptionally skilled' pilots in the R.A.F.

Kenan felt a surge, like an injection of adrenaline enter his blood. He wasn't beaten! Not by a long shot. He looked across the room as Matt stirred. Seeing Kenan on his feet he nudged Sam and the others.

"Kenan?" asked Matt. "Are you okay?" Kenan said nothing but a determined and defiant smile slowly spread across his face. After all, his parents hadn't made it just by giving up! They had kept trying and had made it! *And now,* thought Kenan *so will I!*

"Wheeler!"

It was late morning when Kenan looked at the door as it opened. A chunky built security guard was standing there with a couple of other guards behind him. "Alright guys," he growled. "Let's go, we've got a meeting to get to." The others scrambled up from the floor quickly but Kenan slowly rose from the bench and sauntered over to the guards his hands in his pockets. He looked up at them, a slight mocking expression on his face. This didn't impress them. One of them grabbed him and half pushed, half threw him out of their way.

"Get on with it you disgusting rats!" he shouted. Kenan gritted his teeth, but he knew that his real fight wasn't with these brutes, he knew where they were being taken...to see Lance. The group -including Buster- who was now muzzled- was taken through corridors and rooms up more flights of stairs they down more corridors. At length they went through another door into the bright blazing sunlight. The sky was blue, and they could here the distant sounds of the city carrying on life as normal... not aware that a group of terrified and confused friends were being bundled into the back of a black hover van, not aware that a great evil was hanging just over their heads. Kenan was thrown against the metal of the inside of the vehicle and the doors slammed on them.

"Kenan," whispered Lia. "I'm really scared."

"It's okay," said Kenan as they heard the engine start up. "We're not beaten yet, we'll be free very soon, Lia you mark my words." The van flew quickly and smoothly towards the older part of the city, near the docks, where there were several abandoned warehouses still standing. It landed just outside one of these and the friends were dragged roughly out and straight into the particularly old dilapidated building. Inside, they were steered through broken glass and other debris littering the floor. Finally, Kenan saw their target. A platform at one end of the room, where a figure stood motionless concealed in the shadows. They stopped a few paces from this platform and were thrown to their knees before it. Buster was quickly secured to a pillar and stood there growling, his hackles up.

Slowly the figure dressed in a long dark purple cloak, with a matching hood, over its head walked towards them, then paused before throwing the hood backwards and the cloak back over his shoulders.

It was indeed Lance.

Kenan had never expected to see the King of England in person and had only rarely seen him or heard his voice on the holo-box. In the flesh, he was completely different. The first thing about him was his age. He looked rather young Kenan would say mid twenties at most. He was also rather tall and of average build. He had blonde hair, not dissimilar to Kenan's and piercing green eyes that made you feel uncomfortable if you looked at them for too long. He was dressed, rather casually Kenan thought, in a dark shirt and trousers. But there was no tie or jacket or anything, in fact for you, to tell he was King.

"Well, well," he said his calm smooth voice echoed around the room. "So these are the visitors I've heard so much about and I believe this," he stopped in front of Kenan, "is Master Wheeler himself. What a pleasure it is."

"The honour's mine!" spat Kenan sarcastically. Lance's smile froze.

"What a charming young man," he said, turning and walking along the row of frightened friends. "Come to that what a charming little group here with you," he said. "But tell me please I am a little confused. Why are you all here? Surely you broke into that office block last night with the best intentions right?" No one said a word. They all guessed that Lance knew what they had been up to right from the start. He was just toying with them. "Well?" Lance turned around looking expectantly at the faces before him. "No one feels like talking, no?"

"You know why we're here," muttered Kenan. Lance was immediately at Kenan's side.

"What's that you say? I know. Why, no, I don't. *Do* tell!"

"You've been playing us for fools right from the start." Growled Kenan. You killed Tony Orkas, you arranged for Terry to get beaten up. You hid those spheres all over the city and you nearly got my best mate killed!"

"Ah, ah, ah," said Lance holding up his hand. "*I* never did any of those things. True, I arranged them but I never carried out anything… physically." Lance's smooth and cocky voice had been getting on Kenan's nerves far too quickly and that last remark, made his temper snap… the one he hardly ever dared to use.

"NO YOU DIDN'T DID YOU!" he shouted jumping up and facing Lance. "BECAUSE YOU'RE A **COWARD!** YOU GET OTHER PEOPLE TO CARRY OUT YOU'RE DIRTY

WORK BECAUSE YOU'RE SO **AFRAID** OF
EVERYTHING LEAKING OUT… THE **PROOF** THAT
YOU'RE HEAD OF A CONSPIRACY, TO TRY AND
TAKE OVER THE **WORLD!**" He lowered his voice and
growled: "All over five little glass spheres!" He was standing
almost nose- to- nose with Lance and was so angry that his
eyes seemed to go almost black. Everyone, even Lance's
body- guards were too stunned to move. The King, however
stood his ground without batting an eyelid.
"I'm sensing a lot of bad feelings here," he said finally
"Maybe some guilt or some remorse." Kenan blinked. "Tell
me," continued Lance walking past Kenan, his voice still calm
and low. "What is it that's bothering you exactly?"
     "I don't know what you're on about," muttered Kenan.
     "I think you do," smiled Lance. "You know exactly what
I'm talking about or more to the point, *who* I'm talking about.
Do the names Kenan and Liz Wheeler mean anything to you?"
Kenan gritted his teeth. This was the last thing he needed. "Or
how about George Henderson?" Kenan stared at him.
     "What?" he whispered. Lance sneered back.
     "Well, you are responsible for all three of their deaths
aren't you my boy?"
     "Okay," snarled Kenan. "Staying off the subject of my
mum and dad, how am I responsible for the death of George
Henderson?"
     "It's quite simple really," smiled Lance, slyly. "If you had
never gone to the Henderson mansion for help… none of them
would have ended up in this mess." Kenan suddenly felt his
knees give way and land on the cold floor. He felt sick. What
his enemy said was making a horrible kind of sense. He
looked at the ground as Lance continued. "You skipped up to
that mansion with the little password Terry gave you and tried
to play the big hero. You honestly thought that you could
outsmart me? Me and my operation that's been running for
years? Oh, but then you began to take an interest to other
things didn't you hmm? A certain Naomi Henderson? And by
coincidence she seemed to like you didn't she. That's why
she's where she is now!" Lance's smooth talk and calm tone

had come to an abrupt end. But he wasn't the only one who was ready for an argument.

"You're a liar!" shouted Kenan.

"Oh wake up Kenan!" shouted Lance. "You think I enjoyed ordering what I chose to happen to her? You really think I'm that sick and twisted?"

"I don't know!" shouted Kenan. "Are you? You tried to kill an old man! That didn't seem to bother you too much!"

"But the Henderson family are different," shot back Lance. "A well respected and well known family amongst the right circles. Not the sort of people *you* would ever even *dream* of mixing with. You can't imagine what I felt when I learnt Lord Henderson had been murdered." There was a long silence then:

"You felt nothing," muttered Kenan.

"I beg your pardon?"

"You heard me," growled Kenan. "You felt nothing. Shall I tell you who's really responsible for his death? Yeah. YOU."

"And how do you work that one out?" scowled Lance.

"You said this so called operation of yours has been running for years right? Therefore you must have planned all this way before I came into the picture. You arranged to have George Henderson and Naomi cut out of the scene because they had the right stuff, the right information, the right connections. What they knew about you could have brought down your empire in a second. They had intentions and ideas that could have changed this country around, maybe even the whole world. You knew that but wanted to do things your own way so planned to get rid of them. In power for nearly fifteen years now, you've had all the time in the world to plan this operation and not worry if people died in the process, so don't you dare accuse me of a murder I haven't committed! This isn't about spheres, or searches on the internet, it's about you staying in power for as long as possible and I see now the spheres of the seasons and the Shrine of Orkan were only meant to lure me and Naomi here, so you could kill her!"

A long silence followed. Finally, Lance sighed, then shook his head with an ominous chuckle.

"Well, indeed," he said at length. "Aren't we clever to work all that out eh, Kenan. I see you're in need of a real challenge."

Chapter Twenty-Four

"What do you mean a challenge?"

"You're more intelligent than I anticipated," said Lance. "I think we need something that's on your wavelength." Signalling to one of the guards to free Kenan's hands, Lance also nodded to another one nearby and the quickly went out of the room. "I learned, from a reliable source," continued the King "that even though you live a life of hardship and poverty, you also have your fun. You're familiar with the term air-surfer I take it." Kenan nodded slowly as he stood up. "Well then let's have a little fun and games of our own," grinned Lance. He snapped his fingers and one of the guards threw back a huge metal shutter down one side of the room. Kenan and the other had assumed the only thing that lay beyond this wall was the outside, but instead it opened the room up to reveal an extension to the warehouse, still dark and dingy but this part looked different somehow, people had been working here, large objects were assembled around the room in between the chains and cables that still hung from the ceiling. Hoops, barriers and suchlike were placed at strategic intervals around the room... it only took Kenan a couple of seconds to realize... it was an obstacle course! "It's really very simple," said Lance as Kenan looked. "Three circuits around the course, whoever clears all the obstacles and crosses the finish line first, two out of three times, is the winner…and just to show my sportsmanship, you can make a request and if you win, I'll grant it, but I expect you to make a bargain to."

"Yeah sure," said Kenan. "Give us the last sphere and let us go."

"Of course, if you win," said Lance. "But if you lose I expect you to not only give yourself up but your friends as well."

"What do you mean?" said Kenan. "Forgive me for sounding thick, but aren't we at your mercy already?"

"I meant with your lives!" sneered Lance. Behind him,

Kenan heard his friends gasp. He thought a minute then smiled.

"Me? Take you on and beat you? No problem. You'd better just be ready to hand over that sphere." Once again, Lance only sniggered.

"Who said anything about taking me on?" he growled a faint trace of a smirk on his face. Before Kenan could react, the first security guard who had left the room, reappeared through the door dragging someone forward.

"Naz?" Kenan felt like crying. She was alive! The others cheered when they saw her but something wasn't right. She didn't look right at all in fact. It only took Kenan a second to realize it. Her eyes. She was looking straight at him, but there was no recognition in them at all. She wasn't focusing on anything. It was almost like she was under a kind of...

"Mind control!" beamed Lance. "Isn't it wonderful! The most modern way of eliminating all free will and bending it to your own wishes."

"No kidding," said Matt quietly. "She's totally out of it." Kenan couldn't get a grip of the situation at all! As much as he tried to make eye contact with Naomi, she just stared straight through him. He turned to Lance.

"You monster!" he yelled. "What have you done to her?"

"Oh come now Kenan, it's really not that bad," replied Lance. Then with a sly note in his voice he said, "I mean it's not as if we can't change what's wrong with her. Just give us some time... why don't you change your end of the bargain to help her out instead of the payment of one silly old sphere?"

Kenan's head was in turmoil. Lance was clever. He had planned this all along.... right from the start, but what else could Kenan honestly do? It took him one more look at Naomi to decide... he had to help her.

"Deal," he muttered.

"Great," laughed Lance clapping his hands. "Are you ready Naomi?" Naomi nodded. Kenan blinked. She could hear Lance. Maybe she could hear him as well.

"Naz?" he murmured. She didn't even look at him.

"Don't even try it Kenan." Lance grinned. "I can control

who she listens to and when. And since I don't want her to listen to you... she won't. It's that simple!"

Oh is it? Thought Kenan to himself. *If she can still hear, there's a chance I can still get through to her!*

"Charles?" Lance was talking again. "Fetch the young lady an air surfer won't you, something tells me she won't be able to use hers anymore, after the whole fan episode hmm."

"Is there anything this guy *doesn't* know?" remarked Matt. Kenan was thinking much the same thing. Then he looked twice at what Charles was carrying. It was an air-surfer. It *had* to be an air-surfer, but it was black in colour but longer with a much more sleek, and aero-dynamic shape.

"That's the new model air-surfer!" squealed Lia. "The Three Thousand. The fastest model yet! They cost a bomb!"

"But won't that give Kenan a slight disadvantage?" whispered Sam worriedly.

"Maybe," said Matt as they watched their two friends mount their air-surfers at the start and finish line. "But he's out run police cars and god knows what else on his own air-surfer before now."

"Yeah, but with so much at stake here," said Sam. "I'm not sure I like this."

"Same here," muttered Lia. "I don't like it one bit."

"Sh!" hissed Nick. "They're about to start."

Kenan was looking at the course slightly nervous but more than confident that he could clear it easily. He looked across at Naomi whose eyes were also fixed ahead.

"Naz?" he whispered. "Can you hear me?" No response.

"Okay!" exclaimed Lance. "You both know what you're racing for so let's go on my mark. Three, Two One, GO!"

Naomi immediately shot ahead of Kenan as they pulled away from the line. Once he'd recovered from the shock, Kenan suddenly realized that this was going to be a lot harder than he'd anticipated. What ever it was that was driving Naomi, it was working one hundred and one percent! He quickly pulled himself together and chased after her. Lance was shouting something after them but Kenan couldn't hear, the air was rushing past him again and once more he felt the blood pumping round his system with more fury than ever. The obstacles were really no challenge to him at all: Under a low beam, over a high one, through a hoop. There wasn't much difference between this and the obstacles he cleared at the old industrial estate course. But having said that, Naomi was a lot faster than him... too fast. His air-surfer was old and though reliable, it was just no match for the Three Thousand! More and more distance was building up between them. He knew he had to think fast and act faster. He focused hard on trying to catch up with Naomi but it just didn't work and within hardly thirty seconds of leaving the start line, Naomi was over it and on her second lap. Kenan was only five seconds behind but to him it seemed more like fifty.

There has to be a weakness to that air-surfers speed, he thought. But, from what he could see, there wasn't. The chip that monitored brainwaves was extremely fine-tuned and was able to react at the slightest change of the rider.

Kenan knew that to reach Naomi he'd have to fight fire with fire. More than ever now he focused once more on catching up with her. Every ounce of determination and focus filtered down to his own air-surfer. The memories he and Naomi had shared, the happiness the laughs, his heart seemed to beat faster as he remembered. He needed more than just speed now, he needed his air-surfer to respond with the same urgency and devotion he felt, he needed it to *understand* him! As if on cue, the board gave a slight shudder.

"Come on, old girl," muttered Kenan. "Don't break down on me now!" As if in reply, the air-surfer gave another slight shudder, but then, began to speed up. Slowly at first but then quicker...the gap between them was closing. "Naz!" he yelled. Naomi actually looked round, though her eyes weren't focusing on him it was still a result. But that wasn't all. With her concentration broken her air-surfers speed, dropped sharply and Kenan was able to start catching up with her.

"What are you doing?" yelled Lance from the ground below. "Don't slow down! Speed up!" He turned to Charles and shook him by his collar. "You told me that that air-surfer was unbeatable!" he shouted.

"I- thought- it- was," stammered Charles. "It has to be, it's the latest model!"

"No," growled Lance letting Charles go. "It's *too* sensitive in picking up the brainwaves. If her concentration is broken just a bit, Kenan's got the advantage." Lance wasn't the only one who had worked this out. Kenan had too, and an idea was rapidly growing in his head. If he could divert Naomi's attention, just a little there was a chance she would slow down enough and he'd win the race. It had to be worth a try. "Naomi!" he called again. "Please, I need to talk to you- whoa!" he narrowly avoided a barrier blocking his way. Naomi's concentration was back on the race ahead but Kenan had closed the gap between them and was steadily keeping pace. He decided to try again. "Naomi! Please! Stop this! This isn't you!" Naomi looked at him, now beside her. Kenan sidled round until he was nearly facing her, and almost air-surfing backwards. He was determined to try and keep eye contact but every time he did Naomi just looked right through him .

"NO!" yelled Lance's voice from below.

"Huh?" Kenan suddenly realized what had happened. He had won the second lap without knowing it. He had been inches in front of Naomi by trying to get a reaction out of her and had taken the lead. The next lap decided the race! He had to win, if not for himself at least for his friends and Naomi's sake. He decided to take advantage of the slight lead and focus on winning. Unfortunately Naomi had the same idea but strangely, her air-surfer was no longer overtaking Kenan's but staying more or less alongside it. "Naomi," pleaded Kenan as they both avoided another obstacle, "you've got to snap out of this. You're not a slave for someone else. Nor is anyone else here. C'mon wake up!" But still there was no response. Kenan gave up. He had tried but there seemed to be no way to reverse whatever had been done to her. They were now on the home stretch and still neck and neck. Naomi's eyes focused more intently but her air-surfer was going full speed. Kenan looked at her. *One more time* he thought. He stretched out his hand and reached for Naomi's. "Come on," he whispered as he took hold. "It's me. Naz... Please?" He closed his eyes in desperation, then...

"Kenan?" With a jolt he looked up. Naomi was blinking, she was focusing, she was back! "W-what's going-?" she began, but her sentence was cut short.

"Ooh, it looks like it's going to be a photo finish!" Kenan glared at the figure on the ground. Lance. He had a smarmy look about him at that moment. Worn only by those who know whatever happens, they can't lose. Kenan didn't like it at all. "How close," grinned the King as the two friends descended towards the floor. "And not only that, Kenan you lucky boy, you got your little lady friend's mind back where it belongs."

"Yeah," muttered Kenan jumping to the ground "so it seems we may as well keep up the original end of the bargain, the sphere please."

"But we haven't seen whose won yet," mocked Lance. "Don't you think we should take a look at the result?" At that second, a three dimensional image flashed up from a small grey box Charles held. It looked like a holo-box but it was obviously much more high tech than the one Kenan and the others had acquired from a rubbish tip. Kenan looked up at it. It was a holographic picture of him hardly a minute before...Naomi and him to be exact... the second they had crossed over the finish line.

"Ha!" exclaimed Matt. "Kenan won! I knew he would!"

"Look again," grinned Lance. Matt blinked but his expression still didn't clear.

"I am looking," he said. "And it's quite clear that Kenan was ahead of Naomi.

"Not quite," said Lance pointing towards the bottom of the image. Everyone saw what he meant. The tip of Naomi's air-surfer was ahead of Kenan's. Everyone on Kenan's side - except Naomi who still didn't quite know what had happened-protested.

"The shape of the air -surfer shouldn't matter!" exclaimed Sam. "If it had been a fair race and you'd given her the same one, Kenan would've won it hands down."

"You're a cheat!" agreed Nick. "You knew right from the start Naomi would have the advantage with that shaped air-surfer. Kenan won! He's clearly positioned ahead of her!"

"You can't argue with the majority, Lance," said Kenan facing him. He held out his hand. "I want the sphere now," he continued. "A deal is a deal right?" Lance, at first, looked uneasy before he took something from inside his cloak... but it wasn't a sphere. It looked more like a thin gold staff with a rounded handle. Quick as lightning he had struck out at Kenan with it, and Kenan felt a searing pain run straight through him! He let out a gasp and sank to the floor.

"I've tried to be nice!" growled Lance. "I tried to be reasonable and treat this whole thing with a sense of humour, but now... I'm afraid that, that won't happen."

"What- is- that?" stuttered Kenan looking up at the staff.

"My own personal body guard," smiled Lance. "It releases, an electric current. Strong enough to kill instantly, but for you..." he held the staff dangerously close to Kenan's face, "I think I'll make it nice and slow." Kenan didn't dare to move. Neither did anyone else. Suddenly Lance struck out again. The force this time was a lot harder. Kenan actually skidded back a yard or two across the floor with another gasp.

"Leave him alone!" screamed Naomi as she made to run at them. Lance turned around and pointed the staff at Naomi with a menacing gleam in his eyes.

"Don't worry," he growled. "You're next!" Kenan took a second to try and tackle Lance but his enemy was too quick for him. He turned round and this time held Kenan by the collar of his sweatshirt and held the rod against the left hand side of his torso. Kenan wanted to scream but no sound came out. The pain was indescribable! This was more to it than just plain electricity. It seemed as though blood from the heart of the most evil being that existed, had been squeezed into the very force that drove the current round him! After what seemed like several excruciating hours, though it was only a matter of seconds, Lance dropped Kenan to the ground. Coughing badly and with his breathing shallow Kenan could barely move. But he was determined if he was going to fall, he'd fall fighting! He pulled himself to his hands and knees and tried to catch his breath. Lance was holding the staff at the ready, his face deadpan.

"Stop it please!" yelled Naomi running towards Lance. "Naomi... don't..." choked Kenan. But Naomi was too close. In a split second, Lance had raised the staff and bought it down at horrifying speed. Kenan, weakened, badly hurt, but thinking faster than Lance was acting, leapt between Naomi and the staff and this time he didn't even think about the pain. He dropped to the ground and felt himself slipping into unconsciousness. With his vision blurring, he looked up at Lance, who had raised the staff above his head ready for the final blow. Two bodyguards were restraining Naomi, and his friends were still bound and helpless. He didn't want to give up, this couldn't be the end but he couldn't even move. He laid his head on the ground and waited. He heard Matt and the others shout:

"No!"

Naomi was screaming but he couldn't go on. There was a faint whistle of the staff coming down.

This is it, thought Kenan. Then:

BANG!

Chapter Twenty-Five

That was the last thing Kenan expected to hear. For a second afterwards there was silence. Next two louder bangs! *That's it,* thought Kenan, his eyes still closed. *He's won and I'm history.*

"I tried guys, he muttered. "I tried my best," as he heard something else.

"Damien!"

Damien? Kenan dared to open his eyes. He was still where he had been when he had closed his eyes. He moved his hand. *He could move it?* He was still alive. He looked up and a chaotic scene greeted him. Damien was walking towards the group, his long trench coat flapping behind him. In his hand was a gun… obviously what Kenan had heard. On the floor were Lance's bodyguards; the only two in the room and with one lethal shot wound in his chest was Lance himself- dead! Also behind Damien was Terry looking at the scene his face pale and scared. Upon seeing Kenan lying badly hurt on the ground he ran over to him. Damien was standing over Lance. He took up the staff, and looked at it before throwing it carelessly aside. He set about freeing Matt, Sam Nick and Lia. Naomi was already accompanying Terry with Kenan. He was lapsing in and out of consciousness.

"Back up, back up!" ordered Terry as everyone began to crowd round him. "Give him some air!" Kenan could vaguely make out Damien's face and his distinctive voice saying:

"He needs some 'C145' now."

"No" muttered Terry. "That will kill him instantly the state he's in. I've got the right stuff back at my flat." After this, Kenan blacked out.

"…But will he be okay, grandpa?"

"He's had quite an ordeal Delia. The best thing he can get now is rest."

"But the job's not finished yet-"

"I'll do it. I should have right from the start!"

"Terry?" Kenan half opened his eyes. Terry rushed to his side.

"How are you feeling kid?" he asked. "Like I've been hit by a truck," mumbled Kenan.

"Any pain?"

"My head hurts a bit." Terry smiled.

"That's what I thought. You'll be fine in a little while. I gave you a homemade remedy when we got you here. It's wonderful for injuries of any sort but the side effects can include headaches." Kenan nodded slowly. He was back in Terry's flat, lying on the sofa. Outside, velvet blackness covered the city. Then other things began to appear. Delia was sitting at the end of the sofa. On the other side of the room were Matt and the others, all of them asleep. Naomi was in Terry's armchair also asleep. Buster was on the floor, but as near to the sofa as possible.

"They stayed up for as long as they could," said Delia following Kenan's gaze. But they gave up about an hour ago." Kenan lay there wondering about how long he'd been out cold for. It felt like barely five minutes but his brain was still coming to terms with all that had happened with Lance. Lance! If Kenan could have got up and gone back to the warehouse he would have, but all he could manage to say was:

"Terry…Lance… Damien… I couldn't get the sphere… what's going on? What's happened?"

"Whoa, whoa steady," eased Terry. "One thing at a time. Lance is dead." Kenan blinked. The utter coolness in his voice was a little unnerving.

"Dead?" repeated Kenan. Terry nodded. "But…" Kenan couldn't understand. "Damien, killed him. Won't this be treated as a murder case? He- he'll be killed himself surely for this."

"No, Kenan," said Terry. His voice was barely above a whisper. "Damien has been doing this for many years. He knew exactly what to do in the exact amount of time and even how to get past the security without detection and most importantly how to dispose of any and *all* evidence that points at him or anyone else for that matter."

"But how did he know I was there?" said Kenan. "And how did you manage to tag along with him?"

"I was told you were there, we both took the same route and unknowingly met up half way. He remembered me being his tutor and thought I may be able to help."

"Who told you I was there then?"

Terry smiled nodding in Naomi's direction.

"She phoned me. She said she wasn't certain but was pretty sure you'd gone after him with who ever else would go with you. She's not normally wrong about things like that and she said she was on her way to the car park to try and stop you herself. I told her to stay put but she wouldn't... you have a very good friend there Kenan. They are very few and far between." Kenan nodded.

"I broke a promise to her," he muttered.

"Sorry?"

"I promised I wouldn't put myself in danger anymore and I did, and this time she got involved to." Terry shook his head.

"It was bound to happen sometime Kenan."

"Well, it's not going to again," said Kenan. "Not to her or any of the others."

"I doubt we'll have to worry about anything like that happening again," said Delia. "You haven't shown him what you found have you Grandpa?" Terry stood up quickly.

"No!" he said smiling. "Kenan, take a look at this." Then to Kenan's surprise Terry held up a shining green sphere.

"Is that...?" Kenan started.

"The sphere of summer," said Terry. "The last one."

"But where...?"

"Lance's staff," said Terry. "The sphere of summer the one that provides life, powering something designed only to take it away. It was inside the handle of the staff all the time. That's why an object so small could produce so much power. Lance was a clever man, Kenan. He knew that with the advanced technology today, he could quite easily get some kind of reliable energy source out of it." Kenan closed his eyes. Spheres? Energy? He'd had enough but he still had so many more questions to ask.

"So why did Damien come to the rescue? I'm not his best mate or anything, what's he got to gain?" Terry was silent for a long time.

"It's time you knew Kenan," he said quietly. "You already know that Damien leads a double life?"

"I had suspicions," said Kenan grimly. Terry nodded. "He was once the head of the royal council that served Lance," he said. Kenan raised his eyebrows. He hadn't exactly *not* expected this, but it was still very hard to believe. "And you know that Lance has no blood relatives? Well, at least, he only had his father up until fifteen years ago."

"What happened to him?" Kenan asked. Terry shook his head mysteriously.

"Very suspicious circumstances Kenan. He was just found in bed one morning by a servant. He just stopped breathing, apparently. I say Lance and Damien had something to do with it though. This was after your parents died you see, so Damien was promoted straight in under Lance's wish."

"But Lance... surely he wouldn't kill his own dad?" said Kenan in disbelief. Terry shrugged. "No one knows what happened. There was no poison in his blood, no sign of physical harm like a stab or shot wound... so they couldn't accuse anyone of anything but he was in the prime of life and in good health. I don't suppose anyone will ever know." Kenan was quiet for a minute then said:

"But why would Lance want to lure me and the others there to face him?"

"It wasn't your friends he was after Kenan, it was you."

"But why? Look at me, Terry, I'm a no one, I live on the streets I'm not even important enough to get a criminal record."

"Are you sure?" asked Terry. "What about your background, your mum and dad? They weren't no-one's."

"But what's that got to do with me?" asked Kenan beginning to feel edgy.

"About a hundred years ago," said Terry "a decree was passed under the most secured meeting between parliament and the Royal family ever. It stated that in the event of no blood relatives of a monarch being alive or able to take the throne that their steward should."

"Wait!" exclaimed Kenan. "Are you saying that Damien knew what he was doing before he started working for Lance."

"Indeed," replied Terry. "You've got it in one. My guess is that Damien killed Lance's father under his wishes, then Lance ascended the throne, but because of the circumstances surrounding his father's death, Damien had to wait for a reasonable length of time before killing Lance himself- fifteen years to be exact." Kenan went to say something but Terry held up his hand for silence. "There's more," he continued. "A relative, or a successor to the steward could also substitute if that person couldn't take the job on, providing he was crowned and all the rest of the mumbo jumbo that goes with it. In short, that relative was perfectly within legal rights to become King... or Queen if they were female."

"So now Damien can be King!" exclaimed Kenan. "That's bad! That's very bad... but I still don't get it why was I lured there?"

"Haven't you listened to a word I've said?" Terry was speaking very quietly and very seriously. "YOU are of direct blood line to your parents. THEY were the stewards to the last king, King Lance the first. That law still stands Kenan. Stewards are above the royal council and above Damien. He's a fraud, He always has been...YOU-are-in-line-to-the-throne!" Kenan blinked, slowly shaking his head.

"Nah," he said turning pale. "I'm not... I can't..."

"Yes you can and you are," said Terry.

"But Terry..." Kenan was lost for words, who wouldn't be? Finally he managed to stutter: "Look, I- I live on the streets, I have all my life. How on earth can I make the biggest jump on the social calendar just by the job my parents had?"

"Very easily," said Terry. "And now we have all five spheres we can go down to the shrine then we'll help you take your rightful place..."

"But I can't be the future King of England!" exclaimed

Kenan. "Don't you see Terry, I'm not cut out for this. I'm not even any good at handling my own group of friends so how am I supposed to handle running a country?"

"You've handled saving the world pretty well," said Terry. "You have the makings of a great ruler. Please believe and trust me Kenan. We have to sort things out one step at a time, let me help you." Kenan sighed. He did believe Terry, and he did believe that right now he needed all the help he could get, but what about the others? What would they say? What would their families say? And Vicki? How could he explain all of this when he wasn't even sure of what was going on himself? Another voice spoke up.

"I knew it."

"Naz? You're awake?"

Naomi had opened her eyes and was looking at Kenan with a piercing gaze.

"I told you didn't I?" she said quietly. "When we first met I told you, you had great potential, though I couldn't pick up what it was, I knew there was something about you, and now we know what."

"Shouldn't we be getting on with something a bit more important right now?" said another voice. It was Delia. Terry quickly stood up still holding the sphere.

"Absolutely," he said. "We should put this sphere alongside the others and maybe the weather will sort itself out."

"I want to come with you!"

"Cedric! When did you get here?" exclaimed Delia.

"When I couldn't reach you on your phone." he replied. "Terry shouldn't leave his front door on the latch so often either... but I heard every word," he continued looking at Kenan with a somewhat large amount of new respect, "and I want to help as much as I can." He looked at Delia. Delia looked at Kenan. Kenan looked at Terry. Terry looked back at them before he shrugged, he knew he was beaten.

"Very well," he said finally "but you must promise not to breathe a word of what you see and hear to anyone else." Cedric nodded.

"I promise," he said.

"We'll leave a note for the others," continued Terry. "We may be gone for some time." He looked at the four teenagers who were looking eagerly back waiting to go. "I must be out of my mind," he muttered.

*

It was a good while later when the group headed by Terry, were walking along the tracks looking for the broken light. Naomi and Cedric were clearly more nervous than they thought they would be, Kenan was still not feeling one hundred percent, but Delia and Terry were both looking more serious than ever. In less than a minute from descending onto the tracks, they had found the light and the usual rumbling of the door sliding open filled the air. It took quite a long time for Terry, Delia and Kenan to persuade Naomi and Cedric that the lift was safe.

"We'll be right there waiting for you at the bottom," Kenan told Naomi. "Just trust me." Naomi nodded. She had to admit she was a little relieved Cedric was with her to and that he looked twice as scared as she felt. Eventually, however, they all managed to make it down the shaft to the shrine - Cedric complaining of feeling very sick- without too many setbacks. The first thing Kenan noticed was the spirits they were still gliding about and seemed very restless. Naomi was entranced.

"This is amazing," she whispered. "But a little scary. Something tells me they don't like to be interrupted like this."

"Interrupted?" exclaimed Cedric. "Doing what? They're not exactly playing chess now are they?"

"Be quiet," hissed Terry. "They are aware of our presence but won't hurt you while I'm here. Just don't acknowledge them too much. They like fear, they were created to chase out any intruders who showed terror at the sight of them. As long as we all stay calm, nothing bad will happen. Kenan, I need you to come here with me." Kenan obediently followed Terry to the shrine. Terry had the spheres in a bag he had bought with him. First he gave Kenan the sphere of spring and Kenan placed it on it's corresponding symbol. Then he quickly put the sphere of autumn into place, and finally the Sphere of Summer. The last sphere was aligned with the others, but the ritual was far from over. "Quickly," said Terry. "Get back across the ledge. Unless I'm mistaken something else is yet to happen." He and Kenan ran back to Naomi, Delia and Cedric. As Kenan turned and looked back towards the shrine he could see the five spheres now glowing brightly. One was ultra violet, (the clear one) then the others matched the spheres colours: Blue for winter, pink for spring, gold for autumn and green for summer. As the light grew more intense, something else seemed to be happening, something seemed to be coming out of each glass ball.

"Look!" exclaimed Naomi. "Is... is that..?"

"Snow?" murmured Kenan.

They were right. Snow seemed to be erupting, with the light from the sphere of winter. As they looked, they could see something happening with the other balls. Pink blossom was flying out of the light from the sphere of spring, green leaves were coming from the sphere of summer and a mixture of golden and brown leaves were coming from the autumn one. They flew around the gigantic cavern a swirl of colour. Kenan also realized that the temperature seemed to rise and fall as each wave of objects passed them. The snowflakes bought a freezing cold wind with them, followed immediately by a blast of warm air with the summer leaves. The objects swirled several times around them, before all converging together back over the spheres. There they met and melded together until finally it just appeared to be a blurred ball in the centre of the room. All this time the light from the spheres had been glowing getting bigger and brighter. It had now transformed itself into beams of light that seemed to rise upwards intertwining so it formed a single multi coloured beam that shot up and hit the roof cavern, with no-where else to go it stayed there getting brighter and brighter. Just when Kenan was sure he couldn't bear to look any longer, the two spirits, still gliding around aimlessly came into contact with the beam.

At first they seemed un-effected then Delia squeaked.

"Look! Grandpa! It's got eyes!"

"Not human eyes though," remarked Kenan. "They look more reptilian."

"Check that," said Naomi. "The whole face looks reptilian."

The spirits had indeed not only acquired a long snake like body but now had faces that looked a little like:

"Dragons?" said Kenan. "Terry, you summoned dragons to guard this place?" He didn't know whether to applaud him for braveness or recklessness. The dragon spirits (for that's indeed what they were) had now turned their direction on the group.

"Keep still," hissed Terry. "They won't hurt you as long as you don't alarm them." The spirits glided around them seeming to size each member of the group up but not in a menacing way. They seemed more anxious than anything. If Kenan hadn't known he was awake he would have passed it off as a dream. These were the most elegant creatures he had ever seen. Suddenly the first larger dragon turned in mid flight then turned directly upwards, Kenan was sure it was going to slam into the roof of the cavern but instead, just before it did, it turned transparent and passed through the rock disappearing from view.

"Where's it going?" whispered Kenan.

"It has a storm to destroy," whispered back Terry. "They are guardians in every sense of the word. They protect the shrine and earth as one. Their dimension is the world of the spirits, but they cannot exist without us. Think of it as a mirror image, a parallel universe if you will. Travelling through the dimensions drains them of their powers but the light of the scared spheres restores them and gives them the strength to fight. Once their task is done they will be able to return from where they came... and this right now Kenan is what you've been working towards, you really are the Chosen One." Kenan couldn't feel more proud at this moment. He also felt incredibly lucky and privileged to be a witness to any of this at all. He turned around to look at his friends behind him.

Naomi was still watching the remaining dragon entranced as was Delia. Cedric, however, who had been shaking more and more throughout this whole ordeal clearly hadn't bargained on any of this happening. He let out a kind of high squeal and began to run a round looking for a place to hide shouting:

"Let me go! I can't take this anymore!"

"Cedric!" exclaimed Terry. "Please! Calm down." But Cedric was beyond 'calm down.' He was running around aimlessly, strangely resembling a fat frightened pig. The dragon spirit stopped its peaceful gliding and turned towards him before letting out a roar of confusion and Cedric replied with another loud squeal. The dragon began to chase him around the cavern. Cedric yelled again and made a mad dash for the lift. The dragon pounced causing the unfortunate boy to jump aside, missing the lift, then just running around in circles.

"Help him!" shouted Delia. "Grandpa what will that thing do to him if it touches him?"

"I don't know," remarked Terry looking very uneasy. At that moment Cedric fell over and could only watch in frozen fear as the creature loomed over him!

"Cedric!" yelled Kenan running towards him. "Get out of the way!" he pushed Cedric away in the nick of time but the dragon had already pounced... and Kenan found himself with arms outstretched either side of him and head thrown back as the spirit passed through him. It was so cold it hurt. Kenan felt his strength disappear dramatically. Time seemed to slow down, his head filled with a vision as he saw the other dragon, already miles out to sea fighting a ferocious beast. Black in colour it churned, it roared it flashed with electricity... no this was no beast, this was the storm itself, but nothing like one Kenan had seen before. It seemed to have its own mind, its own movements. He himself felt his own strength drain as the dragon struggled against its opponent. Terrified beyond all rational thought, Kenan saw the dragon frantically snap and claw but to no avail. He closed his eyes as the thunder pounded in his ears and the lightning threatened to blind him. But, no sooner did he open his eyes again, the vision vanished and he found himself standing alone. There was no sound, no storm, no people, nothing. As he surveyed his surroundings, trying to determine where on earth he could be, a mist began to appear all around him. Shaking with fear Kenan watched as a magnificent silver dragon slowly walked forward and stared at him. It lowered its huge head, sniffed him, raised its head again…and began to speak!

Chapter Twenty-Six

"So, you are the chosen one."

"What?" stuttered Kenan.

"But you know that already of course." The dragon's voice was deep and calm but it was such a huge beast that Kenan was well and truly afraid. It looked a little different from the spirit one that had passed through him. Although having the same long neck, this one had a body, silver in colour, with glistening red eyes. There were wings visible, folded across its back and its long legs walked along with the same elegance as a horse. Kenan couldn't take his eyes off this magnificent creature.

As the seconds passed, it slowly dawned on him that the dragon had no intention of hurting him and he began to survey what was around him. There were no other dragons in fact there were no other creatures at all. They were in a barren grey wasteland and the mist now seemed to have turned into a thick smog so that he could see barely five yards in any direction.

"W- where are we?" he managed to ask. The dragon looked back down at him.

"You honestly have to ask that?" he said. Kenan looked round but he really didn't recognize anything that was round him, even though he lived under a car park this had to be the most miserable place in the world.

"I - I'm sorry," he said. Not really knowing why he was still afraid. "I really don't know..." Walking past him, the dragon gestured for Kenan to follow.

"A little change, and you don't even recognize your own home?"

"What?" whispered Kenan. The dragon stopped walking and looked straight ahead. As the mist slowly started to lift, Kenan followed his gaze... and couldn't believe what met his eyes. It was a city, there was no doubt about that but it was mostly in ruins. Many of the skyscrapers looked like they were half built or they had been bombed.

Wind whistled through the empty streets and papers blew about with other debris. Kenan caught a tatty sheet of paper as it flew past him. It was a newspaper.

It was smudged and dirty but he could just read the headline: 'More Bombing Expected!' Kenan blinked then looked back out towards the city with parts of buildings strewn everywhere. He didn't want to recognize where he was but the layout of remains began to look familiar.

"Tell me," he whispered, "tell me this isn't London."

"Where we are standing now, is look out point," said the dragon looking sadly out into the mist, "and I'm afraid that *is* London… in the not too distant future."

"But how?" whispered Kenan beginning to feel sick, "what happened?"

"Evil succeeded," said the dragon.

"What?"

"Evil won. It took control of the worlds greatest leaders and Armageddon happened."

"You're not making any sense!" said Kenan. "Are you saying…?"

"Everything, everyone is dead," said the dragon bluntly.

"No," whispered Kenan.

"Everyone you ever cared for, your friends, family they're all…"

"Shut up!" screamed Kenan. "I don't want to hear any more! How did this happen? I got all the spheres, they were all aligned what happened?"

"Remember," said the dragon, "think back to the prophecy." And as Kenan cast his mind back, he remembered, the ancient text written before him, especially the lines: *For he will appear at the same time as a great evil, and when he does he, and he alone will be have to carry out the tasks ahead and make the most difficult of decisions to ensure our survival…*

"Okay," said Kenan slowly, "so I have to find this – this evil right and destroy it. Who is it? Who's responsible for all this?"

"Your journey must be made alone," said the dragon. "I am not of this world and thus, if I was to divulge advice from

this dimension to be taken into your own realm, the two
worlds would collide, bringing even more chaos and
disorder." Kenan sighed, not afraid to show he was losing
patience. He didn't see the harm in a name or a hint this
dragon could have given him but he was not about to argue
with it. He looked out again towards the ruined city.
"Mankind is on the edge of extinction," he said. "Everyone I
ever cared for is dead." He shuddered. Did that mean that in
this dimension he was too? "There must be some way I can
find out," he whispered. "Some way I can end this."

"There is," said the dragon. "Think back again to the
prophecy. All the answers you will need to know are in there."
Kenan did and as he ran through it again, he recalled one of
the last passages: *Search within your soul, for the answers and
you will not fail, for they will be the right ones...*

"So I just follow what I think is right? Instinct? Is that all
you can give me?"

"Destiny must be followed," said the dragon as the mist began
to clear a little. "You will know when the time comes what
you must do. It is down to you what path you take but as the
prophecy states, search inside yourself. Look into your soul
and your heart, listen to them and make the right choice. My
brother will continue to fight the storm that rages. I must go
and join him, this will be long
battle but you are the Chosen One, our strength reflects off of
your own, the fate of all is now tied between the bond we
share. We must fulfil our destiny as you must now fulfil
yours."

"But I still have so many more questions!" insisted Kenan.
"You must help me!" Everything was beginning to grow
lighter and the dragon was starting to fade away.

"You will know," said the dragon. "Trust me, trust in
yourself and you will do the right thing."

"No!" exclaimed Kenan. "Wait please!" But in a
blinding flash everything vanished and Kenan felt himself
falling to the ground. He was back in the shrine. He lay
there for a few seconds completely exhausted as he
watched the spirit if the dragon fly back overhead and just

as the first one did, disappear through the roof of the cavern.

"Kenan? Kenan! Are you okay?" Naomi and Terry were the first ones up to him (Delia and Cedric puffing along behind). Kenan sat up. "Did you see it?" he breathed.

"Yeah," said Naomi, "it went straight through you, thought we'd lost you for a second. You looked totally out of it."

"No, no!" exclaimed Kenan. "The dragon," the actual dragon battling the storm... or the other one, the one that spoke to me. It showed us a vision of the future!" Naomi looked at Terry.

"Kenan," said Terry, "that spirit went straight through you. It didn't stop, nothing changed. It couldn't have spoken to you anyway it went through in two seconds." Scrambling to his feet, Kenan looked at the four concerned faces.

"I know what I saw and heard," he muttered. He turned and looked up at where the two spirits had vanished, "and that's all I need to know," he whispered to himself.

"So you're telling us you were in a different dimension and talking to a dragon?"

"Yes!" Exclaimed Kenan for the fifth time. "Why don't you believe me Naz?"

"It's not that," said Naomi a little untruthfully, "but it just sounds too freaky to be real." Kenan glared at her.

"So you're calling me a liar?"

"No!" Naomi took a deep breath then continued; "I'm just saying that from where we were standing, that dragon went straight through you."

"Well, that's when it happened," said Kenan, "I don't know maybe they have the ability to stop time....but I tell you one thing Naz, it was scary… very scary."

"Yes but Kenan you've told us all this," said Terry who was standing with them, "what did it mean when it said destiny must be followed? We have done all we can surely."

"I was hoping you could help me out there," sighed Kenan. "Lance is dead, Damien's proved he's on our side,

King or not. He wouldn't have bothered saving us if he was truly *that* evil. I mean there's no-one left is there? I've got to know before it's too late. If I fail, the world fails with me."

Kenan, Naomi and Terry were back in Terry's flat on the balcony watching the sun come up as the city began to stir. When they had got back, it turned out that Matt, Sam and the twins were still asleep. Kenan felt slightly relieved at this as he had so much to think about he really couldn't face explaining it all to them as well. He was also pleasantly surprised for Terry to reveal that his and Naomi's watches had been re-claimed, as had his air-surfer but now he was back to worrying again. Cedric and Delia were looking something up on Cedric's laptop. Despite the calmness of the early morning, the three people on the balcony were anything but calm. They knew that the world was saved but they also knew what could happen next. Surprisingly, Kenan wasn't worried about the prophecy but much more on what the dragon had shown him. Now as he looked over London with the orange sun on the eastern horizon, a new feeling of hope rose up inside him. He wasn't going to let the city fall into ruin; he was going to prove the spirit wrong!

"Kenan, hey, Kenan guess what?" Kenan turned around. Delia and Cedric were both walking towards him with the laptop between them.

"You're somewhat a bit of a celeb," grinned Cedric, "look hard enough on the internet on the right sites and you can find practically anyone!" He pointed to the screen. Kenan didn't know how they had found out but there was a web page displayed with a whole fact file on *him!*

Name: Kenan Stuart Wheeler.
D.O.B: 12th June 2299.
Gender: Male
Eye Colour: Blue
Hair Colour: Blonde
Parents: Mr. Kenan Paul Wheeler, and
Mrs. Elizabeth Caroline Wheeler.

"Hey," smiled Delia. "It's June the eleventh today right?

Who's the birthday boy tomorrow then eh?" Kenan just smiled back.

"Wow," breathed Naomi. "That's got to be you right Kenan?" Kenan blinked. He couldn't see how it couldn't be him as the description fitted him perfectly but, as he asked, why would there be a fact file on him?

"It's from a website going through every thing and everybody connected with the royals," said Cedric.

"So it's true," said Delia, "and if what Grandpa says is accurate then that means... You're our rightful King." Kenan shook his head.

"We've been through this," he said "I'm not. Anyway-" he carried on talking before anyone could argue, "-I need to try and find this new evil that walks the streets before we go looking into all that properly but first I need to get some sleep."

"Me to," said Naomi. "I've got get back otherwise James will have the whole of London out searching for me. He knew I was coming to see you guys but I don't think he thought I'd be staying out at all." Kenan looked back at his friends in the room behind them. As if reading his thoughts, Terry said,

"Don't worry. I'll tell them you've gone back. You'd be best to let them sleep for now." Kenan nodded. As Naomi bade farewell to Delia and Terry, Cedric walked up to him looking very meek and mild.

"Um Kenan," he said sheepishly. "I'd just like to say well thank you."

"For what?" asked Kenan, puzzled. "Well, for saving me from that dragon," said Cedric. "I know it wouldn't have hurt me," he continued "but I was just so terrified..." Kenan held up his hand for Cedric to stop talking.

"It's okay," he said. "Honestly I would have done it for any one of you guys." With a look of respect on his face, Cedric smiled broadly and lowered his voice as he said:

"You have the makings of a great ruler in you, Kenan, don't let anybody tell you any different." In a whisper he added: "I don't deserve people like Naomi and you for friends, but the pair of you definitely deserve each other."

Kenan's eyes widened. Cedric was the last person he had expected to give him such advice. He held out his hand and Cedric shook it eagerly.

"Okay," said Naomi walking up to them. "Are we ready to go?"

"Yeah," said Kenan, "let's go home."

Kenan stopped his air-surfer just outside Naomi's room and she opened the window wide before stepping through it noiselessly.

"Keep that up and you'll be on your way to being the next cat burglar," he grinned as he kept the air- surfer steady in mid air. Naomi turned around and smiled. She looked exhausted but happy. Kenan knew how she felt. "You're going to be okay here? Naomi nodded.

"Mum's not back yet," she murmured quietly, "but James is here so I should be okay."

"If you need anything," said Kenan, "you know where I am." Naomi smiled.

"Thanks, Kenan," she whispered quietly. They looked at each other for one long minute, and before Kenan even knew what was happening Naomi had gently taken his hand in hers and pulled him towards her. Startled Kenan grabbed onto her shoulders through the window as he quickly regained enough composure to keep control of the air surfer. It was only when he looked up, he realized his face was just inches from hers. There was another silence, but this time there was no awkwardness or blushing. Naomi slowly leant towards him as Kenan did the same... just as Buster who had come with them shifted impatiently on the board. Losing his balance again, Kenan fell back from the window. Naomi laughed as Kenan scolded the dog.

"I think he wants to get home," she giggled. "Maybe he wants sleep too.

"I'll give him sleep," scowled Kenan. "I'll knock him out if he does that again!" Naomi only smiled some more.

"I'll let you go," she said quietly. "Hopefully see you tomorrow at some point."

234

"Yeah," muttered Kenan, still glaring at Buster, "hopefully." He waved as Naomi quietly pulled the window up and waved back. He flew back over the gates and looked down at Buster.

"And they say you're mans best friend?" he muttered. Buster wagged his tail.

It was that afternoon when Kenan awoke from a long undisturbed sleep. The first thing he saw was the sunlight outside. He couldn't believe it. Was the whole weather fiasco really over? Then he remembered something. Literally jumping up out of the blankets, he ran towards the lift and quickly pressed a button but he couldn't wait for it to reach him and took off at a sprint up the stairwell. He didn't stop once till he reached the top. He flung open the door and turned to look over the city…it was the most wonderful thing he had ever seen! The sky was a beautiful azure with not a cloud in sight, with the sun making every thing metal gleam and shine. The trees had blossomed again and their brand news leaves were now rustling in the light June breeze. Kenan couldn't believe it, after so long now this was a dream come true for him, but he wasn't the only one who was taking in the sight.

"Isn't it beautiful?"

"Huh?"

"We were wondering how long you'd take to wake up? We wanted you to admire the view while there was still decent enough light." Matt, Sam and the twins stood there smiling at him.

"Not too bad a result eh, mate?" grinned Matt thumping Kenan on the back. "That's something to remember isn't it? Saving the world at the age of fifteen!

"Which reminds us," said Sam. "Now we know it's your birthday tomorrow but we decided we should have a celebration tonight…"

"Whoa, whoa, whoa," exclaimed Kenan. "A party, for me?"

"Yes, a party for you," smiled Sam, "well, in our books anyway. You see there's a street party happening a few blocks from here; it's actually more a public thing held by residents and businesses of the square…they do it every year to promote 'local business,'" Sam held up two fingers on each hand making the 'quote' sign. "You know how they're always on about supporting each other and the local community," she continued. "So we're letting them supply the food, drink and music then we all slip in amongst them while they're busy and help ourselves. As far as I've heard it's open to the public, well that's us isn't it?" Kenan could hardly believe what he was hearing. He was so happy he could hardly speak so instead, gave Sam a hug and Matt held out his hand for a high five. This, they understood better than any words Kenan could have used.

"Is it okay if I hang out here for a bit? It's just I want to be around friends right now." Kenan nodded at Naomi. Not long after the announcement of the party, she had turned up looking very tired but brightened up a bit when the group had welcomed her like an old friend. Kenan had already invited her to come along with them that evening and she had accepted gratefully.

"So," he said as he sat down on the ground, "what do you want to do until it's time to go? We've got about two hours to wait otherwise."

"I don't know," said Naomi, restlessly. "Sorry for coming down here like this, but I couldn't stand waiting around at home."

Kenan nodded he didn't even want to think what was going through Naomi's head at that moment, but he promised himself to help her. She looked so sad, even when she tried to smile or laugh at a joke, he could tell it was all put on. Suddenly, a thought struck him.

"Hey," he said, "I've got an idea of what we can do." Naomi looked up expectantly. "Let's go somewhere *I* like to go whenever I'm feeling a bit down."

"Where would that be?" asked Naomi surprised. Kenan only winked.

"You'll see," he said mysteriously, "come on, jump onto

the air-surfer, it's not far…"

As the air-surfer picked up speed, Kenan followed the well-known route without a sound. Standing in front of him Naomi squinted as the breeze from the movement of the machine through the air became stronger.

"Nearly there," said Kenan, "when I say so I want you to close your eyes okay? Naomi turned around to look at him.

"Why?"

"It has more of an impact if you close your eyes before you get there," he replied smiling.

"How do you know I won't 'accidentally' open them before we get there?" grinned Naomi. In reply, Kenan reached out and held his hands over her eyes.

"There," he said. "Next question?"

Within a few more minutes, they were descending towards lookout point. "Keep still," said Kenan to a giggling Naomi.

"We're nearly there." They landed smoothly on the ground. No one else was there.

"Come on," said Naomi. "It can't be that great, wherever we are."

"Trust me," said Kenan. "Okay, I want you to walk forwards, slowly mind you. Not too quickly." With his hands still over her eyes, Naomi had no choice. Slowly she walked forwards.

"Stop," said Kenan. "Right, take a look." He took his hands away and Naomi blinked a couple of times, then gasped. The city lay before them, as far as the eye could see. Long shadows were thrown towards them as the sun, though still high in the sky, had slowly started to descend against amazing backdrop blue fading to a mysterious yellow like distant horizon.

"Kenan," whispered Naomi. "This is- amazing! It- it's gorgeous!"

"Told you so," said Kenan following her gaze. "Now do you understand why I couldn't let the world be destroyed? I couldn't bear to lose something like this, one thing no one has to pay for and everybody can enjoy. I always come here if it gets too much. It just seems to make all other problems seem so insignificant." Naomi nodded. For a while, the two friends looked out over the city, as yellow ball on the horizon seemed to sink further every minute. More and more lights became visible as time drifted by. Naomi sighed. Looking over her shoulder, Kenan's gaze moved from the horizon to her face.

"Feeling better?" he asked softly.

"Yeah," said Naomi, finally turning away to face him.

"It's calming in a way... sorry...I know I'm not making any sense." Kenan shook his head.

"Perfect sense," he smiled. There was a silence for a minute then, Naomi said:

"Thanks for being such a good friend. I don't know what I'd do without you, any of you guys for that matter, but you've helped me through such a bad time... I'll never forget it." Kenan only smiled but he was spared from having to say anything as Naomi embraced him in a cuddle that was nothing short of pure affection. No awkwardness was between them now, and Kenan suddenly realized that maybe, there was a chance Naomi had the same feelings for him, he did for her... but he wasn't prepared to ask. He wanted to stand there all night, for the moment not to end, but a faint bleeping sounded and Naomi pulled away, looking for something. It was her watch.

"We'll miss your party if we don't hurry back," she said looking at it, and hitting a button to stop the bleeping.

"You set your watch to go off for it?"

"I'm not about to miss a friend's party am I?"

"Okay," said Kenan not looking as if it was okay at all. They both got back onto the air- surfer. As they took off, Naomi steadied herself while trying to get a last look at the scene. Nervous about her falling, Kenan took hold of her hand, while she got settled. Oddly enough, he forgot to let go...

Matt, Sam and the twins met Kenan and Naomi half way to the town centre, which was peacefully quiet. The evening air was warm and Kenan couldn't help but forget about the dragon's prophecy, surely nothing *that* evil could be amongst them now. As he threw discreet glances at his friends, he felt the old happiness swell up inside him again. This was just like before, no worries, no problems, no stress. They got to the town a little early, food and various other things were still being put out. The man who ran the breakfast bar had now changed his stock to burgers and hot dogs. Long tables ran down the closed off streets and a small number of people were carrying out sound tests and checks on a large sound system. Despite this there were already a lot of people walking around, some in large groups others in twos or threes. Within the following half an hour things began to get going. Music started, crowds began to appear, some carrying more food and all with ridiculous amounts of drink. Kenan and the others decided to just mingle in until people began to loose concentration of what was going on... and they didn't have long to wait. As evening drew in and music blared louder people began to drink more, loosing concentration or start getting tired. Some people with young children disappeared while others took drinks back home with them, but there was plenty enough for Kenan and the others. The others soon included Terry, Delia and Cedric for obviously as Terry was a resident they were more than welcome.

It was as Kenan was looking around that he noticed someone wasn't joining in the celebrations. Naomi was standing alone just staring at the ground and not taking the slightest bit of notice of anything else around her. Kenan walked over to her.

"You okay Naz?"

"Yeah," she muttered. "I was just thinking about some – stuff." Kenan looked at her questioningly.

"Like?" he prompted.

"Just...everything that's happened I'm trying to decide whether it's been good or bad. I mean I know I've changed for the better since it started and I've made friends, real friends who appreciate me for me but..." she trailed off. Kenan decided not to pester her so just stood quietly to give her time to carry on. Eventually Naomi looked up at him and said:

"I don't want to lose any of that now," she murmured, "and well, unless you want to stay friends we won't see each other again." Kenan laughed.

"Are you crazy?" he smiled. "'Course we'll still be friends, just so long as it's okay with you. I keep my friends for life, not just when I need them."

"Really?" said Naomi her brown eyes suddenly shining.

"Yeah," replied Kenan. "You want to be friends, we will, and," he winked at her, "I don't care what your mum or *anyone* else thinks of me anymore! None of this appearing through windows or having to hide all the time!" For a second, Naomi looked as though she might burst into tears of joy but instead she looked towards the stage and a smile appeared on her face again.

"Hey," she said. "Hear that? I love this song! Come on let's see if you're a better dancer than me." And before Kenan could protest, she had grabbed him by the hand and pulled him into the packed dance area.

It was without doubt the best birthday celebration Kenan had ever had. The clock tower in the centre of the square read one in the morning before anyone began to feel tired. Finally nearly an hour later, people began to call it a night.

"Come on," Kenan mumbled as he rubbed his eyes, "we've got to get home."

"Okay," giggled Lia, as she set down an empty glass, one of many she had had that evening. "Nick's here, Naomi's here, Sam and Matt... aren't." Everyone began looking around. But the two were nowhere to be seen.

"Matt!" Yelled Kenan. "Sam! C'mon guys we're going!"

"I don't think you'll find them by yelling," laughed a voice from somewhere in the thinning crowds.

"Delia. Have you seen them?"

"Oh we saw them," laughed Cedric (who Kenan couldn't help but notice had his arm round Delia's shoulders) "they seem quite content to stay put I think."

"But where are they?" asked Kenan who really couldn't see what Delia and Cedric were on about.

"You really want to know?" smirked Delia. "Grandpa told us they're behind the stage, he saw them when he left about half an hour ago." Kenan set off at a marching pace.

"They'd better shift unless they'd rather stay," he muttered.

"Hey guys!" he shouted as he rounded the huge stage, "come on everyone's waiting... oh sorry."

"Sorry for what?" exclaimed Sam looking extremely flustered, unusually close to Matt.

"Yeah," said Matt turning scarlet "we're coming." Kenan raised one eyebrow. It didn't take a rocket scientist to work out what had been going on but he kept his mouth shut, aside from the one little comment to Matt as they walked back.

"By the way," he grinned, "you may want to take a look at that mark on your neck. It looks like quite a nasty bite to me."

Matt called him something rude.

Chapter Twenty-Seven

No one really knew how long it took them to walk back to the multi story that night but it was definitely safer than air-surfing. Everyone had had one too many that night and, as was drink driving, air-surfing after drinking alcohol was a serious offence. Upon their arrival, the twins stumbled away and left Kenan, Naomi, Matt and Sam alone.

"Not a bad night I s'pose," mumbled Matt.

"What do you mean 'I s'pose'," remarked Sam. "I don't to think it was bad at all."

"Mm hmm," said Matt, "Okay, it was very good."

"Some bits were better than others eh?" teased Kenan. Matt and Sam glared at him. Naomi looked at the three, puzzled. There followed an awkward silence. Finally Matt got to his feet muttering:

"I'm tired. See you guys in the morning okay?"

"Wait up Matt," called Sam running after him. Naomi looked at Kenan.

"Should we go after them?" she asked.

"Nah," said Kenan lying back on his blankets. "I think they just want to be alone." Naomi's eyes widened.

"Do they…?" she started, "I mean… they aren't are they…?"

"From what I saw," smiled Kenan. "It looked highly suspicious." He closed his eyes and shrugged. "Each to their own I suppose." They were both quiet for a minute. At length Naomi cleared her throat.

"Kenan?"

"Yes."

"Would you mind if I stayed here tonight?" Kenan opened his eyes.

"If you can find a spare blanket you're more than welcome, if you don't mind sleeping on the ground. What about your mum?"

"She's been delayed. She's coming back in the morning now instead of tonight."

"And James?"

"I told him I was staying at a friends."

"Oh," smiled Kenan, sitting up, "so you planned to stay here all along right?"

"No," said Naomi turning her face towards the box as she dug around for a blanket, "it's just I was planning on staying out but not necessarily here, I didn't know where the night would take me," she finished lamely. Kenan continued to look at her, but Naomi had become very interested in hunting down an elusive blanket. Finally she turned to face Kenan.

"There isn't one here," she muttered.

"What?"

"You don't seem to have a spare blanket." Kenan got up and walked over.

"I'm sure I had one," he said as he began chucking things out of the box. Naomi walked over to where Kenan's blanket was. She was now so tired she didn't care where she slept but she needed something to keep her warm. After searching fervently, Kenan gave up.

"You have mine," he said as he crammed everything back into the box.

"What will you have?" asked Naomi immediately.

"My jumper," smiled Kenan. But Naomi didn't return the smile.

"You must have something," she insisted. "Look you have the blanket-"

"No!"

"Yes!"

"I said no!"

"Okay!" exclaimed Naomi. "What do you suggest we do?"

*

"Come on Naz, quit hogging it will you."

"It was your idea to share."

"Yeah well, I wish I'd kept my big mouth shut now," grumbled Kenan. He tried to pull a tiny bit more of the blanket over him but Naomi was holding onto it tightly. In the end Kenan turned onto his back and looked moodily at the ceiling. After a while:

"Kenan?"

"What?"

"Are you still awake?"

"No."

"Oh okay."

"Why?"

"Just wondered."

There was another long pause then: "Do you think it's true?"

"What?" Kenan was beginning to get irritated.

"Well, the prophecy." Naomi turned towards Kenan and looked at him. Kenan didn't look back at her. He didn't quite know what to say, as he wasn't sure himself. Finally he said:

"It's not worth worrying about Naz. To my knowledge the world's safe and that's all that matters."

"That's not the answer to my question," said Naomi, "because if you're going to be in danger I think we should know."

"Why?" muttered Kenan, "so you can jump in the line of fire to try and save me? Let's get one thing straight Naz." Turning on his side to face her he continued; "If something happens to me I'm going to at least make sure it happens away from you guys, because I don't want any of you in danger, because you feel you need to help me."

"So you're willing to risk your life, possibly lose it for us?" said Naomi.

"Yes," said Kenan. "Is that such a bad thing?"

"No, no. I guess not in that sense," said Naomi "it's just…" she didn't finish her sentence. But Kenan hated any conversation left unfinished.

"It's just what," he prompted. Naomi sighed.

"You have no idea what it's like to lose family do you?"

"Err yes I do," snapped Kenan. "Hello? Guy who's responsible for his parent's death speaking!"

"No wait, I didn't mean that?" stuttered Naomi. "But, and please don't take this the wrong way Kenan, you don't

244

remember your mum and dad, where as my dad…" she lowered her voice a little then said, "we were talking, a few days ago about stupid trivial things, like our next holiday and what we were doing at the weekend. Then my nan, she died of totally different circumstances yes but…" Naomi swallowed hard. Kenan was now looking at her. "The bottom line of it is," said Naomi shakily, "I've lost two members of my family, in such a short space of time and I don't think-" she squeezed her eyes tight- "I could bare to lose someone else that – that I care for." At this, Naomi hid her face in the blanket. Kenan felt awful. He had never thought of his friends feelings before and now he suddenly realized how they'd feel if he did plunge into something reckless.

"Hey," he whispered, gently resting a hand on Naomi's arm. "I'm sorry okay? It's just that I'm not used to people being so considerate. I guess I do take you guys for granted when I shouldn't." Naomi looked back at him her eyes now wet with tears but yet determination still in them.

"Never take anyone for granted," she muttered, "that's what I've learned." Kenan nodded. His head suddenly seemed to weigh like a ton of lead. He lay back down on the pillow. Naomi moved closer as Kenan sub-consciously put an arm round her. Despite the month being June, it was a cold night.

"Goodnight Naz," muttered Kenan.

"Happy Birthday, Kenan."

He could have only had a few hours sleep but when Kenan awoke, just before dawn, he wasn't at all tired. In fact he felt better than ever. After all he reminded himself, it was his sixteenth birthday, and that wasn't something you could claim it to be every day. Naomi was cuddled up right next to him still asleep one of her arms now across him. He looked at her for a couple of minutes wondering where her dreams had taken her hoping for her sake it was as far away from reality as possible. He lay there for a few minutes enjoying the peace and quiet of the early morning and the warmth of Naomi next to him, his arm still around her. It was at that moment he realized that he was totally one hundred percent happy for the first time perhaps in his whole life, his main concern now was too look after her and be there for her. He still remembered his promise to keep her safe and he only hoped that somehow he could fulfil that promise *and* the prophecy. After a few more minutes, Kenan withdrew his arm from around Naomi's shoulders and, as quietly as he could, got up. There was just one thing he wanted to do alone that morning. In the distance, he heard the clock striking five.

Great he thought *there's still loads of time.* He cast one more look at Naomi, to make sure she was asleep, picked up his air-surfer and took off in the dim light towards look out point.

Look out point wasn't ever really designed to be the way it was. It was basically a huge mound of earth that had been pushed out of the way when the newer part of London sprang up. Kenan liked it so much because depending on what way you were facing you could watch the sunrise or set from pretty much anywhere you sat. That morning he looked out over the city as the huge orange ball slowly rose up from the horizon. The sounds of life just waking up, were few, it was still early, but that was just the way he liked it. Living in the city all his life meant there were very few occasions when it was quiet and peaceful like this. He had learned to treasure them, as much as possible. A lot of things were going through his head per second, far too much to handle at any one time but as he sat looking at the pink and orange sky he felt somewhat calmed. Maybe the world was safe after all. Maybe the dragon was wrong. As he continued to look out, he saw someone was coming towards him up the steps to the summit where he sat. The early mist meant he couldn't see very clearly, but he could tell it was a girl.

"Kenan?"

He recognized that voice, it was Naomi. He couldn't help feeling a bit annoyed. Why had she bothered to follow him at this hour?

"Naz, what are you doing?"

"I came to find you and ask you the same thing," she said

looking a bit ruffled.

"Look, I just wanted some time out to myself okay?"

"What's that supposed to mean?"

"It means that I've got to think things through and figure out the prophecy...." Naomi turned pale.

"Y-You're still going to-?"

"Yes I'm still going to save the world," said Kenan. "From what ever else it is that's going to happen... IF it does happen," he added.

"But I thought we'd been through this last night," stuttered Naomi.

"No," said Kenan. "We didn't go through anything last night. You talked, I listened."

"Then you didn't listen very well," snapped Naomi. "Because you're already putting yourself in danger going out like this, alone."

"Why does everyone treat me like a kid all the time!" exclaimed Kenan. "I'm sixteen years old-"

"Yeah! Just!"

"And you can talk! You're hardly ever at home, just when your mum needs you the most-!"

"Don't you dare try and put me on a guilt trip Kenan Wheeler!"

"Then why don't you shut up and listen to me!"

"Don't tell ME to SHUT UP!" screamed Naomi. Kenan turned away from her, half in despair, half in disgust. Naomi had the unfortunate ability to act like a spoiled brat even if she didn't mean to and that was one thing that annoyed him the most.

"This is pointless," he muttered.

"What is!" growled Naomi.

"This whole conversation, we're not actually moving onto an intelligent subject are we?"

"So what do you want me to do?" snapped back Naomi. Kenan stood, hands in pockets, his back still to Naomi and said quietly:

"Leave." Naomi's attitude left her immediately.

"What do you mean?" she whispered.

"I've got to do this Naomi. One way or another. I have to figure this out and finish it once and for all. I don't want you around if something bad happens," said Kenan in a low voice. "You don't need anymore hurt so I want you to go home and forget about me and the others." Naomi looked stunned then upset.

"Y- you know I can't do that," she wailed. "You can't just ask me to-"

"I'm not asking you," said Kenan coldly, hating himself for how harsh he sounded, "I'm telling you," he finished, his back still turned. Naomi's sadness turned to anger again.

"Fine," she muttered. "We'll behave like brats." She walked back towards the steps as Kenan finally turned and looked at her. She glared back as she said:

"I'm not involved anymore," and she was gone, vanishing down the steps, out of sight. Kenan watched where she had disappeared for some time, half expecting but more half hoping, she would come back. When it became apparent that she wasn't going to, he slumped to the ground and buried his head in his knees. He felt cold. Shivers running down his spine.

"What am I doing?" he muttered to himself.

"Yes, what are you doing?" That voice made him look up sharply, but there was no one there.

"Hey," he called out. "Who's that?"

"You know," replied another voice, this one was a female voice. Kenan whirled around but there was no sign of anyone around at all. A breeze picked up suddenly. And as the wind rushed past him he distinctively heard something else. "Don't give up Kenan. You can't afford to now." As the wind rushed past, Kenan closed his eyes but immediately his head was filled with a terrifying vision. Both dragons were now just off of a coastline, though what one he didn't know and he felt a surge of physical pain and anxiety go right through him as he watched the storm physically swell, it was of gargantuan proportions now. They were still fighting it but he knew they were losing. He was running out of time – he had possibly an hour or two...

He picked up his air-surfer… he was not staying here a minute longer. Freaked out and still fuming from his row with Naomi, he headed back to the car park.

When Kenan got back however, he immediately felt awful that Naomi was not with him. After all he had been the one that had asked her to go, but at the same time he had made the point he'd been arguing all along… he wasn't a little kid anymore and one way or another they'd all have to accept whatever fate dealt them, he made a promise not to hurt her… this was truly the only way he could keep that promise. Buster ran up to greet his master as usual but Kenan only glowered at the dog, who put his ears and tail down and quickly backed away. Kenan sat down hard on the ground then lay back with his eyes closed. *What's come over me?* he thought, *I'm acting like a jerk to all my friends, this isn't me at all, this is crazy!* Crazy! The word kept repeating itself over and over again in his head. *Maybe I am,* he thought to himself after all how could he explain what had happened with those freaky voices. Had they even been real?

"Kenan! Kenan! Wake up!" For one wonderful minute, Kenan thought he was asleep and this horrible nightmare was over and he'd wake up and it would turn out to be a happy birthday after all. But when he opened his eyes, Naomi had gone and Buster was peeping out at Kenan over a box. It was all still real. He blinked a couple of times then looked up at Matt, who was running towards him, face deathly pale and eyes wide with fright.

"What's up?" he asked as his friend stopped in front of him. He noticed he was carrying the holo-box under his arm.

"You've got to look at this man!" exclaimed Matt, shaking so much he could hardly set the machine up properly. He managed to calm down enough to show a news-clip on, in which the reporter blared:

"And finally, following the authority given earlier this month, the official go ahead has now been given to destroy the multi –story car park situated in Queens Way on the outskirts of borough. The building was erected only fifteen years ago but has not reclaimed the money it cost to build and is costing the taxpayer thousands for it's upkeep. The local government has invested in a quarter-of-a-million-pounds-worth of dynamite to end the unfortunate building's existence tonight as approved by the local council..."

Matt snapped the box shut.

"You'd have thought they'd have said something to us about it," he said angrily.

"Maybe they want to get rid of us along with it," growled Kenan.

"Well, they're gonna have to fight for it," exclaimed Matt. "C'mon Kenan," he continued standing up. "We can't let them blow up this place no matter how crappy it may be, we've got to find some people who are against it! They won't destroy our home that easily!"

Chapter Twenty-Eight

Naomi walked glumly down the street, her hands buried deep in her pockets, her eyes still stinging with tears. Going further and further into the city, the words she had last spoken to Kenan echoed in her head: *I'm not involved anymore!* Why on earth had she let her temper get the better of her? But she reminded herself, *he* had sent *her* away...had she any real reason to feel guilty? Anger was boiling up inside her. Kenan thought he knew everything just because *he'd* been chosen. She'd risked her life for him, her own father had even *given* his life in order to give them a fighting chance and he re-paid her by sending her away. Anger became too much for her. She stomped into another side street and carried on walking not noticing even where she was going. She journeyed further and further into to depths of London's darkest and meanest streets until suddenly she stopped as she looked up for the first time and realized she didn't have a clue where she was. She quickly brought her wristwatch out from under the sleeve of her hooded jumper and opened the 'maps' option. So intent was she on finding out where she was, that she didn't hear the soft footfalls behind her, not until a strong arm grabbed her from behind! Another hand was clapped over her mouth and a mean face leered into hers.

"Scream and you die!" he hissed. Naomi's eyes were wide with terror as she felt herself dragged backwards by the person behind her and slammed up against the wall. Four more brutes emerged from the shadows bringing the total standing around her to six. The watch was ripped off of her. "Nice stuff," sneered the fiend, studying it. He just made out the logo on the back. "Henderson enterprises?" He looked in the most horrible way at Naomi. "Heeeey," he grinned, showing some awful teeth. I know who you are. You're *his* daughter aren't you."

"Leave me alone," whispered Naomi.

"Leave you alone?" laughed another one. "And miss out on this. "Come on daddy's girl, what else have you got on you. Aren't you like the richest kid under sixteen this side of London?"

"Please," Naomi felt a sob rising in her chest. "Please just let me go."

She was cornered again as the one with bad teeth leaned closer. "Come on," he sneered. "I'm sure you've got something else you can give us now..." he paused before gently stroking a strand of her tawny hair between his rough fingers. Naomi trembled at his touch and quickly moved her head away but he only moved his hand to the other side of her face. "I'm sure we can reach some sort of agreement," he continued as he moved slowly towards her... she could smell the tobacco and alcohol on his breath.

Kenan, she thought desperately. *Please help me! **Anyone!***

"Naomi!"

"Cedric?"

Whether it was coincidental, or he had been following her for some time, Naomi was never more pleased to see him at that moment.

"The police are on their way!" he hollered. One of the thugs went to grab something from the back pocket of his jeans, when an ear-splitting cracking sound issued from somewhere in the distance. A second later they felt it... the ground quivered. Naomi shot a glance above her, she could see flocks of birds flying as fast as they could, all heading in one direction. The gang quickly released her, the watch was dropped as they departed. Naomi ran out of the alleyway, as the ground continued to shake growing more and more violent every few seconds. She saw Cedric's gaze was now fixated above them. Naomi followed the direction in which he was staring and was locked to the spot in fear. A gigantic black cloud was moving towards them. It rumbled with what sounded like a hundred thunderstorms and crackled with electricity. It seemed to have a mind of its own, the movement of it reminded her more of a snake; twisting and writhing back on itself moving all the while as a fierce wind picked up,

increasing its speed. The ground was now well and truly
shaking and as Naomi felt the first spot of rain on her face, her
blood seemed to run cold... The storm had arrived!
   "Run!" she managed to scream. They took off at a sprint.
All around was sheer panic. Full grown men and women
screamed and children cried. But the sheer force of the storm
hadn't arrived yet. As the ground continued to shake a
crunching sound made her and several other people turn
round, they watched in terror as a building behind them
started to crumble.
   "Come on!" screamed Cedric grabbing her hand, and
dragging her back into the throng. "Move!" They ran as fast as
they could but more and more people joined them. As chunks
of buildings smashed around them, people doubled back and
ran in the opposite direction resulting in more mayhem all the
while the black cloud above churned and rumbled. In the
confusion, Naomi lost her grip of Cedric's hand. "Naomi!" he
cried as he was pushed away from her by the crowds. Naomi
saw him and made to dash across to him but with a deafening
crack she saw split in the ground coming towards them faster
and faster. Realizing the path it was on she pushed her way
through the crowds but the crack moved faster slicing the road
in two right between them and they were separated.
   "Cedric!" she screamed, "Help me!" But Cedric couldn't
even get near her. Searching desperately for something that
might help them, he suddenly had an idea. "Naomi!" he
yelled. "I'm going to get help okay? Whatever you do try and
stay visible and safe at the same time!" With that, he took off
at a run towards a distant but visible building that loomed up
in the distance.
Back at the multi story Kenan and the group, which included
Damien and Vicky had been discussing ways to save the car
park. Damien hadn't really contributed very much to the
conversation and seemed very pre-occupied. It was clear
Vicky had dragged him along, but hardly ten minutes after
converging pointless ideas, they were interrupted as tremors
shook the ground they were on.
   "W-w-what's h-happening?" Sam exclaimed as she held

onto a shaking pillar to stop her-self falling.

"It's a q-quake!" yelled Matt following suit, "let-ts get out of here!" Kenan, however wasn't shaken up.

"I don't think it's gonna collapse," he started to say, but Lia interrupted him.

"Kenan forget it! Better safe than sorry right? C'mon let's move!" She started to drag him out from under the building but before they could get out they saw a fat figure running towards them. It was Cedric, drenched in sweat and breathing very laboriously, he approached them with a distant look of triumph on his face but his normal pig like eyes, Kenan noticed were wide with fright. Something was definitely wrong.

"Cedric!" he exclaimed breaking from Lia's grasp "Cedric what's up whoa!" He struggled to support his exhausted friend as Cedric crumpled to the ground in a clearly painful heap. He struggled to say something but was panting too hard. "Take it easy," said Kenan as people began to crowd. "Just catch your breath."

"No time!" wheezed Cedric. "Kenan - please! The earthquake it's… I mean there's… it- it's Naomi! She's down there! She's trapped, the crowds will crush her if we don't move now!" There was a stunned silence in which Kenan was heard to murmur:

"Naz," then louder. "Naz! Hold on!" Matt was already running towards him with his and Kenan's air-surfer. "Show us where she is!" yelled Kenan yanking Cedric up from the ground and onto the board.

"But I've never ridden one of these…"

"It doesn't matter I'm driving," snapped Kenan. "Let's go!" He took off with Matt in hot pursuit. The others exchanged worried looks, and then rushed to get their own air-surfers. Damien however stood where he was. Vicky watched as his eyes began to gleam with the horrible shine that always signalled the start of trouble for others.

"What are you smirking about?" she muttered.

"I've had an idea," he growled. "Come with me if you feel like watching something really funny." He took off at a quick stride following the general direction Matt, Kenan and Cedric had taken.

Back on the main streets, Naomi had desperately tried to find a safe place to hide whilst she waited for Cedric's return. However, this was easier said than done. The noise and confusion was unreal and many people seemed to be trying to do the same thing. She was running out of places. She continued to run with them but as the crowds thickened she soon tripped and cowered as best she could from the hundreds of feet. But the horror didn't stop there. Any transport that had been missing from the street she was in seemingly appeared all at once and thundered past, people still in between vehicles, and more kept on coming...

Matt swooped down over the crowds, desperately looking for Naomi, whilst Kenan let Cedric descend from the disc safely. As he straightened up, Matt rushed back towards him shouting:

"There! Kenan! Look down there!" Kenan saw her, cowering with her hands over her head hoping that somehow she'd stay alive.

"Naz!" Naomi looked up.

"Kenan!" she yelled.

"Hold on!" He called back. Gritting his teeth, Kenan found he hardly had time to think twice and took off into the rush weaving in and out of people to reach her.

On the roof of a building, which was the least affected by the quake, Damien and Vicky watched. Damien seemed to be following Kenan's every move closely but Vicky kept looking from one to the other. She had a horrible feeling she knew what Damien was plotting and only hoped she was very wrong. From their air-surfers the group tried also to trace their friend's movements but it was difficult, so much was happening so fast. Back on the ground, Kenan kept *his* eyes focused on Naomi. He only had another hundred yards to go, fifty, twenty, ten but then, Wham! He found himself skidding across the floor as some one tried to grab the air-surfer from under his feet in a vain attempt to use it for himself. Kenan grabbed the air-surfer back and when the man protested

Kenan aimed his fist in his opponents stomach and wrenched the board from his hands as the man fell backwards. Kenan turned to Naomi.

"Okay," he said, "let's get out of here." They both scrambled on as Kenan tried to make a safe return above the traffic. But it was growing thicker all the time. They narrowly avoided a hover bus, missing it by inches and skimming along the top of it sending up a shower or sparks as they went. Kenan searched desperately for a safe place to land that was out of the way, but all he could see was a solid steel iron staircase leading up from the ground by the side of a block of flats. Some people were already on the lower levels but the topmost ones were empty. Kenan headed towards it, but found there was no room for the air-surfer and themselves to land together. "Jump," he ordered. After a seconds hesitation, Naomi jumped and made a lucky landing on the iron grid that was the floor. Beaming, she turned and gestured for Kenan to join her, but as he prepared to leave the board, a car careering out of control struck it. Loosing his footing, Kenan fell followed by his air-surfer disappearing below the rows of traffic.

"No!" yelled Matt who had seen it first. Everyone gasped as Kenan disappeared.

"Where is he?" exclaimed Sam as more and more traffic flew past. Seconds zoomed by, more and more... every-one's heartbeat quickened... suddenly- a figure sprang up between two vehicles. It was Kenan having managed to reclaim his air-surfer yet again. He flew straight past Naomi who rushed up the flights of steps to stay level with him, but upon doing so she gasped. He was holding his right side tightly; he was badly hurt, but thankfully, still alive.

"Come on!" she yelled gesturing for him to jump to safety. Kenan looked up wincing.

Just give me a minute okay?" he gasped. "I'll be fine here for a few seconds."

Back at the top of the building as Damien and Vicky watched the dramatic scene unfold, Damien gritted his teeth and slipped away un-noticed, as Vicky was too busy trying to determine if Kenan was all right.

"Kenan," said Naomi again. Kenan looked up. Naomi took a deep breath and continued; "I'm sorry about earlier."

"Hey no problem," smiled Kenan straightening up still clutching his side.

Not far away Damien saw what he was looking for, an abandoned taxi. He jumped in the driver's side and turned the car around.

"I know," Naomi was saying "but I am really sorry, I was acting like a spoilt brat, you weren't doing anything wrong except pointing out the truth."

Damien finished turning around and jammed the gear stick into the fastest setting.

Kenan was still looking at Naomi.

"It's okay," he said. "We were both on the edge, forget it okay?"

Damien's eyes narrowed as he focused on what he wanted to hit then put his foot flat on the accelerator gripping the steering wheel, a manic expression on his face.

"Are you sure?" smiled Naomi. Kenan nodded smiling back. Naomi began to laugh with relief but her expression turned to that of terror at something behind Kenan. She went to scream "NO! Kenan look out!" Kenan turned but too late. He caught a glimpse of the mad eyes, he suddenly recognized them as the ones he had seen on Terry's web cam the night he had been attacked and that familiar sneer and the look of triumph. It all happened in a split second.

"Damien?" he whispered, then the taxi hit him!

For one awful minute time seemed to stop. The noise and confusion merely dwarfed what went through the heads of every one watching. From their place on the balcony, Sam screamed out loud and turned away as Matt went completely white. Lia hid her face in her brother's jumper as he tried to keep on his feet. Cedric felt his knees give way and grabbed onto the railing to support himself and above them only a few blocks away, Vicky collapsed to the floor feeling horribly sick. Then things sped back to normal. After hitting Kenan, Damien veered upwards sharply speeding away. Judging by

the direction of everyone's eyes, no one knew it was him...
they were watching Kenan. He had immediately been pushed
from the air-surfer but now harder than the two previous
occasions. The pain in his side was magnified ten times over.
He was falling faster and for longer now. The stampede of
people and vehicles was starting to thin but he hardly noticed.
His hands flailed wildly as they made to grab anything that
would save him, but in vain. He could see things disappearing
above him as he continued to fall. He felt himself hit, the
bonnet of a car, the pain was overwhelming, but he rolled off
of, it had slowed his fall dramatically although he still had a
few more feet to go... -
He hit the ground without warning and the worst pain of the
day engulfed him. As he tried to take in what had just
happened he also tried to forget that it felt like every bone in
his body shattered. It was excruciating! He tried to gulp down
mouthfuls of air but it hurt his chest. He felt something rising
in his lungs and coughed violently. The air above him flecked
with red. Blood. His blood. He coughed up more and more
and somehow, miraculously, heaved onto his side in an effort
to stop himself from choking. But that was all he could do. He
noticed his breathing slowing, his vision was blurring and the
pain was strangely ebbing away.

"Naz," he whispered, hardly able to hear himself, before
his eyes closed.

Above him Naomi was already running down the steps.
Everywhere she looked, all she could see was the horrible
image replaying again and again in her mind. Something in
her heart was burning horribly as it beat faster and faster.
Please, she kept thinking to herself. *Not now, not like this.* She
reached the ground as the last of the people thinned away.
Everything had stopped shaking and now only a cold silence
was left hanging in the air along with the dust.

"Kenan," she called, desperately looking for any sign of
him, straining her ears. She wondered aimlessly scanning the
surrounding terrain. Then she heard a sound, something was
moving behind her. She turned eagerly hoping to see
someone, anyone, she knew, but saw that it was a stupid air-

surfer clattering down. *Air-surfer!* Naomi looked in the direction it had come from and the feeling that her heart really did stop beating re-occurred. She could make out someone but was it…?

"Oh please don't say it is," she murmured running towards the person. As she approached, she slowed her pace. *It was!* "Kenan?" she whispered wishing that miracle upon miracle he'd respond, but nothing. She knelt beside him reached out her hand, then hesitated, before resting it on his shoulder and shook him gently. "Kenan?" she tried again. "Kenan?" panic was now edging into her voice. As slowly as she could she rolled him onto his back but his eyes remained closed she could detect no movement anywhere. "No," she whispered. "Please no." She shook him again harder but still no response. She had to know. Slowly she reached out a hand and felt around the neck where she knew she would find a pulse…or not.

It took her too long to decide as she held out false hope. Finally she pulled her hand way. It was no use, she had to face the awful truth, the prophecy had come to pass, in the end he had risked everything, survived more than most, but in his one act to save her, Kenan had made the ultimate sacrifice... he was gone.

Chapter Twenty-Nine

"Where did he go?"

"Can you see him?"

"He took a pretty bad fall."

"Come on, let's find him." Matt and the others were tumbling over each other to get to their air-surfers on the rooftop. When they had seen Kenan fall they hadn't been able to believe their eyes. Rooted to the spot in horror, they had now found the use of their legs and feet and desperate to see if their friend had survived they mounted their boards and slowly descended towards the dusty ground. A mean, hard face watched them below.

"Go and find him," Damien muttered, "and take your time, because I guarantee he will *not* be moving this time."

"How could you?" hissed a voice. Damien merely glanced at the speaker. Vicky was standing there shaking with anger and grief, her face white.

"How could I what?" smirked Damien.

"How could you WHAT?" screamed Vicky. "You- you killed him you bastard! You killed him! He was like our own and you..." she flung herself at him. Trying to hit, kick or just plain hurt every bit of him she could. Damien fended her off far too easily before grabbing each of her wrists and pulling her close.

"No!" he glowered. "He was never *our* own! *I* took him in because I wanted an heir. I prayed and hoped that he would never find the truth, but when he found the very first thing, that stupid little sphere I knew then that it was only a matter of time before my cover was blown and I had to get him out of the picture!" Vicky sank to her knees, her long hair hiding her tear-stained face. Damien turned back towards the taxi he had returned with.

"Where are you going?" snarled Vicky.

"I'm going back," replied Damien. "I need to go and make final arrangements for the move out."

"Move out?"

"Yes. There is no heir to the throne now, so as second in command to Kenan and Liz, I can now claim my prize! I will not be living under that stinking car park for much longer…if it survives till the end of the day," he glowered.

"David!" screamed Vicky.

Damien spun round his eyes flashed.

"Don't you ever call me that!" he exclaimed. "That name died along with the pushover who owned it!"

Back on the ground, Naomi sat alone next to Kenan. She hadn't moved a muscle, not even lifted her eyes from his lifeless face. So many emotions were running through her head it was difficult to vent one. She was upset, angry, confused, guilty, remorseful in fact she wondered why her face was remaining so deadpan. Not far away a teenage boy whom she couldn't see was taking in the scene as though he hadn't seen what happened. Reaching up his hand to push through his messy blonde hair he realized something was wrong. She had her back to him, and seemed to be rigid with grief.

"Hey!" he called urgently, "are you alright?" There was no response. The boy slowly walked towards her. "Hey," he repeated. Still nothing. As he approached Naomi, he slowed his pace, something was very wrong. He took one more step towards her, leaning forward, peering over her shoulder to see that was wrong. When he did see the figure before them he couldn't believe it.

"Th- that's me? But what…? What ha..." He staggered back a few paces. "No," he muttered. "No, no, NO!" He fell against a grounded hover car in shock. He could not take this in at all. *I'm- I'm a... but I'm still... there... but I'm over... no... no I this can't be happening?* But he knew it was. All he was doing was having an argument with the side of him, that deep down inside he knew was right. He felt so stupid as everything came flooding back. How could he have let Damien get him so easily! He had let them all down. Matt, Sam, the twins Naomi… "Naz!" He whirled round. He could now see some expression on her face, she was close to tears. This made him angry. Damien had ruined everything. Kenan, knew he would have survived otherwise and this filled him with more rage, but what got to him more was the fact he knew there was nothing he could do about it now. He was really... gone, defeated just like that. He'd lost. With this thought in mind he looked glumly over at Naomi and slowly trudged over to her. He knelt down beside her and without even thinking put his head on her shoulder.

"I'm so sorry Naz," he whispered. Naomi blinked. Kenan looked harder at her, could she hear him? She did have a sixth sense after all. "Naz," he said quietly. "Can you hear me?" Naomi began to nod but then shook her head.

"Stop it," she muttered her voice very shaky. "Stupid imagination." Kenan grimaced.

"It's not your imagination, Naz," he whispered. "It's me... I'm here. I'm so, so sorry. I didn't want to put you through any more pain..."

"You lied..." she whispered. "You promised..."

"I can't make this up to you," said Kenan quietly. "I know I can't but please Naomi, hear me now, I will always be there, I will always watch over you..."

"Stop it!" shouted Naomi. And that was it. Try as she might to put on a brave face, she burst into tears. Kenan looked down and saw that his right hand was still being held tightly in hers. In truth, he didn't feel sorry for himself. Not in the least, he felt worse for Naomi... but what could he do?

"Kenan?"

That voice!

Although Kenan couldn't yet see the speaker, he recognized it from so long ago. A female voice, soft and caring, could it be...? He slowly turned around, and the sight that met his eyes was something from beyond his wildest dreams. A man and woman stood barely yards from him and he recognized them immediately, the same people from the sketch Naomi had done for him, and the same from the tombstone in High Gate. He was looking for the first time in fifteen years at his parents!

He shakily pulled himself to his feet. He had always thought that upon seeing them again he'd run straight into their arms

262

but he didn't. He couldn't. He just stood their taking in the wondrous sight he'd desired all his life. His mum spoke again, smiling. "Well? Don't you recognize us Kenan. It's only been fifteen years."

"Of course I recognize you," choked Kenan. "But I- I can't-" he was stuck for what to say. Finally he managed to stutter: "I – I – oh my God I'm so sorry!" That was when he ran, full pelt towards them and collapsed in his mum's arms. He had vowed never to show his weaknesses to his parents had he ever the chance to see them again but now he was positively sobbing, half with happiness but half racked with a terrible guilt. When he eventually let go of his mum, he tried to hide his reddened eyes as he looked at his dad. His dad who hadn't said a word to him so far, said the words Kenan had always wanted to hear from him:

"You've made us so proud." A second after he said this however, Kenan felt awful.

"How?" he muttered. "All I've managed to do is mess things up from the word go. I got you two killed, managed to live fifteen years longer by stealing off decent people and…and-" Kenan's mum exchanged glances with her husband before looking Kenan in the face.

"It doesn't matter what's happened in the past," she whispered, "but you are wrong about one thing Kenan."

"What?"

"It wasn't your fault."

"Yes it is!" exclaimed Kenan. "If I hadn't been up there…"

"You weren't," interrupted his dad. "Come on son, you've got a brain. How could a one year old make it up to the top level of a multi story car park? No, you weren't up there Kenan… someone else was."

"And they- they're the reason you're not… here… anymore?" Both his parents nodded.

"Wait a second," muttered Kenan. "Is this any of this actually real?"

"As real as the earth itself," replied his dad. "This dimension is only different to the other by the tiniest fraction. That's why the living can't see or hear us."

"So what you're telling me is true?" pressed on Kenan, as the words his dad had said began to sink in. "So who *is* responsible for you guys not being there whenever I needed you?"

"We were always there Kenan. Whether you knew it or not, we've always been near, but we can't tell you who is responsible."

"Why?"

"Remember what the dragon told you," said his mum. "Information taken from this world into the world of the living could have drastic consequences..."

"But I'm not going back to the world of the living," sighed Kenan.

"Aren't you?" Kenan stared at her.

"Wait! You mean... I can...?"

"Come now Kenan," said his dad, " With what you've seen and witnessed over the past few days, I thought you of all people would have known anything's possible, but there are several factors you can consider here. Firstly, you are at the moment, at the point where you can still go back, this doesn't always happen. It didn't for your mother nor me, but you being here means that destiny has ruptured somewhere. Sometimes we have one path before us, we live it and follow it until we die, but sometimes powerful untapped forces come into play, the path will rupture and split, before joining back together. You've made no decision to stay with us or stay back there, you are, for want of a better expression, in limbo, you can still choose what happens."

"Secondly," his mum continued, "are you aware of the last word you said?" Kenan thought hard.

"Naz? That's Naomi's nickname," he added.... "it was just a spur of the moment thing really."

"And in that one little word," said his mum quietly, "You used the last breath you took, for the name of someone you care for when you could have tried calling for help to save yourself." Kenan blushed at this.

"And lastly," said his dad. "Kenan, you saved the world. Need I go on? If anyone on this earth deserved another chance it would be you."

"You *have* been watching me," exclaimed Kenan.

"We've never left your side," said his mum, "we were there with you and we're going to carry on being there for you even if you can't see us." Kenan's head had never felt clearer! Finally everything was falling into place.

"So that was you... this morning... I heard you!" he exclaimed as he realised. His parents nodded. Kenan smiled. He hadn't been going crazy at all- he should have known it was them all along. But he realised that he had a choice to make and it had to be made soon. He looked longingly at his mum and dad.

"I've waited so long," he whispered. "I - I don't want to lose you again," he was ashamed to feel his eyes filling up for a second time. He looked at the ground quickly but the next second he felt his mum put both her arms around him and embrace him tightly.

"My boy," she murmured as Kenan finally let the tears fall. "My brave, brave boy. You never lost us, and you never will... whenever you feel lost or angry just talk to us, we'll be there... always." Kenan looked behind him, back at the real world... back at Naomi still crying quietly next to his own body. He made up his mind.

"I have to go back," he muttered. "I can't leave her like this." He buried is head in his mum's shoulder as he hugged her one last time. He didn't want to let go, he simply didn't think he could find the strength within him to do so, but as the image of Naomi flashed through his mind he knew he had to... he had a promise to keep. Finally letting go, Kenan looked at his dad for a goodbye but instead his dad simply reached out and hugged him as well. Then whispered so only Kenan could hear:

"That girl's a stunner Kenan. You go for it." He winked as he pulled away and Kenan winked back. His mum kissed him on the forehead before saying:

"Next time we see you here you'd better be much older do you understand?"

Kenan nodded.

"Now close your eyes and focus." said his dad. "Focus on life, focus on breathing, let it fill you up and when you open your eyes again you will be back... trust me." Kenan nodded again.

"I love you," he murmured as the image of his parents started to fade. Just before they completely disappeared, he heard both their voices in the wind.

"We love you too son, we'll be watching..." He swallowed hard before turning to face his own body. He closed his eyes and wished upon hope that it would work, focusing harder with every second... Suddenly, feeling began surging through him. Once again he felt the hard ground beneath him, Naomi's hand holding his, and something else... a heartbeat! He could scarcely believe it - he was alive! He could feel the muscles in his hand tense as he dared to move it. His eyes flickered. He opened them a fraction and saw Naomi still sitting there.

"Please Kenan," she was whispering. "I'd give anything just please... don't leave me. Y-You can't be dead. You just can't be. I need you Kenan...I love you."

"You really mean that Naz?"

"Wha-?" As if waking up from a deep sleep, Kenan looked up at her. Naomi was thunderstruck.

"What's up?" smiled Kenan. "Looks like you've seen a ghost or heard one."

"Wha-?"

"I mean I've been called many things but a figment of imagination?" He slowly pulled himself up into a sitting position and laughed at Naomi's face. "Hey," he said softy. "It's okay... it's really me." As she stared Naomi's look of shock turned into one of relief and before she knew it, she had thrown her arms back around him in a hug that sent him back to the ground. "Hey, watch it," said Kenan wearily, as Naomi stayed where she was both hands flat on the ground, either side of his head so she was leaning over him. "I still feel pretty fragile here," he sighed.

"Sorry," whispered Naomi helping him back up. "I'm just so glad you're okay, I thought I really had lost you." They were both quiet for a minute before Kenan said.

"You didn't answer my question, did you really mean what you said when I came round?" Naomi looked at him.

"Yeah," she replied quietly. "Pretty much."

"Well," Kenan muttered feeling his cheeks burn up, "well, see the thing is Naz..." *oh come on!* a voice in his head shouted, *as if it's not obvious already!* He cleared his throat... "I... I love... you... too." He was spared having to say anything more, as he felt Naomi's hand still holding his. She leaned forward and gently kissed him quickly. She turned away to hide a smile but she knew Kenan was looking at her. "My turn?" he smiled. It was moment they had both fought against for so long, but now neither of them held back. All arguments, disagreements and social status were forgotten as Kenan gently bought Naomi's face round to his, leaned in and finally, without hesitation they both kissed... and this time for much longer.

Naomi was first to pull away but she rested her head on Kenan's shoulder still muttering to God not to let it be a dream. Kenan's mind, however was beginning to remember, clearer than ever, things that had happened over the past few days right up to that minute. Images like snapshots or stills from a film were filling his head, and with each one he became angrier. It was all so obvious now. *Why* had he let them make a fool of him so easily? Naomi felt him tense.

"You okay?" she asked.

"Yeah," muttered Kenan. "It's just, I need some answers to things that have been bugging me, not from you he added looking at Naomi's anxious face I can get all I need to know from one person."

"Who?"

"Damien." Kenan glowered as he said the name.

"Damien?" echoed Naomi. "Why him?" Kenan turned to look at her.

"Because," he said, his voice barely above a whisper, "he was the one driving the taxi." Naomi's eyes widened.

"What?" she whispered in disbelief. "But... but I don't... understand..."

"It was definitely him," murmured Kenan. "And I tell you

something else Naz, he knew exactly what he was doing. I saw his face... he *meant* to hit me." Naomi sat there stunned. From her brief encounter with Damien and what she heard about him, she, found it very easy to believe, but the fact that he had been so cold about it, so determined, before fleeing the scene... it just showed how evil he really was and how far he'd go to achieve his goals.

"Kenan, look," she began at last. "I'm not telling you what to do but I wouldn't go after him just yet. He'll be on his guard now more than ever and ready to counter attack."

"Yeah," nodded Kenan. "You're right. After all," he let the words slip out of his mouth without thinking, "I promised my mum I wouldn't see her again until I was a lot older." Naomi stared at him.

"Your mum?" she whispered. "You mean... you saw your parents?" Kenan nodded. For a second, he looked as if he regretted coming back but Naomi continued talking.

"Did they speak to you?" Kenan nodded again. "What did they say?" asked Naomi.

"Well, for one," sighed Kenan. "I now know that their deaths weren't my fault. They didn't tell me who was responsible. That, I've got to find out for myself, and was one the reasons I came back."

"What did I tell you?" exclaimed Naomi in the ultimate 'I told you so,' tone of voice, though truthfully she was just as pleased that Kenan was no longer drowning in guilt. "Any other reasons?" She asked. Kenan looked at her.

"I'd have thought that one was obvious," he smiled. Naomi just reached forward when:

"Kenan! Oh Wow! You're okay!"

"Guys!" cried Kenan eagerly. Matt, Sam, and the twins came running up followed by a very puffed out but relieved looking Cedric.

"You survived!" exclaimed Matt. "I can't believe you actually made it."

"What you don't know can't hurt you," his friend muttered.

"What do you mean?" asked Sam. Kenan sighed. They

were his best and oldest friends after all. It would be wrong
not to tell them. So he explained as quickly as he could what
happened, though he was careful to leave out a lot of stuff his
parents had said… that was after all between him and them.
Afterwards though, he wished he hadn't told them, everyone,
looked pale and afraid.

"Whoa," muttered Nick, "that just doesn't seem possible,
any of it… I do believe you," he added quickly. "But jeez…
you've got some courage…"

"Yeah," interrupted Kenan, obviously wanting to move off
the subject. "Look we'll talk about it another time. That's
what's happened; now we need to think of what's-going-to-
happen."

"What do you mean what's-going-to-happen?" exclaimed
Matt. "That's obvious we stay the hell away from Damien and
let him get on with it. We obviously can't let him see Kenan
either…"

"I disagree," said a small voice. Everyone turned to face
Lia who was speaking. She clearly hated being the centre of
attention as she was shaking a little but the words she spoke
were as clear as crystal. "It's obvious Damien was always
dangerous but today he has proved he is nothing less than evil.
We all swore to help Kenan save the world but if we run away
we'll be doing exactly what he wants us to do, give up without
a fight. Well I say, we give him a fight and make him sorry for
everything he's done!" There was a silence after this stirring
speech then Nick exclaimed:

"That's it! We'll run him out of the city, the country even,
and get rid of him once and for all!" Sam eagerly agreed but
Matt and Naomi were still looking nervous. Kenan didn't
know what to do. He desperately wanted to find out what
Damien was playing at but then again, it would only take a
second for the madman to fire a gun at him, and Kenan
strongly doubted he *wouldn't* have a weapon on him.

"I think we should ask Kenan what he wants to do," said
Naomi but as she spoke she saw a small glimmer in his eye
and she was almost certain of the answer he would give them.

"I say we do it," muttered Kenan. Matt swallowed hard

and Naomi closed her eyes sighing shakily. "Let's show that psycho we're not scared of him," continued Kenan. He was still sitting on the ground but his face showed determination that gave all of them, even Naomi, a great feeling of hope.

"Kenan! Kenan! Oh thank God your okay!" Everyone turned around. Terry and Delia were running full pelt towards him. "I saw it all from my apartment!" wheezed Terry. "It's taken us all this time to get here and-"

"You sound surprised?" shouted Naomi leaping to her feet. "You knew this would happen and you sound surprised?" Terry looked confused but annoyed to.

"He's here though, isn't he?" he snapped back.

"Naomi just leave it," said Kenan, rubbing his eyes hard. "Just help me up okay?" Casting one of her evil glances at a very bewildered looking Terry, Naomi took Kenan's outstretched hand and helped him shakily to his feet. It took him a few seconds to stand without support, but he managed it.

"Whoa," said Matt quietly, "you fell all that way and you can still stand up?" Kenan smiled.

"Some miracles do happen," he said, "and I had some help." He glanced upwards at the sky that was now, though calmer, gradually turning darker. "Okay mum and dad," he muttered under his breath. "I won't let you down this time."

Chapter Thirty

It was only early afternoon when Kenan and the group began to make their way back at the car park, but you would have thought the darkest night was closing in on them. Heavy rain clouds were hanging ominously over their heads and the mugginess of the weather was not helped by the lack of wind. On the way back, they had seen hardly anyone on the streets except thieves who were taking advantage of abandoned shops and vehicles.

"I think everyone's still afraid to come out," whispered Lia.

"What I want to know," said Naomi "is why an earthquake happened when the world was supposed to be saved." Terry cleared his throat nervously.

"It's just like the spirit said to Kenan," explained Terry. "The three of them feed off each others strength of heart and spirit. I don't know what happened, Kenan, but you must have felt something that somehow triggered a failure or weakness within them. Maybe you did something without even knowing…" Kenan had already worked it out and he exchanged a glance with Naomi and judging by the look on her face she had also worked it out… it was their argument. Kenan had never felt so low and guilty as he had done then… and Terry was right, it had indeed made the spirits temporarily weaker. He looked up at the sky, hopefully the worst was over… for now.

"It doesn't matter what's happened in the past," said Kenan, "all that matters now is we have to deal with the future now and get through it together."

When they finally reached the car park, which took longer than usual because Kenan had to keep taking a short break every now and then, the sky above them was black and the air was eerily still.

Kenan signalled to everyone to crawl towards some wooden crates that were a few yards from the building and stay there while they came up with a plan. Everyone obeyed and cautiously, one by one peeped over the boxes trying to see if it was safe or not. The scene in front of them was not a welcome one. Kenan, Matt, Sam and the twins felt especially betrayed as friends of their parents as well as a group of people they didn't know, were gathered around talking amongst themselves, evidently waiting for someone, most likely Damien. The people who they did not recognize were clad in leather jackets and tatty jeans with heavy looking boots on. They were also carrying weapons, lots of weapons. Upon seeing this, Kenan and the group ducked back down behind the old boxes.

"We so need a plan right now," groaned Matt.

"I say the head on approach," growled Sam, "let's just go in fists first… we can take 'em!"

"No," said Kenan. "No more people get hurt today. We need to find Damien. He's the one who can give us some answers, not these guys."

Before anyone else could move, something else happened about halfway up the car park: lightning struck the wall of the building and it crumbled away. The storm was now overhead but was obviously yet to break. Kenan suddenly lifted his head as he heard that cold unmistakable voice shout:

"What was that?"

He's on the fifth level, Kenan thought to himself. *At least we know where to look.*

"Okay," he said rounding on the others, "you guys go and get Vicky and whoever else in on our side. I'm going to look for Damien."

"Please be careful Kenan," whispered Naomi. Kenan smiled at her in re- assurance but didn't reply, he had too much to worry about now. He made his way up to the fifth floor and crept around in the semi darkness. As he walked, he saw boxes and piles of dynamite but he couldn't worry too much about this yet. His main priority was to find Damien get him to answer the questions he had planned, and run him out… but he knew it wouldn't work like that. What Kenan didn't notice was that hidden cameras were also in use to check the building was completely empty before its

272

demolition. Right now various images of himself and the others were being sent to the police station and authorities were already on their way, they could not only see the people scurrying around but hear them as well and it wasn't long, before they and Kenan heard Damien's voice roar out.

"VICKY!" Hiding behind a post, Kenan peeped out as from the shadows Vicky appeared, and walked up to Damien. She looked awful, her eyes bloodshot from tears and her hair a tangled mess where she had run her hands through it so many times in grief.

"What do you want?" she muttered wearily.

"Are you ready yet?" snapped Damien.

"No," said Vicky. "Damien-" her voice shook a little, "I'm not going with you ... I don't think I could stand it."

"What?" growled Damien. "You're ditching me? After all I've done for you?"

"After all you've done!" exclaimed Vicky. "You've been a member of this stupid little gang of yours for too long. The only money you earn is through drug dealing and killing people, and now after murdering the kid I took in and raised... you want me to live with you? No way Damien! Absolutely no way! I've waited years for this, a chance to report you to the police, you can come after me now, you can kill me. I don't care. My only interest was to protect him!" She laughed in his face, a touch of hysteria in evidence. "You've just got rid of your trump card, Damien. Your get out jail free card. Didn't bargain on that did we? Didn't bargain on your own stupidity-!" She was cut off as Damien swung a punch at Vicky's face. She was caught with a full force and she went tumbling to the ground! Kenan, who had been getting angrier and angrier through this conversation, now ran out from his hiding place. A gasp ran round the audience but he ignored them and went straight to Vicky's side. She was holding a hand over her eye and painfully pulling herself up. She looked towards him and stared.

"Kenan?" She whispered.

"Yeah it's me," he smiled.

"B-but I saw you…" stuttered Vicky. "Are you really alive?"

"As ever."

"How? I don't understand," Vicky was close to tears but Kenan gave her a hug and whispered:

"It doesn't matter - I'm back."

"Kenan? Y-You…" Damien who had been staring at the scene clearly unable to believe his eyes was slowly allowing himself to take it in. Then with an air of great fake relief he ran towards him. "I swore it was you," he exclaimed "but I couldn't see properly… it was too late to turn…" Kenan stood up and strangely feeling a lot braver than he meant to, walked towards Damien.

"One reason not to kill you!" he snarled. Damien held his hands up and backed away as Kenan forced him further away from his cronies.

"Now, now Kenan. L- listen to me? I know what this is all about… I was only prepared to take over if I was sure you were…. Well, I don't know how to start…."

"You don't need to," said Kenan. "If you know the law passed a hundred years ago, you'll know that I, Kenan Wheeler, am the rightful King of England as from when you killed Lance." He stopped as Damien's eyes widened and another gasp followed by murmuring ran round the group behind them.

"Ah well yes, you know me Kenan," spluttered Damien. "I personally would be only too glad to let you take over, but you see you are barely sixteen years old and it's a matter of what the public think at the end of the day isn't it?"

"We're the public," said another voice. Naomi was speaking. She had her arms folded and Vicky now stood beside her and behind them was the rest of the group, including Cedric and Delia, and several more people with them. "And we think Kenan could do the job ten times better than you." Damien's eyes narrowed. He walked over and faced Naomi.

"And what if he had some difficult decision to make," he growled. "What if something horrible happened?" He continued to grin maliciously. "Would you really risk losing him again? Just after losing your father to? I think you're being a little selfish about all this – Naz!"

"That's enough," said Kenan stepping up behind him. "Either step down or I'll personally push you aside. You've heard your options Damien now choose one, very, very carefully."

"Now, now Kenan. Must we resort to threats and violence?" sneered Damien clearly not choosing to leave without trouble. "I'd just hate to feel responsible for someone's death, wouldn't you Kenan? With enough on your plate already."

"You're a liar," snarled Kenan as Damien slowly walked round him, almost looking like he was studying him. At the word 'liar,' Damien's eyebrows rose but his cold expression didn't change.

"What did you call me?" he asked softly.

"A LIAR!" shouted Kenan. "You lied about my parent's death. Even if I don't know who killed them I, at least, know it wasn't me!"

"Then why accuse *me* of lying to you when you can't even prove your *own* innocence?" exclaimed Damien, turning around and advancing menacingly towards Kenan forcing him away from everyone. The two gangs followed them, out of everyone, Naomi was nearest. Damien was still yelling. "You can't even prove you're Kenan Wheeler without a D.N.A test and you can hardly afford that can you?" He was walking slowly but menacingly towards him, still forcing him to walk backwards. Kenan was unaware of how close they were getting to the open wall of the car-park that had been destroyed by the lightning, until someone shouted:

"Watch it!"

"Wha-?" With a single swift movement, Naomi jumped towards them to try and to stop her friend falling... but was seconds too late, Kenan lost his footing at the exact same time Naomi dived behind him and an effort to stop him. As Kenan fell against her, they both began to fall but with one hand Kenan made a wild grab onto the side of the building, with his other hand he held onto Naomi tightly. Damien stood over them as lightning illuminated the horrific scene to all watching; most of Kenan's group was too stunned to move. Damien sniggered. He couldn't resist the irony of the moment.

"Well, well, well," he gloated as he picked Kenan up by the wrist and held him at arm's length. "I believe I'm experiencing deja-vu, don't you Kenan? You see this is exactly how your parents looked before they both died."

Kenan's eyes narrowed as the words began to sink in, but in less than a second later, Damien had let go of Kenan's wrist, thrown him and Naomi higher in the air and caught Kenan by the throat as they came down! Struggling for breath as he tried to loosen the grip around his throat with his free hand, Kenan was lifted closer to Damien then heard him whisper. "Now I'm going to kill you, the same way I killed them!"

A flashback hidden for fifteen years from Kenan suddenly replayed in his mind. Repressed for all this time, Damien's cruel words had at long last brought it all back in vivid clarity. He remembered seeing his parents fall, their terrified faces, the screams…it was all crystal clear. But that wasn't all that was happening. A kind of explosion felt like it had taken place. Hurt, guilt, betrayal, hate, every bad feeling he had ever experienced came flooding from him. A second before Damien could let go, Kenan lashed out first with his free arm, his hand clenched in a tight fist, which he aimed at Damien's stomach as hard as he could. Winded, the villain stumbled backwards taking Kenan and Naomi with him. The second Kenan felt the ground below his feet, he glanced to see if Naomi was okay then jumped to his feet in a second. He barely knew what he was doing. Striking Damien had only been the start of his rage, now Kenan wanted to hurt him; as much as he could he didn't care about the consequences anymore. Damien was still scrabbling backwards, using his hands and feet, but now he was afraid. He had never seen Kenan so angry. Hitting an old oil drum out of his way Kenan advanced on Damien. The oil spilled everywhere and dangerously near the explosives but Kenan no longer cared. Lifting Damien up with one hand, he placed the other round the collar of his coat and forced him against an abandoned old car.

"IT *WAS* YOU!" he yelled.

"K-Kenan," gasped Damien.

"You killed them and blamed me! You killed Tony, didn't you? And George Henderson and tried to kill Matt and myself! It was all you wasn't it!" Damien whimpered. Kenan tightened his grip on Damien as the groups, especially Naomi and Terry, looked on. They knew the madman had been involved with their loved ones murders but had he directly killed them? "ANSWER ME!" screamed Kenan.

"Alright," choked Damien, "Alright. Yes I killed them…every one of them! But don't think I enjoyed it Kenan," a sickly smile had appeared back on his face as he finished, "they were all way too easy!" It took one look from him to get his henchmen to rush at Kenan. Freed from his grasp, Damien slipped away as all Kenan's gang helped their friend back on his feet. A huge fight ensued in the confusion a cigarette end was thrown in the oil and it flared up but thankfully the explosives were a little too far off to be affected. No one knew who was fighting whom that night. Even Nick and Lia were helping to keep Damien's cronies away from their friend. Terry was the only one who stayed out of the action and he slipped away down the stair well as the police arrived

"You need to find him," he exclaimed. "Kenan Wheeler! He's gone after Damien. We all know what that man is capable of!" The police officer nodded. Using a monitor in their van, they scanned every screen in the building before coming to the very last one, and then saw who they were looking for. Kenan, who was scanning wildly for Damien caught sight of him as lightning lit up everything for a second, he was running towards the stairwell and Kenan took chase. Damien ran to the top level of the building but upon reaching it realised he was trapped. He whirled around in a panic and took from his pocket, a small grey ball, and threw it to the ground. It sent up a cloud of thick smoke. Damien sniggered, thinking his enemy had lost him, but then his eyes reflected

terror as he saw Kenan reach the same level and walk slowly
through the smoke towards him, a look of thunder in his eyes.

"Kenan please…" whined Damien. With no thugs and no
Lance to back him up, he was cowering like a frightened dog.

"I should kill you," snarled Kenan still advancing slowly
towards him. "Don't think I wouldn't do it... believe me
Damien, nothing would give me greater pleasure!"

"K- kill me?" whimpered Damien. "You surely... don't
mean that. It wasn't even my fault, it was all Lance's idea… it
just got out of hand, I swear…"

"Liar," whispered Kenan, now face to face with his
enemy. The floor, five stories down, was now belching out
more smoke and flames, which rose upwards to where
Damien and Kenan were giving an eerie affect. At the bottom
of the building, the police, and Kenan's friends with the
absence of Naomi followed the scene on the police screens
with baited breath.

"What are you doing?" exclaimed Sam to the police
officer next to her, "get up there and help him!"

"We can't do that until the fire service get here and they're
on their way," he replied. "With the explosives in that
building we have to keep a safe distance."

"We can't just sit here!" cried Lia. "The whole building
could go at any moment and he's still..."

"Which is the exact reason, we can't go in there." said the
officer firmly but gently. Lia looked at Matt, Sam and Nick.

"We've got to do something!" she whispered desperately.
Glancing back at the monitor, they heard Kenan who was still
talking to Damien.

"You told me nothing but filthy lies to cover up your own
actions," he glowered, "and I'll tell you something else I
worked out as well." Damien swallowed hard, his face was
pale, he was truly too scared to move. Kenan continued, "It
took you two attempts to kill Lance's father, didn't it? You
see I figured it out. The first time you tried it, my parents
caught onto your plan. They gave you a choice: To leave,
forever, or they'd rat you out… only because they weren't
treacherous pieces of scum like you, even suspecting your plot

they *still* gave you a chance. However, giving you this chance put you in their debt. When they were called up they gave me to you, trusting you to take care of me, but twisted with jealousy, you took me and killed them... and you were supposed to be their friend?" He continued to look at Damien who slowly nodded. "They trusted you," Kenan murmured. His face was stained with blood from the events of the day, but this was now mixed with tears of rage that were streaming down his face. Never in his life had he hated anyone as much as Damien. White-hot anger had been boiling up inside him throughout his speech and now he could do nothing else but scream aloud; "THEY TRUSTED YOU!" Damien didn't reply, he was defeated and he knew it. Down below on the ground Matt silently left the group.

"Where are you going?" hissed Sam. Matt turned and looked at her.

"To help my best friend," he muttered. "These guys clearly aren't going to do anything Sam. I don't know where Naomi's gone either. I've got a horrible feeling she's somewhere in there to." Sam went to say something else but was interrupted as she heard Damien's voice on the monitors.

"Please Kenan," he squeaked. "Please don't kill me." Kenan looked down at him for a minute before saying quietly.

"I don't intend to, Damien. I'm not like some people in this world." Damien managed a relieved smile.

"Oh, Kenan thank you," he grovelled. "Thank you so much Ke- no, no, Your Royal Highness. I am forever in your debt I just..." Kenan held up his hand and there was a long daunting silence. He whispered something as he remembered above all the other things Damien had done to them, the red hand mark around Naomi's wrist.

"You hurt a lot of people Damien. Terry, Vicky, Matt, even me, but your last mistake was when you hurt Naomi. No-one hurts my friends and absolutely no-one hurts HER. I made a promise to her dad... it's like he knew what you were planning." He paused as he managed a smile, "funny the way things turn out isn't it? I'm still here and as long as I am, you won't ever touch her again, I guarantee that." Damien nodded shakily. He went to say something but stopped as Kenan lent an inch from his face and whispered:

"Now get out."

"What-?"

"You heard me. Run away. Leave. However you want to take it. Get out of the city, out of the country if you can, because now, Damien, everyone knows who you are and what you've done, and if you so much as glance back I'll see to it you won't be able to move ever again." Damien was dumbstruck. He stared at Kenan for one long minute before he slowly moved, hands in his pockets as he began to slink away.

"Of course," he muttered. "Who am I to argue with the King anyway?" He turned round looking at Kenan over his shoulder. "Before I go," he said quietly. "I have something here I should have given you long ago." Kenan glared at him. He didn't want to believe Damien but something in his brain moved his feet towards him. Damien took something out of his pocket clenched in a fist... and the next second Kenan felt himself punched, then kicked to the ground. In an iron like grip, he was dragged up by his neck, towards the edge of the building. But also he heard something else, a low whistle. Damien evidently heard it to because he stopped moving. As Kenan's vision cleared, he could make out and air-surfer flying, through the smoke, towards them, and riding atop it was Naomi. As she approached them she jumped off but the board carried on going. It struck Damien hard on the arm and he released his grip from Kenan. He made to strike Naomi but now aware of what Damien was trying to do, Kenan blocked it and hit Damien first. Teeth clenched, Damien knocked Kenan to the ground again and did the same to Naomi. This was too much for Kenan. As Damien pulled a knife from his jacket, Kenan leapt once again and the two of them fell over the side of the building! Still grappling, they both hit the edge of the lift some fifty feet down, rolled off, fell the rest of the way and hit the ground. Both lay there stunned. Miraculously, they had survived. Damien was first to move. He saw Kenan trying to pull himself to his feet and ran at him.

"It will be worth being locked up for life to see you dead!"

he screamed. Grabbing Kenan by his jumper, he forced him into the empty lift shaft and pushed a button for it to come down. He held onto Kenan who was now far too weak to fight back, and leered at him only inches from his face. "I'll tell you what I'm going to do after this," he hissed. "I'm going to kill every one of those friends of yours, and as for Naomi, I think she'd be better living in a life of constant fear and suffering, my only regret is that you won't be able to see me in control of her life. Oh what fun I'll have, and you Kenan, won't be here to see it, but don't worry, at least you get to be reunited with your parents in a few seconds... do say hi from me won't you."

"Tell them yourself!" Damien and Kenan both looked around to see Matt running towards them. He made to go towards Damien, but instead at the last minute, dragged Kenan from his grip and out from under the ever closer descending lift.

"And you," hollered Damien, "are the first on my list, to feel pain!" He went to run at them, but stopped. Something was holding him back... his long trench coat was tangled into the lift cables... and it was coming down towards him. "No," he muttered, slowly realizing what was happening. "No!" he yelled louder. He tried to pull the coat from the whirring cogs and wheels. He tried pull the coat off himself, only getting more entangled in the process all the time shouting; "No, help. Kenan! Please! Your parents, they would help me. I didn't mean - I only said – No wait! Stop! Someone save me!" But it was too late. No one could have reached Damien in time. The villain had bought about his own end. Kenan turned his head away and closed his eyes, trying to block out what was happening. Much as he hated Damien, he would have spared him.

High up on the fifth floor the flames made contact with the explosives and Kenan and Matt tried to shield themselves as chunks of the building crashed down around them.

Chapter Thirty-One

The storm had finally broken. Only minutes after the car park exploded, torrential rain poured down. Steam hissed from the hot debris and the last of the flames went out. Amongst all the confusion Naomi, who had had the brains to pick up the air-surfer she had borrowed as the building crumbled, made a shaky landing, as the others surrounded her.

"They caught everything on the monitors Naz!" shrieked Sam. "You and Kenan are innocent."

"But where is he?" asked Lia looking nervously round. A horrible realisation hit Sam as well.

"Oh my God!" she screamed. "Matt's in there somewhere too... he went to help!" As all of them looked at the huge pile of rubble, there was no sign of life at all.

"We've got try and find them," said Nick, voicing all their thoughts. Naomi suddenly had an idea. She punched a number onto her wristwatch and waited, a faint but distinctive ring sounded, somewhere near the top of the mound. As the group scrabbled to reach the top, a hand reached out of the debris and Matt heaved himself out.

"Guys! A little help here please!"

"Matt! What's going on?"

"I've got him! Got him before that madman did." Matt was pulling Kenan from the rubble and from what the others could see he was unconscious, or worse. Naomi immediately cut off the call. She was too afraid to move, what had happened earlier was replaying in her mind.

"C'mon man," muttered Matt trying to wake him. "You've done this once today... don't do it again."

"If you insist," mumbled Kenan, opening his eyes. Matt laughed with relief. He helped him to his feet as the others cheered. Helping him down the rubble, Matt took his time, to let Kenan find his footing. They both reached the bottom of the pile and immediately both boys were knocked down as Sam and Naomi hugged them both. Sam, for once, was in tears but Naomi wasn't. She was too happy that everything was finally sorted. Reporters, paramedics and the fire service began arriving and the scene though chaotic was somewhat that of a dream. It was over.

Hours later, Kenan and the others (others including Vicky and all his friends families) sat in the lobby of the police station. Most of Damien's followers had fled the scene when the first of the police cars turned up. Those that had dared to stay had been arrested, with several of them actually walking up to the police to give themselves up freely. Everyone had had to give a statement, and with the video surveillance from the car park, everything was backed up. Terry sat there quietly alone and Kenan walked over to him.

"What are you so down about?" he said. "You saved the world."

"*You* saved the world," sighed Terry. "And what have you got now? Not even a roof over your head."

"I've got everything I need over there," said Kenan gesturing to the large group of people. "What's more I don't want anything else…" But before he could say anything else, Naomi's mum and James came bursting into the room and made straight for Naomi.

"Where have you been?" shouted Audrey. "I've been back all evening and no phone call, message or anything." She gave her daughter a hug then in a quieter voice, muttered, "I'm glad you're safe but don't ever do that to me again. Where have you been these past two days?" It took a long time for Naomi, Kenan and the others to tell her all that had happened and by the time Lady Henderson had had time to take it all in, night had fallen and people were getting tired.

"I'd volunteer to put you all up for the night," said Terry but I can't. My flat just wouldn't take you all."

"You can stay for as long as you like in our house," said Naomi's mum. Everyone stared at her.

"There's more than enough room," she said, cheerfully "you've all made sure my daughter was kept safe the last few days so it's only fair. I am forever grateful." A very joyful evening ensued. Lady Henderson seemed to have had a complete personality change as she and James supplied the very hungry and tired group with food and drinks but soon, however, the events of the day caught up with them all too quickly and everyone turned in. Lady Henderson and James made sure everyone was sorted before finally checking in the main sitting room. Kenan and Naomi had fallen asleep next to each other, half sitting, half laying on one of the huge sofas, Naomi with her head on Kenan's shoulder. Audrey looked at them and smiled slightly as she saw her daughters hand interlinked with Kenan's. She turned to James. "Leave Kenan but make sure Naomi gets to bed, I need to make some important phone calls," and with that she whisked away. When she returned and hour and a half later she was smiling broadly. James was back downstairs cleaning up.

"All sorted?" he asked.

"Yes," said Audrey. "Sorted. Tomorrow's a big day for all of us."

When Kenan woke up early the next morning, he couldn't for the life of him think where he was, before the events of the previous day came flooding back and he groaned. It was still too much to take in. His head was pounding as it was, or was that someone pounding a door? He sat bolt upright and listened. Lady Henderson swept past him looking bright and bubbly.

"Good morning dear," she called. "Sleep well?" Kenan nodded still bewildered by the strange sequence of events. Lady Henderson stopped at the doorway. "Well, come on," she exclaimed. "We can't keep them waiting." Kenan jumped off the sofa and automatically followed her out to the hall. Terry was standing there to, smiling.

"Come on Kenan," he grinned. "We've got some place to go."

As they glided through London in the chauffer driven limo, Kenan, somehow, managed to not ask where they were going. Terry and Audrey were wearing mysterious smiles and were dressed in their best outfits. Kenan felt very scruffy when he looked at them so turned his attention to the window. He felt he knew this route but couldn't think where he had seen it before. It wasn't long till he knew. About an hour later they pulled up outside the gates of an office block; Damien's old offices. Inside police were everywhere. They were ransacking filing cabinets and bagging up huge files, a couple even had whole computers under their arms.

"It's going down all over the world Kenan," said Terry as two police officers stepped aside to let them pass. "There's enough evidence here to have put Damien *and* Lance away for life. You single-handedly uncovered possibly the biggest terrorist group and the most dangerous conspiracy ever." They went through a pair of glass double doors away from the scene of havoc to a quieter area. Terry nodded to another police officer who led them to a small room with very little in it except a desk and chair and a safe. Terry smiled. "Damien took a lot from you Kenan," he said quietly, "but he couldn't take everything. Turns out he didn't even know this stuff existed, he was so pre-occupied with taking over..." He handed Kenan a box. Kenan looked at him questioningly.

"Open it," encouraged the old man. Kenan did and when he lifted the lid his eyes lit up. It was from his parents. There were old photos, trinkets, a bracelet engraved with his mothers name and a signet ring that had clearly been his dad's. Kenan rifled through the box feeling like all his Christmases and birthdays had come at once. There was so much in here, so much stuff that no-one else would even think twice about keeping, but to Kenan it was like a box of pure gold. It was only when he reached the bottom of the box that he saw an envelope dated and sealed. It simply stated 'Kenan' on the back of it. Kenan opened it his hands trembling slightly then as he read through his jaw dropped and his eyes widened. He looked up at Terry who was now grinning broadly.

"An account," he managed to stutter. It was all he could say as he showed Terry the piece of paper.

"My my," said Terry as he read through. "Aren't we just a very wealthy young man?"

Kenan didn't think his head could swim any more than it was already. They were now back in the limo, speeding through London, and he was holding the box carefully on his lap. He could hardly believe it. He didn't even register where they were actually going at all until he saw Lady Henderson lean forward and speak quietly to the driver who had stopped outside a building surrounded by high railings and a gated entrance. From his seat in the back, he could just make out two guards who nodded as the driver wound down the window and spoke to them quietly. Then the gates swung open and Kenan found himself being driven towards the main doors. It was only when they got out did he realise... they were at Buckingham Palace! At the entrance, two more guards bowed and opened the doors for them. Kenan gasped and stopped short as they walked in. It was impossible to describe but it made Naomi's mansion look a joke, as for Terry's flat... well, it was incomparable.

"Well, what do you think?" said Terry. "Your new home!" Kenan found the power to speak.

"It- it's the most- it's the coolest thing I've ever seen!" he exclaimed happily.

"And just think!" exclaimed Audrey. "We're standing in the very hallway all the great royals have walked through, can you imagine it? Can't you feel the splendor of it all?" She was quite clearly in her element but the rest of her words fell on deaf ears as Kenan turned to Terry. He couldn't quite describe why but he felt guilty about all this. It had all happened so quickly.

"It's amazing," he muttered to Terry, "but I can't live here. I just don't feel right and after all I'm not the King yet, not officially."

"Well, what do you think the coronation's for?" grinned Terry. "We've got to get you ready." Kenan blinked.

"Huh?"

"The coronation," repeated Terry impatiently. "It takes place exactly a week from today, it's all been arranged." Kenan went to say something else but Terry had interrupted him again. "Have you forgotten Kenan? For fifteen years you have been 'missing' but the whole world knew you were supposed to be on the throne before you yourself figured it out and now we need to let them see they were right. Let them see the kind of person that Lance truly was. Let them see you, the person we all know you were meant to be, the person we all know you can be... the person you are."

"But I-"

"No 'buts'" exclaimed Lady Henderson. She knelt till she was level with Kenan. "I know it all seems a bit strange," she said. "But I also know you'll find it natural after a while."

"Even if I don't know the first thing about running a country?" They were on the move again. "Even if I can hardly read... or write!"

"Oh we can soon sort that out," exclaimed Terry, "and you'll have people to help you. You're the King of England, Kenan!" Terry's words rang in his ears all that day. He didn't know why he was so afraid. When he had been younger he and the others used to say what they'd do with all the money they could posses. Now here he was with riches beyond his imagination but he didn't have a clue what to do with it. What was worse was that he knew there were a thousand things he could do with it.

*

"Man, Kenan! You're still moaning? I thought that was my job."

"Matt's right," exclaimed Sam. "This is your dream come true Kenan. Stop freaking about it."

"I'm not freaking," said Kenan. "It's just well look, last week was my birthday and we were living on the streets. Tonight's my coronation yeah MY coronation and..." he trailed off. Never in a million years would he have guessed he would have said those words but he had... and they were true. "Anyway," he carried on, "I mean did you ever guess we'd all be living in Buckingham Palace, even if it's just for a while? I certainly didn't!"

"What do you mean just for a while?" asked Nick.

"Well, it's just until the new one is built."

"The new one?" said Naomi. "But where? Why?"

"I'm not quite sure where yet," said Kenan thoughtfully,

"but I can't live in this one you know. Everything in it reminds me of Lance and Damien... we all need to forget them.

"So what's happening with this one?" asked Naomi.

"I'll keep it open," said Kenan. "They still do public tours now and again. Not all of it though he continued. "Part of it's going to be the centre of operations for a new organisation. That's where part of the admission fees will go as well."

"What organisation?" exclaimed Matt.

Kenan took a deep breath. "We're going to get people off the streets," he said, a determined expression in his eyes. "We're going to help out the homeless, and those who need it most, everyone else society has given up on... just like they did to us. I'm going to change that once and for all." This was greeted by a round of applause.

"That's gonna be great!" exclaimed Matt. "Can I have a job there huh? Can I have a room there too? En-suite bathroom please!"

"No way!" exclaimed Kenan grinning. "You guys are living with me in the new one!" Everyone stared at him. "Well come on guys," Kenan continued. "You can't expect me to leave you lot just like that can you? Like I said this is too much for me. You can all have a wing of the new palace to yourselves and families." Kenan didn't quite know why everyone was looking so shocked. It wasn't as if he had never thought of sharing a big place with them. Now even Buster looked surprised.

"Kenan," said Matt finally. "You are the best!"

"You said it!" joined in Lia.

"I tell you something," said Delia. "It'll be cool when it's finally built. You can design it however you want.

"And we've got to have a pool," cut in Matt. "With gold - no - platinum tiles all around it." At once everyone erupted in what they wanted done with the palace, all except Kenan. He stood up and looked out of the window, staring into space. So many things had happened in the past week, so quickly, it was surreal. Naomi walked over to him and put her hands on his shoulders.

"I know it feels weird," she whispered. "But you'll be fine. I know you will!" Kenan turned around to face her.

"I'm not so sure though," he muttered. "What if I'm not cut out for this Naz?"

"You are," she whispered. "Trust me and more importantly, trust yourself." Quickly, making sure no one was looking, she gave him a kiss on the cheek and smiled.

"Thanks Naz," smiled back Kenan.

"Kenan!" exclaimed Delia who was looking out of another window.

"Grandpa and Audrey are back with some new clothes for tonight. Come on let's see how you look!"

Later that afternoon, Kenan peeped out from behind a curtain and looked outside at the crowds beyond the gates. His stomach turned over. He wished more than anything that the ceremony was still taking place at Westminster Abbey. *That's where they used to be held,* he thought miserably. Though he knew the real reason he thought this was, because he knew that he could have possibly escaped. But no, it was taking place in the palace. Everyone had come to him... after the coronation, he knew he would have to go out onto the balcony and possibly make some sort of speech to them, and the millions watching all over the world! Down below, he could vaguely pick out the sound of people gathering in the main hall. All his friends had gone to get ready. With his stomach still churning, he turned away from the window and looked at himself in the mirror one last time. He had to admit the clothes were a perfect fit, a dark suit and a brush through his hair (that he had refused to even have trimmed) was defiantly all he needed. Lady Henderson had arranged the whole thing properly, all the V.I.P people had been driven or flown in, the tables in the dining hall groaned under the weight of food and drink, and everyone had been bought a special outfit but he, Kenan, had had a range to choose from. It was as he stood there getting used to the feel of the suit, he saw the reflection of someone else standing in the doorway. He turned around sharply.

"Hey relax, it's only me," laughed Naomi. Kenan sighed. He was still jumpy it would take more than a few days to get all the stress and tension out of his system.

"Are they ready?" he guessed. Naomi nodded.

"Ready and waiting. I'll go down now, you follow in a minute." Glancing at Kenan's nervous face her smile faded. She cleared her throat. "You know most people in your position would definitely be a little happier about this," she said gently. Kenan half smiled.

"Would they?" he muttered. Naomi didn't answer, she was a little taken aback but waited for Kenan to explain. He walked over to the window, looked out over the palace grounds and continued. "I don't know Naz, it's just me. Maybe, I'm the most ungrateful person ever to walk the earth but... I don't want this." He turned to look at her. "I never wanted it. You know that."

"How can you be sure?" she whispered. "I know it's a big change but..."

"A big change?" exclaimed Kenan. "Naomi, it's huge. I can't get my head round this no matter how hard I try."

"Considering what you've been through in the past few weeks, that's quite extraordinary," said Naomi a faint smile on her face.

"What we've all been through." Kenan reminded her. He turned to look at her. "You, Matt, Sam, everyone. I couldn't have done it without you and I'll never forget it." Naomi remained silent as he looked back out through the glass.

"It's your decision," she said at last, "only you can make it."

"I know what I want," he replied quietly, "but is it the right thing?" He looked back at her, somewhere his eyes were pleading with her, almost as if he wanted her to make the choice for him. "Is it the right thing to do?" he whispered.

"Ask yourself what's in your heart," she said finally. And that's when Kenan remembered the words from the prophecy, 'the most difficult of decisions' that he now faced, but more than ever before the line that he had tried to follow over and over again: 'Search within your soul, for the answers and you

will not fail, for they will be the right ones...'
Ever since he had read it, ever since that fateful day when
Naomi had revealed the true extent of what they were up
against, he had tried to follow it. Sure, it had got him in
trouble and he'd made a few slip ups along the way, but it had
got them to where they were. They had survived, they had
won. How could he go against that now? How could he ignore
the one answer screaming at him inside his head? He looked
back at Naomi, who smiled back. "You know you'll make the
right choice," she whispered as she walked over to him and
put her arms around him, "and whatever it is," she added
hurriedly as he went to interrupt, "I'll stand by you."

"Kenan? Kenan man we gotta go, everyone's waiting."
Matt knocked on the door after being sent upstairs to find the
guest of honour. There was no answer. "Kenan?" repeated
Matt opening the door slightly. "Naomi?" Only silence
answered him. "Come on you guys, the joke's over, they're
waiting..." He trailed off. It was too quiet, too still, they
weren't there. He was just about to turn and leave when he
noticed something bundled into a corner behind the door...
Kenan's suit. Completely confused, Matt checked the gigantic
wardrobe... all of Kenan's suits were there, every single one,
in fact the only thing missing was his jeans and t-shirt... Matt
scratched his head unable to make head or tail of it all. It was
as he closed the wardrobe that he noticed something on the
glass table nearby. It was a note, and what caught his eye the
most was his name was written on it. He picked it up. He
recognised the scrawled hurried writing immediately, it was
from Kenan and read:
Matt,

*I knew you'd be the one to find this, you always know
where to look to find me, but not this time. I have made a
decision and it does not involve taking the throne. I just can't.
You remember when we used to live on the streets and say if
we had all the money we could dream of, I never thought that
it could be a reality and now that it is, I don't want it. The last*

few days I have learned so much more, about friendship, life and freedom and that is what I choose. Money makes you wealthy, it doesn't necessarily make you rich. We have all seen enough death and bloodshed over the throne and it has made me realise I'm just not ready. Maybe someone, older, wiser would be better suited... maybe someone like Terry? So yeah, I am leaving for a little while, I'll come back, and one day, maybe, I will be ready to take on the responsibility, but not yet, I never realised but I had all along what I want now and that is freedom. So until we meet again Matt, take care.

Kenan

Matt read the letter, and re-read it three times. At first he didn't quite know was emotion was right for the moment and it was another full minute before he started laughing. He didn't know why he chose to do it and didn't care. He just laughed and laughed. Then he ran, He ran from the room, down the hallway and down the stairs, and he knew why he was laughing. Kenan had stepped down, stepped aside. He had left them in complete mayhem that was bound to follow in a few minutes. But for Matt, right now this was *his* moment. *He* would be the one to break the news, *he* was going to be the one to hand the letter to the officials and have the spotlight just for a moment before whatever was going to happen, happened. This was *his* moment, at last and he was going to make the most of it...

Far away from the palace at look out point, a black and brown alsatian trotted around happily sniffing the surroundings. Some distance, away two figures stood hand in hand, a familiar board like object on the ground next to them, looking over the sprawling city before them.

"So," grinned Kenan as he put his arms around Naomi's waist, "where shall we go first?"

Claire Louise Gristwood was born in North London but moved to Hertford with her family at the age of four.

As a child she was always writing short stories and comic strips based on a mixture of her own characters and childhood heroes. The interest in comics inspired her to study art and design at college though she still continued to write in her spare time.

Upon finishing college she decided to go back to her true passion of writing, and has since written several sci-fi and fantasy genre books. She now currently lives in a small town outside of Hertford with her family.

Made in the USA
Charleston, SC
16 March 2013